# EXPOSED

# EXPOSED

## CIRCLE OF THE RED LILY

BOOK ONE

ANNA J. STEWART

CAEZIK
ROMANCE
ARC MANOR
ROCKVILLE, MARYLAND

SHAHID MAHMUD
PUBLISHER

www.CaezikRomance.com

Cover Designer: Authors on a Dime

ISBN: 978-1-64710-067-4

First Edition, First Printing, November 2022
1 2 3 4 5 6 7 8 9 10

An imprint of Arc Manor LLC

www.CaezikRomance.com

*For JoAnn Munso.*

The greatest gift my mother gave me was naming you as my Godmother.

I endeavor to follow your example by leading with love.

# PROLOGUE

ONLY the walls had heard her scream.

Old, crumbling, stone walls dripping with her terror.

The now-familiar drug-induced fog in her brain refused to lift, trapping her in the unending cycle of confusion and fear. How long had it been this time? Days? Weeks? Months? He always waited until she was asleep and every time she closed her eyes, she expected it to be the end. Sleep was his weapon of choice. Sleep and the drugs.

It never stopped.

When, *when* was it going to stop?

She never expected to die at twenty-three. But she would. Death teased her with sweet relief, but not even death seemed to want her. Yet. The thought of escape, of release, however she might attain it, brought a chilling anticipation of peace.

Acceptance had taken … time. Time that had turned her mind to mush and her will to dust. She couldn't remember the last time she'd screamed. But she had screamed. So long and so loud her throat was scraped raw and she coughed up blood. Eventually, the screams had quieted and turned to tears which flowed into a rage that filled the windowless room with a fire stoked by every breath she took.

But it hadn't mattered. Nothing did.

It didn't matter how hard she pounded her hands, her palms, her fists against the intricately carved wooden door without a knob. It didn't matter how many stone grout lines she'd dug into. She got nothing for her pain except raw fingers and ragged, shorn nails. Routine had set in.

Routine had worn her down even in the oddly luxurious room she was locked in. A room filled with images of the others who had come before; framed photographs of the other women whose screams were trapped in these walls.

Portrait-perfect faces touched by the same, careful hands that had touched hers.

It was a room out of time that spoke of glamour and beauty, even as it served as her prison and torture chamber. Amidst the glitz and delicate fragrance of the red lilies he replaced every morning, for a while, however dim, hope burned.

Until he'd come.

Until *they'd* come.

When they'd used, abused, and violated her in ways she could never have imagined, they had killed what little belief she'd still had left that there would be an end other than death.

She wouldn't see her parents again, or her beautiful little niece. She couldn't bring herself to think about her sister—her twin—who would feel her loss so acutely it would be as if a part of herself had died. And what about her dog? What breath she had, hitched in her chest as tears trickled out of the corners of her swollen eyes. She'd only had him a few weeks; he was still a baby. A sob pushed against her lungs. What was going to happen to Barksy?

She wanted to find comfort in the only thing she still had—the solitary half-heart charm that hung around her neck, and the only thing of hers he hadn't taken from her—but she couldn't. Desperation arced through her, pinpricks of energy that sputtered and died after impulse. She willed her arms, her hands, her feet to move. He'd be back soon. The last time he'd brought her food, wearing that blank, plastic mask that left only his piercing black eyes bare, he'd told her his plans.

He'd been so proud of how he hoped to play with her again. Pose her again.

Rape her. Again.

She'd struck out, panicked, flailing, catching him hard against the side of the face. She'd heard the mask crack; the sound splitting through the silence of the room. He'd gone stone still, as if in shock, holding a hand to his exposed cheek as he processed her attack.

She'd dropped to her knees, ducked her head even as she reached up with both hands to grab at his tailored, elegant jacket.

Apologies got her nowhere. She hadn't expected them to. She'd needed to play her part to the hilt even if it meant paying an exacting price later. The price she always paid for disobeying and shattering his imaginary world like the mirror it was.

He wouldn't hit her. He wouldn't dare mar the skin he took such prodigious care of or muss the hair he'd painstakingly dyed, scalp burning, platinum blonde. Instead, he'd bent down and slowly, deliberately, locked his hands around her throat.

When he squeezed, when his gaze bore into hers, she'd clawed at this jacket, struggling to keep air in her lungs until she felt one of the buttons catch between her fingers. When he cast her away, she'd held on and tugged, falling to the ground in a heap, the button clasped securely in her fist.

She'd lain there, barely breathing, forehead pressed against the cold stone floor as he quietly withdrew from the room and closed the door.

She'd had a choice to make while emotions cycloned inside of her. She thought she'd been so smart, not eating the food this time, but now he only brought her water; water that was most certainly drugged. He'd honed his weapon of choice to a deadly edge. She looked down at the button in her hand. Triumph of a sort surged through her. With one swallow, she could use his pretentious clothing against him.

It would cost her her life, but if her gamble paid off, it might also, someday, cost him his. Someday, someone would have to stop him. Maybe … maybe she would be the one. Even if from the grave.

Curled into the smallest corner of the room, she placed the button in her mouth. Hands trembling, she lifted the bottle to her lips and drank, swallowing the button with deliberate thought. Arms wrapped around herself, she rocked herself in comfort, waging a war with exhaustion, gaze pinned on the door. Waiting.

Waiting …

She woke up on the bed.

Lying flat on her back, hands clasped under her breasts, she could feel the soft fabric of whatever he'd dressed her in this time. The surreal antique chandelier glowed over her, hypnotizing her with the glittering lights.

She could smell the chemicals in the makeup he'd slathered on her face, her neck. Her breasts above the exposed skin of her chest. She tasted the toxicity of the thick lipstick he'd painted on her dry lips.

She was tired. So tired of hurting. Of fighting. Of feeling.

Her eyes drifted closed. What she wouldn't give not to be able to feel.

"It's time."

She started awake, eyes going wide as he loomed over her. *Time for what?*

His mask had been replaced, but the white plastic was now black, making him appear faceless in the shadows.

Certainty descended.

She'd go to her grave never having seen her killer's face.

His hands slid under her, lifted her into the air then cradled her against his chest. As he walked to the door, chills erupted all over her body as a cool breeze bathed her skin. She could hear breathing. Steady, quiet, purposeful breathing. Not his. And not hers.

They weren't alone. She sobbed, but the sound caught in her throat.

Had she the strength, she would have panicked at the line of masked faces, the suited figures watching as she was carried past.

Even if she had the energy—the will—she couldn't fight. There was no way to escape his prison. He'd taught her that.

Darkness loomed. Shuffling footsteps echoed all around her as the shadows closed in around. Watching.

Something was different this time. Whatever hope she still possessed was quickly doused by the bright lights of the cavernous room she was carried into.

The air was frigid. The stone walls arched into a dome over her head. She could see a sliver of the moon through a center, round window at the top. Her hands turned to ice and she nearly cried out in shock as she was placed on a solid, unforgiving concrete platform. But no sound emerged from a throat clogged with horror.

The room was silent save for the ever-so-light breathing of its occupants.

She'd lost count of the masks she'd seen, of the faces she imagined behind them. Five? Ten? A dozen? More?

All she could do now was stare up at the night sky shining through that one, small circular bit of glass and pray.

A sudden rush of water erupted. Impulse had her wanting to look, to see exactly what was happening, but the drugs had done their job and paralyzed her into ignorance. Light sprinkles of moisture landed on her face, on the back of her hands. Soaked through her dress from beneath.

She could hear the area around her filling up and then, as suddenly as it started, the water stopped.

It took all her effort to breathe, in terror managing to open wide eyes that had stopped cooperating long ago.

He waded into the water to stand beside her, looking down at her with such … compassion, such reverence, she wondered if this was all some nightmare in her mind.

"It's time." His tone was solemn, respectful and … grateful.

He lay the flower—a solitary, blood-tinted lily—onto her chest.

Dread and panic skittered through her body like ants escaping a fire. She couldn't move. Couldn't blink. Could barely breathe. The heartbeat she'd clung to all this time began to slow. Slower … slower …

His face shifted behind the camera. The same camera he'd used on her time and time again. The platform rumbled under her and began to lower.

She whimpered. A pathetic, hollow sound that didn't come close to conveying her terror. She didn't want to die! She didn't want to …

The water lapped around her face as he leaned in, focused the lens on her eyes and the flower as it drifted into the water, brushed against her cheek.

"There," he murmured. "Almost there. Almost … there. Yes. Ah, yes. There it is. Perfect."

The flash exploded with an odd, dull snap. The click of the shutter echoed in her ears.

She drew in one last, desperate breath as the water closed over her head.

# CHAPTER ONE

*December, Eight Years Later …*

"HEY, hey—if it ain't Miz Riley Temple, photographer to the stars!" The clear-eyed yet ragged-looking homeless man sidled up to the open driver's window of Riley's silver Honda Element as she turned into the parking lot of one of Los Angeles, oldest pawnshops.

Wearing a pair of neon-green parachute pants and a blinding 80s-inspired tank Riley would bet her latest commission he'd unearthed at a local charity shop, she gave silent thanks once again for being born well clear of that fashion-challenged decade. The added reindeer antler hat was a nice festive touch though.

"Come on, pretty lady," the man teased. "Got me some new clothes. You wanna take my picture?"

"I don't think you mean that, Dudley." Riley put the car into park and offered a smile that had the man grinning back. "Last time I took your picture you accused me of trying to steal your soul."

"That was then, pretty lady. This is a new day!" Dudley raised both his arms and his voice. "I am a new man! Come on. Take my picture and I'll prove it. I guarantee you never snapped a man as good looking as me."

"I'll think on it." She'd played this game with him often enough to have learned her lesson. Dudley's moods and stability shifted with each sunrise, but today had clearly been a good one for him. Her gaze shifted to the home he'd made for himself out of a collection of boxes and pallets. He'd added an array of worn blankets and sleeping bags for insulation and—for want of a better term—ambiance. "Follow me to the back." She drove on and pulled into the space that, at this point, should have had her name on it.

The late-afternoon sun beat down before Friday night locked its weekend hold around the City of Angels. A non-obligation Saturday awaited her, one she planned to fill with, God help her, sunrise yoga with her fellow apartment-house tenants and friends, followed by a mimosa brunch, heavy on the mimosas. If she was lucky, she'd cap off the day with a crap ton of ridiculous reality TV that never served as a much-needed reminder of how normal she her life was by comparison.

"I was worried about you," she told Dudley as he sauntered around the corner, glancing over his dark brown shoulder as he hunched his hands into his pockets. She bent into her back seat for her bag. "You weren't here the other day when I came by."

"Church down the street—they added a bunch of new meetings." Dudley inched his chin up, pride shining in his ebony eyes. Tight ringed curls covered his head, which barely reached Riley's shoulder. She put his age somewhere between forty and Medicaid with wise, jaded eyes that still carried a hopeful hint of innocence despite life's challenges. Reaching into the oversized pocket in his pants, he pulled out a yellow plastic coin. "Got me my thirty-day chip."

"That's great, Dudley. Congratulations." Riley pushed as much encouragement into the praise as she could. She'd done it before. No doubt she'd do it again in the future. "I've got something for you."

"For my thirty days?"

*More like for my own peace of mind.* "Sure." She pulled two plastic bags out from her back seat as Dudley moved closer and gave her a good whiff of Los Angeles street funk. "This one's to help you get ready for the rain and cold." She glanced up as the sun took its usual late afternoon sabbatical behind a bank of fast-moving clouds. "Got you a couple of rain ponchos, some thick socks, and a battery-light-up Christmas tree. Oh, and a new sweatshirt. Like the one from last year, only blue this time. I remember you don't like red."

"No, ma'am, pretty lady. No red. That there's the color of the dead. No red for me." She watched as he dug through the bag with the enthusiasm of a five-year-old discovering a gift-laden Christmas tree.

"And this one." She dangled the other bag above his nose. "Is nutrition. There's some fruit and protein bars and one of those salami sandwiches you like from CrayCray. You'd better eat it soon before it spoils."

"Yes, ma'am, pretty lady. You are God's hand, you know that?" Dudley shook his head and looked into his bags. "God's hand, you are. You want me to watch your car while you visit with Merle?"

"If you'd like to." She hitched her worn silver-gray backpack over one shoulder and locked up. "I don't think I'll be very long."

"Got all day, I have. What about my picture?" Dudley called after her. "You gonna take it?"

"Tell you what." She turned, called to him as she walked backward. "You get your sixty-day chip and I'll take you on a photo shoot at the beach."

His face split into a grin so wide her heart swelled. "You got it, pretty lady. Sixty days!"

"A day at a time," she reminded him as she headed toward the street.

Stepping inside Unburied Treasures was, Riley supposed, what the devout must feel when they walked into church. Rather than incense and devotion, she smelled silver polish, dust, and more than a little a touch of expectation. The door frame was decked out in cheap silver-tinsel garland accented with red, gold, and green ball ornaments that had definitely seen better days.

She'd been six the first time she'd stood in front of this building that offered what her childhood mind saw as a magical portal into the past. Her grandfather had promised a unique adventure on the other side of the scarred glass door. Reality had not disappointed. Enchanted by all the bits and baubles her child mind couldn't yet identify, she soon learned each and every item offered promising tidbits of history: a story. People's lives. All encapsulated in trinkets that had, at one time, meant something to someone.

Of course, now Riley saw the pawnshop for what it was: a rundown, barely hanging on business that thrived on return customers and people selling off pieces of themselves in order to survive.

The blinking neon sign with the blown-out "p" declared the store open. Hard to believe this rundown area of downtown was such a short distance from the upscale neighborhood she resided in, but that's what you got in LA. An entire menu of varying neighborhoods stretching across the financial divide, offering everything anyone could ever possibly want or need. And more than an unhealthy amount of everything no one should.

Riley glanced at her watch. An hour until closing meant Merle would be in a chatty mood. At least she hoped so. She had questions and as of this moment, Merle Paddock was the only one with answers. Besides, nothing got the old man chattier than the promise of a cuppa tea before Vanna performed her nightly vocabulary reveal.

The buzzer sounded as she pushed open the spider-web-cracked door. The second she stepped inside, the air was filled by a screech and scream that had Riley covering her ears. "Merle, what the holy hell is that?"

"Oh, Riley! Hello!" The paunch heavy, bespectacled man behind one of the many glass counters held up both hands as if in surrender before he spun his wheelchair around and disappeared through the doorway behind him. "Sorry. Sorry!" The English accent he clung to after more than thirty years in the States carried through the store above the din. "Bagpipes. About three audio files piled up on each other. It's a new security feature I'm playing with." The fact he had to yell to be heard seemed to escape his notice. "I'm experimenting with audio deterrents that complement the security cameras."

"Shame on you," she yelled back as the store went blessedly silent. "Bagpipes are the instruments of the gods. How dare you defile them this way!"

"Spoken like the true Scots descendant you are." Merle's familiar disapproving scowl was in place when he re-emerged, partially decked out himself with a Santa hat and that typical twinkle in his eye. As diabetes had wreaked havoc with his circulation, he'd been relegated to peering at his customers over the edge of his display counters for the past few years. That said, he zipped around this place better in his wheelchair than Riley did on two good feet.

"Your grandfather, God rest him," Merle went on, "would agree with you about those bloody pipes, sadly enough. Ask me, they could drive a saint over the brink. Guess the noise won't do me any good if it drives away my regulars. I just want to scare off the would-be thieves that don't wanna be noticed."

"Try the Chipmunks." Riley shook her head to clear the remnants of noise. "They chase me away every time."

"Chipmunks, check!" Merle raised a triumphant fist.

"What happened with the security-cage entry system you told me about? I thought you were going to look into investing in one?"

"Exceeds my current budget." Merle waved her back. "I've got the pot on for tea and I have some of those shortbread cookies you like. Flip the open sign off, will you? Don't usually see you twice in one week. What brings you by?"

"Oh, a couple of things." Riley pursed her lips, debating, once again, how much to share. The initial photo negatives she'd evaluated earlier this afternoon could be nothing. Probably were nothing.

Or, if the gnawing in her stomach could be believed, they might very well be a very big something.

Riley chewed on the inside of her cheek. Living life in Hollywood, the eternal land of make-believe, often meant Riley questioned, or at the very least battled, reality. She was probably just being silly. Honestly, she was close to dismissing that niggling little voice in her head that was telling her she'd stumbled on something no one was ever supposed to see. That little voice had rarely, if ever, steered her wrong in all of her thirty-two years.

She clicked off the sign, ending the gentle hum of neon as she wandered through the store.

She performed her usual visual scan of the shelves holding everything from musical instruments to old collectibles, typewriters to exercise equipment that doubled as designer-clothes racks. Framed movie posters from Casablanca to the latest Bond installment hung high on the walls adding that necessary Hollywood touch that was a prerequisite for any shop in downtown LA.

Some of the glass counter display cases were filled with jewelry; cheap knockoffs mingling incestuously with the real deal. Other displays showed off pricier designer items or a limited array of weapons that included engraved brass knuckles, a pair of nunchucks that at one time had reportedly been used by Bruce Lee in a movie, and a selection of knives.

She stopped briefly at the tall tower cabinet filled with cameras and equipment. As if they had a mind of their own, her fingers reverently brushed the glass as she tamped down the longing coursing through her. From a stereoscope viewer to a 1929 Rolleiflex twin lens, to a Polaroid camera from 1948, every cell inside of her itched to get her hands on any one of them. Viewing today's world through a decades-old lens was a special and sometimes her preferred point of view.

There was little she loved more than adding to the collection of cameras her great-grandfather had started back in the 1920s. But frivolities like new old cameras would have to wait until monthly expenses were seen to. Her top priority had to be hiring a new building manager to replace the one who had quit Temple House three weeks ago without any notice.

As always, Temple House—the twenty-plus tenant apartment building she'd partially inherited from her grandfather when he'd passed—came before everything else. It had come first for him, and it always would for her. "Ho ho ho. Responsibilities first," she murmured and bid a silent but hopefully temporary farewell to the camera display. "Sometimes being an adult really sucks."

She joined Merle in the kitchen that serviced both the store and Merle's back apartment. Dropping her bag on the floor by the stove, she took a seat at the small square table against the wall. His living space was tidy and practically outfitted for a man of limited mobility. Accented with throwback appliances and an odd floral wallpaper she suspected reminded him of England, cozy was a word that came to mind. "I was worried about Dudley," she told him.

"Dudley." Merle shook his head. "Now there's a man who always lands on his feet. He's had a good couple of weeks. Got a new thirty-day chip."

"He showed me." She knew Merle and Dudley had an unofficial arrangement to watch out for each other. Of course, reliability issues had cropped up now and again, but the two men had coexisted peacefully for more than a year. As for the other reason that had brought her here … "I wanted to ask you about that old film you sold me the other day."

"As much as I adore you, Riley." Merle shot her a warning glare. "You know my stand on refunds."

Riley laughed while Merle poured the tea and infused the air with cinnamon and spice. "I'm not looking to return the film." Far from it. Her gut was telling her she'd come across something special even before she'd actually developed the negatives. Her photography work kept her head above water, but the paparazzi jobs—her main source of income—made her stomach turn even more than normal these days. What she wouldn't give for one of her accidental, non-invasive pictures to pay as well as scandal and controversy.

She took a deep breath, ran a finger along the edge of a solitary plastic daisy drooping out of an old jar. "I was hoping you might tell me where you got it?"

"You've never asked me that before." Merle frowned and pushed a plate of cookies closer to her. "Why do you want to know? You develop it already?" Interest piqued, his eyes narrowed. "What's on it?"

"I'm still working with it." It wasn't exactly a lie. She'd only gotten a quick glimpse at a few of the negatives. But they had been disturbing enough to bring her back to Merle's doorstep. "Old film takes a lot of time to bloom and develop its secrets."

Developing old, lost film wasn't just a hobby for Riley; it was an obsession. One that had begun at age five when, after the death of her parents, she'd come to live with her grandfather, a onetime Hollywood portrait artist who'd worked in the studio system back in the late 40s and early 50s. The second that Douglas Temple placed a camera in Riley's hand, she'd found her calling. Over the years, she'd established her own path in the industry; eked out her own opportunities and ways of doing things as a part-time loathsome paparazzo. But nothing beat the rush of the undiscovered treasures lurking in a rusted 35mm canister.

While she had arrangements with multiple pawnshop owners and antique-store dealers around town when it came to photography equipment, Merle, an old friend of her grandfather's, was always her preferred go-to.

She wasn't a cheapskate about it, either. She was willing to pay top dollar for potential. Her form of gambling, she supposed. She never knew what would be revealed in the darkroom. She might make a living using the most up-to-date technology, but her heart belonged to the images of the past.

As far as she was concerned, rolls that lay forgotten for decades were like rare diamonds waiting to be freed from the earth. It also helped that the hobby kept her sane as she trudged through the sometimes-muddy trenches of Hollywood.

Riley shifted in her chair as the knot in her stomach tightened. "I know you don't like to share where you obtain a lot of your … merchandise. I'm not looking to hone in on your system or anything, but—"

"But what?" He turned on his appraiser look. "You're going to have to be straight with me if you want an honest answer about where that film came from."

"I don't want to get ahead of myself." She shook her head. "I honestly don't know what I'm dealing with yet. But some background might help me flesh out those answers."

"You're thinking it's something big? Something you can cash in on?"

Always with the bottom line: money. "Possibly."

"Enough to front me some cash to pay for that security cage I've got my eye on?" Merle pressed.

"Maybe." Riley shook her head, grinned, and sipped her tea.

"Well, in that case." Merle's expression brightened. "That might just change an old man's mind. There's only one problem."

"What's that?"

"The box I found that film in didn't come from one of my usual sources. Young kid, said his name was Nestor. Didn't give me a last name. Looked skittish. Brought in a big box of stuff early last week. Mostly junk, near as I could tell at first. Books, trinket boxes. Trophies. Couldn't seem to unload it all fast enough. I gave him fifty for everything and he seemed grateful."

Riley would bet Merle had already made a profit on the junk box, given how much she'd paid for that film. "So there's not really anything you can tell me."

"Didn't say that." Merle's mouth twisted. "Got the feeling he might be back, so I started a customer card for him."

God bless Merle's old-fashioned heart. "What else was in the box?"

"Had an estate sale come in that looked more promising, so I didn't go digging any deeper yet. Just blind luck the film was in that shoebox on the top." Merle swung his chair one way, then the other, as if deciding which way he needed to go.

"I don't suppose you'd be okay with me taking the box home with me?" She didn't give him a chance to argue before plowing ahead. "Just a couple of days. I promise I'll bring it all back next week. I'll even pay for the privilege."

"Now that's a none-too-gentle push." Merle's brow furrowed to the point his bushy gray eyebrows obscured his eyes. "What on earth's on that film that's got you wanting to cannibalize my potentially ill-gotten gains? Not that I'm confessing to anything criminal, mind you."

Riley pressed her lips into a thin line. Speculating at this point was only going to result in more questions and that was one thing she did not need.

"Never mind!" Merle let out a huge, chest-deflating sigh. "I know that look. It's the same one your grandfather got when he was bluffing a poker hand. Take the box if you want. But only if you promise to tell me everything as soon as you can."

"I'll even do so over Christmas Eve dinner at Temple House, how's that?" She hoped her smile didn't look as relieved as she felt.

"Will Moxie be there?" Merle's eyebrows recovered and rose halfway up his forehead.

"I will make certain Aunt Moxie is in attendance," Riley teased. The two of them in the same room always provided a substantial amount of entertainment. "What about that card on Nestor?"

"Maybe I should start charging you by the request." He spun his chair and rolled up to the register. "Give me just a second ..."

She gave him more than a few seconds while she drank her tea and nibbled on a star-shaped cookie. That had gone better than anticipated. Merle could be as moody and unpredictable as his alley-dwelling tenant, but she also knew how fond Merle was of mysteries. Heck, his bookshelves were filled with them.

With her nerves abated, Riley took a bigger bite of cookie and reached for another. Something about shortbread and tea always left her felling a bit sentimental. Both were firmly tied around memories of her grandfather. He and his sister, Riley's Aunt Moxie had made it their mission to keep her entertained, occupied, and distracted long enough to pull her through whatever grief her five-year-old self had been feeling after her parents' death. Tea and cookies had gone a long way in that department. Her parents were ghosts in her memory, but her grandfather? He'd loom large over Riley for the rest of her life.

"Here it is." Merle snapped the card out of its holder and handed it to her. "Guy was cagey at first, but I got some info out of him. Probably didn't realize he slipped and mentioned Constant Care Storage off Western Avenue. Place has been there longer than I've had my doors open. They might have some information for you about him."

"Fabulous." She took a quick picture of the card before handing it back. "And don't worry. When and if I cash in, a security cage will be on the top of my list."

As anxious as she was to talk to the storage center's manager, she finished her tea and ate another couple of cookies. Or three.

Before she headed out, she checked the storage facility's website for office hours. She'd have to head over there this weekend to talk to the manager. "So much for my Real Housewives bingeathon tomorrow." She sighed as she hoisted the box off the floor and into her arms.

"What's that?" Merle asked as he wheeled behind her to the door.

"Nothing important. I'll be by next week." She kissed Merle's whisker-rough cheek. Her dilemma as to how to juggle the box and open the door was solved for her by the elderly couple who walked in. "I'm sorry, he's closed."

"Oh, heavens. That's too bad." The frail-looking man, stooped, a bit wobbly, and more than a little wrinkled, heaved a sigh as he clutched his wife's hand. "A lovely young man at the record store told us we'd find an excellent selection of autographed albums. I was hoping you might have an Ornette Coleman or Charles Mingus? Our son's a jazz collector and we want to get him something special for Christmas."

"Let them in, Riley, for heaven's sake." Merle's voice boomed as he waved them inside. "I've got bills to pay. Come in, come in. Charles Mingus, you say?"

Chuckling to herself, Riley maneuvered around the couple and headed outside. Stashing the box in her car took no effort because she'd purchased the small SUV precisely for its storage capability. A dim light shined from the openings between the blankets and sleeping bags on Dudley's house. She could hear him, inside, singing *Here Comes Santa Clause* to himself as he munched away on the food she'd given him.

No sooner had she closed the liftgate on her car than her phone rang. One look at the number and she accepted that her dinner plans with Aunt Moxie were about to change. "Carlos. Long time, no hear. How's my favorite hotel manager doing this fine Friday night?" She climbed behind the wheel and started the car.

"I bet you say that to all the hotel managers in town," the middle-aged man teased and Riley smirked. He wasn't wrong. "You asked me to let you know when Tiffany Small checked in again. I put her in bungalow twelve, your favorite. She's ordered room service for two. Also booked a couples massage for nine tonight."

*Yes!* Riley gave in to an enthusiastic fist pump. As much as she had a love/hate relationship with being part of the rank-and-file paparazzo, some celebrities just begged for attention. Tiffany Small had attempted to build her reputation on family-friendly characters made of cotton candy, angel wings, and pixie dust. Unfortunately, she'd spent an equal amount of time bouncing around nightclubs, harassing her production assistants, and having knock-down screaming matches with her timid, Midwestest, Bible-quoting saint of a mother. The dichotomy of personalities had definitely left the producers of her show scrambling for cover and Riley thirsting for a "gotcha" pic.

"Carlos, you're a gem." She tapped her dash GPS, opened favorite destinations then chose Fairfront Suites. "She checking out in the morning?"

"Yep. One night. Same commission?"

"Ten percent if the pictures sell." And these days any photos of Hollywood's new "It" girl would. Of course, the price would depend on who her bungalow bunny happened to be. Riley had her money on her TV co-star. "I'll up it to fifteen percent if there's a bidding war. Thanks for the head's up."

"Anytime."

She glanced at the dashboard clock. Just after six. Plenty of time to still salvage at least some of her Friday night. Rather than turning left and heading home, she made a right and drove toward East 11th Street where the boutique hotel was located.

It wasn't every town where its traffic had its own reputation. Heck, at this point it should have its own Facebook page. All anyone had to do was mention Los Angeles freeways and the chaotic image was planted.

Driving in the area had been the butt of late-night jokes for decades, but within the humor lay truth. Many a blood pressure had been raised and more than a few instances of road rage induced, thanks to these streets. Riley had always looked at driving in Los Angeles as a special kind of game; one she frequently won because she refused to be baited by the congestion that was literally the heartbeat of the city.

The trick, she'd discovered when she'd learned to drive, was to embrace the insanity. Plan ahead. And, above all, avoid freeways whenever possible.

On evenings like this, when her mind was racing with questions around images she couldn't quite forget, a drive was the perfect solution. She never ceased to be amazed by the city she called home. There wasn't a block that didn't contain some small crumb of history or opportunity for entertainment. Not that it was perfect. No place was, especially a town built on desperate dreams. But that didn't make LA any less of a home or, more importantly, any less ideal for her.

She fit as easily into LA as a studio head in a leather chair. They were made for one another.

Riley parked across the street from the back side of the hotel, gave quick thanks to the parking gods for opening up a spot just as she arrived, and within seconds popped open the back of her car. She pried up the carpet and opened the custom locked storage system she'd had built into the floor. If she ever needed a spare tire she was out of luck, but with thousands of dollars' worth of camera equipment stashed inside her vehicle, she needed things as safe as possible. She'd also invested in a state-of-the-art security system that could border on illegal if her colorful ex-felon of a mechanic could be believed. What better person to install anti-theft devices than a reformed car-thief who called herself Nightmare Halle?

Inside her purse, Riley's phone buzzed. Stopped. Buzzed again. Irritated, she dug for her phone, saw Merle's name on the screen. She clicked decline and tossed it back into her bag. She'd call him back once she was done.

Riley had been sneaking into hotels long enough to have the routine and costume down pat. She tugged on a simple black skirt over her jeans which she quickly shimmied out of. Off came the sweater which was quickly replaced with a white button-down over the white tank she wore. She toed out of her sneakers and slipped on simple black flats, tied her hair up into a semi-neat ponytail and, after flicking through the dozens of name tags she kept in a pop-out compartment in the side of the car, found one for "Vicky," a customer relations representative at the Fairfront Hotel.

She was not one for camping out or staking out hotel entrances, the latest fad restaurant, or even the red carpet. Nope. She had better ways to spend her time and, instead, had spent years cultivating relationships and investments into reliable sources who got her in and out of places quickly, efficiently, so she could exit with significant money shots.

She grabbed her smallest camera bag, loaded it with an extra 55 mm wide-angle lens, and strapped one of her oldest Canon digitals around her neck.

With her car locked up and secured, she hurried across the street, then slowed her pace as she keyed in the default code into the keypad on the back gate.

The boutique hotel was one of the smaller ones in the downtown area, but it was its hidden oasis behind the three-story building that served as the main attraction for a good portion of local Hollywood talent. Privacy abounded amidst the lush forestlike greenery accented with beautiful landscaping that spoke more of the tropics than West Coast cement. The winding paths snaked in and around various bungalows that for the most part lay dark and dormant. If one paid the right people, their stays went unnoticed. For the most part. Riley had found great success riding karma's coattails.

Bungalow number twelve was closest to the back gate, tucked away behind a thick grove of shrubs that Riley was more than familiar with. She stood back in the shadows for a few minutes, getting a few initial shots to lay the groundwork for where she was. One thing she liked to include in all her sets of photographs was a trail that proved she'd taken them where she said they were.

As she reached into her bag for the additional lens, the front door popped open and a room-service waiter emerged. The irritated expression on his face matched the sharp under-the-breath mutterings that drifted toward Riley on the evening breeze.

"Poor guy," Riley muttered, even as she silently lambasted the actress occupying the bungalow. People got what they doled out and Tiffany Small had earned a karmic backslap in spades since first coming to LA from Montana eighteen months ago.

She wasn't the kind of young woman who could be neatly pigeonholed into a category, which didn't always lead to success. But her natural comedic talent, along with her ability to easily shift from sweet, dark-haired, misunderstood teen to pumped-up red-headed bombshell was keeping her on the top of the current "it girl" heap. That said, Ms. Small was of the generation who believed publicity, good and bad, all led to one thing: stardom.

Riley smirked. A universal truth that kept her solidly employed.

Riley adjusted the lens, took one more picture of the front of the bungalow, then made her way to the shrub-obscured window. Lucky number twelve. She'd been here often enough before to have worn a path, most recently capturing do-no-wrong romantic lead Evan Bennington snorting enough cocaine to send him not only to the moon but on a round trip around the universe. One he'd come down from that trip, he'd shifted his social calendar to include an extended stay in rehab. She didn't take any credit for that. She hoped his awakening had to do with his sudden desire to stay alive rather than the embarrassment at having been caught. Riley's focus wasn't on exposing people; it was exposing hypocrisy and that she would never apologize for.

Noticing the addition of holiday poinsettias and pots of holly, she daintily ducked down in the shrubbery, the skirt snug around her knees as she lifted the camera.

She'd exposed her share of affairs from this position; helped end some marriages while others had been strengthened. Contrary to a lot of her fellow paparazzi, she had lines she didn't cross. Granted those lines were getting thinner and further between considering the new reality was to over share everything on social media.

Lurking in the bushes for over an hour, however, came with its own set of frustrating complications. Riley squirmed and cringed. Dammit, she had to pee! She shifted again, winced, and cursed herself for not thinking of it sooner. Maybe luck would be on her side and she'd get the shot she needed before …

High-heeled footsteps echoed down the path. Riley shrank into herself, curling into a ball even in the thickness of the bushes. When she heard the harsh rap of knuckles on the door, she popped up, just enough to watch as the door opened and Tiffany Small, dressed in her trademark yellow, stepped back to allow her mother inside.

"Well, crap." Riley sank back down, frowned, and lifted the camera. No illicit tryst. No marriage to bust up or relationship to expose. Didn't stop her from snapping photos as the two women's voices began to rise.

"I'm tired, Mama. I don't want to do this anymore. I want to come home. Please." Tiffany's plea had Riley's spine stiffening as the young woman dropped onto the sofa near the window. "Please let me come home."

Tiffany's mother stepped into the frame, her angular face flushed with the anger that sparked in her eyes. The blue Valentino suit fit her oddly, as if she had picked it off the designer rack of a thrift store. "We had a plan, young lady. You're not living up to your end of things."

"*You* had a plan." The exhaustion in Tiffany's voice had Riley lowering her camera, but only for a moment before she shifted her focus on the older woman.

She could see it now. The camera never lied. Resentment. Disappointment. Anger, all etched into deep makeup covered lines. She could see Tiffany's mother's desperation, her determination to live vicariously through a daughter Riley would bet had been far more beautiful than she'd ever dreamed of being.

"It was your plan, Mama. You made it. Not me. People hate me. *I* hate me!"

"This isn't about being liked. Your face should be plastered on every tabloid all over the country," her mother railed as Riley snapped frame after frame, capturing the anger as it erupted toward Tiffany.

And just like that, any irritation Riley might have felt for the young woman vanished. The pain in Tiffany's voice, on her face? That was real anguish. Riley shook her head, disappointed in herself. How many times did she have to learn that no one in this town was what they appeared to be?

"A scandal is the only way important people are going to look at you," Tiffany's mother spat.

"I've been seen by important people," Tiffany said. "Trust me, they don't just look."

"Sometimes there's a price to be paid for what we want."

"There is no we! This isn't what *I* want. This isn't who I want to be!"

"It's who you *are.* It's who I've *made* you," her mother snapped. "You're going to be a success. You're going to be a star."

"Why? Because you weren't?" Tiffany demanded. "Because you didn't have the talent—"

Riley rose up as the slap cracked like a whip in the air. Riley released the shutter, checked the digital display. "Got it, you bitch."

Satisfied, Riley pushed to her feet, shoved the camera into her bag and stepped clear of the bushes. Straightening her shirt and skirt, brushing a leaf off her shoulder, she headed back down the path. She was at the gate when she heard the voices rise again.

Riley hesitated, hand on the gate handle, toes scrunching in her shoes. She dropped her chin to her chest and sighed. "Damn it!"

She set her bag under one of the small cement benches and returned to the bungalow. After she knocked, she stepped back and waited for the door to open. "Good evening, ma'am," she ground out a sickly sweet greeting Tiffany's mother.

"What is it?" The woman demanded, anger still shimmering in her glassy eyes.

"I'm sorry to disturb you, but I wanted to let Ms. Small know our masseuse had a cancellation and that she'll be arriving at least an hour earlier than expected. Ms. Small?" She said as Tiffany stepped into view. The upcoming starlet wasn't on display tonight. The yellow T-shirt and jeans, the bare feet, the simple, low ponytail all put the real Tiffany front and center.

The young woman wasn't a good enough actress to hide the sorrow in her eyes, nor was she fast enough to cover the welt on the side of her face. The welt that looked as angry as the woman standing beside her shell-shocked daughter. Riley stepped forward, but her mother grabbed Tiffany's upper arm and squeezed it as if in silent warning. "I hope that'll be all right?" Riley said without missing a beat.

"Yes, it'll be fine, thank you." Tiffany managed a weak smile. And there she was, Riley thought. The real Tiffany Small. The authentic Tiffany who deserved to live whatever life she wanted to live wherever she wanted to lead it. "Thank you for telling me."

"Yes, ma'am," Riley said. "Is there anything else I can do for you?" *Like drive you to the airport? Or punch your mother in her fat mouth?*

"No, you can't. Thank you." Tiffany's mother slammed the door in Riley's face.

"All right then." Riley pivoted and headed over to retrieve her bag. If there was one thing Riley loathed it was a bully. But there were ways to deal with bullies.

She returned to her car and uploaded the images to her laptop. She refrained from tweaking too much. There wasn't any need as the images spoke for themselves. After typing a couple of emails, she sent the attached photographs to her favorite local news anchor as well as the police. She started to close the computer, reconsidered. "What the hell. Mommie dearest wants to be a star? Let's say we make her a star." She shot off a third email to a tabloid editor friend who could circulate gossip faster than a goose could crap grease. She'd get scale for it, enough to make her bank account happy, but it would be worth taking the hit for. "Just so it's not a total waste of an evening."

She locked her equipment back up, grabbed her cell and climbed into the car, waiting for Merle to answer her call back.

"I'm sorry," she said when an unfamiliar voice answered the phone. Younger than Merle. No accent like Merle, but definitely male. "I must have dialed wrong?" But that didn't make sense. She'd tapped Merle's name. "I'm trying to reach Merle Hargrove."

"Riley Temple?"

"Who is this?" she countered, an odd, slick, greasy feeling slithered into her stomach. She knew that tone. That officious, serious, down-to-business tone. "Why do you have Merle's phone?"

"My name is Detective Quinn Burton, ma'am."

"Detective?" Riley repeated, as if from a distance. "A detective with what department? Burglary? Fraud?"

"No, ma'am." There was a pause before he spoke. "I'm with homicide."

# CHAPTER TWO

"WE can likely mark Riley Temple off our list of suspects." Detective Quinn Burton slipped Merle's phone back into the plastic evidence baggie and, after casting his new partner a brief glance, handed it off and stepped out of the way of one of the crime techs. "She was shocked. And angry."

"This is Hollywood," Detective First Grade Wally Osterman said with a derisive snort from behind the disposable mask clutched against his nose and mouth. The younger man had the nose of a bloodhound and didn't do well at murder scenes in particular. Ironically, it was the smell of blood that tended to make him sick. "You sure she wasn't acting? She was his last call. Maybe he was identifying his—"

"No one's that good an actress. Not even in this town. And we can confirm her whereabouts, to be sure." Shoes crunching, Quinn made his way through the EMT debris, destroyed displays, and shattered cabinet glass. After more than fifteen years as an LA cop, Quinn had learned how to tamp down on his anger; to keep an emotional distance.

But something in Riley Temple's voice had grabbed hold of him. Grabbed hold and refused to let go.

Sometimes .... He crouched and resisted the urge to rescue the autographed Charles Mingus album, soaked with the victim's blood. Sometimes this job was too damned much even for him.

"Tis the season, huh?" Wally scoffed. "Takes one evil son of a bitch to come after Merle Paddock. Man's a freaking legend around here. You know, my grandfather used to hock his guitar here when he was short on rent. Merle always kept it in the back room for when he could afford to buy it back."

"Merle's known for his big heart." Attacking a beloved character like Merle wasn't just ballsy, it was risky. Nothing united a community faster than going after someone who had attacked one of their own.

Wally hop scotched over the pile of costume jewelry. "This is one of those 'world's officially gone mad' cases, isn't it?"

"The world went mad before either of us was ever born." Quinn scanned the floor, a frown furrowing his brow. The jumble of rings and watches and jewels sparkled amidst the glass. He reached out a gloved hand, lifted a necklace free of the wreckage. He angled it in the overhead lights. "Something look off to you with this robbery, Wally?"

"Wallace," his partner corrected automatically. "And no, not really." The newly promoted detective stepped behind Quinn and peeked around the cashier counter. He wore a snug suit jacket and slacks that made him look like a kid dressing up for his first school dance. "Cash register's empty. Apartment behind the store's been tossed as well. Wheelchair's on its side back here, like he was dumped out of it then dragged out before anything was destroyed. Tells me they didn't like something he said or did. Neighborhood's got its problems. Plenty of addicts and homeless—"

"No addict or homeless person would have come after Merle." Quinn grasped the necklace in his palm. "He helps them. Protects them." He stood, let the jewelry catch in the light. "I'm pretty sure these are real diamonds."

"No shit?" Wally's eyes went first year detective wide. "Why would a thief leave something like that behind?"

"They wouldn't." Quinn gestured to one of the techs to bag the necklace and wondered how many other valuable items had been left behind. "Something's off. Almost as if ..." he trailed off. It was too early to speculate that this hadn't been a robbery at all, even if that's what it felt like. "I need some air."

Quinn strode out the broken glass doors of Unburied Treasures and into the police-light illuminated night. Even in the crime scene aura of violence and change, he found an odd peace on the other side of the crime scene. Outside, he could close his eyes and draw the city in his head as a source of comfort. The old RCA Records building, Echo Park, the countless mom-and-pop hole-in-the-wall eateries he prided himself on patronizing. But there was no comfort tonight. Not one bit of it.

The pair of patrol cars that had been first on the scene sat parked haphazardly in the street. While one patrolman directed traffic around the blocked-off area, others had taped off the store's entrance and the alley next door. Quinn's department-issued sedan was double-parked nearby where a crowd had begun to form, cell phone cameras clicking away.

Quinn snapped off his gloves and shoved them in a nearby trash can on the other side of the crime scene tape. Homicide was the goal of a lot of cops when they signed up for duty. It had been his goal from the start. But there was one thing they didn't teach at the academy: being called to a homicide always meant you were too late.

Dammit. He was really tired of being too late.

His hand automatically dipped into his jacket pocket, then fisted when it didn't find what he needed. "Picked a bad month to stop smoking." And a bad night to offer to be on call. With a handful of detectives swinging between shifts, the main investigators in their unit—Quinn, Wally, and Detectives Perkins and Powers—managed to cover the crimes committed in their designated area of Los Angeles fairly easily. But Perkins and Powers—or as they were known, P-Squared—each had families. Well, in Power's case her marriage was hanging by a very thin thread, but Quinn's lack of attachments made him easy pickings when his fellow cops asked for him to cover their weekend shifts.

That said, Quinn could have gone the next twenty years without seeing Merle Paddock's life smashed into oblivion.

"Just last through the year," he reminded himself. "Then you can be done with all this if you want."

Even as he said it, that tiny, doubting devil that took up too much space in his head danced its irritating little dance on his soul. For a moment, Quinn gave in and listened, breathing in the somewhat clean Los Angeles air as he started the process of bidding adieu to the job he loved.

Nights like this often led him into dwelling on the what-ifs, but those thoughts always circled back to the one, firm truth of his life. He was a good cop. Correction—he was a damned good cop. Countless commendations and certificates of merit aside, he was proud of the work he did. He had an instinct for it and a dedication to it that was becoming far too rare. He'd learned to listen and trust his feelings while still keeping the realities of the job firmly in place. If he had his way, he'd stay where he was in robbery homicide until his pension came due.

But Burtons didn't settle for a detective shield and a permanent spot in one department. Oh, no. Quinn was expected to follow the family tradition of clawing his way all the way to the top of the LA law enforcement food chain. His grandfather's run as chief had lasted more than ten years which came on the heels of his great-grandfather's tenure. Quinn's father was poised to double that, a feat unheard of in the toxic sludge of Los Angeles politics. As for Quinn?

He stomped an invisible foot on that dancing devil to grind him into silence. He was taking every second of this month to make the decision whether to jump onto that ladder or not.

That nicotine craving of his kicked into high gear. He almost gave into temptation and asked one of the lookie-loos for a cigarette, but he forced himself to detour to the parking lot to check on the second forensics team instead.

An explosion of tires screeching and horns honking had him turning to the street where he saw a woman racing across traffic. She wore a stark button-down white blouse tucked into a knee-tight black skirt and flats that made his arches hurt. Keys and cell phone clutched in her hand, shoulder-length dark hair flying around her tear-stained, flushed face, she leapt onto the sidewalk with no indication she planned to let the crime scene tape slow her down.

"I'm sorry, ma'am." One of the female patrol officers stepped effortlessly in front of her, both hands up to stop her. "No one's allowed beyond the tape."

"I'm family." Her breath hitched on a sob she was clearly trying to stop. "Merle's my fam—"

"Miss Temple?" Recognizing her voice, Quinn moved toward them. "It's all right officer. I've got this."

Relief swept across her face even as caution rose in her eyes. "Detective Burton?"

"Yes. Come on through." He lifted the tape, flicked his gaze to the name tag pinned over her heart as he drew her away, lowering his voice. "I planned to call you once we were done with the scene."

"Where is he? I want to see him." She hugged her arms around her torso and squeezed, tried to catch her breath. "Where's Merle?"

"They're taking him to Cedars-Sinai. It was touch and go for the EMTs, but they got him stabilized."

"He's *alive*?" She reached out and grabbed his arm, letting that trapped sob escape. Once it did, she released a breath and closed her eyes. "I guess I assumed when you said homicide—"

"I'm sorry. I should have been more clear during our conversation." Not that there had been much of an exchange. He'd barely gotten another sentence out before she'd hung up on him—probably to drive on over here. "Patrol units responded to the store's silent alarm. We were actually called to the secondary scene."

Her dark eyes opened. They were clearer now. Sharper. And far more leery. "Secondary scene. Someone else was hurt?"

"Yes. I'm afraid they were killed." He looked down to where she continued to cling to him. "In the parking lot. There's a homeless—"

"Dudley." She shoved past him, running through the parking lot gate. One of the crime scene techs shot to his feet. "Please. Let me see …" She turned pleading eyes on Quinn. "Let me see him."

Intrigued, Quinn didn't have to ask if she was sure. Certainty was written all over her face. He nodded to the techs and they moved aside, the police on the ready to intervene if she moved too close to the evidence, or pollute the crime scene in any way. She was careful, respectful even, as she moved deliberately before crouching in front of the opening of the makeshift dwelling. A tiny Christmas tree with no more than a dozen teeny light bulbs glowed dimly in the space.

A soft, grief-filled sound escaped the control he saw her fighting for.

"Give us a few minutes?" Quinn asked the techs. The parking lot's solitary light flickered, as if it, too, was exhausted from the night's events. There weren't any cars around, save for the SUV belonging to the crime scene team. For a downtown Hollywood lot, the place was pretty clean. The Jenga construction of the victim's residence told Quinn he—Dudley—had been living here for some time.

Quinn bent down and rested a gentle hand on Ms. Temple's shoulder. "We haven't found an ID for him yet. You said his name was Dudley? Dudley what?"

"He never said." She shook her head, tucked her hair behind her ears as she pressed her lips into a hard line. "He showed up about a year ago, tried to steal a pair of shoes from Merle's shop." A sad smile touched her lips as she reached for a yellow plastic disc lying on the blanket.

"I'm sorry." He caught her hand, held it gently. "I can't let you touch anything."

"Right." She shook her head as if clearing her thoughts. "I knew that. He was just so proud … sorry."

So was he, Quinn thought. It was clear this man had meant something to her. "You were saying? About Merle and Dudley? Dudley tried to steal some shoes?"

"He made a right mess of it. Knocked over a bunch of displays trying to get away. Instead of calling the police, Merle fed him dinner and offered him a deal. He could camp out here in the lot if Dudley kept his eyes on the place at night." She reached out again, this time to touch the man's lifeless hand, but refrained from making contact. "Guess, maybe, it wasn't such a good deal after all. He looks like he's sleeping."

"It would have been quick." Two bullets. One to the head. One to the heart. Gunshots around this part of town, at this time, caused as much concern these days as errant firecrackers. "I know it doesn't mean much."

"It doesn't mean anything. He was harmless," she whispered. "He was harmless to everyone except to himself. Why kill him? Why …" She stood, looked back to the gate. "This doesn't make any sense. Why is Merle alive but Dudley's dead?"

There was no guarantee Merle was going to live, but Quinn kept that to himself for now. It was, however, a very good question. "Did you see either Merle or Dudley recently?"

"I was here earlier this evening." She nodded, confusion crossing her face. "I wanted to ask Merle about some film he sold me."

"Film?"

"I'm a photographer." Her gaze seemed cloudy, as if she was still trying to process the situation. "Developing old film is a hobby. Merle comes across a lot of it from estate sales." She looked back at Dudley's sleeping bag covered home. "I only left a couple of hours ago. He and Dudley were both fine."

He caught sight of Wally heading their way and waved him over. "Where did you go after you left here?"

"The Fairfont Hotel."

"Did anyone see you?"

"Yes." She blinked. "Right. Sure. I guess you need to know that."

"If you don't mind?"

"The two women in bungalow number twelve." She shrugged. "I spoke to them. I'm sure they'll remember me."

"Am I right in assuming they'd remember you as Vicky?" Quinn gestured to her name tag.

She touched her fingers against the plastic, but rather than removing it, she simply shrugged it off. "Like I said, I'm a photographer. I got a tip about a celebrity checking in to the hotel."

"So when you said photographer." Wally voice held clear disdain. "You meant—"

"I meant photographer." Her voice was so cool her words could have triggered an ice storm. "I've got time-stamped photographs on the camera in my car if I need an alibi."

"Can't hurt to cover all our bases," Quinn cut his partner off and earned his own glare from Wallace. "You were a frequent customer of Merle's then?"

"I've been coming here since I was a little girl. He should have sprung for that stupid security cage," she muttered. "Always too damned cheap to invest in protecting himself. He considered everyone who walked in those doors a friend."

"We didn't see any security cameras either," Wallace said.

"Then you weren't looking closely enough." She shifted her attention to Quinn. "Bookshelf over the cash register. Collector's copy of Ian Flemming's *The Spy Who Loved Me.* You'll find a camera in the spine. And another in the front display cabinet by the door. In the eye of the Lucky Cat statue."

Appropriate or not, having her come back to the scene was proving a gold mine of information.

Wallace didn't seem to agree. "Not going to do us much good without the computer it fed into. Thieves must have taken it."

"Wally—" Quinn warned.

"He was frugal, detective. Not stupid. If you check his apartment," Ms. Temple said with obvious strained patience, "the bookcase in the living room slides out. His computer system's in there. Not that he needed one for the Wi-Fi cameras." Ms. Temple turned her cool stare on Wallace. "I didn't catch your name."

Quinn didn't know much about this woman beyond her obvious devotion to her friends, but he knew enough not to want to be on the receiving end of that tone.

Wally shifted to attention. "Detective Wally—" He cleared his throat, straightening up. "Wallace Osterman, ma'am."

"The store security feed uploads to a Cloud account," she told them. "You'll find the IP address and password in the Rolodex—"

"Rolodex," Wally snort laughed and scribbled in his notebook as he shook his head. "Man, these old guys are a hoot."

"So glad my friend's assault could entertain you, Detective Osterman." Her glare eased a fraction when she refocused on Quinn. "The information's under John Robie."

Quinn's lips twitched. "Clever."

"Merle thought—thinks so," she agreed, clearly impressed Quinn got the joke even as Wally stared blankly between them.

"John Robie was Cary Grant's name in *It Takes a Thief,*" Quinn filled in his partner. "You work in Hollywood, Wally. Watch some movies."

"Wallace," he corrected.

"Can we get back to it, detective?" The techs called from their vehicle.

"Yes, sorry." Quinn waved them back over as the three of them shifted to stand beside the parking lot entrance. "Ms. Temple—"

"Riley's fine. You're going to find my prints in there." She gestured toward where Dudley's body lay. "Whenever I came by, I brought him some necessities. Food, clothes." She flinched. "The Christmas tree."

Quinn nodded. "Then we should probably take yours then for elimination—"

"No need," Riley interrupted him. "I'm in the system."

Quinn bit the inside of his cheek to stop his amusement showing. "Should I guess?"

"Harassment?" Wallace jumped in like a twit. "Stalking?"

"Trespassing, actually." And just like that, whatever light there was in her eyes vanished. "Unless you have more questions for me, I'd like to head over to the hospital and see Merle."

"Give me a second to call the ER." Quinn pulled out his phone. "If he's awake and stable I'd like to talk—"

Across the street a car alarm blared. Considering most alarms these days barely registered, Quinn dismissed it. Until Riley's cell phone vibrated and blared the exact same sound. "Shit." She craned her neck to peer over the crowed. "I don't believe this."

She was off in a shot, ducking under the crime scene tape before getting swallowed by the crowd of onlookers. With images of having to scrape what was left of her off the street, Quinn ran after her, grabbed her arm and yanked her back before she dived into traffic.

"Hey!" Riley shouted into the night toward the small gray SUV parked beneath the solitary traffic light across the way. "Get the hell out of there! Get away from my car!" She turned and glared at Quinn. "Let go of me!" She did her best to wrench free of his hold, but he only tightened his grip. A Cadillac Seville blasted past, horn blaring as it nearly skimmed her toes.

"Nothing's worth getting run over for," he muttered angrily in her ear.

"Easy for you to say," she snapped. "Do you know how much camera equipment costs?" The hoodie-clad figure struggled to drag something out of the back seat. A bandana covered the bottom portion of his face that, for an instant, was illuminated in the glow of the streetlamp.

"Officers!" Quinn shouted over his shoulder and then shouted some quick orders—too quick for Riley to comprehend. Two of the uniformed patrol men ducked under the tape and stepped into the street to bring the cars in both direction to a halt.

"About time," Riley grunted and yanked herself free. "Drop the box!"

Quinn stuck close, focusing his attention on the would-be thief who glanced toward them, eyes shifting with anger. After one hard tug on the box, the thief's feet slipped in the shattered window glass. The oversized, filled-to-capacity box tipped out of his hold and spilled its contents onto the street.

For a split second, the thief stood over the strewn pile of junk before throwing a solid, frustrated gloved-fist punch into the side of Riley's car. He looked back at them one more time before he sprinted away like a jackrabbit. Halfway down the street he jumped into an idling sedan waiting in front of a vacant dry cleaners.

The car pulled away so fast, smoke plumed off the asphalt.

"Let them go," Quinn ordered the patrol officer running up behind him as the car made a sharp right at the corner. "I got most of the plate number. Riley?"

"Stupid shoes." She stood beside her car, panting, hands on her hips as she glared down at her feet, then over her shoulder at him. "I'd have caught him if I'd been in my sneakers."

"Or you'd be joining Merle in the hospital."

Her mouth twisted beneath narrowed eyes. "I didn't need your help, detective." It was the way she said it, as if his title was somehow toxic to her lips.

"Next time I'll just let you turn yourself into roadkill then."

She opened her mouth, then snapped it shut as Wally jogged over, an additional patrol woman at his heels. "You get a plate?"

Quinn rattled off the few numbers he'd caught in the dim light. "Toyota. White. Probably 1990s model. Don't know how many street cameras are around. Could be worth a check and see where they go. Riley ..."

She had moved away to pop open the back of her vehicle and was rummaging around inside as Quinn and Wally joined her.

She pulled open a shoulder bag, searched it, set it aside then touched a hand to the souped-up, sticker-covered laptop. Lifting up the spare-tire panel revealed a custom storage system that put Martha Stewart to shame. Her sigh of relief accompanied her bracing her hands on the SUV as she dropped her chin to her chest. "It's okay. It's all here."

"Must not have had time to get to it," Wally said. "Or know where it was. That is one impressive installation, ma'am." He said it as if he was surprised.

Quinn frowned, stepped back to take in the damage done to the side window and the very deliberate punch that had left a slight dent in the door. "You had a high-end laptop in plain view in the back of your car and they went after this box of junk?"

"What?" Riley poked her head around the side of the car. "Yeah. I guess." She blinked, something akin to recognition registering in her eyes before she looked away, as if guarding her thoughts. "Who knows what they were thinking. Crazy, huh?"

"Yes," Quinn said slowly. "Crazy."

"What's in it?" Wally stooped over and picked up a rusted metal box and a couple of worn paperbacks, pulled the box over and dumped them in.

"What's in what?" Riley asked as she added in a package of golf balls, an overstuffed accordion file, and an ancient calculator.

"The box." Quinn retrieved a now-broken track trophy from behind the front tire.

"Just ... junk. Is that everything?" She ducked down, checked under the car as the officers brought over the last of the items. "Just toss it all in there, thanks." When she bent down to pick the box up, Wally shooed her away and hefted the box into the back seat once more. "Any more questions, Detective Burton?" She rubbed her hands down the side of her skirt hard enough to rip the skin off her palms.

"You should come into the station, make a report on the attempted theft," Quinn told her, but she waved him off.

"No point." The snap in her voice told him she didn't appreciate his suggestion. "I'm well aware that small-fry crime doesn't register high enough to waste your time. Do you mind?" She stopped in front of where he stood, blocking the driver's door.

"Your insurance won't cover any of the repairs without a police report." Quinn tried again as he stepped aside.

"I've got it handled."

Right. She didn't need his help. "If you're sure." He opened the door and stepped back, closing it once she was inside. "You going to head to the hospital and check on Merle?" he asked after she started the engine and powered down the window.

"Yes."

"With a busted window? You lucked out just now. No way someone doesn't steal your equipment a second time."

She pressed her lips into a straight line, as if angry with herself for needing the reminder. "Right." She tucked her hair behind her ear, something she'd done earlier over Dudley's body. A sign of stress? Or maybe uncertainty? "I guess I'll head home first. My friend Mabel ..." She waved off her own thought. "More information than you need. Appreciate you letting me see Dudley, detective. Thank you ... for taking care of him." There it was again. That tone. She was dismissing him. "If you have any other questions, let me know."

Oh, he had questions all right, but now wasn't the time to push. "I'll be in touch." Quinn motioned a gaping Wally to keep quiet. "Good night, Ms. .... Good night, Riley."

She was spooked, he thought as she drove away. Spooked, scared, and definitely angry. Anger that was clearly directed at him and his fellow officers and not, as one would expect, at the person responsible for harming—and killing—her friends.

"It's not just me, right?" Wally moved in behind him. "That whole car thing was super weird, wasn't it?"

"Definitely weird. Too coincidental. Who would dare to rob a car with so many police cars in attendance? That's bold as brass, even for hardened criminals." There was definitely something more to Riley Temple—and her box of junk—than met the eye. But his curiosity on that topic would have to wait. "Do me a favor?" Quinn asked his partner as they walked back to the crime scene. "Grab your laptop and meet me inside."

He made his way back into Unburied Treasures and, ignoring the click of the techs' cameras, headed to the front counter. A solitary card sat nearby with the name Nestor and the name of a local storage facility. He flipped through the ancient Rolodex, finding John Robie's information amidst the hundreds of names and contact information. He pulled the card free, snapped a photo with his phone then motioned one of the techs, a young woman with yet-to-be-jaded eyes, over. "Make sure this Rolodex gets brought in with the rest of the evidence, will you? And these cards." He indicated the one he'd pulled out and the one on the counter.

"Sure thing, detective."

"What's got your spidey senses tingling?" Wally asked as he joined him.

"Spiderman you get, but not classic Hitchcock." Quinn shook his head in exaggerated disapproval. "Don't know if this relationship of ours is going to work, Wally."

"Wallace." The correction came without the usual irritated tone. "That the IP address and password?"

"Unless Riley Temple lied to us." But she hadn't. Not about this at least. It took a few minutes for the site to load and for Wally to figure out exactly where the most recent footage was stored. "Okay, here we go. This is the live feed here. See?" He turned, waved up at the camera that displayed the same action on screen, with just a fraction of a delay. He returned to the computer, tapping on another icon. "Here—this is the archive." He clicked on the time box. "Going back to opening hour."

"Good. Riley said she came in this afternoon. Let's fast forward through—"

"On it." They slowed down for customers coming and going, then reduced the tracking speed again as Quinn's eyes scanned the screen. "So here's Riley Temple arriving," Wally murmured. "Time stamp is three-forty five this afternoon. Lines up with what she told us."

"I'm not worried about her arrival time. She's got her eye on something in the cabinet, there." He pointed then glanced to where the tall cabinet once stood. The cabinet that now lay smashed on the ground, along with a handful of vintage cameras. As she was a photographer, he'd bet that sight would break her heart. "Okay, yeah. Slow it down here. See that?" He tapped the screen image of Riley, her arms filled with the box from the back of her car. "Clever woman." He shook his head. "No wonder she got squirrely. She likely figured out the guy was probably specifically after the box." Riley didn't know what was in the box because it had been in Merle's shop until shortly before the assault. He stood up, pressed his hands into his lower back. "No audio on the surveillance footage?" Quinn asked.

"No. And I don't think the box is the only issue." Wallace paused the playback to display Riley stepping back to let an elderly couple shuffle in the door. After a quick exchange, Riley left and the couple entered.

Merle wheeled into the frame and the three of them chatted for a few minutes before the owner waved for them to follow him into the back of the store. Not long after, the old male customer, no longer stooped and delicate, returned to the front door and locked it. When he turned to face the camera that he didn't realize was there, the age and frailty disappeared.

"Can you zoom in on his face?"

"Yeah, sure, but I don't think there's any doubt he's the one responsible—"

"For the attack on Merle—yeah, I know. That's not ... what I'm ... looking for." He peered closer. A disguise. A good one, but the man was definitely wearing one. Seemed like overkill for a simple pawnshop robbery. The resolution was crap, but some things shined through. "Yeah," he murmured as he nodded. "I'll bet two months' salary that's the guy who broke into Riley's car."

"Really?" Wallace didn't sound convinced. "Near as I could tell, he was wearing a mask—how could you be sure?"

"It's the eyes." Caught in the spotlight of the one working lamppost. Cool, dead eyes. "Keep the video going." It wasn't pretty. But viewing the footage definitely shifted the direction of the investigation. He'd been right. This definitely wasn't a straight-forward robbery. Despite having a rather joyous romp destroying the store after looking for something they were clearly disappointed not to find, the assailants hadn't taken a thing other than the cash from the register to make it *look* like a robbery. "We need that other camera footage. Can we play them side by side?"

"Yeah, give me just a sec ..." Wally's deft skill with technology was one of the reasons Quinn had agreed to take him on as a partner after his last one took early retirement. "Let me just sync it up timewise and ... here."

The laptop screen divided into two windows. From the second angle, it was clear Merle had been attacked well before the store had been trashed. But he hadn't gone down easily. "They thought he was down for good." That was when they began trashing the store, hopping and jumping around like cartoon senior citizens on meth. "But he wasn't. He hit the silent alarm button—just then. Did you see it? You can see his fingers over the edge of the counter." Quinn stepped back, found the button by the register. "They didn't expect that. They got careless."

"And angry," Wally added as the male suspect slammed the camera display case into the floor. "I can see where that's our car puncher."

"They dragged him out from behind the counter. He's still moving at this point." Despite knowing Merle was still alive and hadn't been shot, he still cringed at the image of one of the intruders aiming a pistol at the back of Merle's head. At the last second, his accomplice said something before she hauled him out of the store. "Literally dodged a bullet," Quinn murmured, watched as Merle dragged his cell out of his pocket. "Must have been when he called Riley." Quinn slapped a hand against Wallace's shoulder, squeezing it in excitement. "Wait, what was that? There. Go back about a minute and freeze it." He looked up at the cracked mirror hanging on the wall behind a rack of coats and classic T-shirts. "There was a flash in the mirror."

Quinn walked over to stand in front of the cracked mirror. He looked at his reflection, and the large square window behind him. He turned, strode across the store back toward the register. "The camera display case blocked the window before the attack, but not after." He peered outside where his lab techs were continuing to work the scene. "Dudley's tent is right below this window. That could have been a muzzle flash we saw in the mirror." Something shifted inside of him, the same something that uncoiled whenever he saw a case opening up in a new direction. "They shot Dudley *after* attacking Merle. Not before."

"Wouldn't they have killed him on the way in if they were worried about witnesses?"

"Maybe they didn't care about witnesses," Quinn reasoned out. "They'd planned to kill Merle, but got scared away. Maybe they needed someone—or make that anyone—dead."

"Again? Why?"

There was only one reason Quinn could come up with.

To lure back the one person they knew had walked out with a box before they realized what it likely contained. To lure Riley Temple back to Unburied Treasures.

## CHAPTER THREE

EXHAUSTED to the point of feeling disoriented, Riley drew the final eight-by-ten photograph out of the fixer bath. She'd been up all night. Even if she'd been of the mind to sleep, how could she? But she could focus on something important. Something that might shed light on why Merle had been attacked. Why Dudley had been killed.

In the dim red glow of the darkroom light she held the picture up and stared, resignedly, until the image was burned into her mind.

It didn't matter how many of the pictures she developed from the roll of discarded film. It didn't matter how vehemently she tried to convince herself the next picture would be different, that she wasn't seeing what was clearly there.

The next picture, and the next, only confirmed what the first one had shown.

A beautiful young woman, perfectly posed, elegantly arranged.

And, at least in the final images, one hundred percent, dead—presumably drowned, from the water shimmering around her.

Riley gave up trying to shake off the chills that hadn't stopped racing up and down her spine. She'd seen dead bodies before. Hell, she'd seen one just last night. Tears tightened her throat as she blinked them back.

Even before Dudley, she'd come across her fair share. Homeless people on the street who had succumbed to the elements. An addict who had OD'd in an alley. The up-and-coming action actor who had drowned during an early morning swim at the beach. Victims of a four-car pileup on the freeway that to this day made her fasten her seatbelt every time she got into a car.

She'd seen all of that and more and, drawing on her grandfather's advice, used those experiences to build up her tolerance to the harsh realities of the world. That was what she loved about photography. There was no hiding or lying or deception. Moments of time caught in undeniable permanence. Truth. Plain and simple.

But this woman, these pictures .... Nausea rolled in her belly, slick and greasy. These pictures depicted something else entirely.

*Murder.*

Riley snapped off her rubber gloves, tossed them aside, and pulled out the tall metal stool to give her aching, numb legs a break. She hated what she was thinking, that there was an odd, macabre kind of art in the story the pictures conveyed. A chilling, soul-scorching art.

Every shot was different. Full body. Upper torso. Front facing. Back. Full-on zoom-in facial portrait. Like a presumably drugged-then-lifeless doll being manipulated into the viewer's desired positions. And in every one of them, she saw an attention to detail and an effort to showcase the play of light against whites, silvers, grays, and blacks. Various background details blurred in and out, ruining some shots, accentuating others.

Dark, shimmery fabric draped perfectly over the woman's curves, accentuating the cleavage offered by the hint of lace peeking out. Her hair, inky black, was barrel curled, invisible pins holding thick rolls of her hair in place around her round face, that even after being submerged in water never lost their styled form.

She had a face, a look, a feeling out of time.

Even before Riley started her own business, she had attended enough professional photo shoots with her grandfather to recognize the sublime talent of a makeup artist. There was nothing casual about these pictures. Smooth pancake makeup covered any imperfections in her skin, not digital touch-ups. That pale complexion that for so long had defined cinematic perfection.

Dark color stained her slightly parted lips. If Riley had to guess she'd say her lips were a deep, rich, blood -ed. The same red of the flower petal draped over one of the woman's shoulders.

That was the only common element in each shot.

One solitary glorious lily.

And in the bottom left corner, as if burned into the lens, there was a crown—or was it a flowerlike logo?

She scrubbed her hands down her face. What on earth was she looking at? Other than the obvious.

Riley's heart ached for the woman. She was young; there was no denying that. Twenty maybe? Certainly not significantly older than that. There was an innocence in the vacant, black-eyed stare that would have vanished beneath the weight of existence had she continued to live.

Riley wanted to be wrong. She'd wanted to find a flicker of light, a flicker of life in the very last frames, but there was none.

Instead, she'd been captured at her most perfect. As she'd drawn her last breath.

Riley gnawed on her lower lip. Whatever these pictures were, they weren't normal. They were ... evil. Evil enough she was second guessing herself over not being more open with the detective at Merle's store. *Is there a connection? Will they come after me, next?*

"Okay, now you're being stupid." With the artistic talent shown in these photos, it was surely just some really good simulation of a death—for some kind of performance art maybe. Riley swallowed her doubt, but the bitterness of previous experience with the LAPD lodged squarely in her throat. "This whole situation is getting too maudlin, even for you." She pressed her fingers into her eyes, then jumped at the knock on the door.

"Riley Jessica Temple, you've been in there all night." Aunt Moxie's voice was almost stern, and most definitely frustrated. "You come out now for some air and sustenance or I'll go down to the basement and throw the breaker switch to kill the power to the whole building."

Riley leapt to her feet, knocked over the stool, and flipped the switch that turned off the safety light and unlocked the door. She pulled it open just enough to stick her nose out and caught the distinct aroma of long-simmering cider and the pine needles from the tree they'd had delivered two days before. "You hate the basement," she accused. "You wouldn't dare."

"Try me."

Riley narrowed her eyes as she evaluated her options. Fewer things were more certain in life than Moxie Temple's determination to defy expectation. She'd made an entire career out of it, actually. A career that even decades later continued to afford her occasional employment opportunities. Add that to the fact that should Moxie carry out her threat, Riley would have to visit every one of their twenty-plus tenants and apologize for a power interruption .... That would seriously eat away most of her Saturday.

"Don't have to dare now." Moxie smirked and shoved a banana at her. "I can see it in your eyes." This week's hairstyle for the eighty-year-old actress was 1940s sideswept pin curls in a highlighted copper, accented with a familiar blue-patterned band. Moxie's eyes, currently narrowed and shooting green, irritated laser beams in Riley's direction, carried the same determined glare her older brother—Riley's grandfather—had possessed. "Consider the night shift over," Moxie announced. "Sun's coming up and you've got yoga on the roof in a half hour."

"Yoga, ugh." Riley groaned and rested her forehead against the door. "I forgot."

"Not like you to forget even the promise of a mimosa. Lock it up and move it out, Baby Cakes. I've got places to be and things to do."

"I haven't been Baby Cakes since I was ten," Riley mumbled, but at Moxie's added glare, she stood up straight and flashed a smile. "Yes, ma'am." She snapped open the banana and shoved a bite into her mouth. "Out in five minutes."

"I'll be counting! One. Two. Three ..."

"It's a good thing I love her," Riley muttered as she reclosed the door.

"I heard that!"

Riley grinned, polishing off the banana in record time before yanking the photographs off the drying line and placing them into an empty folder.

Normally she'd stash the folder in one of her tall metal filing cabinets, but she bypassed that option and instead hurried through her connecting office into her bedroom suite. Aunt Moxie had never been much of a snoop, and it wasn't often she ventured into Riley's area of their shared four-bedroom apartment, but given what these pictures *could* represent—that she was still convincing herself surely didn't represent—she wasn't going to take the chance of triggering an interrogation session with her great aunt.

Until Riley had a better idea of what those pictures were, until she confirmed they weren't some weird prank … no. She shook her head and shoved that thought out of her mind. Detective Quinn Burton had been right in his assessment of her predicament last night. The so-called thief had ignored a pricey laptop to go for the box. That alone meant these pictures were worth something to someone. Maybe because they showed some kind of kink fetish that would embarrass the owner? Either way, she couldn't have imagined they'd be something to kill over.

She hoped to discover the two incidents were completely unrelated.

Keeping the photos to herself and as secret as possible was absolutely the best course of action until she found out what the deal was. She didn't want to put anyone else in jeopardy.

In her walk-in closet, she pulled down the box labeled 'favorite high school mementos' (a total fabrication as she had none) and stashed the folder inside. After changing into her workout clothes, she returned to the darkroom to clean up.

With the photographs out of sight, her darkroom already felt … lighter somehow. *Out of sight, out of mind,* Moxie always said. In this case, Riley found that concept impossible to embrace. The images felt toxic somehow, but also filled with, what? Promise? That film was at least two, maybe three decades old. Now, finally, the metal canister they'd been stored in had been allowed to spill its secrets.

Whether those secrets proved lucrative? Well, that was something she'd have to mull over, wouldn't she? Until then, she was on a time crunch thanks to Moxie, and she picked up speed getting the room spot-check clean once more.

She'd grown up in this building; in this very apartment and more specifically in this darkroom amidst the bottles and basins and cylinders. When most girls had been playing with Barbie or Polly Pocket, she'd had timers and lenses, and cameras of every type. She'd spent hours perched on the tallest stool, enraptured by her grandfather's stories as he unspooled, developed, enlarged, and printed moments of time caught by film rolls all but forgotten by modern day.

She'd made this room her own since Douglas Temple's death eight years ago; when Moxie had insisted on remodeling the living space to give them both a joint home and each have their privacy. They shared kitchen and entertaining areas, but had separate bedroom suites. That the darkroom would be hers had been a given and Moxie had turned the extra bedroom into a small screening and meditation room.

As for Riley and her darkroom, she'd repainted the cabinets, covered the wall in a faux brick panel that added that New York loft appeal, added storage for a less cluttered, more organized appearance, and kept it dedicated to developing the long-lost and forgotten film she collected from pawnshops and estate sales around Los Angeles.

Normally Riley displayed the results as art or gave the framed photos as gifts, but most of the pictures got filed away for potential exhibitions and shows, a dream so out of reach at this point she wasn't sure why she bothered dwelling on it.

Digital photography, not futile dreams, paid the bills. On top of her paparazzi work, she offered family portrait sessions, headshot packages, and interior showcases for websites and commercial advertising. Word of mouth and an up-to-date website earned her the majority of her jobs. Of course she'd always be considered a pariah by some—Detective Burton's partner for example, but his attitude and inappropriate humor were typical of cops in her experience.

Detective Quinn Burton? Riley found herself frowning. He'd been more of a surprise. Not one she should still be thinking about, she told herself in a not-so-gentle tone. She knew what most people thought about the paparazzi and honestly, at times, she agreed. Stalking celebrities, attempting to capture them at their most vulnerable—it wasn't a profession that lent itself to expanding friendships or building up positive karma, let alone pride in one's profession. But until performers' extra-curricular activities stopped paying, she' keep on keeping on.

Yeah, Detective Burton's partner had definitely flipped her bitch switch last night. But Detective Burton?

She scrunched her lips. He'd flipped another switch entirely.

She let out a slow, deliberate breath. Even through the haze of anger and grief, she'd have to have been ten years in the grave herself not to have noticed the appealing package that man came wrapped in. Tall, with the healthy build of a man who took fitness seriously, but not to the extreme, he kept his light brown hair neat, but not particularly styled.

He'd looked oddly comfortable in a crisp white button-down shirt, pressed slacks, and dark blazer. She liked that he'd foregone the tie. He was professional in his appearance without looking overly stuffy. Unlike his partner who, to Riley's jaded eye, looked as if he was trying too hard.

The fact Detective Burton got the inside joke on Merle's Rolodex system had earned him definite bonus points, as had his obvious irritation over his partner's comments. But he lost them again for his chosen profession.

Any other time, Quinn Burton may very well have landed on the top of her to-do list. But that title of detective just pushed all the wrong buttons for her. Besides, thinking about him this way, or in any way, was completely inappropriate. Him being a cop aside, now was not the time to pull anyone new into her life, no matter how attractive. Or distracting.

Besides, he struck her as a throwback; a man of, well, honor, and Riley didn't exactly have the inside track on that quality.

An honorable woman would hand over potential evidence in a pair of crimes that struck far too close to her heart, not stash them in her closet. An honorable woman wouldn't be planning on tracking down where those photographs came from. An honorable woman would trust the authorities to handle things, but experience had taught her long ago that didn't always pan out.

Riley also wasn't big on trust. It needed to be hard-earned.

Loyalty, on the other hand? Justice? Revenge even?

Those she embraced with relish.

"Extra-large double shot macchiato."

Quinn glanced down at the paper coffee cup Wally set on his desk. It was obvious his partner had taken a bit of a break, changed his clothes, and had the refreshed appearance of one recently showered. Envy prickled against irritation even as a surprising wave of gratitude washed over him. "Thanks."

"Looked like you needed it."

Quinn wasn't about to argue. This was fast turning into one of the longest weekends of his life and it was only Saturday. "Maybe I'm wrong." He picked up the cup and drank until his system rebooted. "Maybe this partnership has hope after all. Wallace." He emphasized his full name for the first time.

Wallace's youthful face broke into a molar exposing grin. "Told you I'd grow on you." His boyish features had served him well as an undercover in Narcotics and Vice, but Robbery/Homicide had a different vibe and higher expectations. He was going to have to trudge through a lot of bullshit and ribbing to find his place here. "Also, I figured I owed you after last night." Wally circled around to his desk that was butted up against Quinn's.

"You did okay." Quinn returned his attention to his computer screen, not wanting to open the chitchat door any further.

Late Saturday morning in Robbery/Homicide often reminded Quinn of weekend detention back in high school. There were just enough people around to keep things interesting, yet with less supervision than normal to reduce expectation. Meager, discount store decorations provided occasional explosions of holiday cheer at officers' desks. A collection of cardboard elves were taped up on the desk sergeant's window, thick ropes of tinsel sagged and draped over cubicle dividers. A Charlie Brown-inspired tree held together by sheer force of will sat on the corner of Detective Perkins's desk, its faded silver star on the verge of tipping over the entire display.

"I was just going over your report before we submit it," Quinn told Wally.

"Does 'going over' mean rewriting?"

"Only in a few spots."

Instead of click-clacking on his keyboard, Wally rested his arms on his desk and looked at Quinn. "I was too snarky last night, wasn't I? With Riley Temple," Wally added at Quinn's obvious confusion.

"I need to learn not to insult potential witnesses about their chosen professions. Or anything else."

"Something tells me it didn't matter how you dealt with her." There was no question she had issues with cops. She was guarded around them; distrustful even while dealing with her grief. He'd been on the job long enough to read people. Normally he just accepted it and moved on, but with Riley? With Riley Temple, he had this deep seated desire and need to know why. "But in the future, it would be best not to alienate or offend people who might be of help."

"Right. Lesson learned." Wally nodded again. Continued to stare while drinking his own coffee.

"Something on your mind, Osterman?" Quinn gnashed his back teeth together as he stared at his screen. "Stop chewing on it and spit it out."

"Nothing really. I was just ..." he gestured to Quinn's screen. "I thought you said we could eliminate Riley as a suspect."

"We can." Quinn clicked on yet another link, scanned the new bit of information he was storing for future use. "I have."

"Then why are you reading up on her?"

Because he found her fascinating. Because Riley's reaction to someone breaking into her car presented a myriad of questions he wanted answers to. Because despite being spooked over the incident, she did her best to hide it while still looking at him with a glare that could have fried bacon in an instant.

But for the most part?

He was curious because he could not get her out of his head. It had been a long time since a woman had actually fascinated him. "I'm reading up on her," Quinn said carefully. "Because I think she knows more than she's saying about this case. I want to know who I'm dealing with before I talk with her again."

"We. Before *we* talk to her again, right?" Wally hid his all-too-knowing grin behind his coffee. "If you're worried I'm going to give you grief over being interested in a beautiful woman—"

"You giving me grief didn't factor into my thoughts at all." Before Wally took the opportunity to expound, Quinn added, "For the record, her solitary charge of trespassing goes back twelve years. Probably in her early days as a pap. She'd set up camp in Cameron

Hayward's front yard hoping to get a shot of him coming home from rehab."

"Cameron Hayward," Wally mused. "I remember him. Wasn't he in that TV series about the gas station owner who finds a talking moon rock behind the bathrooms?"

"Moon Talk," Quinn muttered. "My kid brother was obsessed with that show. It has a rabid cult following on YouTube."

"I don't get how truly awful shows sometimes get the most mileage. So Riley got arrested staking out Hayward?"

"In a way. Turns out in Riley's excitement to get the shot, she'd accidentally camped out in the yard next door to Hayward. Those owners called the cops and Riley was arrested just as Hayward arrived home. She missed the shot and earned herself a criminal record."

"Bad timing's kind of a thing with her, isn't it?" Wally commented. "Sure seemed to have issues with us cops."

*Yes,* Quinn silently agreed. *She most definitely did.* And after following his gut, he had a pretty good idea as to why. "Gotta hand it to her, though. With the trespassing, she owned up to her mistake. Pled guilty, got six months community service, which she served by teaching photography at one of the local youth centers. Since then, no arrests. Or citations." Heck, he hadn't even found a parking ticket on record, and that was a near impossibility living in Los Angeles.

She struck him as a quick learner. She'd struck him as a lot of things.

Plenty of women had made an impact on him over the years. Hell, he'd even married one of them for all of two minutes. But it had been quite some time since a female of substance had landed on him with this much force.

For the first time in a long time, he was very curious to test just how big the fallout might be.

"She has an impressive Hollywood pedigree," Quinn observed.

Wally cringed. "I feel safe in saying she would not appreciate being equated to a participant in the Westminster Dog Show."

Quinn chuckled. "Agreed. Before her grandfather became a cinematographer, he was a major studio photographer. I bet he had some stories about the Golden Age."

"The golden age of what?"

"I'm getting you a subscription to AMC for Christmas," Quinn muttered. "The Golden Age of Hollywood. The 30s, 40s, and 50s. You know, the old movie studio system." Even if they didn't live and work in Los Angeles, the term should not have drawn a complete blank from his partner. "Something tells me you'd best refrain from asking those kinds of questions around Riley. Her great aunt is Moxie Temple. And before you ask," Quinn said sharply when Wally opened his mouth, "Moxie played Sally Tate in the Montague Mystery Series. You can't live on this planet and not have heard of those movies."

"Those I've seen." Wally looked entirely too proud of himself. "She was that Rosie the Riveter character who solved murders like Miss Marple, right?"

"If you want to define her in a demented CliffsNotes kind of way." Quinn took another big glug of his coffee.

"LT is here." Wally's voice lowered to the same, cautious tone it always did when their boss made an appearance. "I thought he didn't come in on the weekends."

"Only if there's an emergency." Or a case with political ramifications. Even as Quinn turned in his chair, he caught sight of the middle-aged, Black man making his way toward his office. Well, this couldn't be good. Lieutenant Conrad Gibson's normal attire of an LAPD upper-echelon uniform had been replaced by navy sweat pants and T-shirt. His usual easygoing expression laid hidden deep beneath a locked jaw and irritated gaze. "Morning, LT."

"Burton." He stopped long enough to glancing longingly at Quinn's coffee cup. "It's one of those days I'm sorry I gave up caffeine. Join me in my office?"

"Ah, sure." Quinn and Wally both stood, but Lieutenant Gibson waved Osterman back down.

"Just Burton," Lieutenant Gibson clarified before he continued on.

Wally looked as if the lieutenant had just kicked his puppy.

"Go grab him a vanilla Frap," Quinn told his partner as he grabbed his coffee and followed his boss. He shot Wallace an additional "trust me" look over his shoulder that had Wallace racing for the stairs. After crisscrossing his way through the maze of desks, he rapped his knuckles on the doorframe. "Problem, LT?"

"My oldest has a basketball game starting in ten minutes and I'm here talking to you." Gibson slammed a file drawer shut and sank into the chair behind his desk. "What do you think?"

"Sir, if this is about Wally's …" He trailed off the second Gibson's eyes narrowed. "Never mind." Clearly Wally's tiff with witness Riley hadn't made it onto the gossip train. "Should I sit or ask for a blindfold?"

"For now? Sit," Gibson said. "But close the door first."

Strange. The skeleton shift wasn't normally a concern, but he did as Gibson requested then took a seat in one of the two padded chairs across the desk.

"The Merle Paddock case." Gibson picked up a pen, tapped it on the desk as he sat back in his chair. "I didn't find the report in the system yet."

"Finalizing it now, sir."

"Bring me up to date then."

He did, keeping his thoughts—and feelings—about certain aspects of the attacks to himself for now. "I spoke to the station nurse this morning," he said as a conclusion. "Mr. Paddock is stable, but considered critical. They've got him sedated and in ICU for the time being. He has a concussion, three broken ribs, massive bruising, and four broken fingers on his right hand."

Gibson cringed. "Poor bastard."

"Once we got a look at the second camera footage, we saw where they stomped on his hand after he hit the silent alarm. He broke their routine, their plan."

"You think they had a plan."

Was that doubt in his boss's voice? Quinn couldn't be sure. "I do." A plan that had come to a sharp halt thanks to Riley's car alarm.

"So what do you plan to do next?" Gibson asked.

"Considering Merle's health issues, his prognosis isn't great, but I'm keeping a good thought we can question him," Quinn admitted. "Could be touch and go for a bit. Could also be a while before that happens."

"Okay." Gibson nodded. "What about the homeless man who was shot?"

"Kim's already sent up his prints. Wally ran them and they came back to a Dudley Waniker, age thirty-eight. Served one tour in Afghanistan. Honorable discharge. No legal residence since he's been stateside. No marriages on record. No living relatives. Multiple arrests for trespassing, drunk and disorderly, the usual. According to Riley Temple, Dudley and Merle had a friendly relationship."

"Riley Temple." Gibson's brow arched and he continued to tap his pen. "There's a name I haven't heard in a while." He looked at Quinn, who simply returned the stare. "You did some digging around."

"Yes, sir. I picked up on some ... animosity from her last night. A phrase she used sounded familiar." And not in a good way. "Small fry crime." Quinn grimaced. "According to my father, that was a favorite saying of Detective Joe Pantello."

"Pantello," Gibson practically cursed his name. "The man never should have been given a badge if you ask me. Got passed around from department to department faster than the clap makes its way through a whorehouse. The force became a better place as soon as his ass was out of here. We have Riley Temple and her camera to thank for that, actually."

"You're talking about the Ernie Walters incident." Quinn had been a newly minted detective at the time, earning his stripes in Vice, but word had gotten around fast once those photos hit the internet.

"Incident makes it sound like a blip on Pantello's record. That man shouldn't have died," Gibson said with more than a little vehemence in his voice. "Pantello's dereliction of duty and callous disregard for the attack left Walters bleeding internally. Tragic error in judgment. One that should have been addressed sooner."

"According to the report I read, Riley witnessed the entire episode."

"She'd been working on a freelance piece about the rising problems of the homeless. Instead of looking at it from law enforcement's perspective, she turned it around and befriended a group of homeless teens. Ernie Walters was one of those kids. He got jumped and brutally assaulted by suspects unknown. Riley was the one who found him and called us. The patrol officers who arrived on the scene took his statement but before they could call an ambulance, Pantello—off duty at the time—drove by, stopped, and after assessing the situation—"

"Said police shouldn't be bothered with small fry crime," Quinn finished for his boss. "An hour later, Ernie died in the ambulance on the way to the hospital." There it was, Quinn thought even as the bile rose in his throat. "That would explain her issues."

"Riley got pictures, but she also recorded the entire incident on her phone. That recording," Gibson added, "was never made public."

"I can't imagine the woman I met last night would have been happy with that," Quinn observed.

"She was not. But she got her point across by sending her pictures to the media. Something we couldn't stop. She got credit for the pictures and a boost to her reputation. She agreed to turn over the recording as long as Pantello was made to answer for it. He lost his job, his pension, his wife took off with the kids, and he pled guilty to involuntary manslaughter."

"Eleven months in jail," Quinn said. "Yeah. He really paid."

"I'm not going to debate department history with you, Quinn. You of all people know nothing's perfect within these walls. You also know things are never as black-and-white as they seem from the outside."

"Not arguing with you on that, sir."

"My concern comes from Riley knowing the victims in this case. She's not going to just sit back and let you run with it."

"No, sir, I don't believe she will." He hesitated, trying to find the right words. "But I think there might be something more to this case than a botched robbery and murder." He gave his boss a rundown of the videos and his still tenuous conclusions after the attempted break in of Riley's vehicle.

"Tread carefully," Gibson warned. "Riley's one of the few paps in this town people actually like. The Temple name carries some weight in a lot of circles. She's got friends. Connections. And she's not afraid to use them. Especially against us."

"She's not the only one with connections," Quinn reminded Gibson. "I am curious about something, sir. Why the Saturday morning interest on the Paddock case? You could have just waited for us to file our report."

Gibson was back to looking irritated. "Let's just say it's caught the interest of some higher-ups. How long do you think it's going to take to wrap things up?"

"It'll take as long as it takes." He eyed his commanding officer. "Or until someone tells me to back off." It was a bullshit bluff.

Quinn's boss was well aware of Quinn's tenacity when it came to the cases he was assigned. He'd run clues and evidence into the ground, even if it meant steamrolling over political agendas. It was his job; one he took seriously. "Is someone about to tell me to back off?"

Gibson continued to pin his gaze on the pile of files on his desk. "No." He blinked, shook himself out of whatever semi-trance he'd been in. "No one in this office, at least. Keep going with what you've got. But keep me in the loop. And get that report filed ASAP."

"Yes, sir." Quinn stood, coffee still in hand. "And the reason you didn't want Osterman in on this discussion?"

Gibson glanced out the window into the bullpen to where Wally had just returned. "Kid's still green. Despite three years in Narcotics and Vice, he doesn't know what you or I do. That politics and self-interest have as much a hand in how things play out as anything else. Tell him what you need to, but keep in mind he hasn't established his filter yet. He's chummy with a lot of people outside this department as well as other divisions. Anything you want kept secret, you keep to yourself, understand?"

"Sir." Quinn nodded. "Am I right in assuming you'd prefer any developments be reported privately and verbally?"

"For now," Gibson said with a slow nod. "Yes. Now do us both a favor and close this case fast and clean. The sooner it's in the books, the sooner you cut ties with Riley Temple, the better. For all of us."

"I think she's dead."

Someone poked Riley hard. In the ribs. Then in the arm. On the nose.

"Don't be ridiculous," a voice spoke close to Riley's ear. "No one ever died during yoga."

Riley reached up, batted the annoyance away.

"See? Not dead. Ri-ley." Her name came out in melody. "Time to get up now. We have mimosas waiting."

"Mmmmmm." Riley sighed and smiled. "Mimosas."

"Thought that might do it. Oh, wait, Barksy, don't—"

Something large and furry landed on Riley's chest, right before a very wet and very large tongue swiped up the side of her face. Riley laughed, wrapped her arms around the familiar Australian Cattle Dog and gave him a squeeze. "I'm awake, big guy. Enough kisses." When she opened her eyes, she found not only Barksy, but four other pairs of eyes staring down at her. Heat rose into her cheeks and she groaned. "I fell asleep, didn't I?"

"Ironically during corpse pose. Okay, Barksy, that's enough." Mabel's shoulder-length dark blonde hair sat piled on her head in a messy knot as she crouched down and tugged on Barksy's collar. "Let her breathe, boy."

"Dammit, I wasn't fast enough with my camera," Sutton O'Hara mumbled and glared down at her cell. "That was almost blackmail material, you know."

"Nothing scandalous about a public romp with the perfect male." Riley gave the dog a good deep fur scrub.

"I hear that," Mabel said. "Come on, boy. Off." Barksy heaved out a sigh and did as he was told, but before he left, he landed a paw right in the center of her solar plexus. After more than eight years, the dog still didn't seem to recognize his own size. Or strength.

"Ooof." Riley huffed out air. "That'll hurt later." She sat up, rubbed her gritty eyes. Sunrise yoga on the roof of Temple House was appointment get-togethers for Riley and her four best friends. It was even more special during the holiday season, when the spacious outdoor retreat was accentuated with twinkling lights and a Christmas tree situated in the back corner, under the covered outdoor theater area.

Yoga was one of the few things the five women had in common and thus a great friendship was birthed. They came from such vastly different backgrounds, worked across the professional spectrum, but yoga and mimosas—okay, alcohol of any kind—had forged the bonds of friendship shortly after the four other women moved into various apartments in Temple House.

Riley stretched, drawing as much chilly, fresh morning air into her lungs as she could manage. "Sorry, guys. Really long night."

"So we assumed." Laurel Fontaine, with all the elegance her name evoked, moved her high-priced defense attorney self out of view long enough to come back with a couple of tall, filled champagne flutes. Also tall, she was dark featured, and carried herself with a confidence and grace Riley could only imagine possessing. Add to that the fact that Laurel could effortlessly fold her body into yoga poses even the most practiced yogis avoided, and she was pretty much the perfect woman.

"We woke up to a Riley Temple special edition this morning," Mabel announced in her usual over-caffeinated way as she carried over three more glasses. "At least, we think we did. Careful, Cass. I filled that one too full."

"There's no such thing as 'too full' where mimosas are concerned," Cassia Davis murmured before sipping. She lowered herself onto the yoga mat she'd dragged over from the other side of the roof. "One of us has her doubts that Riley is responsible for the social media trending topic of the day."

"I didn't say I have doubts," Sutton scoffed as she sat and took up the last space in the circle. She had the look of a fresh-faced Midwest farm girl, which made no sense seeing as she was from upstate New York. "I'm just not jumping to conclusions."

"I'm not following any of this." Mimosa in one hand, Riley held out her hand to Barksy who eagerly padded over to plop down beside her. "What are they all talking about, huh, Barks?"

"Okay, you can't tell me the Tiffany Small thing wasn't you." Mabel retrieved a plastic bin of pre-schmeared bagels and cream cheese. "And no carb complaining out of you two." She pointed a plastic knife at Laurel and Sutton. "The school science fair is coming up and Keeley's in planning mode—so no, I didn't have time to make the homemade granola bar recipe you gave me, Sutton."

Sutton eyed her bagel dubiously.

"Just as well, since we've outlawed chia and hemp seeds from our mimosa time," Laurel reminded them then grinned at Sutton. "Sorry about that."

"Whatever." Sutton, a dietitian who specialized in nutrition programs for the elderly when she wasn't providing personalized home-delivered meals, shrugged. "What's a cheat day for, anyway?"

"Well, bagels work great for me." Riley grabbed an everything bagel and shoved it into her mouth. "No." Her mouth full, she shook her head at a whining Barksy. She chewed for a blissful minute, and then added: "And okay, yeah, I might have caught a moment or two between Tiffany and her monster mother. Why? Fallout already?"

Laurel smirked, curled her legs in and daintily plucked a piece of bagel free. "Mommie dearest—"

"Hey, that's what I called her last night," Riley interrupted.

"Apt description. She's being investigated for assault," Sutton said. "Police showed up at the Fairfront Hotel first thing this morning and took her in for questioning. Word has it Vegas bookmakers are laying odds on whether Tiffany presses charges."

"She will if she wants her life back," Riley said. At their curious looks, she filled them in. "The brat show was all an act," she said at the end. "Poor kid just wants out. Or at least, she did last night."

"Might change her mind without that albatross around her neck," Mabel said. "That action shot you caught was trending on Twitter from the jump."

"I'll bet she signs a TV movie deal about her life. Tiffany Small: The Real Story. And she'll star in it," Laurel added. "Any takers?"

"That's a sucker bet," Sutton snorted. "Hey. You okay, Riley?" She reached out and jostled Riley's knee. "Sleep issues aside, you look stressed."

"The Tiffany story no doubt buried the lead." Riley attempted a smile but failed miserably. "Someone attacked Merle in his store last night."

"Oh my God. That sweet old man who owns the pawnshop?" Sutton tapped a hand against her heart. "Who would do such a horrible thing? Is he all right?"

"He's stable," Riley said. "I talked to his nurse before I came up here. He lied on his medical information file and listed me as his daughter apparently. They're letting me visit later this morning." The image of a laughing, teasing Dudley floated through her mind. She ducked her head as tears filled her eyes. "They killed Dudley."

"They—who?" Laurel demanded. "The same person who attacked Merle?"

Riley nodded. "He was such a nice guy. Troubled, sure, but he was just living his life. Then he wasn't." She refrained from saying anything more, but the fear she was somehow responsible grabbed hold. She'd been through this before. Losing a friend to violence. It never got easier. Because it made her feel better, she plucked off a chunk of bagel and gave it to Barksy.

"Don't feed him that, Riley," Mabel whined. "Cheese makes him fart." Barksy gobbled up the treat and shot what could only be described as a gloating grin at his owner.

"It's part of his charm," Cassia's quiet voice carried more than a little humor. The least chatty of the bunch, Cassia Davis tended to live in a very encapsulated bubble, keeping herself safe from the outside world she had difficulty traversing. It had taken a lot of cajoling and urging to get her to join yoga and other activities with the rest of them, but every week she got a little more comfortable on that front.

She didn't suffer from agoraphobia exactly, but Riley and the others had frequently wondered and worried if their friend, despite her ongoing therapy sessions, needed additional professional assistance.

"Easy for you to say, Cass." Mabel scowled. "You don't have to live with the stink bomb." Cheese issues aside, Mabel reached out a hand to pet him, her other hand absently reaching up to clasp the half-heart pendant she never removed.

Riley's heart twisted. Barksy was more than just a pet to Mabel. He was the remaining lifeline she had to her twin sister who had disappeared a little more than eght years ago. Sylvie Reynolds had only had Barksy a few weeks when she'd vanished after attending a private party in the Hollywood Hills. But the dog had given Mabel and her parents something—someone to cling to as they moved through the grieving process to finally accept Sylvie wasn't coming home.

As if reading Riley's thoughts, Barksy turned his head, let out a soft whine, and rested his chin on her knee. Riley wanted to confide in her friends about the other events of last night. The attempted theft in her car. The photographs burning a hole in the box they were hidden in. But all of those things combined felt like a serious danger zone, one that could put her friends at risk. Until she knew more, until she believed she was safe, she wasn't going to push it.

"I hate to bring up a sore subject," Laurel said, "but how is the search coming for a new building manager?" Her question was clearly one the other women had been curious about as they turned expectant eyes on Riley.

"Right. Building manager." Riley closed her eyes. She'd almost forgotten. "Not getting that many applicants, unfortunately, and the ones I have gotten so far—"

"Let me guess," Laurel interrupted. "Background check issues?"

"Candidate number one had two restraining orders out for stalking. Candidate number two, who I actually had hopes for, inadvertently admitted to being a kleptomaniac and number three—" She shuddered. "Let's just say she should be working on horror movie sets given her predilection for modern torture devices. She showed me pictures," she added at their blank stares. "I've got three interviews for potentials on Monday. Why?" Riley asked. "What's going on? Something wrong with your place?"

"No, not yet," Laurel said as she reached for another bagel, rolling her eyes at Mabel's "ha ha, gotcha with the carbs" expression. "But we thought we should warn you. Moxie's started to, um, help."

"Help? Help how?" Riley sat up straight. "Don't tell me—"

"I saw her coming out of Mrs. Yen's apartment yesterday afternoon," Sutton said. "She was wearing her Sally Tate getup. Blue headband, rolled up shirtsleeves. Sneakers. Toolbelt."

"And overalls," Mabel added. "Don't forget the bright-yellow overalls. Looked like she'd stepped right off the screen."

"They were black-and-white movies," Laurel reminded them. "Moxie's trying to help you, Ry."

"Truth." Sutton nodded. "I brought Lucas and Addie over Thursday morning before school for some dramatic pointers for the Christmas play auditions. Before we left, Moxie said she had plans to take some of the responsibility off your shoulders. She's worried about you."

"So her plans are to act as building handywoman and fix us right into the poorhouse. Gotcha." Lord, this was the last thing she needed. That said, no wonder her aunt had sounded so concerned when she'd banged on the darkroom door. "I'll drop in on Mrs. Yan before I head to the hospital. Any idea what needed—"

"Heater and AC," Cassia said and earned surprised stares from the rest of them. "Mrs. Yan lives above me. I heard someone banging around, then one big clang and, well, I think Moxie dropped something in the heating ducts because there's a constant rattle in the vent over my bed now."

"Well, well," Laurel said with a waggle of her brows. "Lucky you."

"I'll ramp up my manager search," Riley assured them and polished off her bagel. "Now that I've had my nap, I've got to get going."

"You want some company at the hospital?" Laurel asked.

"No." She shoved up and stepped out of the circle. "Thanks, but it isn't my only stop." First thing was heading over to Nightmare Halle's Auto Shop for a new back window. "I'm going to get the Christmas decorations out to keep Aunt Moxie occupied today. Anything else crazy happens around here, text me." She stopped, turned, held up both hands. "Wait. On second thought, don't. I'll just be … surprised when I get home."

# CHAPTER FOUR

"HELLO, detective." Senior Lab Tech Supervisor Susie Soloman, her goldfish eyes magnified behind thick, bowl glasses, looked up at Quinn after he pushed through the swinging doors to the evidence lab. "What brings you down to our little evidence cave on a Saturday?"

"Just because you're in the basement doesn't mean it's a cave," Quinn teased her despite his exhaustion. Whatever jolt his macchiato had provided had long since drained away.

The older woman was one who typically embraced life, but most especially during the holidays. In spring she dressed in bright colors that made her look like a wayward Easter egg. For the Fourth of July, she'd worn a red jumpsuit that turned her into a walking firecracker. But she pulled out all the stops at Christmas time. With today's attire, thanks to the white lab coat and colorful striped scarf tossed around her neck and tiny top-hat headband, she could have doubled as Frosty's wiser, goofier older sister.

In the background, music played over the sound system, classic carols that reminded him of snowy trips back east to visit his maternal grandparents during the holidays.

"Well, most of us spend so much time here it's like we've been turned into bats." She pointed to the ceiling. "I'm thinking about installing some sleep swings, so we don't have to go home anymore."

Quinn chuckled. "If you do, I want pictures of Gregory strapped into one of them. I still owe him for the exploding talcum powder in my locker."

Susie tutted and shook her head. "That was two years ago, Quinn. Get over it already." She set the evidence bag she'd been about to open aside. "Here to visit or need something?"

"Ah …"

"You need something. Okay." She snapped off her gloves. "Let's have it."

"The homicide connected to the Merle Paddock assault. I was hoping you were done running prints on one of the pieces of evidence?"

"Charlie was working on them a while ago." She waved Quinn over and led him down the narrow aisle to another workstation. "Sent him on an early lunch. His wife's about to have baby number three and he's already losing sleep. What piece?"

"Plastic sobriety chip. Yellow. I'm hoping it just had the victim's prints on it."

Susie sorted through the pile of processed items, drew out one from the heap. "Here it is." She ran the number through the system. "Only usable prints belonged to Mr. Waniker."

"Great. Can I have it?"

"It's your case." Susie shrugged. "As long as you sign for it." She printed out a release form, handed it to him with a pen. "Don't see how it'll be useful. It's just a chip."

"No. It's not." Quinn sliced open the plastic bag, handed it back to Susie to keep with the rest. "I'm hoping it's also a key."

After driving home for a quick shower and change, he headed back downtown to Cedars, where parking proved surprisingly easy given the hospital's patient capacity. The holidays pulsed all around him starting with the giant, lighted tree in the medical facility's lobby and the garland-wrapped stairways. By the time he checked in with the ICU nurse's desk—that looked more like an elves' workstation with its cartoony décor and bright red, green, and gold tinsel ropes laid out across the counter—it was closing in on noon.

"Hello." He presented his badge to the weary looking Santa hat-capped nurse behind the desk. The plastic badge around her neck displayed the name Alicia. "Detective Burton with LAPD. I wanted to check on Merle Paddock's condition. See if he might be able to answer a few questions for me."

"I'm afraid not, detective." She turned her head into the light and the freckles on her dark skin went on full display. "He's still under heavy sedation."

"Right." He nodded, offered a regretful smile. "Well, it was worth a shot."

"Maybe his daughter could be of help?"

"His daughter?" Quinn said slowly. As far as he knew, Merle didn't have any close relatives. "That would be . . .?"

"Ms. Temple. She's been sitting with him for a while. Room six."

"Of course." Quinn nodded and smiled. "Ms. Temple. I think that might work out just fine. Thanks." Quinn slid his hands into his pants pocket, grasped the plastic token between his fingers and headed down the hall.

Like most people, hospitals were not on the top of his must-visit list. He'd been fortunate not to have spent a lot of time in them. That said, he always found the *beep beep* noises, the blaring alarms of medical equipment, and the whooshing of ventilators disturbing. Room six was only a few doors down from the nurses' desk. Sunlight streamed through the trio of windows, adding a sense of calm to the overwhelming sight of tubes and wires and hookups working hard to keep Merle Paddock alive.

He stood in the doorway for a long moment. Riley had pulled one of the high-back cushioned chairs beside the bed, kicked up her feet and, with one hand holding onto Merle's, she looked to be sound asleep. His shoe squeaked as he stepped into the room and her eyes shot open. In an instant, she dropped her feet to the floor, sat forward, and, squeezing Merle's hand, looked toward the bank of machines.

"Sorry," Quinn murmured as her sleep-fogged eyes cleared. "Didn't mean to wake you."

"Oh. Detective." She blinked, shoving a hand into her loose hair before she twisted one way, then the other in a way, Quinn supposed, to ease the stiffness in her spine. "Hard to get comfortable in these chairs. If you were hoping to talk to him—"

"They're keeping him sedated, I know." He stood at the foot of the bed and only then did he notice the wrist restraints on the old man.

Riley followed his gaze, then looked up at him, sadness filling the dark depths. "He woke up a few hours ago, but the painkillers have left him disoriented. He didn't know where he was or what was happening. He tried to pull everything loose, so they had to …" She touched her fingers to the cloth straps. "He must have been so scared."

"It'll get better as they wean him off the meds," Quinn assured her. "I remember my grandmother having similar issues when she was admitted for her gallbladder. Older patients, they get confused more easily, especially if they don't have loved ones around as an anchor. You know, like a daughter."

Riley pursed her lips. "Are you going to arrest me for familial impersonation, detective?"

"No." He pulled out the token, held it between two fingers and offered it to her. "I asked the lab to push it through printing and eliminate it as evidence. Thought maybe you'd like to have it."

"Oh." She accepted it, staring down at the yellow plastic circle sitting in her palm. "That's so … okay. Wow." She swiped at her eyes. "Stupid tears. They've had a mind of their own today. Thank you so much." She closed her fingers around the coin and brought it to her heart. "I know it's silly, but he was so proud of this. I just wanted something …" she broke off, took another breath and let it out slowly. "Thank you."

"Since Merle isn't able to answer any of my questions, maybe I can pick your brain for a bit? There's an amazing empanada shop a short walk from here. I bet you could do with some fresh air. Buy you lunch?"

She inclined her head, her gaze suspicious yet curious. "This is only the second time we've met and you've already uncovered one of my weaknesses."

"Lunch?"

"Empanadas. I'm too tired and too hungry to refuse. Thanks." She stood, leaned down and pressed a kiss to Merle's forehead. "I'll be back to see you soon. Stay with me, Merle," she whispered with so much affection Quinn felt his heart clench. "I'm not ready to let you go yet." After slipping the chip into the front pocket of her jeans, she lifted a small gray backpack off the floor and swung it over one shoulder.

Quinn followed her out, and they silently made their way through the maze that was one of Los Angeles's largest nonprofit medical facilities.

"Last night you told us you've been visiting Merle's store since you were a little girl." Quinn held open the exit door for her, then once outside led her right.

"He and my grandfather were good friends. They could talk or argue about anything and it would go on for hours." She reached back for the second strap and secured her pack across her back. "Weekly visits were the norm. Tea and cookies in the kitchen, the two of them talking while I explored all the things in the store."

"Like the display cabinet filled with cameras?"

She turned her head, brows raised.

He shook his head at her silent question. "I watched the security tape footage. You stopped at that cabinet when you came in. Like it was a ritual for you."

"It is. Was." Her jaw locked and she glanced away. "I don't even want to think what the place looks like now." She stopped walking, seemed to need a moment before she spun on him. "Can I be told when the scene's been … what do you say, released? I want to get it cleaned up for him for when he comes back."

Assuming Merle came back. Or even wanted to. There would be a lot of physical and mental fallout from the assault. It wouldn't be easy for him to return to a place that now connected to something violent in his life. "Seeing as you're his next of kin—"

"Haha." Her smile didn't come close to reaching her eyes. "Needs must. And sometimes lies are necessary."

"I'll beg to differ on that idea, but it's a conversation for another time." He took her elbow and guided her down the block. When they stopped at the corner for the light, he added, "I can make sure you're notified when we're done with the scene. And I'd be happy to recommend some local crime-scene-cleanup businesses. I'm sure his insurance company can be of assistance arranging everything."

"Thanks." She nodded. "That would be a big help." Distracted, she stepped down off the curb. A silver sedan zoomed around the corner against the light and would have knocked her right off her feet if Quinn hadn't grabbed her arm and yanked her back. "Jesus." She pressed a hand against her chest, eyes wide with anger-tinged fear. "What is it with the two of us and traffic? That wasn't my fault, was it? The light turned, didn't it?"

"It did," Quinn said slowly as he looked after the car. "And no, it most definitely wasn't your fault." He kept hold of her arm as they crossed. "Hope that didn't ruin your appetite."

"It's a bit early in our relationship for me to share such intimate details, detective, but I'm going to let you in on a little secret."

"Oh?" That sounded promising. "What's that, Ms. Temple?"

"Very little ruins my appetite." She stiffened her spine and, as they approached the open door of Peruvian Oven, took in a chest-expanding breath. "That smells heavenly. You might have ticked up a few notches in my book, detective."

"Quinn. You calling me detective makes me think I should have you in cuffs."

"Does it?" The look in her eye boasted amusement and, if he wasn't mistaken, temptation. "Nah, I'll stick with detective. It sounds sexier."

"Does it?" He echoed and arched a brow, curiosity evident.

"Careful. There's a reason I'm still unattached at thirty-two." Her grin faded as his eyes sharpened. "I have the reputation of leaving skid marks on men's hearts." Her gaze angled down. "And other parts of the human anatomy."

He couldn't have ignored the blast of heat that ignited inside of him if he'd tried. Heat that shot through his entire body and settled somewhere south of his belt. His interest in Riley Temple took an unwise and decided shift from professional straight into personal, hovering somewhere around carnal. "Consider me intrigued." He waved her inside. "And challenged."

They ate lunch outside, beneath the cloud-banked sun that grasped for a final blast of heat before winter fully descended. The distant

sound of emergency vehicles acted as background music to the neighborhood surrounding the medical center. A handful of apartment buildings and even more small businesses boasting unique eating and shopping experiences added to the holiday touches of weatherproof greenery and colorful candy canes looped around lampposts.

The small circular metal table outside the mom-and-pop eatery was just big enough to hold the tasting selection she'd embraced after getting a look at the menu. She'd needed something to focus on after the less-than-subtle acknowledgement that her passing attraction to Detective Quinn Burton was most definitely not one-sided.

Being attracted to a cop, a detective no less, created all sorts of complicated, fuzzy feelings inside of her. Whether complicated was a bad thing or not, was something she had yet to decide. She didn't trust cops as a species. Good or bad, she had her reasons. But on a one-on-one basis she tended to be a little less ... judgy.

She'd watched him fill their soda cups, debating with herself over whether coming to lunch with him had been a wise idea. A girl had to eat, but getting entangled with him, getting to know him on a personal level ...

It seemed to just be asking for trouble.

"There's a pasty food truck that sits at the park a couple of blocks from my place. Their empanadas are to die for," she said as she unwrapped one of the paper bags. Each pastry parcel, neatly enclosed with a perfectly crimped toasty edge, was branded with its filling name. She went for the Carne Asada first and sank her teeth into the perfectly cooked strips of beef and spicy garlic and jalapeno sauce. "Mmmm." She grabbed a napkin, hunched over the table. "My food truck might have just gotten bumped to second place. Definitely need to pin this place on my phone."

He rifled through the bags until he found the Samosa Veggie. He took a bite, chewed, and smiled as he nodded. "Carmen's got a magic touch with these things. First came across this place my last six months as a patrol officer. Couple of stupid kids playing armed robbers thought they'd be clever hitting them first thing in the morning."

"First thing? Let me guess," Riley said. "No money in the till?"

"Their criminal careers ended the day it began." He inclined his chin toward the young man exiting the shop with two large paper bags tagged as deliveries which he lifted in greeting when he spotted them.

"'Sup, Quinn?"

"Same old, Marcus," Quinn said as the young man hopped on one of the two bikes stashed near the curb. "Carmen's husband called the cops on Marcus there and his brother Tony. While they waited, Carmen fed the boys. And talked to them. Not an unfamiliar story, but she found out their mother was struggling to find work after their father took off. The boys couldn't think of another way to help."

"So they turned to crime. Ah, our education system doing us proud." Riley patted a hand against her heart.

"Now their mom works with Carmen in the kitchen, Tony manages the front of the store, and Marcus runs the website and online ordering system."

"And you found a new place to eat," Riley teased. "I take it you didn't arrest the boys."

"Would have. Probably should have. Carmen wouldn't let me."

"So everyone lives happily ever after."

"Happier maybe," Quinn said. "Word got around the department about Carmen and now"—he gave a head nod to two patrol officers as they headed inside—"Carmen's got enough cops coming and going throughout the day she doesn't have to worry about another robbery." He eyed the street beyond. "Neither does anyone else around here."

"Well, your good deed for the day is done, detective. You've restored my fragile faith in humanity."

"Or maybe just in cops."

Riley's food turned to glue in her mouth. Someone had been doing their research.

"Something you said last night struck a chord. I tend to remember everything I hear," he added at her suspicious frown. "Weird talent, I know, but small fry crime definitely left me thinking."

She eyed her lunch. "Should I be waiting for the arsenic to take effect? I don't have the best reputation with your fellow law enforcement friends."

"I think you'd be surprised how many fans you have. We're not all Joe Pantello, Riley. And the majority of us are not his fans."

"I know that." She glugged soda so she could swallow.

"Good." He nodded. "I wasn't sure, given how things went last night."

"Last night I was not at my best. I tend to get testy when my friends are attacked and murdered."

"I take it your faith in humanity remains a bit shaky."

Feeling slightly more at ease, she offered a smile. "No more so than the San Andreas fault." Riley took another bite and opened another bag containing the spicy corn empanada. He'd been curious enough about her to go poking into the past. The fact he hadn't stayed away after learning the truth about her past with the LAPD told her something important. He didn't shy away from the truth. "Viewing life through a camera lens means nothing's hidden. I see everything."

"I imagine you do." Quinn gave her a long, considering look. "You said you were at the Fairfront Hotel last night. Bungalow twelve."

She focused back on her food. "Uh-huh."

"There were two women you spoke with. Would that have been Tiffany Small and her mother?"

"Checking on my alibi, detective?"

"Confirming a theory." He leaned his arms on the table, his lunch forgotten. "Why'd you send the pictures you took to Juvenile Crime? Tiffany Small's nineteen."

"It was the only direct email address I had handy." There was no point denying what's she'd done. Besides, some things weren't worth lying about. "I figured once news broke, if that wasn't the right department to handle it, it would get to where it needed to go." She dunked the corner of her corn empanada into the side of chimichurri sauce and nearly swooned at the spices dancing on her tongue. "I heard her mother was taken in for questioning, so I guess it worked."

"Oh, it definitely worked. Word has it Tiffany's agent is trying to spin this for a TV movie deal."

"Damned if Laurel didn't call that one," she muttered under her breath. "Totally should have taken that bet."

"A lot of people in your profession would have seen the bigger picture," Quinn observed. "The financial picture. There's a lot of profit to be made in exposing shit like that. How much did you get from the news outlets?"

"Nothing." Yet. She shook her head. "And don't go declaring me some kind of saint, detective. I'm too much of a bitch for that."

"Not from where I'm sitting."

"That's because I'm something shiny and new to play with." Now that's what she'd call projecting. "You haven't come close to seeing how tarnished I am beneath the surface."

"Tarnish has never looked so appealing before."

She shook her head, managed a laugh. "There are three things I loathe most in this world, Detective Burton." She ticked them off on her fingers. "Bullies, hypocrites, and users. My friends call those my issue buttons. Once they're pushed, there's no telling what I'll do. And they're pushed. A lot."

"I do believe we've dug down to the bedrock of your shaky-trust syndrome."

Her smile came easily now. Dammit, she really liked this guy. "The number of people I trust and can completely rely on wouldn't take up all ten of your fingers. The truth I live by? People are never what or who they pretend to be. There's always something ... more. Under the surface. Lurking. Waiting to be exposed even while people do everything they can not to be."

"Is that the purpose of your photography?" Quinn asked before he resumed eating. "To expose the person behind the image? That would make you a paparazzo with an agenda."

"Everyone has an agenda," Riley told him. "Once I accepted that, life got quite a bit easier to survive."

"Harsh way to see the world." It wasn't often he encountered someone more jaded than the cops he worked with.

"Ask Dudley if I'm wrong." Bitterness coated her words. "You can find him in the morgue, in case you forgot."

"I didn't forget," he said quietly. "And point made."

She wasn't entirely sure she liked the look in Quinn's eyes. As if he was trying to pry her apart and puzzle her back together. She also didn't care for the idea of anyone trying to figure her out, especially when she worked hard to be a complete and open book. The secrets she did keep, they weren't for anyone to discover. They were hers and hers alone.

"I don't agree with you, however," he said after a moment. "I don't believe everyone has an agenda, Riley."

"Sure they do. Take you for example." She polished off the last of both empanadas, then broke the Dulce de Leche dessert pocket in half, slid his portion toward him. "You want to ask me something. Something you aren't sure I'm going to be honest about. So you bolstered your chances by softening me up." She leaned back, pulled the sobriety token out of her pocket and set it on the table. "Or are you going try to claim giving me this was just a kind gesture to ease my grief?"

He sat back in his chair, his features tightening as he looked down at the coin, then back at her. "I'll admit it struck me as a good way to connect with you on a more emotional level."

"We already connected," she told him. "The tragedy of last night aside, I'd say we definitely have some chemistry brewing between us, despite your unfortunate profession which, for the record, is a major turnoff for me." The only one she'd uncovered so far. "What else do you want?"

His lips twitched. "Now there's a loaded question."

She scooped a finger into the pastry and brought the cream to her lips, her eyes boring into his as she licked her finger clean. The way his pupils dilated, the way his breath hitched ever so slightly in his chest, had her feeling more than a little triumphant. "Let's clear the debris out of the way, shall we?" She swallowed, and tried not to think about the way her own pulse was hammering in her throat. "I think it's a given there's a very good chance we're going to end up in bed together."

"If you can get over the fact I'm a cop," Quinn said with a nod. "Definitely a safe bet."

*Smart. So smart.* "So let's say we use the rest of our discussion and lunch to determine how fast that's going to happen. The sooner you ask what you want to ask, the faster we can get back to the more interesting aspect of our growing … connection. Fair warning, though. Whatever the question is, I'm going to make you earn your way into my bed."

"Who says it's going to be your bed?"

Oh, yeah. She grinned. He was definitely going to be fun.

She could see it: amusement, shock, and just a teeny bit of admiration, maybe? There was little she enjoyed more than pushing confident, handsome, firmly settled men utterly and completely off balance. All they needed was the jumping off point and she was more than ready to dive in. "Ask your question, detective."

"What was in the box you took from Merle's store yesterday?"

"Junk." It took every bit of focus she had not to blink. She nibbled at the last of her dessert, attempted to feign disinterest at his inquiry as she relished the flaky pastry. "Just junk. Nothing important."

"Maybe by the time you came back to the shop to collect that box," his lips barely moved as he spoke, "you'd already found what those two assailants were looking for, didn't you? Let me guess. The film you mentioned?"

"What film?"

"I already told you I remember everything anyone's ever told me about anything," Quinn said. "It's a gift. And a curse. But I remember. What's on that film, Riley?" He shifted his head ever so slightly, the interest in his gaze no doubt reminiscent of how he interrogated suspects. "What are those pictures of?"

"I don't know." It wasn't a lie. Not completely anyway. She only had strong suspicions, not actual proof of a woman's murder and until she had a more solid idea, she was keeping them to herself. "I'm still working with them."

"But you know they're what the guy who broke into your car last night was after. Or at least you suspect it. I saw it on your face the instant you made the connection. You were scared."

"Now you read minds?" Her first instincts about this man had been right. He was dangerous. But for so many more reasons than she'd initially thought.

"I do a lot of things. You told me to ask, and I'm asking. Funny how you're just dancing around an actual response. Makes me think I'm right about what I'm thinking."

"And you, like so many men, hate being right." It took an effort to keep her tone light.

"Let's try something simpler. How's your car?"

"Got the window fixed this morning." Cost her a pretty penny, too, but an unexpected rush job with Halle always cost. "And just to circle back and be clear, you're not as good as you think you are."

"Neither are you." Flat determination shone in his eyes. "I want to see those pictures."

"You can. Just as soon as you get a warrant." She gathered up her trash, wadded it up so her hands had something to do other than fidget. "The only thing you have is a vague memory of me mentioning pictures during a conversation where I was clearly distraught. I doubt it'll get you very far with a judge."

"Don't underestimate my powers of persuasion. And I don't believe you do distraught." His eyebrow arched. "Ever."

For the first time in her life, she understood the appeal of playing cat and mouse. If only she could be sure which creature she was. "Let's say I did develop that film and I do have some photographs. In theory," she added at his arched brow, "the second I show them to you, I lose control over them and become irrelevant to anything that comes after."

"Worried about a payday?"

The accusation struck hard, but given the way she made her living, could she argue? It wasn't as if the thought hadn't crossed her mind as well. What she was worried about was that the photos would get buried in an evidence box somewhere along with the mystery of who that woman had been. At least she'd known Dudley's name. That poor woman, whoever she'd been, she may very well have disappeared into the ether of this town.

"Who isn't worried about a payday?" she played along. "But that's beside the point. While I'm more than happy to dance around with you all the way into one of our beds, that doesn't mean I'm remotely close to trusting you where other things are concerned. Once you have those pictures, you have no reason to keep me in the loop."

"I asked for the pictures, not the negatives. Nothing stopping you from developing more."

"So you're going to semantics me to death."

"What makes you think I'd shut you out? Oh, right." He snapped his fingers. "Trust issues. You know I can charge you with withholding material evidence in a murder investigation?"

"You can try, but my lawyer would have me back out in minutes. Laurel Fontaine." She fluttered her lashes. "Maybe you've heard of her?"

"The name's not completely unfamiliar." Massive understatement given the sour expression on his face. "Semantics aside," Quinn sat forward, rested his arms on the table, "my interest in those pictures has more to do with you than what they might show. I'm worried about you, Riley."

"Are you?" She leaned her chin in her hand and batted her lashes. "Do tell."

"I'm not being some macho, misogynist douche here." But his patience was clearly wearing thin. "For the record, I had that gene knocked out of my DNA by a very progressive, ball-kicking older sister."

She refused to laugh. Instead, she set her jaw and watched him.

"I need you to realize what you're potentially up against here, so please listen to me." He kept his tone, and his eyes, controlled, flat, and focused entirely on her. "Whoever attacked Merle killed Dudley to lure you back to the store, Riley. They know who you are. They broke into your car, which means if they didn't have your license plate number then, they sure as hell do now. It's not a big jump to find out where you live. I'm worried they'll come after you next."

"Please," she scoffed even as his warning sent a loud bell clanging inside of her. "You're just trying to scare me into doing what you want me to do."

"That's not what I'm doing," he snapped. "If you want to brush me off, fine, but the surveillance tape shows me everything I need to know. Both those assailants looked you straight in the eye before you walked out with that box. Did Merle mention your name when you waved goodbye? Not many Rileys around, I'd bet. Not even in this town."

She swallowed hard. "My building's secure."

"And it's not like you ever leave your building. They tossed that place looking for something and near as we could tell, they didn't find it. I'm convinced they left Merle alive in case they needed to come back. And you'd be easy pickings in the hospital should you start spending more time there. But that aside for now, here's the really important part: as that alarm rang and the cops were on their way, those two killers took enough time to walk around into the parking lot and put two bullets point-blank into Dudley while he slept and listened to Christmas carols. They knew you'd be back the second you heard someone at that property was dead. They knew and they were waiting for you."

"Stop it." Closing her eyes did nothing to stop the images from flashing through her mind. She couldn't bear the thought that lovely, harmless, lovable Dudley had been killed because of her. Because of something she'd done. Or seen.

"This wasn't an impulsive attack, Riley. They made mistakes, but they knew what they were after. Whatever you have, whatever is on that film, is worth two people's lives so far. The more you fight me on this, the more reckless you seem. And the more I'm convinced you aren't safe as long as you have it." His eyes hardened. "Neither is anyone around you."

Panic threatened to lock around her throat. "Now you're just—"

"Being paranoid? Manipulative? Sure. Fine. Whatever it takes. Nothing Wally and I picked up off the street by your car was remotely interesting or valuable."

"Not true," Riley protested. "There was a first edition Jackie Collins paperback in that box. And a bunch of Sydney Sheldons. Tell me those aren't collectible."

He didn't bat an eye. "That guy took the chance, with three patrol cars and one detective unit less than a block away, to try to steal that box out of your car. You aren't stupid, Riley. Stop pretending this is news to you. You're worried about being kept out of the loop? Really? Is that what Dudley's life meant to you?"

"Low blow." She couldn't look at him any longer.

The two officers were sitting at the window counter inside, chatting, eating, and tossing an occasional glance in hers and Detective Burton's direction. She didn't want to cause a scene, not when he was making entirely too much, terrifying sense. She pushed to her feet, grabbed her trash to toss, then returned for her bag.

"Don't make me turn this into something official, Riley."

"Don't threaten me, *detective*," she snapped and slung her bag over her shoulder. "And don't presume to know anything about me other than what you've read on Google."

"I prefer DuckDuckGo, actually—"

"If I had any pictures—" She felt like a feral cat, desperate to lash out and hiss. "I'm not saying I do—"

"You did last night."

"Today's a brand new day. *If I* had them—those pictures are going to lead me to who killed my friend."

"It's my job to get there first."

"Right. Because a dead homeless man from a parking lot is on the top of your priority list. Like that other, equally dead, young homeless teen Pantello had 'helped,' too."

"I'm not Joe Pantello." The icy tone in his voice coated her in shame.

She already knew he wasn't anything like that asshole detective who had been more concerned with getting his rocks off than saving a young man in crisis. *Of course* Detective Quinn Burton was different. He wouldn't have shown up at the hospital if he wasn't.

He certainly wouldn't be sitting across the table from her now. Unless ...

Unless he was willing to do anything to get his hands on that film.

"I've seen enough discarded homeless lying in the street to know that their deaths are rarely paid attention to, let alone addressed," she said. "I'm not going to let you use Dudley's death as the next rung on your career ladder."

"Now hold on—"

That irritation sparked into anger, but she was already chugging ahead. "Shall we go back through your department's history with selective truths? Hell, this entire city is built on a graveyard of lies and secrets.

"How do I know the second I turn over those photos they won't just vanish into the ether of the LAPD, like my video did? How do I know you and your partner aren't already moving beyond last night and straight into whatever headline-grabbing crime happens tomorrow? Or that the second I even try to go public with whatever pictures I might have, you tag me as a quack-a-doodle-doo." Her lungs burned as if she were an out-of-control steamroller. "Merle's attack and Dudley's murder barely registered a blip on the local news, but those pictures of Tiffany Small and her Crawford wannabe of a mother? Lead story. Number one trending on Twitter while potential movie deals get talked about. Tell me again," she leaned closer and stared him in the eye, "that you give one damn about what those pictures might actually represent."

"I can't tell you anything until I've seen them." His calm, careful tone sounded vastly more dangerous than his outraged one. "And for the record, I don't control the media."

She glared at him, battling against reason that left her wanting to believe he was different. That he was someone she could trust. But she couldn't take the chance of letting those photographs out of her control. Not when she could use them to find the people responsible for hurting Merle and killing Dudley.

"I'm going to tell you something you clearly need to hear." He finally moved, rose to his feet and, touched a gentle hand to her jacket clad arm. "I hear you, Riley. I've heard everything you said and I'll remember every—"

"Word. Yeah, so you've said." She huffed out a breath and like a five-year-old in the middle of a temper tantrum felt the overwhelming urge to stomp her feet. Dammit, did he have to be so ... understanding? Did he have to counter every single belief she'd held most of her life about cops?

"Despite disagreeing with you, I hear what you're saying," he continued, "Painting everyone in this town with the same tainted brush isn't fair. Just like me calling you a paparazzo would probably irk you a teeny bit."

She was giving herself a headache with all the glaring she was doing.

"I work with a lot of good people, Riley. Are all of them perfect? Of course not. Are there days I hate my job? Yes. Just like you do sometimes, I'm sure. But I wouldn't still be carrying a badge if I thought everyone was corrupt and out for themselves. But that's a discussion for another day." He stepped closer, took hold of her upper arms and shifted her until they were nose to nose. Until she could feel the heat of him pulsing through his hands, radiating from every inch of his toned, taut body. "You might think you're protecting yourself, but as long as you keep those photographs to yourself, you're exposed, Riley. And not just to the two people responsible for what happened last night."

"Now what are you talking about?" The confusion she'd fought to keep under wraps seeped into her voice.

"I've encountered my fair share of criminals over the years." He moved in, the warmth of his breath brushing over her cheek. "I know hired killers when I see them. They didn't finish the job. They didn't get what they came for. And I don't think they're going to stop until they find it."

Her wall of resistance cracked, but she'd be damned if she let it crumble completely. "And what? You think taking the pictures off my hands suddenly puts me in the safety zone?"

"No, actually, I don't. You're a target. You're in their sights. And you're probably going to stay there until this all plays out."

"If I'm in their sights, then you know who to look for when I end up in the morgue next to Dudley."

For the first time since they'd met, she saw anger spark in his eyes. "That isn't remotely funny."

"It's a little funny." It was also a complete bluff; one that threatened to make her heave up her lunch. "Give me a couple of days. I just need some time—"

But he wasn't looking at her any longer. His gaze had shifted over her head, into the street, his frustration and anger fading behind cold realization as his eyes sharpened. The revving of an engine erupted in her ears, followed quickly by the screeching of tires. As she turned out of his hold, she scanned the line of cars and caught the silver sedan out of the corner of her eye.

The world shifted into slow motion as an arm extended out of the open window.

"Get down!" Quinn yelled. "Now!"

It occurred to her, when Quinn's arm wrapped around her shoulders, that an odd dull, popping sound exploded toward them. He dragged her in front of him and threw her to the ground. She heard glass exploding as she landed face first, her chin impacting the sidewalk hard enough to make her head snap back.

She tried to breathe, but couldn't, not with Quinn flattened on top of her. He pulled himself off her, onto his knees beside her, still holding her in place with one solid hand. The echoes of screams and cries and running footsteps erupted all around. Cars screeched to a halt as another raced away, the acrid smell of burning rubber the only thing left in their wake.

"Riley?" Quinn shifted, his hand still on her back and she lifted her head. He was holding his weapon with his other hand, poised to shoot, ready to defend. "You hit?"

She did a quick mental inventory, shook her head as the pressure of his hold released and she sat up. "No, I don't think so." She patted a hand down her front.

"Good."

"Detective?" One of the officers, a young woman with tightly braided hair and wide yet controlled eyes, raced out, her own weapon drawn as she dropped down beside them. "Everyone okay?"

"We're good. People inside?"

"They're fine. We heard you in time."

Riley looked around. Passersby were visibly shaken, packages and bags littering the sidewalk. Some people were getting to their feet after hitting the ground. A baby screamed in its mother's arms, the stroller tipped over, wheels spinning. An older couple comforted each other as they visibly trembled in each other's embrace.

"Window's shot to hell," the officer said. "Some cosmetic damage for sure, but no one was hurt. My partner's calling it in."

"Tell him to ask for Detective Osterman and that his partner's already on scene," Quinn said. "Riley, you okay on your feet?"

"Yeah." She pushed up, locked her knees, touched her head and felt glass fall from her hair. "Did you set that up? Because that's one hell of a way to convince me you might be right, detective," she tried to joke, the humor never quite forming behind the terror-filled sob that caught in her throat. Someone had shot at her! Shot! At her!

He reached out, caught the back of her neck and hauled her against him, covering her mouth in a quick, hard, powerful kiss that drained the adrenaline coursing through her system—gave her a more pleasurable shock to distract her with. "Damn it," he murmured against her lips before he slid an arm around her shoulders and held her tight. "Sometimes I hate being right. That was too close."

She nodded, unable to speak as she clung to him. Her mind was spinning, was too full of the ghost sounds of bullets, glass, and the trembling acknowledgement that this man threatened to upend every aspect of her life. And yet somehow, impossibly, she felt safe here, standing in this man's—this *cop's*—arms. Arms that had locked around her as if he was never going to let her go.

"I need to go check on Carmela and the others," he said into her hair. "I want you to sit on the stool in the kitchen and wait for me, okay? They won't be back," he insisted at her shocked expression, as he led her to the enclosed space when food was prepared for the restaurant. "Too many witnesses. You'll need to make a statement when Wally and additional officers get here." He slid his gun back into his belt holster. "Then I'm going to take you home."

"You are?" She hated to admit it, but that sounded like a good idea.

"I'm taking you home." He caught her face between his hands, stared into her eyes until she had no option other than to blink. "And you're going to show me those pictures."

## CHAPTER FIVE

"I'VE never let anyone drive my car before."

Quinn didn't have to be looking at Riley to know she was glaring at him. He could feel her stare, like radiation lasers burning through his Southern California-tanned skin. But if glaring and complaining got her back into normal Riley mode, he was happy to speed it along. He wasn't the kind of man who second-guessed himself, but ever since he'd seen that gun, he couldn't stop wondering what would have happened if he'd been even a fraction of a moment later in reacting. "I guess you get to mark this in your book of firsts then."

While he was drop-to-his-knees grateful she hadn't been physically injured, it was only a matter of time before the reality of what had happened hit her. Someone trying to kill you wasn't an easy thing to process. The fall was coming. Whether he'd be there to catch her again remained to be seen.

"Are you sure this isn't you attempting to exercise those misogyny muscles your sister kicked out of you?"

"Pretty sure." Even in stressful situations, the woman had a knack for pulling a smile out of him. "Just don't expect me to parallel park this thing for you. I don't think my ego could take the ensuing commentary."

"Ah, he's human after all. What'd you to do to your partner?"

"Huh?" He stopped at a red light, rested his hands in his lap and admired the surprisingly comfortable mini SUV. "What about Wally?"

"Wallace," she corrected. "He really likes to be seen as a full-grown detective." She chuckled, thinly. "He looked seriously pissed off when he arrived."

"Yeah. I ditched him earlier." Relieved when the light changed before he hit Santa Monica Boulevard, he focused his attention back on the road. Weekend traffic didn't hold a candle to weekday rush hour, but it still wasn't anything close to pleasant. A car two lanes over blasted its horn when a motorcycle zipped across to turn at the corner. "I didn't want him around, so I could hit on you. He probably thought I was cutting him out of police action."

"I'd say half of that statement is true." She arched a brow when he glanced at her. "Maybe I'm not the only one with trust issues."

"Change isn't my forte," he admitted. "My last partner and I clicked from the start and we worked together for more than five years. With Wally—"

"Wallace."

"Right. Wally and I are still finding our footing. Partnerships take time to develop and work the kinks out."

"Only if you're hoping it doesn't work out. Tell me something."

"Shoot." He looked at her again. "Too soon? Cop humor."

"It's the twenty-first century, right? We've got technology for everything these days. Heck, we've got cars that drive themselves."

"Only if we let them." Until Quinn witnessed George Jetson himself blipping by, he'd continue to think self-driving vehicles were a bad idea.

"Honestly, I think I could blink Morse code and accidentally order a food delivery, so tell me, how on earth does it take almost four hours to deal with a crime scene and take witness statements?"

"At least I'm getting you home before the sun sets. But to answer your question, it takes as long as it does because when all is said and done, we're dealing with human beings, most of whom don't deal well with violent surprises like drive-by shootings. And to be fair, that last hour is all on me."

"I'm not complaining about you helping install plywood panels into the window frames of the restaurant. Although to be fair, I'm not entirely sure that wasn't self-serving. I bet you earned free empanadas for life."

"Nah. Just six months." He grinned. "And that was only because I told Carmela I'd help her walk through the insurance claim. Not that she needs help," he added. "Woman probably could have deflected every one of those bullets if she hadn't misplaced her amazonium bracelets."

"Huh."

"What?" Was he mistaken or did she look ... impressed?

"I wouldn't have pegged you as an old-school comic book reader. Most Wonder Woman fans think the bracelets were forged from Aegis, Zeus's unbreakable shield."

"I'm a purist for origin details. Issue number 52 clearly explained her bracelet's origins, although I like what the TV series did by calling it feminum."

"That whole Nazi story line when they took over Paradise Island?" Riley turned in her seat, eyes bright like a tween discovering her first boy band crush. "My favorite episodes, for sure. Although the one with Rick Springfield is a close second."

"One of many fun guest stars," Quinn agreed. "Might be time for another bingeathon." Her sudden silence had him frowning now. "What?"

"Nothing." She shifted back and stared straight ahead. "I'm mainly annoyed that I like you."

He chuckled. "Wait until we talk about *Battlestar Galactica.*"

"Depends on if you mean the original or remake. And for the record," she added. "If you don't love both, we can't be friends. Take the third off-ramp," she told him.

"I know exactly where I'm going, don't worry."

"Let me guess," she said. "You have an unhealthy and intimate relationship with Google maps."

"No, I had a great Uncle Silas."

"Didn't we all?"

"He worked as a stuntman for Columbia Pictures back in the day," Quinn said. "He used to take me and my brother and sister on tours around town to visit all the city's famous and not-so-famous landmarks. Temple House was one of his favorite places."

"I can't imagine why." Her smile seemed genuine. "I'm sure it's history as a boarding house for Hollywood actresses and extras—"

"*Female* Hollywood extras. And backup dancers. And starlets," Quinn cut in. "Don't forget the starlets. Lana Turner, Veronica Lake, Rosalind Russell, Marilyn—"

"Hate to disappoint you, but Marilyn never lived at Temple House," Riley said. "She visited a few times though, according to my grandfather. They actually played chess one evening. She beat him," she added with a fond smile. "That was one of his favorite stories to tell. There's a picture of the two of them together on one of our bookcase shelves."

"No Marilyn at Temple House? Good thing Uncle Silas is gone. That news might just break his starlet-loving heart." Quinn had such a clear image of the place in his head; it was as if he'd lived there at some point. "I remember the downstairs lobby that doubled as some kind of meeting place for studio execs?"

She nodded. "They called it Hollywood Switzerland. Lots of hush-hush meetings people weren't comfortable holding in public. Considering how the rumor mill ran even back then, no one could visit a studio office without everyone finding out. But pop over here for a drink and chat in the lobby of Temple House? That was a whole other matter."

"There was a summer, back when I was ten," Quinn recalled. "Temple House opened for tours. I think Uncle Silas brought me maybe half a dozen times. I remember eating tuna sandwiches and vanilla pudding out on the patio."

"We opened it up for the building's seventieth anniversary. My grandfather's idea," she added. "The *LA Times* did a big retrospective on the building's history that spring so there was massive interest. The admission and tour fees paid the property taxes for a few years."

"I thought about becoming an architect after one of those tours," Quinn recalled. "I always thought it was so interesting, how the original plans for Spanish architecture was overtaken by Art Deco. The combination created this new kind of mishmash of styles."

"That's what happens when new investors are brought in at the last second. Powell Film Studios had the original idea, but not the cash on hand to get the building completed. The head of the studio at the time made a deal with the competing studios to get in on the construction and have a place for their stable of actresses to live. By the way, don't mention the word stable around my aunt in reference to Temple House. She takes exception to the term." She paused, wincing. "Speaking of Moxie. I don't want her to know about any of this."

"The pictures you've unearthed or the fact you were almost killed a few hours ago?"

"Both. Any and all of it." She took a deep breath as if trying to pretend someone hadn't taken some serious shots at her. "Just … tell her you require my photographic expertise or something."

"So you want me to lie." Quinn arched a brow. "Interesting."

"I'm asking you to help me protect her, detective. She's eighty years old. I don't want her weighed down with all … this."

"I get it." Some things weren't worth joking about. "Where should I park?"

He didn't realize just how long it had been since he'd even driven past Temple House until he stepped out of her car and closed the door. "Not a bad security setup," he acknowledged as she grabbed her bag and, taking the keys from his hand, activated the car's lock. "Last time I was here this was just an open lot for the residents."

"We had a lot of insurance claims because of car break-ins," Riley explained and indicated the high, spiked iron fence and coded keypad gateway. "My grandfather bit the bullet and invested in an upgrade about fifteen years ago. He wasn't one to do things halfway."

"Did he keep the lobby bar? What about the piano and the fireplace?"

"All still very much on display and intact. Although, with the number of kids in the building, we stock the bar with water and snacks rather than liquor. That we keep locked up, mind you."

"I would have killed for my very own snack shop in my house." Quinn pushed open the walk-through gate that led them down a short path to the sidewalk. "And the screening room. Tell me there's still a screening room."

"I'm beginning to think your interest in me has nothing to do with photographs and everything to do with the building I live in."

"The building you own," Quinn corrected.

"Co-own," she said. "Yes, the screening room is still there, upgraded for modern viewing capabilities. Although we still have a bunch of the old projectors down in the basement. We invested in some decent theater seating and can accommodate up to fifty people. Comes in handy for birthday parties and building events. Every couple of years Aunt Moxie hosts a Sally Tate film festival. We bring in a bunch of residents from local nursing homes and make a big event out of it."

"Sally Tate back on the big screen." Quinn didn't try to hide his excitement. "How do I get an invite to that?"

"First Wonder Woman, now Sally Tate?" She arched a dubious brow. "I'm onto you, Detective Burton. No man is this perfect." Riley grabbed his arm, stopped walking. "I've been buzzing around so fast the last couple of days, I didn't stop to think. Your last name. Burton. Are you related to Chief Burton?"

"Only slightly," Quinn admitted. "He's my father."

"Your father. Wow. Okay." Her brow furrowed. "Sorry. Should have made that connection sooner."

"No reason you should be thinking about the police chief." Quinn didn't like to make a big deal out of it. He'd be lying if he said the rumblings of nepotism didn't rear their ugly heads every once in a while, especially around promotion time. But most every cop in the department had some anchor hanging around their neck. His happened to be a Los Angeles powerhouse with a badge.

"Isn't your dad like third-generation chief? That makes you—"

"Detective Burton. The same detective who shared his favorite empanada restaurant with you." He guided her around the corner toward the front entrance of Temple House. "I'm a fourth-generation cop." Whatever happened in the future, he was always going to be that. "That's all there is to it right now."

He remembered the three stone steps leading up to Temple House's double glass door entrance being larger than this. The wide and deep entryway opened up after Riley keyed in a code on the pad by the door, below the intercom system connecting the entrance to each apartment. Quinn glanced up, nodded approvingly.

"Good security setup. Cameras are a good brand. Reliable. Do you have in-house security?"

"No. We hire out to a private company who monitors all the entrances and elevators."

"What about the roof? The alley? What's the coverage there?"

"How did you know about the … ah, the tours." She nodded as he pulled open the door when the click sounded. "No cameras on the roof. We've limited access to a handful of residents. Key entry. We consider it private, personal space, but open it up once in a while for when the weather's particularly glorious. Don't make me start worrying about one of the few things that brings me joy, detective."

"Something to keep in mind, moving forward, is all," he said as a not-so-subtle reminder of the afternoon's events. But he found those concerns pushed aside the second he stepped inside Temple House.

Quinn's memory had not failed him. While time had clearly marched on, at its core, the essence of glamorous old Hollywood remained, pristine and glowing. From the white marble floors to the beautifully maintained architectural details, Temple House was absolute perfection.

Or at least it probably was on a normal day when it wasn't caught up in the chaos and celebratory atmosphere of Christmas gradually staking its claim.

The thick, round columns and cathedral-style arched windows on either side of the expansive space that meticulously displayed stark black photo frames displaying countless classic Hollywood personalities and legends. The lobby area itself reached up two stories, with higher windows displaying elegant, gold-accented stained glass. Marble tiles stretched the entire expanse. Everything mingled into perfect harmony.

Immediately to the right of the entryway sat the highly polished curving open-sided bar with brass foot rails. Matching bar stools sat in groups of three, sectioned apart. The mirrored wall behind was lined with shelves, filled with antique glasses and bottles, while various refrigerators made up the back counter area. Racks of snacks, healthy and otherwise, sat in easy reach of little hands while bowls of fruit sat on display for a quick grab-and-go nosh.

The spicy aroma of mulling spices and hot apples filled the air. With Christmas music playing over hidden speakers, all that was missing was a gentle snowfall, which Los Angeles had rarely seen.

Quinn went and stood on the top of the raised dais above the welcoming crowded heartbeat of Temple House. A couple dozen people pinged around like errant pin balls draping garlands, hanging ornaments, and situating quirky holiday characters in hidden peeking spots around the lobby.

"I guess the lobby tree arrived." Riley almost had to yell over Pentatonix beatboxing their way through the holidays. "Moxie's favorite annual project. We have an arrangement with a local Christmas tree farm for the tenants and always get a huge one for the lobby." She pointed to the eight-foot spruce being arranged in the far left corner by the enormous fireplace. "This is good." She patted his arm. "She'll be distracted and won't ask me a lot of questions." She turned at a scampering sound, her face lighting up. "Hey, guys. Okay, hang on." She dumped her bag and dropped down to embrace the three dogs who had scampered over to her.

One of the dogs, a rough looking Golden Retriever eyed Quinn suspiciously.

"Who put this hat on you, Elliot?" Riley clucked her tongue and removed the pointy elf-hat. "That is so undignified for a dog of your status." Given the dog's pained expression, Quinn surmised Elliot clearly agreed.

"Aww, Aunt Riley, it took us forever to get straight." A young girl with bright blonde hair tied up in tinsel and bows slid onto her knees and wrapped her arms around Elliot's neck. "He liked it! Hi!" She beamed up at Quinn. "Are you Aunt Riley's new boyfriend?"

"Keeley, that's not funny," Riley warned. "Come here, Barksy. You too, Yoda." She brushed a hand over the graying head of a sturdy-looking guard dog before lifting the Yorkie with one hand, giving him a quick kiss on his head. "Lord, but I swear the holidays are hardest on the animals. Let's get this garland off of you."

"Does your Aunt Riley need a new boyfriend, Keeley?" Quinn stepped down and crouched to offer his hand to each of the bigger dogs as he spoke to the little girl.

"Nah, nobody *needs* one," Keeley said matter-of-factly. "But my mom says—"

"Never mind what your mother says about my relationship status," Riley warned. "This is Mr. Burton. I'm, um … I'm helping him with something for his work."

"Wow," Quinn mouthed when Keeley was preoccupied with the dogs. "I don't know why, but I assumed you'd be a better liar," he murmured into Riley's ear when he stood and moved closer.

"I am," she confirmed. "Except with people I care about. Where is your mom, Keeley?"

"Phone call." Keeley reached up and took Yoda out of Riley's hands. "We've got sugar cookies and gingerbread over on the table. Come on." But rather than taking Riley's hand, she grabbed Quinn's and tugged. "There's hot apple cider and wine for the grown-ups," she said loudly over her shoulder. "Aunt Moxie's pouring."

"Should I be worried?" he asked Riley.

"Only if no one's monitoring the rum," Riley warned with a look that had him laughing. "Hi, Mrs. Yan—Clark." She waved at the forty-something couple digging into one of the dozens of ornament and decoration boxes strewn about the lobby. Elliot and Barksy trailed behind them and made their way around the tree to give it a good sniff while a young boy and girl—around the same age as Keeley—popped out from behind the familiar fireplace that years before had transfixed Quinn. "Help yourself to some food," Riley told him. "Just be warned, it's sugar season around here until New Year's. I need to make the rounds, real quick, otherwise we'll never make it upstairs. Oh! Hey, Aunt Moxie."

Riley stopped short when she spun around and came face-to-face with her aunt. It was a face Quinn had seen all his life on screen, but looking at her now, in person, melted all those years away. He wasn't easily starstruck. How could he be when you could barely turn around in this town without running into a famous face? But Moxie was of an entirely different generation. She'd worked with some of the giants in the industry and made it to the end of her career with only a few bumps along the way, something that made her all the more remarkable.

"I've been calling you for the last couple of hours," Moxie Temple said with a flare of concern in her green eyes. Green eyes that seemed to sparkle when she shifted her gaze to Quinn. "Now I think I understand why you've been incommunicado. Hello, young man. Are you here to interview for the building manager position?"

"No, ma'am."

"Well, that's a shame. You'd be nice to have around. Riley?" Moxie gasped, caught Riley's chin between two fingers and raised her face to the light. "What on earth happened here? You look like you've been dragged down Mulholland, face first."

"It's nothing. I … tripped." She angled a warning look at Quinn. "Detective Quinn Burton, this is my great aunt, Moxie Temple." She batted Moxie's curious hands away from her face. "Stop that! I'm fine."

"Detective?" Moxie finally shifted her attention, then spun on her niece. "Tripped? I'm not a simpleton, Riley. What happened? Something happened."

"Riley's helping me out with some photographic issues that cropped up in a case, Ms. Temple. And I'm afraid that scrape on her chin is my fault. I didn't catch her fast enough." Ready to distract the older woman, he added, "I'm sorry to intrude. I had no idea there was a party going on."

"No intrusion possible at this time of year. If I had my way, there'd always be a party going on," Moxie said with a laugh that didn't sound quite right. "Would you excuse us for a moment, Detective Burton? I need to speak with my niece for a moment."

"Quinn, please. And of course." He made his way over to the coffee table and ladled up a cup of cider then did a cup of the mulled wine for Riley, who he watched out of the corner of his eye. They exchanged a few words then Moxie pushed an envelope into her hand. Riley stared at it for a moment, sighed, nodded and shoved it into the back pocket of her jeans. After giving her aunt a reassuring hug, Riley moved into the crowd while Moxie returned to overseeing the decorating of the tree.

"Detective Burton. This is an interesting place for you to turn up."

Quinn stopped mid-sip and stepped back toward the fireplace to face the dark-haired woman standing behind him. It took him longer than it should have to recognize her, but when he did, he almost did a double take. "Laurel. Wow. Yeah." He offered a guarded smile and his hand, which she accepted easily. "Riley mentioned you were her lawyer. Do you live here, too?"

"I do." Laurel nodded slowly, as if taking inventory of him.

"It's nice to see you," he said. "I almost didn't recognize you without whip and chair."

Laurel Fontaine offered her trademark smile that had won over countless juries for her high-priced clients. "That's almost the nicest thing you've ever said to me, Quinn."

"You know, there's a pool bet going around the courthouse that you don't even own a pair of jeans." He looked her up and down, trying to reconcile the elegant, designer-wearing, no-nonsense defense attorney with the jean-clad, classic-rock-t-shirt-wearing woman standing in front of him. "I really should have gotten in on that action. Are those sneakers? I could have cleaned up on that one."

"Keeping people like you off guard and unbalanced is my raison d'être," she teased, but maintained that cool façade that earned her numerous nicknames among her law enforcement friends. None that he found remotely amusing. "Riley mentioned me, did she? Tell me something. What topic were you two discussing that she felt the need to drop my name?"

Quinn ducked his chin to hide his smile. He could definitely see where the two of them were friends. "Just polite conversation."

"Must have been an interesting one." She held up a manicured hand. "Don't worry—like you said, I don't have my attorney shoes on this evening." She glanced down at the well-worn sneakers. "Besides, I prefer to interrogate police officers on the stand not at apartment building Christmas-decorating parties. Lucas?" Laurel called out to a young boy untangling a string of Christmas lights. "Be careful with those, okay? Remember last year …"

"That's why I didn't plug them in this time." Lucas stuck his tongue out of the corner of his mouth. "Addie bet me I couldn't get them to work. If she's wrong, she has to make my bed *for a week.*"

"Sibling motivation." Laurel leaned over and poured herself some of the mulled wine. "A concept that's lost on me. How's your sister doing these days, Quinn? I haven't seen Cheryl in court lately."

"She's taken an extended leave of absence from the DA's office." Knowing Laurel, he was pretty sure she already knew that. "She and Marcie are expecting twins next month."

"Twins." Laurel's eyes widened. "Ouch."

"Double ouch," Quinn agreed.

"So what are you two talking about?" Riley popped up between them like a hyped-up rogue Whac-A-Mole. "Do you know each other? It looks like you know each other. Thanks." She accepted the cup Quinn had poured for her. "So? How do you know each other?"

"Well, aren't you hyper this afternoon," Laurel said. "Have you been eating sugar straight out of the bowl again?"

"Nope, not yet." Riley grinned. "Just a couple of Mrs. Sullivan's bourbon balls. Who's going to spill info first?"

"I've found myself on the wrong side of a few of Laurel's interrogations in court," Quinn admitted. "But we were actually talking about my sister. She's pregnant with twins, so Laurel's missing one of her favorite courtroom adversaries. I'm filling in as a proxy."

"And doing a marvelous job of it. For the record," Laurel said, "and because I'm just full of the Christmas spirit, I'll admit I consider Quinn one of those rare breeds of cop who actually takes his oath and duty seriously. Never caught him being anything other than completely open and upfront."

"Wow." Riley blinked in shock. "I don't think I've ever heard you heap praise like that on anyone before. Merry Christmas, indeed."

"Stop," Quinn grinned. "I'm blushing."

"Mabel, hey—you finally joining us?" Riley stopped a pretty, petite blonde as she rushed past.

"I wish. I got a call from a new"—she eyed Quinn as she tugged on a long, blue coat—"client. Can one of you watch Keeley and Barksy until I get back?"

Riley glanced at Quinn, clearly torn between what he was here for and wanting to help her friend. Laurel, being the overly attentive woman she was, reached out and touched Mabel's arm. "Of course. We'll hang out here and help decorate and if you aren't back by the time we're done, I'll bring them to my place."

"Thanks," Mabel said. "Keeley, baby?" She called her daughter over.

"Moooom." Keeley stomped over. "I asked you to please stop calling me baby."

"Right—sorry, baby." She grabbed Keeley's head and pressed a kiss to the top. "Sorry," she said again. "That's going to take some work. Aunt Laurel's got you and Barksy for tonight."

"Way cool." Keeley immediately brightened. "Can we watch *Poltergeist* again?"

"No, you can't," Mabel warned Laurel. "That movie gave her nightmares for weeks. Honestly, can't you watch the Muppets or something?"

"Aw, Mom. You ruin everything."

"Don't worry," Laurel said when Keeley raced off to find Barksy. "I'll find something eight-year-old appropriate. And for the record, she waited until I was asleep before she dragged that out of my Netflix cue. Go. Do your good work."

"Yeah, okay. Sorry I didn't get to meet you—whoever you are," Mabel added with a glance at Quinn. "Maybe next time?" She turned questioning eyes on Riley before she headed out.

"She didn't mean client in the traditional sense, did she?" Quinn asked. "What does she do?"

"She's an accountant mostly," Laurel said.

"And the rest of the time?" Quinn asked Riley.

"She's a Rape Victim Advocate. She—"

"Ah, I know what she does then," Quinn said, thinking of the myriad of women—and men—whose cases he'd worked over the years. Rape Victim Advocates were exactly what they sounded like: a voice for the victim and, at times, a much-needed barrier of protection as they made their way through what would forever be a different world. "You're right, Laurel. It's definitely good work. Seems like you all do good work," he added with a tight smile. That dose of reality was enough to push him back into detective mode. "Speaking of, we have some work to do in your darkroom, I believe, Riley?"

"Ah, right. Darkroom."

"Is that code for something?" Laurel asked. "If it isn't, it sure seems like it should be."

"Right now, it's code for 'mind your own business.'" Riley fluttered her lashes at her friend before inclining her head toward Quinn to indicate the elevator at the far end of the lobby. "You need help with the munchkin, give a holler."

"Don't let her hear you call her that," Laurel called.

"Call me what?" Keeley yelled.

"Nothing!" Laurel swept around and grabbed an oversized glitter-covered star to add to the tree. "Where should we put this?"

"Consider me impressed," Quinn said from behind Riley as she led him into her third-floor, loft-style apartment.

She felt like a locomotive engine being pushed up the hill by an inordinate amount of steam. There wasn't enough of her to contain all the emotions pinballing around inside of her. "Oh?"

"I didn't really think Temple House could be improved upon," he continued. "I think I see even more homage paid to its history than I remember from when I was a kid. Did Frank Sinatra and Sammy Davis Jr. really have a post-*Ocean's 11* wrap party here?"

"No. But they stopped for a few drinks before." Riley headed through the open area and into the kitchen where she dumped her bag on the expansive kitchen island.

"Want to talk about it?"

"Talk about what?"

"That." He pointed to her jeans.

"You want to talk about my butt?"

"Not while you have that expression on your face. This." He moved closer and pulled the envelope out of her back pocket. Even as he dangled it in front of her nose, she felt her blood pressure spike. "I would have thought getting shot at would have put you in a bad mood, but turns out all it took was a registered letter."

"Give me that." She snatched it out of his grasp, but rather than crumpling it up and throwing it in the trash like she wanted, she flicked it onto the counter. "That's nothing."

"Clearly."

"It's nothing I want to think about right now," she clarified.

"Looks important. It's from Powell Film Studios."

"Yes, it is." What was she going to do? Lie when he was staring right at the return address? "You want something to drink? I was thinking about putting on a pot of coffee."

"You're really not going to open it?"

"Oh my God. No wonder you became a detective. You must have been a nightmare as a kid on Christmas morning," she said. "I already know what it says." It was just a reiteration of what the previous letters had said. Deciding caffeine might not be the best solution for her mood, she headed to the refrigerator and the wine. "Go ahead and quell your curiosity."

"It is a prerequisite for my job." He picked it back up, hesitated. "You're really okay with me reading it?"

"Uh-huh." She pulled out the bottle of Merlot she and Moxie had opened last night and poured herself a glass. "You want some?"

"No, thanks. I think that cider gave me a cavity." He slid his finger beneath the seal and pulled out the film studio letterhead. "Wow." He looked up at her and she rolled her eyes, debated whether to dive into the chips or wait for actual food for dinner. "You really should read this."

"It probably says the same thing the last three letters did," she told him. "Granger Powell, aka, the head of Powell Films, wants to buy Temple House. I'm tired of telling him it isn't for sale."

"You sure you don't want to consider the offer? This is a lot of money, Riley."

"I don't want a lot of money." She shrugged when he clearly didn't buy her bluff. "Okay, I don't want to get a lot of money *that* way. PFS had their chance to counter my great-grandfather's offer to buy the place when the studios wanted to tear it down. One of the many consequences of the change in the studio system, by the way. They didn't need their *stable* any longer, so why keep the boarding house? Great-Grandpa Temple made a lowball offer, in cash, and Granger Powell's grandfather took the offer immediately. Now that Granger's got the studio off of life-support again—"

"The guy's a mega-mogul, Riley. You could probably ask for anything from him if he's this interested." He handed her the letter. "Especially since it looks as if he's sweetened the offer."

"Please." Riley glugged some wine and snatched the paper. "He's already offered twice its market value. What more could he—" She nearly choked when she got to the third paragraph and slammed her glass on the counter. "That son of a bitch." She pressed a hand against her heart. "Thank God Moxie didn't open this. I can't even—" she gaped at Quinn. "He thinks he can bribe us into selling by offering Moxie a co-starring role in a remake of the Sally Tate movies? That's low, even by Hollywood standards."

"Is it?" Quinn didn't look convinced. "He's not telling you you'd have to move out or anything. He just wants to buy the building. Maybe it's worth a conversation."

"Of course he'd want us out," Riley spat. "He'd want everyone out. What else would he want with this place? Probably wants to turn it into high-priced—"

"It's already high-priced," Quinn said.

"Not by Powell standards, it isn't. Dammit." She slapped the letter down. "I'm going to have to tell Moxie about this and it's going to be a whole thing." She hated—no, she *loathed*—Granger Powell for putting her in this position. "I'm not selling my home."

"Okay." Now it was Quinn who shrugged. "Just saying that if someone offered me that much cash—"

"Please." She planted her hands on the black marble countertop. "Finish that sentence in some way that doesn't lower you in my estimation. Money might make some things easier, but it complicates everything else. I've got tenants who love living here. It's not just my home or Moxie's. It's theirs. We're a family. We look out for each other. We're ... a microcosm of societal perfection and we're connected. If I—if we—sell, they'd all have to find someplace else to go and not everyone can afford to move. I'm not letting that happen. I don't care what offer Granger Powell makes me, this is *Temple* House. It has been for the past forty years, and it will continue to be until I'm dead in my grave."

It took her an extra beat of a moment to realize what she'd said. Quinn was quick, but not fast enough to hide the warning expression that crossed his face.

"Stop it!"

He frowned. "Stop what?"

"I know what you're thinking." It was the same thing she was thinking. It was only a few hours ago she had come close to booking a ticket to that very final destination. "I'm done talking about this. I'm also pissed off enough now to show you those photographs. Wait here."

Before she headed into her bedroom, she detoured into the darkroom in an effort to find a moment of peace. The contentment curtain dropped around her instantly as she stepped inside and for the first time in hours, she felt the bands of tension loosen from around her chest.

She stood in the middle of the room and inhaled the familiar, comforting scent of hours spent doing what she loved most.

Damn Granger Powell. He'd been trying for more than a year to entice her and Moxie to sell and now he may have just found a way to put her and her great-aunt at each other's throats.

Tempting Moxie with her greatest dream—a dream Riley's great-aunt had been chasing for most of the past thirty years with guest appearances on TV shows, murder mysteries of the week, game shows, talk shows, anything to stay relevant—was a low blow. Of course Moxie had maintained a modicum of success after Sally Tate, but that had been a role of a lifetime. What Powell offered was a way for her to go out the way she'd come in.

With a cinematic bang.

Riley clenched her fists, pounded them against her thighs and repressed a throat-searing scream. Moxie deserved every bit of happiness she could attain. She'd do anything to give Moxie that chance at a comeback.

But why did the price have to be Temple House?

"Riley?" Quinn knocked gently on the open door before he pushed it open. Doing so pulled her out of the shadows as light streamed into her sanctuary.

"Yeah, sorry." She swiped her hands across her cheeks, mortified he'd caught her crying over a stupid letter. "I just needed a few minutes to wallow."

"It's the first time you're tempted, isn't it?" He leaned a shoulder against the doorframe. "To sell Temple House."

She turned, braced her hands against the back counter. "Not for me .... But I hate him for it," she whispered. "There are only two things I love in this world. Well, maybe more than that, but Moxie and Temple House? They're the two I'd do anything for, and he knows it. He's asking me to play one against the other to get what he wants, and you know what?" She scrubbed the last of the tears off her face. "That really, really pisses me off."

"Are you going to tell Moxie about the offer?"

"Of course I am." She lifted both hands helplessly into the air. "How can I not? We own this place together. It's ours, which means it's not only my decision to make. This place, this room," she gestured to the comforting, shadowy space that had given her everything she'd ever needed in life, including a purpose. "What would I do without it?"

"Why don't you start with talking to Moxie and see where things go? There's no need worrying about something that might not happen. She might feel the same way you do."

"She's eighty years old, Quinn." Tears filled her eyes again and pushed her right over the edge into whining. God, she loathed whiners. "This is a lightning-strike offer. There won't be another chance for a comeback for her." When he straightened and started to move toward her she shook her head, pointing to the panel inside the door. "Turn on the light, will you? I'll go get the pictures."

Embarrassment pushed her into her bedroom, into the closet, and had her pulling down the box containing the photos. Photos that had already cost too high a price as far as she was concerned. She should just give them to him and be done. Whoever the dead woman was, she was long gone; probably forgotten. Who was she to unearth a mystery that by all rights should probably stay buried?

Her treacherous mind wouldn't stay quiet. *But what about her family? Didn't they deserve answers?*

She stopped in the doorway and watched Quinn wander around the darkroom. He had his hands in his pockets, as if afraid to touch something. The curiosity was evident on his handsome face, a face she was becoming quite accustomed to seeing. Okay, that knowledge wasn't going to calm her down at all.

With his back to her, he shook his head. "I can't begin to fathom how you do what you do with all this stuff. It's like some insane scientific laboratory that conjures a weird kind of magic."

Riley hugged the box to her chest, trying to dismiss the affection squeezing her heart as exhaustion and stress, but couldn't quite manage. She *was* tired. *And* overwhelmed. *And* irritated. Maybe she just wanted to feel something, *anything* other than the weight of responsibility she heaped onto her own shoulders. It was normal, wasn't it, after a close brush with death, to want to feel more alive?

Or maybe, Riley thought with more than a flash of irritation, she should be honest with herself and admit that she wanted *him*.

She walked over to him, set the box down and, when he turned, she stepped close. Lifting her hands, she caught his face between her palms and stared, utterly and completely into his eyes. He didn't move. She wasn't entirely sure he even breathed, but as she rose up on her toes, his hands slipped around her waist.

Even before she kissed him, she could feel the debate raging inside of her. The teasing banter they'd engaged in over lunch was one thing. It was playful, hopeful, and more than tempting. But now, feeling his arms around her, knowing what it felt like to be held by him, that throwaway comment of him taking her into her bed didn't seem nearly as casual. The distance between their lips shrank with every breath she took.

She pressed her lips together, as if anticipating what he'd feel like, what he'd taste like, but still she kept enough distance to postpone her fall into temptation.

"Are you going to close the deal or not?" His rumbling question had her lips twitching.

"Well, since you asked so nicely." She pressed her mouth to his, anticipating, expecting that same head-spinning reaction she'd felt back at the restaurant. As she drew him closer, as his mouth softened against hers, there was no equating then and now.

There was no before. There was only this.

His mouth moved over hers, expertly, commandingly, and the fire built from her toes, winding its way up and through her body like a whirling dervish, devouring everything responsible for rational thought. It wasn't enough. Wasn't nearly enough. She clung to him, her hands moving to his shoulders, gripping tight as his arms locked and he pressed his palms flat into her spine. Her arms felt heavy as she drew them around his neck and, after a moan of acceptance, opened her mouth to let him in.

She met him stroke for stroke, pary for pary, as his entire body sank into the kiss; sank into her. He pivoted until the counter pressed into her back. In one graceful, glorious move he bent, grabbed her behind the thighs and hauled her up and onto the edge. She didn't want to let his mouth go. She didn't want to let him go. There wasn't an inch of him she didn't want to feel, to touch, to embrace.

Riley raised her legs, felt him cradled between her thighs and, smiling against his searching, demanding, torturous mouth, she locked her feet behind his back and pulled him in.

She caught his gasp in her mouth, felt the passion inside of her building to the point she couldn't breathe. His hands left her hips, slipped under her shirt and expertly moved to the clasp of her bra, which he unsnapped with little more than a flick of his fingers.

"You've done this before," she murmured against his lips, pulling back only enough to watch his half-closed eyes open.

"No," he said in chilling seriousness. "No, I haven't. Not like this." She thought he was going to kiss her again, but instead he dipped his head and locked his mouth to the side of her neck as his hands, his fingers, his thumbs, moved under the front of her bra to tease her straining breasts.

"Oh." She dropped her head back, felt the pressure building between her legs even as she reached down and grabbed the waistband of his jeans.

"Riley!" Moxie's voice echoed through the apartment seconds before the front door slammed.

"Shit," Riley groaned and dropped her forehead onto Quinn's quickly rising chest. "The woman has the timing of a tornado."

"We can't find your grandfather's Scottish Santa statue!" Moxie yelled. "The one we always put by the lobby door. Riley?"

"In here," she squeaked as if she'd been breathing in helium. "Be out in a minute!"

"A minute might be pushing things ..." Quinn teased as he nipped at her ear. She batted at him, pushed him away.

"I'm not having sex in the darkroom with my aunt in the other room. Oh no!" She felt the blood drain from her face. "The letter. We left it on the kitchen counter. I need—"

"Go." He stepped back so she could jump down. "I'll wait here."

She turned, backed away, and angled a very purposeful look at his bulging crotch. "Guess I'll have to wait to open my Christmas present."

"You'd best leave now before I pull you back and lock the door," he warned. "Great Aunt Moxie be damned."

Feeling inappropriately giddier than she had a right to, she hurried into the kitchen, relieved to find Moxie digging through the hall closet. She snatched the letter off the kitchen counter and shoved it back into her pocket.

"I swear I just saw that statue in here just a few weeks ago," Moxie grumbled.

"I think I put him in the basement lockup." Standing behind her aunt, casting an uneasy gaze back to the darkroom, Riley twisted and tried to straighten her shirt, but the fabric wouldn't cooperate. Then she realized her bra was not where it was supposed to be. When Moxie started to stand, Riley pounced. "Is that it?" She pointed to a box in the corner and when Moxie dived in to check, Riley shimmied out of her bra, pulling it out of one of her shirt sleeves.

"Honest to goodness, girl. That's not big enough to hold Santa. Hang on." She stepped over a giant garbage bag filled with old crocheted pillows that had, at one time, been a hobby. Sometime between the diamond art painting and the candle making phases. "I'm going in. I know that stinker's in here somewhere."

"Right. I'm sure he is." Riley spun around, then dived for the counter and stashed her bra in the upside-down elf cookie jar by the stove. "Did you find him?"

"Don't worry, I will. Why don't you go back to doing whatever you were doing in the darkroom with Detective Sexy Pants." Moxie popped her head around to look her in the eye. "And might I suggest you lock the door this time?"

Riley's cheeks went cinnamon-candy hot. "You couldn't possibly have seen—"

"Didn't have to see. I was your age, once upon a time. Had my share of darkroom dalliances, too, if you must know."

"I mustn't," Riley groaned. "I really—" She stopped, replayed the conversation. "Detective Sexy Pants?"

"No good?" Moxie flung a paper bag filled with fake holiday flowers out of the closet. "Laurel thought it was a little too on the nose. Don't worry. We'll come up with something more appropriate down the road." She stood up, planted her hands on her hips and gave Riley one of her looks. "Go on already. No use you wasting time with me when you've got things you could be doing."

Riley walked away, mainly because if she didn't, she might just scream. "How am I not in therapy?" she asked herself as she returned to the darkroom. "Okay, I don't know if you suffer from performance … anxiety. What's wrong?" She wasn't entirely sure why her stomach clutched at the sight of Quinn using a magnifying glass on one of the photos, but it could have to do with the somewhat dazed and shocked expression on his face.

But that expression vanished when he lifted his gaze to hers.

"Sorry. Just thinking." He set the glass down. "These pictures are … disturbing. I'm trying to imagine someone playing dead for the camera."

"You think she's acting?" Of all the reactions she'd imagined the good detective having, that hadn't cracked the top one hundred. "Quinn, that woman isn't playing at anything. You can see the progression. She's dying. On film. And here? After she's been in the water?" She stepped forward, tapped a finger on the final image. "She's dead."

"Maybe."

The distance in his voice pushed her deeper into resolve and incredulity. How could he not see what she did? And why did it bother her so much that he didn't?

"Did Merle tell you where he got the negatives?" She didn't hear Quinn in his voice now. All she heard was cop. The hair on the back of her neck bristled even as the little voice in her head sang "told you so."

"Merle didn't get the negatives, he got the film," Riley explained carefully. "There's a difference. I can walk you through the process—"

"Where did he get them?" The urgency in his voice churned up new bubbles of doubt. "Where did the box they were in come from?"

"A customer." It was all he was going to get out of her as long as he refused to share what he obviously knew. There was no denying that guarded, suspicious glint in his eyes. A glint that removed any lingering doubt the pictures represented far more than just a macabre photo shoot. He did believe they were real—he was just downplaying his reaction. She was trying to decide what would piss her off more: him *not* believing her, or him pretending he didn't. The later won out. She bristled.

He set that last picture on top of the others, closed the folder, and picked it up.

"What are you doing?"

"I'm taking these with me." It wasn't a question or a request, but a flat-out statement.

"Fine." She shrugged. "I'll just develop another set."

"No." He didn't flinch. He didn't hesitate. He ordered. "No, I want the negatives, too."

So he was going back on their deal after all. Disappointment crashed through her. She should have known. "Why?" she challenged. "If you're saying they're not what I thought they were—"

"The negatives, Riley." Every word sounded like an expertly aimed shot from his gun. "Give them to me."

She crossed her arms over her chest and planted her feet as if standing in front of a linebacker. "No."

"What do you mean no?"

Her fists clenched so hard her nails bit into her palms. It should have come as a relief, the offer to take all of this out of her hands. Heck, wasn't she just thinking it wasn't worth the emotional exhaustion to keep dwelling on them? But she didn't feel any sense of relief by his command. Instead, she felt only a stomach-churning sense of dread and heartbreaking disappointment. She'd probably just broken the world record for almost-hook-up to bust up.

"There's not really anywhere to go with the word, detective." The title tasted more than a little bitter on her tongue now. "No, you can't have the negatives."

His gaze hardened. "This isn't a game, Riley."

"Sure it is. You want those negatives so badly, then tell me what's going on in that thick skull of yours. What do you see in those pictures that I don't?" That she'd missed.

He glared, narrowed his eyes, clearly participating in an internal debate he wasn't willing to share. "I'm not in a position—"

"There's only two of us in this room." She reached out and pushed the door closed. "You can speak freely. It's soundproofed."

He looked at her just long enough to raise her temper.

"There's no way you're walking out of this apartment with the negatives, detective." So much for thinking he was cut from a different cloth than his fellow cops. Dammit, sometimes she hated being right. "You've got the pictures, not the negatives—*like we'd agreed.* Consider that your win." She inched up her chin at his disbelieving stare and reiterated. "The negatives are mine. I paid for them. Merle and Dudley definitely paid for them."

"You don't trust me."

"Right now? No. Give me a reason to. You said I could keep the negatives. Now you're reneging." She wanted to trust him. More than she'd wanted anything in a long time. She stepped closer, resisted the urge to touch him. That wouldn't take either of them anywhere good at the moment. "You know who she is. Tell me."

"I didn't say I know who she is."

"People must get rich playing poker with you, detective." She narrowed her gaze, peered into eyes that not so long ago had been clouded with desire. "You can't bluff worth a damn. You want my cooperation? Tell me who she is and maybe I'll change my mind."

Now who was bluffing? She wasn't going to change her mind. She was going to get to the bottom of those photographs. She was going to identify that woman. And, because it was clear no one else planned to, Riley was going to get her and Dudley the justice they deserved.

"I can't tell you who she is."

"Because you don't want to."

He looked about to argue, but changed his mind. "If you're determined to keep those negatives—"

"I am. Unless you want to serve me with a warrant." And he couldn't do that without showing his hand, not only to her, but to the system he so valiantly trusted.

"Don't think I'm not considering it," he said, and for the first time sounded as exhausted as she felt. "You keep those negatives to yourself, Riley. Don't show them to anyone. Do you hear me?"

"Hard not to." She pointed around the room. "Soundproofed, remember?"

"Unbelievable," he muttered before he yanked open the door. She followed him to the front door, stood in the doorway as he headed down the outer hall to the staircase beside the elevator.

"You could just tell me who she is, Quinn." She couldn't resist one more attempt. As angry and disappointed as she was, she still liked him; maybe even a little more than she had a few minutes ago. And didn't that just irk beyond belief. "Just tell me who she is, and we can figure out the rest together."

He stopped three stairs down, cell phone in hand, file tucked under his arm. When he looked back at her she felt time shift into slow motion, as if she could pull him back and rewind the past few minutes in the hopes of changing the outcome.

"Just tell me," she pleaded.

"I don't know who she is." He walked down the stairs and out of sight.

Riley closed the door and leaned back against it, a hand clutched against her chest as if she'd lost something important. He'd lied to her. Flat-out lied. He knew who that woman was, she had no doubt. But that wasn't the question pressing down on her the hardest …

"Found him!" Moxie announced and held a kilted Santa up over her head in triumph. "Riley? Everything okay?"

"Yeah, everything's fine, Moxie." She waved at her grandmother as she headed back into the darkroom. The magnifying glass lay where he'd set it. She picked it up, turned it between her fingers as she considered.

"He saw something. Something I didn't. What was it?" she mused. It wasn't the woman he'd been looking at, she realized now, but one of those details she'd dismissed. A detail that had been important enough for him to magnify. "All right, detective. Challenge accepted."

She returned to her bedroom, retrieved the negatives she'd stashed with the pictures. "Let's do this again. Only bigger," she murmured as she bid another night of sleep goodbye. "Pay attention to everything, Riley. This time, don't miss a thing."

# CHAPTER SIX

QUINN should have called Wally to pick him up outside Temple House, but the last thing Quinn needed right now was a car ride filled with endless questions and passive-aggressive woe-as-me declarations. Yes, his partner was ticked to be left out of the loop, and maybe he had a right to be, but right now Quinn's mind was racing faster than a rookie at his first homicide. He needed time to think, not to coddle and reassure.

He needed to figure out the right approach to take.

He needed to go back in time and somehow tell Riley to destroy the pictures before he could see them. Before she'd even developed them.

He Ubered back to the hospital to pick up his car, making a quick detour into the ICU to check on Merle's condition. No change. By the time he drove out of the parking lot—his wallet significantly lighter given the parking charges he'd incurred—he was back to circling the same questions, over and over. Questions he might not have had if he was anyone other than a Burton.

The file of photographs sat like a ten-ton boulder on the passenger seat, tilting everything off-balance. He didn't have to ask the questions that were now begging to be asked; he didn't have to pursue this at all. But he also knew Riley well enough to suspect his inability to process the reality of those photographs in a rational manner pushed her right over the edge of curiosity and into full-blown investigative mode.

Riley wasn't going to let this go. Not because it might be the right thing to do—to find a murderer—but because she was as tenacious as he was. Were their roles reversed, he wouldn't be walking away from it either. But that didn't mean he wasn't wishing she would.

There had been something beyond determination and grit in her eyes when they'd looked at the dead woman's image together. He'd seen pity, and anger. And that all-too familiar desire for … in his case, he'd call it justice. But Riley?

He couldn't find any other word to describe the expression other than rage.

It wasn't often Quinn felt like a failure, so riding this out was a particularly nasty journey. He'd always prided himself on being controlled; of being able to handle any situation that landed in his lap. But situations like this weren't everyday occurrences. Those photographs were as good as a time bomb. If … no, when—because with Riley involved, the explosion was inevitable—when the truth bomb went off, the resulting fallout would be devastating for so many people.

Not to mention impossible to recover from for some.

For once, he appreciated the time it took to make the drive to the suburb of Glendale where his parents had moved shortly after Quinn's younger brother had graduated from high school. Their dream house. Their retirement house. At least, it would be when his father finally hung up his shield.

It was a family joke, one even Quinn's mother laughed at. Alexander Burton was a cop right down to his marrow. Being part of the police department wasn't just a calling for the Burtons; it was in their DNA. Quinn should know. That gene had definitely been activated the second Quinn himself had taken his first breath. But his father? His father was a different breed of cop. He was …

Quinn swallowed the bile rising in his throat. The idea something Quinn himself had come across might tarnish his father's, for the most part, unblemished reputation …

No. He couldn't let himself go down that road.

His father was the most honorable man he'd ever known.

Quinn clung to that idea, to that mantra, as he made his way through the suburban area that, at least in this moment, looked nearly utopian. Elegantly designed homes with lush lawns or ecologically water-resistant landscaped front yards. Christmas lights burned bright in every color of the holiday rainbow, from solitary strings outlining peaked roofs, to blinking orchestras of color illuminating more than a solitary yard. Inflatable characters bobbed and danced in the night breeze, but none of it sadly brought him anything close to a sense of peace.

His pulse ratcheted up incrementally as he made the final turn into the driveway and parked behind his mother's white Prius. Quinn and his brother were on call next weekend to string up the lights, but until then, his mother had set out the oversized lighted gift boxes that glowed in bright golds and reds on the lawn. Quinn almost smiled at his mother's sneaky way of supporting her hometown football team, the San Francisco 49ers.

Quinn could see the light on in the front window of the two-story home. His father's office lay behind those curtains. A sanctum sanctorum they'd jokingly named it after a Sunday family superhero-movie binge.

The sun had set and the cool pre-winter air blew in over the mountains to hit Quinn's skin like chilly slaps. File in hand, Quinn walked slowly, trying to think of the best way to approach his father, but there was only one way to open this wound and that was with straight up, in-your-face honesty.

The enormous front door was nearly obscured by an oversized wreath giving off the combined holiday scent of cinnamon and pine. Before Quinn could knock, the door opened.

"Quinn." Alexander Burton's face split into a welcoming smile.

He stepped back, and waved Quinn inside with a hand holding a newly opened bottle of beer. Even though he and his dad were a similar height, and his father had greeted him with a friendly demeanor, it was times like this that Quinn felt like he was six years old again and in slight awe of the man. Known for his patience and cool head, there was no one who could gnaw on a case more thoroughly than Quinn's dad.

“This is a surprise. What brings you by?”

“Is Mom here?” Quinn stood in the foyer, looking up the curving staircase as he clenched the file in suddenly numb fingers.

“She’s at Cheryl’s, driving your sister nuts by now, I’m sure. Why?” Alexander’s eyes—the same dark color as Quinn’s—sharpened. “What’s happened? Is it your brother?” He pulled his cell out of his pocket to check if he’d missed a call.

“No, no, nothing like that.” Quinn swore, then cringed. “Language, sorry.”

“You’re apologizing for your language?” Alexander’s eyebrow arched. “Now I am worried.”

“I need to talk to you about something, Dad. It’s … hell, I don’t know exactly what it is, but we need to talk about it. Now.”

“Okay, come on into the kitchen. You can help me finish the pizza your mother can’t know I ordered for dinner. I heard you got called in on the Merle Paddock assault. There was a homeless man killed in the parking lot, wasn’t there? Sorry. I read the report earlier.” Alexander tapped a finger against his head. “Dudley. His name was Dudley Waniker, that’s right.”

It was just like his father, Quinn thought. There wasn’t a victim in this city Chief Burton didn’t commit to memory. He took his oath of office—to serve and protect—as seriously as most people took their dedication to breathing. Whether Riley Temple would see him in the same light was another question. One that left Quinn frowning while he followed his father into the kitchen.

He did his best to block out the photographic evidence of his family plastered all over the mocha painted walls. He didn’t need reminding his familial obligation should have him prepping for that climb up to the role of chief one day. He also didn’t appreciate the way the pictures of his parents, sister, and brother taunted him with pulsating potential disappointment, if he failed to make that leap.

“The Paddock case is partly why I’m here.” He barely knew where to start. “I came across something unexpected thanks to one of the witnesses we questioned.”

“I wasn’t aware there were any witnesses to the crime.” He motioned for Quinn to sit at the kitchen island, one that oddly enough reminded him of the one in Riley's loft apartment. Dammit, why did everything about her have to have made an impact?

"I'm using witness in the loosest way," Quinn said. "A friend of Merle's, she was visiting with him before the suspects walked in." Time to rip the first of many bandages off. "Riley Temple."

Alexander's eyes went wide for a moment, then he retrieved another beer from the fridge and handed it over. Quinn gratefully twisted off the cap and took a long drink. "Definitely a name I wasn't anxious to hear again," his father finally said.

"Because of the Pantello situation?"

"You've been talking with your lieutenant." His father snorted with obvious disdain. "The negotiations with Ms. Temple regarding the *situation* with Pantello were complicated but they gave us the result we needed."

"You spoke with Riley personally?" He couldn't fathom how that conversation might have gone.

"No. But I observed the discussion. She's a tough one. I liked her, actually. Surprised myself that I did, but there you are. Connect the dots for me, please. How does Riley fit in with the Paddock case?"

As succinctly as he could, Quinn gave his father the expanded version of the report Wallace had submitted earlier in the day. "The reason Riley visited with Merle that afternoon was that she had questions for him about some film he sold her."

"Okay." Alexander set the piece of pizza he was about to bite into down on a napkin. "Am I right in assuming those are the pictures from that film?"

"Yeah." Quinn kept his hand on the file. "Dad—"

"Don't go second-guessing yourself now, son." Alexander motioned his hand away. "Something brought you here. Your gut instinct. Don't ignore it now."

"No, sir." He slumped into the high-backed bar stool and watched as his father flipped open the file, his hand jumping slightly at the familiar face.

His face drained of all color. "Melanie."

"Yeah," Quinn repeated, his mind flashing back to the twenty-five-year-old case as Alexander flipped through the pictures. The shock on his father's face was expected, but that didn't mean the emotions his dad was experiencing didn't strike Quinn hard. "I almost didn't bring it to you. I didn't want to open—"

"Old wounds." Alexander nodded, almost absently. "This is why you asked if your mother was home."

Now it was Quinn who nodded. "I remember this case was …" he struggled for the right word, "… complicated for you."

"It was," Alexander confirmed, even as he seemed lost in the images. He frowned. "In a lot of ways, it still is."

The beer did little to settle Quinn's stomach. Twenty-five years ago, he'd been seven. Young enough to still to worship his father yet old enough to know when something was off in their house.

There had been a period of a few months, around the holidays, when his father hadn't been around as much. He'd been working. A lot. Quinn's mother had done her best to fill the void his father's continued absence created, but it was clear there was something wrong. That their relationship was strained because of it. Something indefinable had scared Quinn to the point he'd taken to sneaking into his father's office at night to sleep on the sofa. Hoping, praying, that his father would come home and tell him everything was going to be okay.

It was, Quinn remembered with absolute clarity, the only thing he'd asked Santa for that year: for his father to come home.

By January, Santa had delivered and it would be years before Quinn understood the truth behind what was going on at the time. Every cop had a case—that one case. The case that kept them up at night even after it was solved, and a victim who haunted them long after the investigation was over.

Melanie Dennings's murder was that case for his father.

His father, however, had not been alone in his obsession. The Dennings murder had become that case for the entire city of Los Angeles, which made it national news. The media had likened the killing to the infamous Black Dahlia case from 1947. That case had ushered in an entirely new era—not only of crimes it seemed, but of criminal investigation practices.

Ironically, Quinn's grandfather had been one of the first officers on the scene when Elizabeth Short's mutilated body had been found. And then history repeated itself with Melanie Dennings and Quinn's father.

Alexander took his time, as if memorizing every detail of each photo before he went to the next. When he reached one of the last images, he set his beer bottle down. Quinn stood up, walked over to the makeshift desk under one of the kitchen cabinets, and retrieved a magnifying glass. "You'll want to use this." He pointed to the bottom right corner. "It's the newspaper that caught my attention. There's not much of it showing, but there's enough to make out the date." It was all Quinn could do not to just tell his father what he'd found, but he kept quiet and allowed Alexander to see it, to read it, for himself.

"November sixteenth." Alexander's hand shook, but after he set the magnifier down, it had steadied again. "She was alive on November sixteenth. But that's not ..."

"If I remember the details from the case file correctly," Quinn said quietly, "Dean Samuels was already in custody by then. If these photos are authentic, there's no way the man you and your partner arrested killed Melanie Dennings."

"That doesn't mean Samuels wasn't involved in her abduction." Alexander's voice had that hollow, distant quality that had scared seven-year-old Quinn into sleeping in his father's office. The same tone that sent chills racing down Quinn's spine now. His dad was disappearing into the case again, as if he were stepping into a bank of thick fog. "All these years," his father murmured. "I barely remembered what she looked like in life. I could only see .... This is the dress she was wearing when we found her. Her makeup, everything in this picture ..." he trailed off, as if lost in the past. "They found her body buried in a grove on a route frequented by Samuels. He pled guilty to her murder. He accepted life without parole."

"He did both of those things after protesting his innocence for more than a year. We were only what, maybe ten years out from DNA being allowed in court? Forensics was iffy—"

"I'm aware of the details, Quinn," his father said.

"Dad—"

"Are these the only copies?"

It was the question Quinn had hoped his father wouldn't ask. The one question that tipped Quinn further into uncertainty. Not over what he'd done by confiscating the pictures from Riley, but whether or not his father would admit that maybe, possibly, mistakes had been made with Dean Samuels. And whether or not those mistakes had been on purpose.

"For now? Yes. Riley has the negatives," Quinn said. "I asked her for them, but—" He shook his head, finished his beer and, because he couldn't sit still for another minute, got up to grab another one. "Given her past experience with the LAPD, I couldn't very well push to take something that rightfully and legally belongs to her. That's all the ammunition she would need to take these pictures public." And these days, the second something like this hit the media, it was guilty until proven … guilty.

"Maybe that's where you start," Alexander suggested. "If she purchased these pictures from a known pawnshop owner—"

"You're thinking they could be declared stolen, and we'd have the right to take them from her." Quinn shook his head, took another drink. "Riley's too sharp for that. Besides, her attorney lives downstairs from her. Laurel Fontaine. I really don't think we want to get her involved with this."

"Laurel Fontaine." Alexander sighed and shook his head. "You're just full of good news tonight, aren't you?"

He walked around the kitchen counter and into the great room that doubled as entertainment central for family gatherings. The Christmas decorations were in pre-arrangement mode, per his mother's usual schedule. Boxes had been dragged down from the crawl space, an area seat aside for the tree that would be delivered next week.

Within the plastic bins Quinn could see hints of homemade childhood ornaments his mother would proudly display front and center of that tree, along with the fabric lighted angel that had once belonged to Quinn's grandmother.

His father sat on the edge of his favorite recliner, beer bottle clasped in his hands. "Dean Samuels killed Melanie Dennings. I'm as certain about that as I am that you're standing in this room with me." He looked at Quinn, but there was something in his father's gaze that had Quinn swallowing hard. Alexander Burton would deny it, but it was there. Fear.

And doubt.

"I didn't want you blindsided by this, Dad," Quinn told him as he sat on the sofa. "I wanted you to have some time to prepare for when it hits, because it is going to hit. Riley already started asking questions and look what happened. Merle Paddock was attacked and a homeless man was murdered. Merle was one thing, but I'm convinced the killing was committed to draw Riley out. It worked." He hesitated. "Someone tried to kill her this afternoon."

"What? What are you talking about?" Alexander blinked as if coming out of a trance. "Is she all right? I didn't see anything come across—"

"She's fine. So am I. Report is forthcoming from Wally. It should hit the system sometime in the morning."

"What do you mean, so am I? Explain." It was the clipped tone that had officers falling in line all over the city, but couched with a father's concern.

"I was with her," Quinn said. "I ran into her at the hospital when I went to check on Merle Paddock. I thought taking her to lunch would be a good way to break the ice with her and get some information about why she'd been at Merle's place before he was attacked. Car drove by and opened fire." The same silver car that had nearly run her over at the traffic light. It had taken him longer than he liked to admit to put those two incidents together, but he finally had. "Middle of the day. Brazen." Desperate, perhaps? "No injuries other than a store's windows. Two patrol officers were on scene." He mentioned their names and gave them both a good verbal report.

"What a fucking mess," Alexander muttered. "All this happened since when? Did Riley tell you when she got the film?"

"Three, maybe four days ago? She's not going to let this go, Dad. Especially now."

"No, she won't." He took a long, deep breath. "Nor should she."

The balloon of panic that had been expanding in Quinn's chest deflated slightly. "No?"

"No. Even if she was the only person who knew about the photos, there would be no keeping her quiet. Not now. She'd just see it as an attempt to enact a cover-up, which would be correct." He shook his head as if puzzling things out. "We need to control as much of this as we can for as long as we can." He looked at Quinn. "Is that possible? Would Riley cooperate with that?"

"If you're asking if I can control *her,* the answer is no." Quinn wasn't about to lie to his father. Not about that at least. He also didn't think dear old dad needed to hear that Quinn and Riley had been minutes away from adding an even bigger complication to this situation. For the first time in his career, he had to wonder if he'd been compromised and what, if anything, he was going to do about it. "What I do think I can do is be up-front with her about some of this. This photography stuff—the connections she has? She's good, Dad. She thinks outside the box."

"Woman missed her calling as a journalist. Or a cop, if she hadn't come face-to-face with the worst of us." He shuddered. "Can't believe I actually said that. She's got an overdeveloped sense of justice, but that's something you can use to your advantage."

"Sir?"

"If she's already been targeted—"

"You're not suggesting we use her as bait?" He never conceived of such a suggestion coming out of his father's mouth.

"She's already bait," Alexander said. "You said yourself it's why you believed that Dudley Waniker was killed."

"That doesn't mean we should use her to chum the waters even more." The statement came out far harsher and louder than he'd intended. "I'm not going to use her that way. Not without her cooperation." To avoid his father's assessing gaze, Quinn took a long, throat-scorching swallow of beer. "But I won't pull the option completely off the table."

"Fair enough. For now, this stays off the books," Alexander added with a flinch. "Dammit, I always swore I'd never put you in this kind of position."

"I don't matter in any of this, Dad."

"Of course you matter," Alexander shot back. "You have an entire future to consider, Quinn."

"And what about your legacy?" Quinn demanded. "I'm not going to trade one for the other. Neither should you."

Given his father didn't give any acknowledgement of agreement, Quinn would bet his father had decided to table the conversation for another time.

"There's something else we need to consider in this, Dad. Someone else. Dean Samuels."

"I don't think—" Alexander's voice deadened.

"I'm going to have to talk to him, Dad."

Alexander shook his head, and looked somewhat defeated. "That won't be easy. As far as I know, Dean Samuels hasn't seen anyone since he was put away."

"You can grease the wheels, can't you?"

His father winced. "I'll see what I can do. It'll be tricky, doing so under the radar, but I've got some friends in the prison system who owe me a favor or two. It'll take some time to find out."

"I wish I could say we could afford it."

"Agreed." Alexander nodded. "Give Riley some leash. We'll open some doors. Cooperate, let her think she's taking the lead—to a point," his father added. "The last thing this department needs is a scandal over a wrongful conviction. Especially one as high profile as Samuels. Shit, I got my promotion to Captain because of that case. There's no good way to spin that and I'm not going to try." He inhaled again. "Maybe your mother's going to get her Christmas wish after all."

"What wish is that?"

"The same wish she's made for the last thirty years. For me to retire."

"It won't come to that." This statement he had no trouble uttering out loud. "We won't let it."

"I'll admit I don't like the idea. I'm not ready to go. I've still got a lot of years left in me and enough good will within the department to see me through. But if I screwed up with Samuels, if I had a hand in sending an innocent man to prison for life?" He shook his head and hung his head in near defeat. "Then, the truth is, I don't deserve this job. You find out the truth, son. You find out the truth and you tell me. All of it. No holding back. From there? We'll figure out where we go. Together. Deal?" He stretched out his hand, which Quinn automatically accepted.

Not as a son to his father.

But as one cop to another.

Riley told herself she'd waited until Sunday afternoon to ring Laurel's second-floor apartment bell because she didn't want to bother her friend, but the truth was Riley had only dragged herself out of bed a little more than an hour ago. Despite only one glass of mulled wine at the holiday decorating party, the late night in the darkroom and spinning carousel of thoughts inside her head made her feel as if she'd just dragged herself home after a three-day don't-ask-me-any-questions girls' trip to Vegas.

"Ah, Vegas," she sighed as she leaned her forehead on Laurel's door. "That sounds so nice about now."

"What sounds nice about now?" Laurel popped the door open and had to catch Riley before she went splat on her entryway floor. "Rough night?"

"I don't know where to begin," Riley said as she righted herself.

"Is there a reason you didn't use your key?" Laurel arched a brow. "Did your brain leak out of your ears last night because of a certain gentleman caller?"

Good God, Riley thought. She'd finally gotten some sleep and somehow woken up in a Tennessee Williams play. "Do you have a few minutes? I have a … problem."

"Considering how you look, I'd say you have more than one. Come on in."

Laurel, barefoot and wearing gray yoga pants and an oversized sweatshirt that announced she wasn't responsible for what her face did when someone talked, she turned off her workspace computer, powered down, and headed into the kitchen.

This model apartment was one of Riley's favorites. It was a two-story loft design, with the main bedroom and bathroom upstairs, a second bedroom and bath downstairs, and an alcove within a giant arched window that Laurel turned into her home office. The kitchen, living room, and dining area were all connected and, like Laurel herself, elegantly designed in crisp white and black with gold accents. Even her Christmas tree looked as if she'd plucked it off the cover of *Architectural Digest.* She even had a perfectly even cascading ribbon in stunning peacock blue that wound around branches like a lover's hand. Riley's cheeks went hot just thinking about where Quinn's hands had been last night.

"Am I right in assuming you aren't hung over because of Detective Sexy Pants?" Laurel pulled open one of the cabinets and began riffling around.

"Seriously, stop calling him that." Riley sighed and hauled herself up onto one of the three stools at the kitchen island. "Moxie disappointed me with that name. It's hardly original."

"And yet incredibly accurate," Laurel sent a teasing grin over her shoulder. A grin that faded pretty quickly. "I was going to put on a pot of pasta to go with the loaf of garlic bread I bought this morning at Servici's. You want in?"

"A carb feast sounds sublime," Riley said, even as her stomach growled. "Mabel's bagels kick you off the carb wagon?"

"And left me lying helpless in the road." Laurel dug into her fridge and came out with a tray of sliced cheeses and olives. "Wine or coffee?"

"Is there such a thing as woffee?" She pried open the plastic wrap and grabbed a chunk of gouda. "Seems like there should be."

"Wow. Okay." Laurel went for the wine and poured two large glasses. "Spill. Info, not wine."

Riley had calculated how to begin this conversation as if she was wading cautiously into the ocean rather than fully diving in. "How long did you work in the DA's office?"

"Long enough that I nearly starved to death." Realizing humor was not on Riley's most wanted list, Laurel pulled back on the sarcasm. "Two years. First two years out of law school. Eye-opening experience, for sure. Why?"

"I think you could help me fill in some missing blanks I've got about this situation I find myself in."

"That was way too big a mouthful for a Sunday." Laurel bent down and pulled a massive pot out from under the sink.

"You're cooking that much for just the two of us?" Riley asked.

"For the month," Laurel said. "You can take some home to Moxie and I'll drop off some with Mabel. Her new case sounds like a rough one. She called me about nine, and asked me to keep Keeley and Barksy all night. Wasn't any trouble, since they'd both already crashed on the sofa."

"Must have been bad." Normally Mabel coming home to Keeley was what kept the rape advocate sane. If she hadn't wanted to be around her daughter … suddenly Riley's own bad night paled by comparison. "Not sure my situation is going to make you feel any better."

"Good thing I stocked up on my coping juice then." Laurel set the pot on the stove, then grabbed another, smaller one and filled it with water. Moving with the grace of a lifelong ballerina—Pilates did that to some people—she got to work on her homemade and infamous tomato sauce by extracting a farmer's market worth of veggies from the fridge. "Do you want to just show me what's in that file so you can cut to the chase?"

Honestly? No, she didn't want to. The last time she'd shown these photos to someone he'd changed personalities as quick as Dr. Jekyll turned into Mr. Hyde. "I feel like this needs an explanation first."

"You do you," Laurel said. "You talk, I'll chop."

"Well, to start, someone tried to kill me yesterday."

Laurel shot half a carrot straight into the air. It landed with a thunk in the sink. She set the knife down, placed her hand on a hip and stared at Laurel. "Well, shit, Riley. Are you okay?" Concern melted away with a flash of recognition. "Ah." She gave a slow nod. "That explains Detective Sex … Quinn showing up with you last night."

"Partially explains, actually." Riley stood and grabbed a box of crackers out of the pantry. What was Laurel thinking, serving cheese without crackers? "Suffice it to say Quinn is probably the reason why I'm sitting here today."

"Okay, I owe him for that, for sure. But let's backtrack a bit here." Laurel got herself together and resumed chopping, albeit a bit slower. "Does someone trying to kill you have anything to do with what happened to Merle and Dudley?"

"Quinn thinks it has everything to do with what happened to Merle and Dudley." Before Laurel could make a snippy comment, she added, "And I think he's right. It all started with some film Merle sold me a few days ago."

It didn't take as long as she thought it would to bring Laurel up to date. By the time she'd reached the point of sharing the photographs, the apartment was filled with the stomach-growling inducing aroma of onions, carrots, garlic, and finely minced crimini mushrooms. After she added four huge cans of San Marzano tomatoes, Laurel put the lid on the pot and tidied up.

"All right, let's see what you think Quinn's lying about," she said with her wineglass back in her hand.

"I don't think he's lying, really ..." she trailed off and, at Lauren's perfectly arched brow, shrugged. Why was she making excuses for him? "Okay, yeah, he lied. I do think he knows who the woman is. But the more I think about how he acted, the more he seemed ... I don't know, protective? Like he was afraid of saying too much, rather than trying to manipulate the situation. Does that make sense?"

"Maybe. Let's see already." She held out her hand and, despite having second thoughts, Riley handed her the folder.

"After I refused to turn them over, he told me—or rather, ordered me—to keep the negatives to myself. He doesn't want me talking to anyone about it."

"If someone tried to kill you over these," Laurel said, "he's right to be concerned. You're out and about a lot, Ry. Collateral damage is a possibility. But rest assured, you picked the right confidant. You and I will see this through."

"No, *we* won't. You're my lawyer and can't legally tell anyone what I'm showing you. That's the only reason I felt safe confiding in you."

"I'll take what I can get. Okay, so ..." She flipped open the cover and set her glass down with a nearly glass-shattering clank. "Holy crap on a cracker."

"That didn't take long." Riley stacked a wheat cracker with an unhealthy amount of cheddar.

"I can't believe you don't know who this is." Laurel gaped. "You, Riley Temple. One of the nosiest—"

"Hey!"

"Sorry, *curious* people I know. This is Melanie Dennings."

Riley frowned, thinking. "Why do I know that name?"

"Because you don't live in a cave. Melanie Dennings, age twenty-four at the time. I think. This was back in 1996? No, 97. She attended this big-ass party at a Hollywood producers' house. Huge names in attendance. Like Oscar night huge. And I use the word house loosely, as it could probably rival Temple House in the square-footage department."

"Straying off topic," Riley told her as her memory awakened.

"Right. So flash back twenty-some-odd years. Melanie's newish to Los Angeles. She's just signed with her first agent, gone out on some auditions. She's living in an apartment with three other wannabe actresses, all repp'd by the same agent whose name totally escapes me at the moment. Clara Sheffeld was one of them. Yeah, she testified at the trial, actually. One of her better performances," Laurel commented. "The other two roommates didn't ever spark on the job. Anyway, someone at the party gets handsy with Melanie—"

"More than handsy I'd say, given the era." One of the more positive things to happen within the industry in the last few years was the spotlight that shone on predatory practices and practitioners. For the most part.

"True." Lauren agreed. "So Melanie calls a cab from the house before she takes off, but there's no way a cab is getting anywhere near the house with all those cars parked, so she waits out on the side of the road. Cab picks her up and heads north, which is actually the opposite direction to where Melanie lives. No one sees her alive again. Cabbie's the only suspect they can land on. Despite him having no record, and being married with two young kids—"

"Killers come in all types," Riley observed.

"Maybe. Guy's also bootstrap poor, so the police hedge their bets and arrest and charge him, figuring he can't make bail. Three weeks after the arrest, they find Melanie's body buried on that North road, maybe three miles from the house."

"Open-and-shut case, then?"

"You'd think, but here's where it gets weird." Laurel's eyes brightened with interest. "I remember being obsessed with this case back in law school. There was this weird, sick kind of romanticism about it. Dean Samuels, the cabbie—he's saddled with a public defender, right? But he actually lands a pretty good one. They make it all the way through the prosecution's case and his lawyer finds this bombshell witness who says he saw Melanie after the time the cabbie says he drops her off at home, only before the witness takes the stand—"

"Don't tell me," Riley muttered. "He disappeared."

"No!" Laurel slammed her hand on the counter so hard Riley jumped. "That's the crazy part. His testimony becomes unnecessary because Samuels changed his plea. In the space of like a couple of hours, he fires his lawyer in open court, pleads guilty, and accepts a sentence of life without parole. Done and dusted. Mark one off for the good guys. He's been in California Prison System ever since."

"This might have the makings of a Netflix reality series," Riley commented, recalling other prisoners who had been sent to LA County's state prison. "But I'm not hearing any reason why these pictures would have upset Quinn so much."

"Aside from the fact that there were rumors of police misconduct—"

"Shocking." Riley rolled her eyes. "Do tell."

"No, not your kind of misconduct. Like serious high-up stuff. But as far as Quinn is concerned—"

"He'd have still been playing Little League at that time," Riley said. "I feel safe in saying he's in the clear for the murder."

"Yes. But his father was the lead detective on the case. His father who is now …"

"Chief of Police Burton." Riley choked on her crackers and cheese and had to glug down wine to start breathing again. "Holy hell."

"Don't go counting those clucking chickens just yet," Laurel warned.

"Excuse me?" Was Laurel not even listening to herself? "It seems pretty clear where this is leading."

"Aren't you the one who's always telling me nothing is ever what it seems in this town? Do not let your personal prejudices against cops get in your way. Not with something this explosive."

"That's not what I'm doing."

"Sure it is, and I understand why, but if you want a clear picture of what's going on, you need to see things from other possible angles. And this case has a ton of them. I know the LAPD and DA's office view me in a certain way."

"Shark," Riley was happy to remind her. "They call you a shark."

"I'm un-impressible, Riley. Seriously, it takes a lot to break through my shields and when it happens, I remember it. This Chief Burton? He's one of the good ones. I don't say that easily. I truly believe he is a good man. Even after seeing those photos." She shook her head, returned to the stove to stir her sauce. "There has to be more to this than we're seeing. What picture was it that Quinn took exception to?"

"Um. This one." She shuffled through the enlarged prints until she pulled the one with the newspaper. "I'm pretty sure he was looking at the date."

"Let me run with that for a bit," Laurel said. "Focus on the photographs and where they've been for the past twenty-something years. Just one thing," she added at Riley's nod, "when you start digging, you make damned sure you're careful. More careful than you have been, considering someone's already tried to shoot you. Until we know what those photos actually represent, there's no telling who is coming after that film. Or coming after you. It could be whoever really is responsible for Melanie's murder. Or it could be—"

"It could be the police who have a vested interest in keeping a potentially innocent man behind bars to save their reputation?"

"Okay, enough already. I know you want to paint them as the bad guys in this, but assumptions may just get you killed. You need to keep a completely open mind. I mean it," Laurel warned. "The Dennings murder was a big deal back in the day. Like seriously scandalous revelations and accusations were made about that party she attended the night she disappeared." Laurel added a healthy amount of salt into her pot, followed by a few spoonfuls of sugar. "You won't just be rocking one boat with questions. You'll be rocking three. At least."

"Maybe one of those boats will turn out to be the Titanic." And maybe Riley would find just the right iceberg to sink it.

"Criminals and potentially corrupt police are one thing," Laurel said in that cautious, I-know-more-than-you-do tone. "But Hollywood connections take you into an entirely different arena. I've worked for a lot of people in the industry, remember. I know what they're capable of." Given her expression, Riley would bet Laurel knew where a lot of bodies were buried, too. So to speak. "I want you to promise me you're going to keep me apprised every step of the way. In fact, hang on." She walked over to her desk, rifled around in one of the drawers and pulled out a flashdrive. "Save everything you come up with on this. It's coded to automatically backup to my personal Cloud storage. I want everything there, you hear me? Everything you find out, I want it on record." She placed the drive on the counter in front of Riley. "You need to be protected. I'm saying this as your attorney. And your best friend."

Why did one little flashdrive carve such a huge pit in her stomach? "You make it sound as if I'm going to war."

"You are," Laurel told her. "By following those pictures, that's exactly where you're headed. Also—and hear me out before you say no—I think you need to give Quinn a chance to explain and come clean."

"I heard you." Riley spun the drive with her fingers. "And, no. I don't need his help."

"You can't do this alone. And I'd bet he's already realizing the same thing. You complement each other where this case is concerned. You know how to get in and around certain areas that are locked off to him as an officer of the law. And he has access to things you can't legally get your hands on." Laurel's hand shot up when Riley opened her mouth. "Like the Melanie Dennings file. Think about that."

"I did think about it. That's why I asked how long you'd worked at the DA's office."

Laurel shook her head and lifted the lid off the pot. "My superpowers don't get me that far. You need an insider. You said you're worried about Quinn using you where this case is concerned, right?"

"I guess."

"He's already proved you wrong on one point. He's not bolstering the blue wall, Riley, he's protecting his father. Maybe he's not the villain you want him to be."

"I never said I want him to be a villain," Riley protested.

"Sure you do, because that makes it easier for you to shut him out."

Riley's mouth twisted as her friend's words hit their target.

"People are complicated, Riley. And they rarely fall into the black-and-white areas of life."

"Yeah, yeah, we all live in the gray areas, I know."

"If it bothers you so much, if *he* bothers you so much, there's another solution. One you might actually enjoy," Laurel hinted.

"Yeah? What's that?"

"Stop wallowing that he isn't perfect and embrace it. Play the game he's started." Laurel arched a telling brow and popped a chunk of cheese into her mouth. "Have a little fun and use him right back."

# CHAPTER SEVEN

"APOLOGY coffee." Quinn gave himself points for not cringing as he set the coffee cup on the edge of his partner's desk early on Monday morning. "Wallace," he added purposely at his partner's suspicious glare, hoping using his full name will placate him. "I should have told you I was going to the hospital to check on Merle. The whole Riley and lunch thing just happened out of that."

Wally picked up the cup, sniffing it as if it contained something suspicious. "It also just so happened you were with her when someone took a shot at her. Make that *ten* shots. Ballistics came in. No match on the bullets. Weapon's not in the system." He drank, inclined his head, nodded, then drank again. "Thanks for this. I guess we still have some work to do on finding our partnership footing."

"Yeah, well, I've been slacking on that, so it's mostly on me." He gave a morning wave to Detectives Perkins and Powers, and cast an assessing glance around the rest of the department that was in full, chaotic swing. In their little department in Hollywood, four detectives was cutting it close on coverage, but they had found a rhythm that worked. "Any leads on the car?"

"Reported stolen two days ago by an elderly woman out in Ventura. She doesn't drive it very often, so she's not entirely sure when it went missing. No sign of it since the shooting but we have an alert out."

"Probably stripped for parts by now." Quinn took a seat at his desk, shifting his Darth Vader bobblehead around to face him. "Appreciate everything you did yesterday."

"It's my job," Wallace said, but the edge in his voice had softened. "Figured I'd save you some time and call the hospital this morning. Merle's doing better. The sedation's wearing off and he's more coherent. Nurse thinks he'll be up for a conversation later today."

"Well, that's some good news." News he didn't particularly want getting around. "How would you feel about going over and talking to him when he's up for it?"

"On my own?"

"Yeah." Quinn leaned his arms on his desk. "I think there are a lot more moving pieces to this case than we're aware of and—honestly?—I'm a little concerned whoever attacked Merle is going to come back around for another inquisition session. Call it a gut feeling," he added with a glance toward Lieutenant Gibson's office. "They won't assign a protective detail on a gut feeling."

"So, this would kind of be a favor you're asking me for," Wallace hedged in typical Wally style. "As in, you're going to owe me one or two in return?"

"Don't push it, but yeah." Quinn owed him that much. Probably more. "Maybe one or two."

Wally's eyes widened briefly as he looked over Quinn's head, then he cleared his throat. "So what do you plan to do while I'm playing bodyguard and hitting on nurses all afternoon?"

"Geez, kid." Quinn pinched the bridge of his nose. "Don't have today end with a harassment complaint, okay? And since you asked"—and since Quinn was trying to be honest with his partner in an attempt to keep him from getting too curious, he decided to tell the truth—"I was hoping to talk to Riley again. We left things a little … well, the evening didn't end as either of us expected it to."

"She get pissed at you for something?" Wallace's voice raised just enough to have Quinn wincing. "I can see that happening. You haven't exactly been embracing your charming attributes lately."

"Don't make me wish I'd poured the coffee over your head," Quinn told him.

"He's only telling the truth." Riley's voice had Quinn cringing. "Your charm definitely veered into the danger zone last night."

"Really?" Quinn sighed, dropped his hand and glared at his partner. "You couldn't tell me she was standing behind me?"

"Nah. More fun this way." Wallace's grin nearly pulled a smile out Quinn. "You want me to head over to the hospital now?"

"Yeah. That'd be great." Quinn spun in his chair and faced a surprisingly amused-looking Riley.

She'd knotted her hair back up but missed a few strands that curled into gentle waves around her face. He wasn't sure he'd ever seen a woman so perfectly fill out a pair of jeans before, from the curves of her hips to that butt he'd had his hands on just yesterday. His fingers still felt warm from touching her. Her T-shirt was the color of peak-season raspberries and the oversized gray sweater was both practical and well-worn. She'd somehow managed to bundle herself up and put herself on display. "Good morning, Ms. Temple."

Her brow arched. "Good morning. *Detective.*"

"Clearly you two have some issues to work out." Wallace grabbed his jacket along with his coffee. He surprised both of them by stopping in front of Riley. "I apologize for the cracks I made about your photography job," Wallace said. "I've been told my attempt at humor comes across as more—"

"Misogynistic, unsympathetic, and rude?" Riley asked with wide-eyed innocence.

"Rude seems a bit harsh," Wallace grinned. "Word is you're the one who got the pictures of Tiffany Small's mother taking that shot at her at the hotel."

"I'd rather that not be a claim to fame," Riley said. "I don't like bullies."

"Well, then, we have something in common." Wallace offered his hand. "Truce?"

She looked down, then accepted. "All right. A provisional one."

"I'll take what I can get." He started to walk away, then snapped his fingers and leapt back. "By the way, since Detective Burton here got curious about you, I did some digging myself. I came across this old report filed by a Christopher Huntington. He's a fellow … photographer, isn't he?"

"Sure. We can call him that." Riley's eyes narrowed. "Why?"

"Nothing. I just thought it was interesting. About six months ago, he called 911 because this small silver SUV nearly jumped the curb while he was attempting to get a picture of Ramona Stillman. Guy took a serious tumble, busted his leg up pretty good, but I thought it was interesting that he mentioned seeing a Sally Tate decal on the back window when the car drove off. I noticed your decal the other night at Merle's. Matches the description he gave."

"You really didn't hear the word 'provisional,' did you?" She shrugged. "Sally Tate has a massive fan base," Riley said easily. "Those decals can be found all over Los Angeles."

"True enough. I'm just wondering," Wallace said, "since you're in the same profession. Who do you suppose would have attempted to run him over like that?"

"Wally." Quinn pushed to his feet, but as he kept his eyes on Riley, she merely smiled and shrugged. Just his luck. She'd committed vehicular assault and appeared to have no qualms about it.

"Hypothetically?" Riley asked his partner. "Well, *hypothetically*, first off, I think running him over is a bit of an overstatement. Secondly, I would guess that Ramona Stillman was walking her daughter to school for the first day of kindergarten. And maybe said photographer had already been lambasted for going after new celebrity parents on their way home from the hospital and showing up in school playgrounds under false pretenses. And, despite being arrested on multiple occasions, he's never received anything beyond a fine. Maybe whoever accidentally swerved is of the belief that celebrities' kids should be off-limits and that douchebags who stalk children ought to be shown the errors of their ways." Her smile actually reached her eyes. "But I'd just be guessing."

"Yeah," Wallace nodded in what Quinn could only describe as grudging admiration. "Yeah, that sounds like a really good guess, actually. I'll keep in touch, yeah, Quinn?"

"Yes, please." Quinn waited until his partner was out of earshot before turning to Riley.

"Did he say he's going to the hospital? To talk to Merle?"

"Yes. Sounds as if he's doing better."

"He is. They're weaning him off sedation, so hopefully I can talk to him myself, soon."

"So, Riley …" Quinn crossed his arms over his chest. "Is this going to be a long conversation or a drive-by?"

She snorted, smacked his arm and, after offering a surprising smile in his direction, plopped herself down in the chair he'd vacated. "What do they call that cop mentality you all seem to have? Gallows humor?"

"Takes the edge off the horrors of the job," Quinn confirmed. He thought about asking about the Christopher Huntington incident, then realized he really, really didn't want to know. "I was going to stop by Temple House later. To apologize."

"That's nice to hear. For what exactly?" She blinked in that hummingbird wing way that she had that was part tease, part evil genius.

"I handled my reaction to those pictures … badly."

"Oh. That." She sighed, cradled her oversized purse close. "I thought maybe you were sorry you didn't finish what you started. With me." She glanced over his shoulder and when Quinn turned, he found not only his fellow detectives eavesdropping, but at least three uniformed officers as well. "You know. On my darkroom counter? I was disappointed not to test the weight limit specified at installation."

"Good God, woman, you're a menace," Quinn muttered even as he found himself wanting to laugh. "Okay, that's enough. Show's over." Quinn told his co-workers over their muted laughter. "You're—"

"Naughty?" She beamed up at him. "I'm also running on about three hours sleep, so I'm probably filterless, too."

Yeah, because he had no doubt her filter was engaged the other times they'd been in each other's company. "Let's take a walk, shall we?" Like maybe out to her car.

"Spoilsport," she muttered under her breath, but she got up and followed him outside. "Were you really going to stop by?"

"I don't say things unless I mean them." He caught her arm, steered her around to the currently unoccupied smoking area. As he inhaled the phantom fragrance of tobacco and nicotine, he found himself longing for a contact high. "Yes, I really was."

"In that case, I'll offer my own mea culpa and say I shouldn't have baited you into that argument about the pictures. You may have noticed, but I have issues with being told what to do."

"I've picked up on that." While he appreciated her apology, he couldn't help but think she was wasn't entirely happy to be making it. "How's Moxie? Did you talk to her about that letter from Powell Films yet?"

"No." She took a deep breath and glanced away. "She left early for breakfast with some of her old movie friends so I'm saving that conversation." A strand of her hair was caught by the chilly breeze. She caught it and tucked it behind her ear before looking at him. Before those stunning eyes of hers scorched his soul. "I do want to talk about the photos."

"I'll start. You were right in thinking I knew who the woman is. Was. Her name was—"

"Melanie Dennings." Riley pressed her lips into a thin line, ducked her head and rocked back on her heels. "Your father was one of the lead detectives on the case. I have good sources," she added at his stony expression.

"You have Laurel Fontaine," he commented. "I've never played the politics game well, Riley. The very idea of doing so doesn't sit well."

"But this isn't politics." Her comment surprised him. "It's personal. I get it," she added when started to respond. "It's family. Family always complicates matters. Especially when you're determined to protect them."

"My father's a good man. He doesn't deserve what's going to land on him over this."

"Dean Samuels didn't deserve a life sentence for a crime he didn't commit."

"Maybe he wasn't there when she died," Quinn said in a forced calm voice. "That doesn't mean he's innocent. Look." He took a slow, deep breath. "There's nothing we can do at present that'll overturn his conviction—"

"Plea," Riley corrected him. "He pled guilty despite there being evidence that could have resulted in a different verdict had it gone to the jury. You're really okay letting a man remain in prison where he probably doesn't belong."

"I'm not, actually," he admitted. "But what I am saying is that it's going to take months to unravel whatever mess we've ... *you've* stumbled on." What Riley Temple could convey with a look was enough to turn his spine to ice. "He's been in for twenty-give years, Riley. Another couple of weeks or months—"

"Could feel like another lifetime." She ducked her head, but not before he saw the grudging acceptance flash in her eyes.

"Contrary to you being well-informed," he pushed just a bit harder, "I'd bet Laurel would agree blowing this up in an uncontrolled way isn't going to serve Dean Samuels any more than it's going to benefit us. The second this revelation gets leaked we lose any chance we have of finding out the actual truth. People are going to start scrambling to cover everything they can."

"Scrambling and panic makes people careless," she pointed out. "They could make a mistake that proves us right. Pushing this into the light might force the issue with more than one faction."

"Or we could inadvertently put Dean Samuels in jeopardy." It was an idea that hadn't occurred to him until now. "This case has lain dormant for twenty-plus years, Riley. What happens when it's reopened? My father might be willing to own up to his role in things, but I can guarantee there are going to be a hell of a lot of other powerful people who won't be. You want to take them on and work on finding the truth at the same time? Or do you want to come at them with the truth and give them no place to hide?"

Her eyes narrowed as she pursed her lips.

"You know I'm right, Riley. We have to come at this from a different way. A quieter way. And when the time is right, we'll blow it open. Together. If you're willing to work with me. And trust me. That's what's bothering you right now, isn't it? You don't know if you can trust me."

"Do you know you can trust me?"

"I think I can." He surprised himself by believing it. "Because I think you're an endgame kind of woman. At the very least, I can trust you enough for us to get a foothold on what we're really dealing with where those pictures are concerned."

"You're right about one thing. I plan to find out who hurt and killed my friends. I plan to make them pay."

"So do I." Although he had no doubt their method of payment differed. The band of tension around his chest eased. "And I'm not saying we don't go where the evidence leads. If I use those photos of yours as evidence in Merle's case, there won't be any going back. Once they're out, they're out. But unofficially, it's something I think we should explore. Together. As a team. Give me a week, Riley. A week of working together and we'll see where we end up."

"And if the only place we end up means going public with those pictures of Melanie Denning?"

"We will go public with them," Quinn said as a final attempt to persuade her. "It's a given. All we're working out now is the timing."

"All right." She nodded, but he could still see the wheels spinning behind her eyes. "For the record, Laurel's the one who convinced me to shift my attitude and approach you. She thinks you're a good guy with decent motives. Despite your obvious stupid man tendencies."

"I'll have to add those qualities to my resume," Quinn said.

"Okay then. It's official. We're a team. We'll start this afternoon."

"Start what?" Why did he feel as if he'd missed an entire chunk of conversation?

"Merle told me who brought in the box, but more importantly, he told me where that person found it." She flashed him a smile that made his cheeks ache. "Interested in the details? Pick me up at Temple House around one. I'm interviewing some potential building managers later this morning, but I should be done by then."

"All right." He wasn't so foolish as to believe for a second she didn't plan to keep her secrets. Just as he planned to keep his. "I'll see you around one. Riley,"—he grabbed her arm when she started to walk away—"we could have had this conversation over the phone, you know."

"We could have," Riley said. "But I think we'd have lost a lot in translation. Plus, I wanted to see your face again." That smile of hers might just be the death of him. "Glad we're finally on the same page. detective."

They might be reading the same book, Quinn thought as he followed her to her vehicle and watched her climb into her car, but they definitely were not on the same page. Despite agreeing to keeping their investigation quiet, he had no doubt Riley Temple was planning on firing them out of a massive cannon that would not only blow up Quinn's entire life, but his father's legacy.

"One step at a time," he told himself as he headed back into the station house. "Just take things with her one small step at a time."

A number of hours, three interviews, and one stress headache later, Riley rested her forehead on the lobby bar and let out a completely unladylike shriek of frustration. She lived in a city of nearly four million people. What was it going to take to find someone competent to take over as building manager?

"Carter Milano, this is all your fault." Why, oh why, did their super reliable, uber capable building manager of nearly a decade have quit on her out of the blue? If she'd had some warning, she could have saved herself so much frustration over finding a new one by planning ahead.

"Uh-oh." Moxie's voice had Riley heaving another sigh. "Interviews didn't go well?"

"That would be the understatement of the decade." Bachelor number one neglected to list his nearly three-year stint in county for burglary. Bachelor number two had a serious hygiene problem that made Riley's eyes water, which brought her to bachelor number three who hadn't been able to stay off his cell phone long enough to answer a few simple repair questions. All of which left Riley with the very late bachelor number four who, if he ever did show up, was already on her shit list.

She lifted her head, then nearly toppled off her stool in her rush to get to her great aunt.

"What on earth? Moxie, what are you doing with that?" She reached a winded Moxie who shuffled over, a familiar blue metal toolbox in one hand. "That's too heavy for you to carry around. You're going to tip over!" Before her aunt could protest, Riley grabbed the box, which rattled in her grasp. "How was breakfast? Wait. You're wearing your Sally Tate costume again. Why? What's broken?" Even as she asked, she felt her day tip into the unsalvageable range.

"The sink in Mr. Fabian's kitchen was backed up. Don't worry. I fixed it. Popped that clog out like champagne cork on New Year's Eve." But then she cringed, twirled a finger in a strand of hair that had come loose from her snood. "But I think his garbage disposal might be on strike. It started spewing sludge like a drunk sailor on leave before I left. I need to look for a manual online."

"Define spewing." With images of the Exorcist child in her mind, she started to pray. "Is it still—"

"Oh, no, honey. It stopped." She waved off any concern even as she refused to meet Riley's eyes. "For now, at least. He just can't use his water until I fix it. And he's not too happy about it, I can tell you. I told him you'd be up to talk to him about it while I figured out how to fix it for good."

"Awesome. I'll add that to my list." Right before she took off to Tahiti. "Why don't you leave the tools with me and head on back upstairs and check the files for the disposal manual? I remember seeing them when I was filing some paperwork." That was a whopper. Riley had digitized all those manuals into her laptop six months ago, but if it kept her aunt occupied, so much the better.

"But Shelly and Carmine in 4B called and said that they aren't getting any hot water. I really should—Oh. Who's that? Another interviewee?" Moxie pushed past Riley to the door to let the young man in. "Hello there."

"Mrs. Temple? My name's David Marino." His voice carried a hint of Texas and sounded barely on the other side of puberty. "I was hoping to interview for the building manager position?"

Riley frowned. "I'm sorry. I don't have your name on my schedule." Toolbox still in hand, she joined Moxie at the door as the young man stepped in.

"N-no, ma'am." His Muppet-round eyes sat sunken into a round, pudgy face. A mass of dark hair was cut short on the sides yet piled high on the top of his head—probably, Riley thought, to appear taller. His gaze darted around nervously as he shoved his hands deep into the pockets of his too-large jeans. "I heard about the opening from Carl down at the Pick and Pack. He said you might be open to talking?" He plunged ahead before Riley could say no. He didn't look like he could lift a piece of lint, let along service an entire apartment building. "I'm a part-time student at UCLA. Engineering. I've always been good with my hands and fixing things. According to my ma, at least." He managed a quick smile. "Sorry. I'm babbling. If you've already filled the position—"

"No, she hasn't. Let they boy in, Riley," Moxie shooed her back and ushered David inside. "He isn't doing anyone any good out there. Come on in, young man. Let's chat a bit."

"Moxie," Riley warned. She didn't want to get the young man's hopes up. One thing this job required was physical strength and confidence, both of which seemed to have passed this young man by. "You have a disposal manual to look for, remember?" Riley flashed her potential manager an apologetic smile. Poor kid looked like he was about to bolt, he was shaking so bad.

"All right, all right," Moxie muttered. "I'm just going to get myself some refreshment first. We're out of Cuervo, by the way," she told Riley on her way around to the bar.

"Do you have a resume and references?" Riley asked David.

"Ah, yes, ma'am. Back at my apartment. This was all spur of the moment, so …" He trailed off, shrugged, and bit his lower lip. "I didn't want to miss an opportunity."

"Well, if this goes well, you can just email those to me, okay? I don't suppose you know anything about water heaters," Riley teased and earned a spark of hope out of the young man.

"Actually, my grandfather had a plumbing business. I used to stay with him on the weekends back in Austin. I'd be happy to take a look."

Then again, maybe the angels had sent him after all. "Let's consider this an interview-by-fire then and we'll see what you've got."

Riley led the way through the lobby to the closed-off basement stairs on the other side of the lobby fireplace. It wasn't an area Temple House residents often ventured into, and if they did, it was only to access the small storage unit each tenant was provided with on their lease. Junk catchers her grandfather had called them. Dusty ones.

She descended the first few steps, stopped on the landing, and clicked on the basement light which provided just enough glow so as they didn't trip the rest of the way down. "Not a lot of light." She shifted the toolbox to her other hand. "Sorry about that. Be careful. There are pipes in weird places down here."

"No problem. I've got cat eyes."

Riley's brows rose. Cat eyes? That was a new one. "We're planning on updating the electrical," Riley explained and glanced over her shoulder as David followed her down. The basement door clicked shut behind them. "As an engineering student, maybe you'd have some suggestions on that front."

"I'm sure I can come up with something."

"I'm not sure how much Carl told you about the job." Riley made her way down the narrow aisle between the gated cubicles toward the east end of the basement. "It's a live-in position. The apartment isn't huge, but it's been recently renovated. Two bedrooms and a full bath. The second bedroom's more of a large walk-in closet, but it's big enough for an office or gaming room." The last she suggested because of his age, then realized she was stereotyping him by assuming he liked video games. "It's located on the ground floor, just off the lobby up …" With the stairs out of sight, she turned and, wincing against the glare of one of the bare bulbs, pointed behind him.

She froze.

The David standing in the shadows bore no resemblance to the innocent young man she and Moxie had welcomed into the building. His bright clear eyes had narrowed and darkened. The hands he'd been keeping in his pockets flexed at his sides, making the gloves covering them stretch and squeak.

The phrase "too stupid to live" shot through her head like a bullet, ricocheting around until it landed with a thud dead center of her chest.

Her wannabe manager appeared to have grown inches in the space of moments, but she realized that's because upstairs, he'd been slouching. He wasn't slouching now.

"You aren't here about the job." Her voice quivered despite her determination not to give into the fear. She tried to swallow around the panic prickling the back of her neck.

"No." Gone was the youthful, hopeful voice she'd heard before. "I want the film."

"What film?" Riley backed away, her hand flexing around the toolbox handle. It suddenly felt so heavy, as if her arm couldn't remain attached to her body if she held on much longer.

"The film you bought from Merle Paddock." He moved toward her. She stepped back. "Where is it?"

"Not here." She shook her head. "I don't have it anymore." She mentally grappled for the image of Quinn and held on. "I gave it to the police."

"Lying isn't going to make this any easier," he said. "We heard you arguing with that cop about it at the restaurant. You didn't give it to him. Now where is it? Upstairs?" he angled his chin up, but Riley's gaze was glued to his hands that reached into his back pocket. "Does your aunt have it?"

Her breath froze in her chest. She'd never said Moxie was her aunt.

"She doesn't know anything about this. You shooting at me yesterday changed my mind about a lot of things." She nearly tripped over an electrical cord stretched across the floor. She caught her balance, only to find herself trapped with her back against the wall. He was closing in. *Just a little bit closer.* That was all she needed. "I don't have it anymore."

"That's too bad." The man shook his head, seemed to draw into himself as he frowned. "They won't be happy to hear that. Not happy at all."

"Who?" She shifted the toolbox in front of her, biding her time, focused her breath as he crept closer still. "Who won't be happy?" His hands came up, stretching a length of rope in front of him. A warning of what was to come. She really needed to update her "ways I don't want to die" list. "Moxie saw you come in," she whispered. "If you hurt me, she'll tell the police everything about you." She strained to memorize every detail of his face and, as he stepped beneath one of the bare blubs, she mentally clicked a shutter to capture his image.

"No." His lips stretched across bright white teeth. "She won't."

Riley threw all her weight forward and plowed the toolbox into his chest. When he stumbled back, she catapulted past him. He dropped down, his hand whipping out and whacked a hand against her ankle. She went sprawling face-first onto the cement floor. The air whooshed out of her and she gasped, reaching out with her hands, trying to claw into the unforgiving cement to pull herself forward.

She tried to scream, but all that came out was a muffled cry. Riley shoved herself up and over, hands and feet scrambling backward as he approached her again. *Get to the stairs. Get to goddamned stairs already!*

"They're all gone. No one can help you. Especially not that old woman." As if reading her mind, a slow, horrific, amused smile stretched his lips. "I was hoping you'd fight me. You're a much bigger challenge than the old man was."

"Merle still beat you though, didn't he?" She couldn't resist a challenge herself; the challenge to make him angrier. She knew firsthand the damage anger did; how careless it made someone. But she also knew her own anger was the shortest path to survival. "He hit that alarm and sent you running."

"Left you with a surprise, though."

Grief punctured the terror coursing through her. Grief and her own rage.

"A sacrifice had to be made." His eyes clouded over as if he'd been caught in some kind of mindless chant. "They demanded one. They always demand one."

"Riley?" Aunt Moxie's muffled voice sounded through the closed door. "Honey, is everything all right? There's a man up here—"

"Shhhhh." Her attacker held a gloved finger to his lips. "You don't want Aunt Moxie hurt, do you?"

"She'd kick your balls into your throat," Riley lied, but as she heard the basement door open she screamed, "Stay up there! Don't come down, Moxie! I'll be up in a few minutes." She was racking up lies faster than a hustler racked up pool balls.

"Why? Riley, what's going on?"

Riley could hear the concern, a tremble of fear, in her aunt's voice and hated him for it. She shoved her feet under her hips and stood up, looking around for something, anything she could use for defense. But there was nothing other than cages filled with musty old boxes and memories.

David's pace picked up and he advanced, snapping the rope tight between his hands as she continued to back away, moving him away from the staircase. As she drew him forward and the door was firmly behind him, she saw a shadow move out of the corner of her eye. A shadow that ever so slowly, crept down the stairs. Moxie?!

Fear paralyzed her. *Go back, go back, go back!* But as the shadow moved, relief swamped her. Too limber—not Moxie.

But who?

Dread choked off what was left of her air. It was another man. A larger, more imposing one. Stealthy. David's accomplice? Oh, God. There were two of them now?

Panic seized her around the chest. She flailed, reaching out, searching, hoping for something, *anything* to help her. She wanted to scream as she grabbed one of the fence posts and pushed herself faster and deeper into the basement.

The back of her head connected hard with one of the pipes she'd warned her attacker about. Even as stars erupted behind tightly squeezed eyes, she grasped the unexpected solution.

She reached up and grabbed hold of the pipe. Straining, she swung her legs back, then forward with every bit of strength she possessed. She connected, her feet catching David in the jaw with a solid thwack, but the second she made contact the dust coating the pipe made her hands slip and she dropped straight to the ground.

She lay there, dazed, head spinning, and saw the second man launch himself over the bottom portion of the metal stair rail. As her attacker attempted to catch his footing, he turned and caught a solid fist right in the center of his solar plexus.

Riley heard his exhale of breath as he stumbled into the cages. She rolled in the opposite direction then, as he sprinted past her, she reached out to try to trip him. She caught only air, then sagged back as he disappeared into the darkness. Seconds later, he scrambled up the metal staircase like a clumsy rat and shoved open the metal panel that led out into the outside alley.

The panel slammed closed behind him.

She groaned, unable to identify an inch of her body that didn't hurt or ache. And her head? Holy hell, her head felt as if she'd been slugged by a two-by-four.

"Ms. Temple?" Her surprising stair savior approached, hands splayed to show he had no weapons. Her eyes had adjusted to the dim light and she could see his short, military style-haircut, the neatly trimmed beard, and intense, concerned, sympathetic eyes. "Are you all right?"

"Remains to be seen." From her splayed position on the floor, she eyed him in the darkness. He took up far more space in the basement than she was comfortable with. "Who the hell are you?"

"Blake Redford. I had an appointment to interview for the building manager position. Your aunt let me in. Here," he held out a hand, "careful standing up."

She let out an ego-bursting groan as he hauled her up. "You're late."

"Yeah, sorry about that."

"Don't you dare apologize," she huffed and, after doing a quick mental inventory, decided nothing was broken. She touched a hand against the back of her head and felt her knees sag in relief when there wasn't any blood.

"Riley?" Aunt Moxie appeared on the landing. "The police are on the way!"

"Great," Riley muttered. "Just what …" She cursed, swayed, and found herself steadied by Blake Redford's solid hands. "Moxie, Quinn's probably going to be here soon." What time was it anyway? "Go wait for him by the door, please."

"DSP is coming back? Hot damn! And here I thought you kicked him to the curb last night."

"Moxie," Riley warned.

"Fine." Moxie huffed. She slammed the door closed behind her.

"DSP?" Blake asked.

"Don't ask," Riley said at Blake's questioning yet amused look as he led her to the staircase. "Wait. Before we tackle the climb …" She considered him for a long moment. He clearly had the strength for the job, and obviously a protective streak—check, and check. "I've got one question for you."

"All right."

"How are you with garbage disposals and water heaters?"

"We get along just fine, ma'am."

"Awesome." Riley grabbed hold of the railing and dragged herself up the first step. "You're hired."

# CHAPTER EIGHT

QUINN didn't think anything of it when he pulled to the right to let two patrol cars, sirens blaring, race past him as he exited the Hollywood Freeway.

Nor did he consider the report coming across the radio of an attempted assault anything other than a typical day's call. But the second he heard the familiar address, his foot hit the gas so hard and fast he nearly plowed through the car in front of him.

He flipped on his own lights and siren and put his long-ago defensive driving course to the test and zigzagged his way around traffic until he screeched to a halt outside Temple House behind one of the patrol cars.

The uniformed officers were just headed through the double glass doors being held open by a familiar, elderly redhead who, once she caught sight of him, propelled herself outside to his car.

He slammed the car into park, shoved open the door and hurried toward her. "Moxie? What's wrong? What happened? Are you okay?" He didn't like the lack of color in the old woman's face, or her slightly glassy spinning eyes.

"Someone attacked Riley. In the basement. He seemed like such a nice boy." She grabbed hold of his arms when he reached her. "It was my fault. All my fault. I let him in. How could I be so careless?"

"I'm sure this isn't your fault. Is Riley all right?" It seemed to take him an age to push the words out, but as soon as he did, she nodded.

"She's fine. Someone helped. I know she didn't want me to call the police, but—"

"It's all right. We're here now." He curled an arm around her shoulders, despite his desperation to see for himself that Riley was all right, and slowly led her back up the stairs and into the lobby. He could feel her shaking.

He didn't see Riley right away, blocked as she was by four uniformed officers and one tall, bearded man he didn't recognize. One of the tenants he hadn't yet met, he figured.

"Where's Moxie? Is my aunt all right? Moxie?"

The second Quinn heard her voice, the bands around his chest loosened. "Moxie's fine, Riley. I've got her."

The fact he could hear her sigh of relief all the way across the lobby was a testament to how completely detached she was from reality. She wasn't even trying to keep her emotions under control.

"I think I need a drink," Moxie said. "There's some Scotch locked behind the bar somewhere."

"Let's start with water," Quinn suggested before he retrieved a bottle from one of the small refrigerators. "See how this goes down first." Because he still didn't like her pallor, he caught her wrist and, pressing his fingers against her pulse, counted for a spell. The beat was a little unsteady, but that was to be expected after a shock. At least now her cheeks were a bit brighter, and she'd stopped trembling. He didn't want to indulge her request for alcohol until he knew what medications, if any, she might be taking. "I want you to stay here, all right? I'm going to check and see how Riley's doing, then I'll be back to check on you?"

"Thank you, Quinn," Moxie murmured and rested her forehead in her hand. "I'm glad you're here."

It was nice to hear, even if it hadn't come from Riley.

The officers parted as he approached with another bottle of water in his hand for Riley. Her face was streaked with tears and smudges of dirt. Her fingers were raw where a couple of nails had been shredded. The towel she held against the back of her head was sopping, sending tiny rivers of melted ice down her arm.

"She won't let us call for an ambulance," Officer Delacroix told him as he bent down beside a shaky-looking Riley. "Shouldn't mess around with head injuries."

"I told them, I'm fine." But he could hear her teeth chattering against the cold and shock. "This is my 'I'm one of the too-stupid-to-live chicks from a horror movie' look. He looked like a kid," she whispered as if speaking more to herself than to anyone else. "Then he sort of transformed, like he turned into the Hulk or something. Little fucker. Should have kicked him in the nuts the second I realized something was off."

Reassured the real Riley Temple was still alive and well, Quinn rested a gentle hand on Riley's jean-clad knee and squeezed. Without even looking at him, she covered his hand with hers and hung on.

"I think you should let them call the EMTs," Quinn told her. "Riley, be sensible," he added when she started to protest. "They could check Moxie out as well. She's had a shock and she's a little unsteady on her feet. As a precaution, let's get you both checked out, all right?"

She begrudgingly nodded, then winced.

Funny. He'd known her such a short time and yet instinctively he'd managed to get her to do something she didn't want to do. Make his request about Moxie, or probably anyone she cared about, and he could get her to do anything. Wasn't that just another surprise for the day?

She finally met his gaze and in her eyes he saw far more than he believed she'd be comfortable with. She wasn't just shaken. She was downright scared. Part of him thought, good—it's about time. The other part of him? The part that had nothing to do with being a cop and everything to do with being a man who cared about her? That part wanted to tear out onto the streets and find the asshole who had done this to her.

"She knocked her head against a pipe in the basement," the man standing beside Riley told him. "I heard it from ten feet away. If she doesn't have a concussion, it'll be a miracle. Sorry." He held out his hand. "Blake Redford. New building manager for Temple House."

"If I'd known you were a tattletale, I wouldn't have hired you," Riley muttered as Quinn stood and returned the greeting, then gave an assenting nod to the waiting officers, one of whom grabbed their shoulder talkie and moved off to call for the ambulance. Officer Delacroix walked over to Moxie to stay with her while Riley's aunt sipped her water.

When Quinn shifted to Blake Redford and sized him up, he got an instant, solid read. Clean-cut with short hair, neatly trimmed beard, and an intense, focused expression. Commanding presence if not a silent one. Pressed, crisp, practical clothes. Nothing fancy about his jeans and T-shirt. He set off military vibes by the boatload so Quinn took a guess. "Marines?"

"Navy," Blake said and held out his hand. "Intelligence, mostly. Special deployment."

Quinn's eyebrows rose, impressed. "Recent discharge?"

"Pensioned retirement."

Quinn frowned. The man couldn't be much older than he was, if that. Pensioned retirement from the military before forty? There had to be a story there.

"Are you two done bonding because I'd really like to …" Riley's eyes went wide and she swayed in her seat.

"Head down." Blake locked his hand around the back of Riley's neck and coaxed her head down between her knees. "Deep breaths. Long in, long out." He glanced up at Quinn when Riley squirmed briefly before giving in, muttering something about not liking being told what to do. "I also worked as a medic for a few months."

"I don't suppose you got a good look at him?" Quinn asked Blake as the distant sound of sirens echoed.

"Not as good as I would have liked. Got this though." Still holding a hand on Riley's neck, he reached into his back pocket and held out a brown leather glove. "Ripped it off his hand after I took a swing at him. Thought maybe you could get prints off the inside."

"Unbelievable." Riley mumbled into her shoes. "I've hired myself a cop."

Or even better, Quinn mused. Former Special Forces.

He took the glove from and handed it off to one of the patrol men with instructions to grab an evidence bag out of the trunk of his car. "How'd he get past you?"

"He didn't," Riley's voice was muffled. "He went out the basement staircase."

"Luck?" Quinn asked Blake, who shook his head.

"No one's that lucky," Blake said. "My guess? He knew the building. He had this planned out. It's the middle of a workday. He wasn't worried about someone being around." He inclined his chin toward Moxie. "She could've easily been collateral damage, but instead he played with them. Drew it out."

"Little fucker," Riley muttered again.

"Indeed," Quinn agreed.

"He knew more than the building. I'm okay." She sat up, took a deep breath and nodded. "Thanks. That helped." Dark circles were forming under her eyes. "I'm only going to say this to you once, Quinn, so I want to make sure you're listening."

"All right."

"You were right. Do not comment," she ordered him. "You either," she shot Blake a warning look. "You'll get maybe three months' worth of good will out of this before I really put you to work on this place."

"Noted and understood," Blake said. "I'm going to go check out the alley, see if he left some kind of trail. I hit him pretty hard. Maybe hard enough to make him puke. One can hope." He walked away, heading out the front door instead of going through the basement.

"Me being right aside …" Quinn took a seat beside her on the old-fashioned circular beige upholstered bench and laid his hand on her arm. "What do you mean he knew more than the building's layout."

"He knew Moxie was my aunt." She kept her voice low as she readjusted the makeshift ice bag. "I never said it while he was here. He knew, Quinn. He knew about her. He knew the building was pretty much empty. He knew how to get out of Temple House. You were right." Her eyes, clear now, brimmed not with tears, but with rage. "They're coming after my family."

"You have got to be kidding me," Mabel snapped the second she pulled back the emergency room curtain and yanked the cell phone out of Riley's hand. "You're in the ER for crying out loud. Get off the damned phone."

"Give that back." Riley nearly fell off the bed diving for it.

"No." Mabel lifted the phone to her ear. "She'll call you back."

"That was important." Riley didn't have to be on the receiving end of "the look" to know she sounded like Keeley in one of her back in the toddler days temper tantrums. She grabbed one of the notebooks she'd pulled out of her bag before it fell off the bed and hoped she could read the scribbled information she'd acquired from the manager of Constant Care Storage.

"You just had an MRI and a CT scan to check for skull fractures. You're supposed to be taking it easy, not—"

"Making calls to find out where this nightmare started?" Without her phone she felt as if a limb had been amputated. "Give me my phone back."

"No." Mabel snapped the curtain shut and, after shoving Riley's legs to the side, sat on the end of the narrow emergency room bed. "Start talking. Or I'll go out there and demand that cop of yours arrest you for public stupidity."

"He's not my cop." The second she uttered the words she realized she'd focused on entirely the wrong subject. "The EMTs gave Moxie a clean bill of health. Why'd they have to load me up—"

"Oddly enough, they were concerned about keeping you alive. Imagine that. Nice gown." She smirked. "Very stylish. Easy access in the back I assume so they can remove that stick up your—"

"Oh, shut up." Riley tucked her legs in and wrapped her arms around her knees.

"Embrace the fear and turn down the attitude," Mabel ordered with more than a little heat. "What happened to you scared the crap out of a lot of us. Forget the intruder you happily let walk into our home. You could have been killed, you know."

"Believe me, I know." Moxie could have been hurt as well and that, more than anything, was responsible for the giant pit of despair in her stomach. The only way to get rid of it, and protect the people she cared about, was to dig deep and find the answers she needed and expose the man responsible—not only for the attack on her this afternoon, but for Dudley's murder and Merle's assault. Shouldn't take more than a day or two. *Ha.* "Is Moxie all right? And Cassia? I didn't stop to think—"

"Cass is fine. A little spooked after we told her what happened," Mabel said in a way that made Riley believe she wasn't being entirely honest about their friend's mental state. "Sutton talked her out of her apartment and, with the kids, they're keeping Moxie entertained at your place. I believe they're going to bake a cake."

"And Barksy?" Riley asked hopefully.

"I don't think they considered baking Barksy." Mabel's serious tone had Riley's lips twitching. "Barksy is definitely on Moxie cheer-up duty. She's worried about you. Moxie, I mean," Mabel clarified and dropped her bag on the floor. "We all are."

"I know." While Moxie thrived on being the center of the universe, Riley prided herself of getting by with little to no attention at all. "You didn't have to come down here. After Saturday night, I figured you'd need some serious Keeley time."

"Keeley got smothered with motherly affection yesterday, so she was more than happy to see me go. Besides, the cake is promised to be chocolate and, like her mother, my child is happy to trade me in for a slice. Although after the last couple of days I'd probably scarf down the entire thing."

"What's going on? You okay?" Riley rested her chin on her knees. She didn't like the overly cheerful tone in Mabel's voice, as if determined to convince everyone everything was fine. "Laurel said this last one was bad."

"It was. But it was worse for an eighteen-year-old girl whose entire life is never going to be what it was." Mabel stared up at the ceiling as if trying not to cry. "Every time I get called out, I tell myself there's no way I can be surprised. I've been doing this for five years. How can I possibly be shocked by what humans are capable of doing to one another and yet .... Jesus, Riley. After they raped her, they branded her." Mabel touched fingers to the back of her neck. "Who even thinks to do that?" She shrugged in a helpless attempt to shake off what clearly continued to bother her. "I helped get her settled in at the shelter. They'll keep an eye on her, help her decide what happens next. Personally? I hope she gets on a plane and heads home to Kansas. Are you going to tell me what's actually going on with you, or do I need to wait and find out at a coroner's inquest?"

"Are you and Laurel having secret meetings about me? That's almost exactly what she said to me yesterday."

"Not yet," Mabel warned. "Our first one is scheduled for tomorrow evening after work. On the roof. With Sutton and Cas. They've already RSVP'd We're going to talk about you."

"Awesome." Maybe there was a bright side to being in the hospital after all. "Did you see the doctor on your way in? When are they letting me go?"

"Laurel and Quinn are waiting to talk to him now and you can bet you aren't going anywhere if they aren't convinced it's safe for you to leave."

"My circle of protectors is getting annoyingly large." Riley rested her forehead on her knees. How could she have been so monumentally stupid to go into the basement with a stranger? How many times had she ranted about fictional characters doing just that on television shows or in horror movies? And yet she hadn't given it a second thought. Part of her wondered if she'd deserved what happened, then she had to remind herself that no one deserved that type of action being taken against them. Ever. "I appreciate you coming down to be with me. I know this isn't your favorite place."

"It's fine." Mabel's tight response left Riley swallowing a good chunk of guilt. "It'll be nice to leave here with some good news for a change." She clutched the half-heart pendant dangling at her throat. "I'm beginning to think I need a break from my volunteer work. Seeing as you seem to need a keeper these days, maybe I should shift my attention to being a personal puppy dog and start following you around."

It was on the tip of her tongue to tease Mabel out of her sour mood, but as she didn't have the guts to do anything close to what Mabel Reynolds did to help rape victims traverse their suddenly different world, Riley couldn't possibly judge. Or advise.

"You need to do what's right for you," Riley said instead. "For you and Keeley. What you do takes a toll, Mabel. It has to. I know you always said you became a rape victim advocate because of what happened to Sylvie, but—"

"That was me projecting. Me deciding what might have … what must have happened to her," Mabel whispered as ghosts seemed to pass across her gaze. "It's so cliché, but the not knowing really is the worst part. Sometimes I swear like I can feel her. Every time I come to see a victim in the ER, I tell myself I'm helping them because no one was there to help her. Even though …" she trailed off, shook her head. "I've accepted I'll never know what happened to my sister, that my parents will never know what happened to their daughter. Being an advocate gave me a place to focus that anger, that pain." She rubbed the center of her chest where Riley knew it felt as if she had a hole in her heart. "Some days, some cases, it just feels so hopeless. Other times it's as if I've lost her all over again."

"You know you can always talk to us about this, don't you? Me, Laurel, Cass, Sutton. It's what we're here for. I know you can't get into specific details about the victims you work with, but with the horror you hear about, Mabel, surely there has to be an outlet for you."

"Why do you think I have a heavy bag installed in my bedroom?"

"Hey." Riley held up her hands. "What you do in your bedroom is your business." They laughed because it was better than screaming, but Riley hoped, she prayed, some of what she offered broke through. When the curtain opened again, Riley and Mabel both looked up to where Laurel and Quinn stood.

"You want the good news or the bad news first?" Laurel asked, her all too wise eyes shifting between her friends in a way that told Riley there was a private conversation in the offing.

"I'll take whichever news says I can go home." Riley was already sliding her legs over the edge of the bed. "Am I being cut loose?"

"You are," Quinn told her. "But you're on restricted activity for the next twenty-four hours. You definitely gave your skull a good wallop."

"There's a word you don't hear very often. Wallop. Wallop." Riley grinned. "That's fun to say."

"Maybe she needs another CT scan," Laurel suggested.

"Wait." Riley stopped her foot from hitting the floor. "Was that the good news or the bad?"

"Totally depends on how your point of view." Laurel beamed up at Quinn. "It's been decided that until we put this whole mystery photo issue behind you—"

"What mystery photo issue?" Mabel asked.

"You'll find out at tomorrow night's meeting," Laurel told her.

"Wait," Riley said. "That's a real thing? It's actually happening?" What happened to keeping the photographs quiet and secret? What happened to not telling anyone what was going on?

"Oh, the meeting is happening," Laurel warned her. "We might even have a guest speaker for the event. An invitation I issued just a few minutes ago when I put two and two together. Right, detective?"

"It's like my universal translator is busted." Riley gently knocked her palm against the side of her head and earned a trio of protests. "Oh, relax. I'm fine." But she needed to not do that again. "You found something out about that date on the paper in the photograph?"

"I did." Laurel confirmed. "We'll talk about it tomorrow night. Because you're going to take it easy for the next day."

"I can't," Riley protested. "I feel fine—"

"She says that like she has a choice," Laurel cut her off. "That conversation you and I had about being careful wasn't even twenty-four hours ago. That's how long it took you to land in this place. So listen up, Buttercup."

"Uh-oh. She used the B word," Mabel murmured under her breath.

"Until this mess you've gotten yourself into is cleaned up," Laurel said. "And whatever psycho killers are after you are caught, we've got a new Temple House resident. Welcome, detective."

"Thank you, Ms. Fontaine." He straightened as if being handed an award. "Pleasure to be staying with you all."

Riley's mouth dropped open. "You cannot be serious." Bad idea. Such a bad idea. "There's no need for—"

"Oh, I think there is and before you argue owner's rights, as one of your tenants and said property's official attorney, I can say right now we're overruling any protest you might come up with," Laurel said in a tone Riley had only heard her use when practicing her closing arguments. "We're beyond this being about you and your curiosity being abated. This is about all the people who live in our building who could have easily been affected today. Hell, they all *have* been affected. Or do you need me to remind you just how close Moxie was to that maniac?"

"You do not," Riley snapped. "And he won't get in again. I know what he looks like."

"Clearly you don't," Quinn cut her off in an equally no-nonsense voice. "Otherwise you would have recognized him from Merle's shop the other night."

Her brain was starting to smoke from being overloaded. "What on earth are you talking about? There wasn't anyone at the shop when I was there except that old … couple." Putting two and two together had never come so slow. "Wait, you're saying that was *him*? Like in some sort of disguise?"

"A high-quality disguise," Quinn confirmed. "There's a reason you never hear about senior citizen hit men. Or women," he added at Laurel's click of her tongue. "It's a young person's game. No one gets to be that old and have that much evil in their eyes. Not in my experience. The killing gets into their soul and eats away at them. The question now is whether your attacker wore a disguise today or if he felt safe enough to walk in face-first. Hopefully that glove Blake ripped off his hand will give us something to start working with. Until then, consider yourself under protective custody."

"That's just not possible," Riley said. "All the apartments are full. Even the building manager's, now that I've hired Blake." She sat up a bit straighter with that tidbit of information. "Sorry about that."

"Don't be," Quinn said. "I don't need my own place." His smile was quick, but sharp. And aimed directly at her. "I'll just take your couch."

From his temporary home on Riley and Moxie's living room sofa, Quinn sat forward and nodded as if his lieutenant could see him. After six hours in the emergency room with Riley and then being run through the lack of evidence in the basement with the crime scene crew, now that Riley was hopefully asleep, he'd enjoyed a surprising and entertaining dinner with Moxie Temple, only to end his evening with yet another terse conversation with his boss.

At this point Quinn wasn't sure where this case was heading, but he also knew admitting that to his superior could open a whole other can of worms.

"Yes, sir, I understand," Quinn said. "I appreciate you giving me some rope on this, LT."

"Just make sure you don't hang yourself with it," Lieutenant Gibson warned. "No one's going to buy you taking time off, so we'll chalk it up to you turning your attention to a prior case that got away from you."

"Use the Peterson murder," Quinn suggested. "That botched burglary didn't provide much evidence at the time, so it fits the bill."

"What about Osterman? You want him with you, or I can reassign him—"

"I'll keep Wallace." Quinn had been giving this a good deal of thought. "I'll give him lead on the Paddock case. He's already established a rapport with the victim and I'd like him to keep an eye on Merle in the hospital. If anyone has their radar pinging, I want Wallace acting as normal as possible."

"You sure?"

"I'm not seeing we have much of a choice if we want to keep things under wraps," Quinn admitted. "That leaves P Squared to pick up the new cases as they come in."

"Yeah, well, they're clear for now, but I can only make that work for a week before it gets someone's attention."

"Doesn't give me much time." Quinn could already feel himself tipping into the darkness of obsession. Rereading of files, rewatching of security footage. Compulsively searching for anyone and anything that connected Riley, those photographs, and their original source. He had more help than expected, though, thanks to Laurel sussing out the truth about Melanie's death and Dean Samuels's arrest date.

"I suggest you make the most of what you do have," Lieutenant Gibson advised. "You get in trouble, I'm your first call. In the meantime, you keep your eyes open and your feet on the floor."

"Sir?" He blinked, certain he hadn't heard Gibson correctly.

"You know exactly what I'm saying. This is one investigation we don't need compromised in any way. Let me know when you've made some progress."

"Translation," Quinn muttered to himself as he clicked off his screen and set his cell down. "Stay out of your protectee's bed."

The front door intercom buzzed, the old-fashioned electrical charge reverberating around the spacious loft apartment. The fact he hesitated a moment before getting up to answer it spoke volumes about his day.

"Don't tell me you're paranoid now." Riley's sleepy voice had Quinn's head snapping around. "Sorry." She didn't sound anything of the kind. Riley did, however, look appropriately rumpled in her hot-pink sleep shorts and matching tank. Her hair was knotted and mussed, and her color was better than it had been back in the ER. He'd say her return of attitude was a good sign except near as he could tell, it had never gone away.

As he stood, he dragged his gaze from the tip of her painted red toes to the top of her tangled hair. Those legs of hers drew him back for a second look. Tanner, more toned than he expected, and far longer than he'd dreamed. Full breasts strained against the stretch of her shirt. Damn. She was one nicely formed female. Suddenly his boss's warning felt more like a premonition in need of fulfilling.

"Didn't mean to spook the bodyguard," Riley said. "And his gun." She pointed to his hand that rested on the butt of his weapon. "If you're that itchy maybe we should rethink this living arrangement. I wouldn't like to be shot by accident. Or by any way come to think of it." The buzzer sounded again, and he headed to the entryway. "You expecting someone?"

"My partner." He punched the outdated button and leaned in. "Wallace?"

"No, it's freaking Santa Claus. Buzz me in already."

As there was no mistaking that voice or that humor, Quinn buzzed him in and faced Riley. "I thought you were asleep."

"I was. Now I'm not. Glad to hear you finally got his name right. Not entirely thrilled with the idea of another cop in my apartment." She held up a hand and waved off an argument. "Don't mind me. I'm the poster girl for hangry. And Wallace had best hustle up here before Mrs. Zamada starts playing security guard at how many men are walking the halls and has patrol officers here for a whole new reason."

"Is she the woman we met when we got back? Fifty-something, bottle glasses, neon-green stripe in her hair? Lives in ..." he thought back to the collection of plants in front of her door. "2A?"

"That's her. And be warned, she's quite fond of her late father's weapon collection. She even offered to let me keep one of his shotguns. Don't worry, detective," she added at his dubious expression. "They're all legal. I think. Then again, she always believed her father was a Russian sleeper agent, so who knows what's real anymore? Hell, for all I know this could be the Upsidedown and I'm an exploded rat in the basement. Coffee?"

"It's after ten." Not amused by the colorful imagery, Quinn unbolted the metal front door and pulled it open, heard the elevator whirring as it delivered Wallace to the third floor. "And caffeine is contraindicated with your pain meds."

"Or it would be if I'd taken one. Don't mother hen me, Quinn. It makes me grouchy."

First hangry, now grouchy. *Quinn, you really know how to pick them.* Strangely enough though, the idea didn't disagree with him. He stepped into the hall that carried through the elegant feel of the downstairs lobby. When the elevator doors popped open, Wallace, who for a change was not wearing one of his throwback 70s suits, but instead had donned dark sweats and a T-shirt, stumbled out. Quinn dipped down and caught the warm, oversized pizza box before it hit the floor. "You brought dinner."

"Yeah." Wallace hefted one of Quinn's duffel bags more securely onto his shoulder. "My dick of a partner called for a favor and interrupted my Chinese food leftover binge. I thought hazing was illegal these days."

"Hazing, yes. We call them trust exercises now." Because he felt sorry for the younger man, Quinn held out his hand. "Computer?"

"Right. Here you go." Wallace readjusted and passed off the computer case.

"Come on in. I'll get you a beer." Quinn motioned him inside, then closed the door behind them.

"Riley has beer?"

"You needn't sound so shocked, detective." Riley approached, a mug of steaming coffee in one hand, a bottle of beer in the other. "I'm a civilized woman. And the beer is courtesy of my friend Sutton. She figured cops and beer go together and since this one's decided to plant roots in my couch—"

"I thought Moxie said it was her couch?" Quinn said.

Riley handed off the bottle after Wallace let go and dumped his bags in the middle of the living room.

"If all this junk is testament to how fast you expect to work this case, my confidence is far from stoked." Riley blinked, a bit disbelievingly, at the pile. "Whatever," she muttered, when Quinn opened his mouth. "Welcome, Detective Osterman. Make yourself at home." Her smile could have injected venom had she bared her teeth. She watched him plant himself in her living room, and huffed. "Wait, he already has." She sniffed the air, then dropped her gaze to the pizza box. "That smells amazing." She reached out and pried open the lid. "Sausage and mushroom?"

"And onion," Wallace confirmed. "He hates onions, so I had them cut them up real small and add them into the sauce."

"Nice." Riley grinned. "I'll get the plates. And the leftover spaghetti you and Moxie had for the dinner I slept through, DSP," she added before she sauntered away.

"DSP?" Wallace asked him

"Don't go there," Quinn warned.

"She seems … what's the word? Nice?"

"It's a ruse," Quinn warned the younger man. "She's pissed and scared and I can hear the wheels spinning in her head." Riley Temple was up to something, which told Quinn things were going to get way worse before they got better.

"Consider me warned." Wallace slapped his hands together. "And hungry. Let's eat."

"Guess Moxie is a sound sleeper," Quinn observed as Riley cleared away their paper plates and snatched up the last piece of pizza. "Thought maybe she'd join us. She strikes me as a midnight margarita kind of woman."

"Once upon a time," Riley smirked. "These days she's done for by nine and she sleeps with one of those earphone headband deals and a night mask. Short of an eight-point-two on the Richter scale, she won't budge until seven at least."

"Especially since you poured her a second shot of scotch before she retired for the evening." Quinn reminded her.

"That, too." Riley's smile was quick.

"How's your head?" Wallace asked.

"Miraculously still attached to my shoulders." Riley dumped the trash and tidied the kitchen before pulling a half-filled cake container off the counter and set it on the spacious dining table. "We're calling this distraction cake," she announced as she cut each of them a slice. "Courtesy of Moxie, Addie, and Keeley. Sutton supervised, so I'm sure it's edible."

"Sutton's the one in 1C, correct? Along with two kids, Addie and Lucas?" Before his lieutenant had called, Quinn had been memorizing the various tenants and their apartment numbers thanks to Riley's meticulous tenant records. "Before that she was in 2D?"

"Correct." Rather than taking a piece of the chocolate cake for herself, she dragged a finger along the plate's frosting line and stuck it in her mouth.

Quinn found himself significantly distracted by the action, then irritated when he caught Wallace grinning at him. "Why the move?"

Riley shrugged. "For one, 1C has a kitchen twice the size as any other in this building. She's a dietitian and personal chef who specializes in senior nutrition, so she's always got something going on the stove. She also needed the extra bedrooms for her niece and nephew after her brother and sister-in-law died." She focused her gaze directly on Quinn. "Am I correct in assuming there's a plan of action in motion where I'm concerned?"

"I'm your shadow from here on," Quinn stated, not the least disappointed or surprised by the surly expression on her face. "And completely approved by your tenants—you're out-numbered." The smile on his face was slow to form, and it made Riley's stomach flutter, despite her annoyance. Quinn then turned a more serious expression on to his partner. "Wallace, the boss is giving you lead on the Paddock case while I do some digging on the guy who came after Riley. That reminds me, any lab report on that glove yet?"

"Should have something tomorrow morning," Wallace said after swallowing a mouthful of cake. "Apparently the fabric of the gloves makes ridge detail a bitch to uncover, but Susie's relishing the challenge and consulting with a forensic specialist she knows. You're really giving me the go ahead on Merle and Dudley's case? I gave Merle your best by the way, Riley. He's getting cranky."

"Means he's feeling better." Riley's voice softened. "I tried to get the ambulance to take me to the same hospital, but the other ER was closer."

"We can make some time to visit him in the next day or so," Quinn assured her.

"Has anyone come forward to claim Dudley's body?" Riley asked.

"Merle asked the same thing," Wallace admitted. "So far we haven't heard anything."

"Then he's ours," Riley declared. "Mine and Merle's. Whatever details you need worked out, signatures, whatever, I'll take care of them, okay, Wallace? Let Merle focus on getting better and tell him Dudley's being cared for."

"You sure you want to take that on?" Quinn asked.

"He's mine," she repeated. "Once Merle's out of the hospital, we'll figure out what arrangements to make. I did some photography work for Angelus-Rosedale Cemetery a while back for some historical archives. I might have earned a favor or two and even if I didn't, that seems a fitting place to put Dudley to rest. I'm not having him end up in some Potter's field."

"I understand." The action was, as he'd come to know her, pure Riley. Her friends were her family and her family were friends.

Wallace nodded. "I'll keep you updated."

"Back to this plan of action?" Riley asked.

"Already told you. Wallace'll take the lead on Merle's case and I'm sticking close to you until the guy who came after you in the basement is taken care of. You don't leave this building without me. Hell, you don't leave this apartment without me."

"It's funny." Riley curled her legs up and braced her heels on the edge of the chair. "You keep saying that as if I'm meant to obey. I have obligations, you know. I do have a job. Distasteful as it might be," she added with a sickly sweet smile aimed directly at Wallace.

"Then I suggest you clear your calendar," Quinn said. "Or adjust your methods. If they came after you in your home, they'll have no qualms about attacking you outside your comfort zone. Or going after someone you care about."

"At some point, are either of you going to share exactly what was in that box in Riley's car? What do you have that they want?" Wallace shoved his empty cake plate away.

When Riley started to speak, Quinn silenced her with a warming look. "It's safer that you don't know everything right now."

"Says you," Wallace shot back.

"That's right," Quinn said firmly. "Says me. Call it pulling rank if you want." Or not wanting to drag the kid any deeper into this than he already was. He had a full, long career ahead of him. Quinn didn't want to be responsible for ending it before it really got off the ground.

"In the meantime," Riley sighed, "little ole me has to rely on the big strong man to play protector." She fanned her face and did her best—or make that worst—Scarlett O'Hara impersonation. "Why, I do suppose I'll just have to—"

"Accept reality—and that reality is me." With Wallace looking down at his cell, Quinn shot her a look that told her to knock it off. "How is your head?"

"It feels like I got slammed repeatedly by an anvil meant for the Road Runner."

"Sounds like an honest answer to me," Wallace grumbled. "Okay, here's the link and the login information for that new ID program you asked about." He sent it whooshing via email to Quinn's. "Once you've got a good digital likeness, I'll shoot it my way and I'll get the composite out there as a person of interest in both Dudley's murder and the attempted assault on Riley."

"We should run the image by Blake before we give it to Wallace," Riley suggested. "He might have noticed something I didn't."

Quinn wasn't sold on the whole ID thing for this guy. Even if they got a match, the guy knew how to hide in public.

"If you two don't mind, I'd like to try to grab some sleep before I head back to my desk tomorrow," Wallace said. "Thanks for the down time, Riley. Glad you're okay."

"Thanks." This time her smile seemed genuine. "Appreciate that."

Quinn walked Wallace to the door, looked back to see Riley seemingly dozing at the table, and lowered his voice. "I found Blake Redford's resume in Riley's paperwork." He pulled the folded-up stapled papers out of his pocket and passed it to his partner. "I want to you run a discreet check on him. Nothing to raise any alarms, okay? Just find out if anything's off."

"Sure." Wallace frowned. "Vibes?"

Not ... exactly. "I'm not a believer in perfect timing. I convinced LT to put a patrol officer outside Merle's hospital room for the next few days." He was biding his time before asking for an additional unit to keep a surreptitious eye on Moxie. Riley was adamant about keeping a lot of this from her aunt, which meant her aunt would be out and about on her normal routine. Once he had a good idea on the older woman's schedule, he'd make the call. "Better safe than sorry and after this guy botched today's encounter with Riley, who knows what's coming down the pike. Stay alert, okay? Watch your back."

"Got it." Wallace nodded. "I've gone back three days before Merle's assault on the surveillance video and no hint of that box being brought in so far."

"We'll search the rest of the way. Let me know what the lab says on those gloves."

"Good to know you trust me with something at least."

"I trust you, Wallace. If I didn't, I wouldn't have had you rifling through my apartment."

"But you don't trust me enough to bring me in on the rest of what's going on." The accusation was clear. Wallace didn't like being kept in the dark.

"It's complicated." There wasn't any other way to describe him being caught in between Riley's photographic discovery of a potential miscarriage of justice, and forever tainting his father's life's work. "It has nothing to do with trust."

"Sure it does." Wallace looked at him for a long moment then smirked. "Never mind. Let me know when you've decided I can ditch the training wheels. *Partner.*"

Quinn almost called Wallace back, but some things were more important than hurt feelings. The tighter the circle they kept with all this, the better, the safer everyone would be.

Riley hadn't been kidding when she said she felt like Wile E. Coyote had been practicing on her. She also hadn't been exaggerating. She'd had her share of migraines over the years, but nothing could have prepared her for the constant ka-thudding that vibrated like a jackhammer in her head. Hard to believe she hadn't incurred a full-blown concussion.

"The price of stupidity," she muttered as she grabbed what was left of her coffee, along with one of the blankets off the back of the sofa. She was curling into her favorite corner when he closed the door to her apartment.

"Well, look at that," he said as he passed by to retrieve his laptop. "You're in my bed after all."

"Not tonight, detective. I have a headache."

He chuckled. "If only they'd given you some pills to help with that."

"Shove it." Prescription painkillers were the pharmaceutical equivalent of being told what to do. Besides, anything other than over-the-counter meds always triggered her gag reflexes. Didn't matter what the meds, she puked it up in a matter of minutes. It made taking antibiotics especially ... messy. "You should also know this whole you staying here thing is ridiculous. The only reason this happened was because we let him in. That will not be happening again."

"Makes him more dangerous in my eyes because he's running out of options. And lest we forget, he wasn't alone at Unburied Treasures. He had a partner remember, and we haven't seen a sign of her since." Quinn settled in next to her, opened his laptop and, after accessing his email, clicked to download the program Wallace had acquired for them. "For the record, I'm not just here to make sure you and Moxie stay safe." Riley's heart tipped a bit at the obvious affection in his voice at the mention of her great aunt. "I'm here because I don't trust you to not go off on your own and make things worse. So if you want to blame someone for me being here, start with yourself."

"I reject your argument."

"I'm shocked."

It surprised her he had a lighter side. Of course she understood the whole gallows humor mentality with cops. Despite her personal issues with law enforcement—and she had a lot of them—everyone needed a way to cope, just like she'd encouraged Mabel. Offensive, borderline humor was definitely one way to deal with reality.

Feeling oddly comfortable and cozy, she tucked the blanket up around her ears and curled up. Watching him fascinated her. He was so thorough with everything he did. Careful. Cautious, but extremely capable. She wondered if he was like that with other aspects of his life. Say with more … intimate activities. And those hands of his …

She squeezed her eyes shut, would have shook her head to erase that thought from her brain if she wasn't afraid her head might somehow topple to the ground. Instead, she focused on his less appealing qualities. "Why are you a cop?"

"My DNA demanded it."

"I'm serious." And she found she was.

"So am I." He clicked a few keys, then sat back and shifted slightly so he could look her in the eye. "My mother used to joke I came out of the womb holding a badge."

Riley winced. "Your poor mother."

"In more ways than one. There wasn't anything else for me. It just … was. Maybe it was middle-child syndrome. The desire to keep everyone happy and play peacemaker. Maybe it was the unspoken expectation to follow in the family footsteps. Don't get me wrong. It was my choice to answer that, well—for want of a better term—call."

"Was it? No, don't react that way," she said quickly when his jaw tensed. "I'm honestly curious." She reached a hand out from under the blanket, touched fingertips to his arm. "I don't think I've ever spent this much time speaking with a cop before. Or maybe I should say, listening."

"Maybe you should have." He turned back to his laptop when it beeped. "It might have uncolored your perception about us."

Riley considered her response carefully. She understood where he was coming from. Her anger, her distrust of him and his chosen profession had to be a warning shot in a war she probably had no business participating in. But that didn't make her feelings—or beliefs—any less justified. "My parents were killed in a home invasion when I was five."

His fingers froze on the keys. Slowly, he turned back to her.

"I thought maybe you knew," she said, a lifetime of practice making it possible for her to speak as if from an emotional distance. "You knew about the situation with Detective Pantello, so I assumed you'd—"

"No." He shook his head. "I didn't. I didn't go back that far."

Unease prickled the back of her neck, but there were walls between them that needed tearing down or at the very least destabilized. It was the only way they'd be able to work together. "That night, it feels a lot like a recurring dream at times. I was up past my bedtime. Because—well, you've met me—bedtime was an early rule I took exception to." She managed a small laugh, one that halted in her throat when he stretched his arm out across the back of the sofa, palm open. She didn't have to think about grabbing hold, only that once she did a surge of strength shot through her and helped her push the words out.

"Rather than fighting me on it, my parents said as long as I was quiet, playing or reading, I could go to bed when I wanted. It was late. I could see the moon outside my window." She frowned. She hadn't thought about that detail very often. "I've never been able to put all the pieces together, but I remember hearing this horrible slamming sound and then the house alarm blaring and blaring. I ran and hid in my closet, pushed my hands against my ears to get it to stop. My mother always sang to me when I got scared, but the only song I could remember was Happy Birthday. I hate that song," she whispered as if in commentary. "To this day it takes me right back to that darkness. The closet. And that horrible, blaring alarm. When everything went quiet, I thought it was over. And then my mother screamed—a primal, horrific, chilling sound that I swear I can still hear sometimes."

"Riley."

How she loathed the sympathy she heard in Quinn's voice. But with sympathy, hopefully, would come understanding. Along with acceptance that not everyone viewed law enforcement with the same rose-colored lens he could.

"There were three shots. Bang. Bang bang." She shook her head as if hearing the gun firing at this moment. "Hours later, I remember hearing the neighbors talking when I was sitting in the back of the ambulance. They'd all called the police. So many of them had called and yet no one came. It felt like I'd spent hours in that closet before an officer opened that closet door. Even then, I didn't feel anything remotely close to safe." There were days she still didn't. "When I was older, I got my hands on the file. Don't ask," she warned at his curious look. "I had my ways. Do you know how long it took the police to come to my house that night? Sixty-two minutes. So much for protect and serve."

He didn't react to the verbal punch. Instead, he said, "Sometimes we're too late."

"Yeah." She swiped at the solitary tear that escaped her control. "When your parents have always taught you the police will be there when you need them and then they're not? It breaks something inside of you, Quinn. Oh, I'm sure there are reasons for why it happened. Budget cuts. Officer shortage. I tell myself they did the best they could at the time. My head knows that, but my heart?" She thought back to her conversation with Mabel in the emergency room and her friend's comment that whoever that eighteen-year-old rape victim had been wouldn't be who she was meant to become. Not anymore. "Trust is a really hard thing to rebuild," she told him. "Especially when it's broken at a young age. It doesn't help when your distrust is proven over and over again."

He shifted his grip and slid his fingers between hers, tightening his hold even as she was tempted to pull away. "It's rare anyone sees the good we do," he said quietly. "The media, social and otherwise—it's all the controversy and shock that gets the ratings. The hits. The attention. The good gets buried beneath the bad. But there is good, Riley. I wouldn't be a cop if I didn't believe that."

"You have no idea how much I want to believe you." She'd been trying to for so many years and yet …

"There's nothing I can say or do to make any of the past go away, Riley." He reached out his other hand, brushed his fingers down the side of her face. "What happened to you and your parents, it shouldn't happen to anyone, but bad shit happens. It's just the way it is. Here's what I can tell you, and I know for a fact it's true because I've been too late as well. Too late too many times to count."

She rested her head on the back of the sofa, her heart pinching around his admission.

"Those police officers who found you in your closet? They're just as haunted as you are. Those scenes that are trapped in your head? They're trapped in theirs. They tell themselves, even all these years later, that if they'd just been a little faster, if they'd only gotten there sooner, things could have been different. They were hurt, too, Riley. Those are the kind of cops you want working the streets. Those are the kind of cops you want on call. The ones who want to do better."

"Is that the kind of cop you are, Quinn?" She wanted to believe. More than anything, she wanted to believe in him.

He stroked his thumb against her pulse. "It's the kind of cop I try to be."

"Mmmmm." She nodded and gently withdrew from his grasp, tucked her arm back under the blanket and rested her head against the back of the sofa. "That's a nice thought to consider. I'm just going to close my eyes for a few minutes, okay? Wake me up when the program's ready to go so I can tell you what that little fucker looks like?"

"Go to sleep, Riley." The cushion of the sofa shifted as he moved closer, and she smiled when he pressed his lips against her forehead. For that moment—that one, brief, pulse-stopping moment—she almost believed nothing could hurt her. "I promise I'll be here when you wake up."

To Riley's surprise—and pleasure—he was.

## CHAPTER NINE

"WHAT'S on your agenda for today?" Moxie's too chipper voice echoed through Riley's still-throbbing head early the next morning. "I'm meeting Edgar for lunch at Rao's. He thinks there's a role for me in a local production of *12 Angry Women*."

"Shhh." Riley turned from her space on the sofa, held a finger up to her lips, and pointed to a sleeping Quinn who was lying half on, half off the same couch. Moxie wore her Chinese red pajamas and gold embroidered slippers. Along with her perfectly combed hair, she looked like an extra from *Flower Drum Song*, one of their favorite films. "He's sleeping."

"Oh." Moxie's eyes went wide, and she tiptoed over like a toddler sneaking up on the Christmas tree. Riley glanced over to where their six-foot tree, which had arrived on Saturday with the rest, remained propped up in the corner awaiting attention and hydration. "Sorry," Moxie said. She lowered her voice to a stage whisper as if Riley hadn't heard her the first time. "I'm meeting Edgar for lunch at Rao's. He thinks there's a role for me in a local production of *12 Angry Women*."

"Men," Riley corrected and earned a smug grin from her aunt.

"Not this production. It's a reimagining."

"Do you need me to drive you?"

"Edgar is sending a car for me." Moxie beamed. "He always treats me like a queen."

Always was right. Her great aunt's agent was three years older than Moxie and still had his ear glued to every major studio and production office in Los Angeles.

"I'm thinking the Henry Fonda role—"

"Shhh." Riley pointed at Quinn's unmoving form.

"No need to shush her," Quinn opened his eyes and sat up in one envy-inducing fluid move. Only a cop, Riley thought sourly, or perhaps a mother, could shift so easily to alert from sleep. "I've been awake since you started tapping on those laptop keys."

"Sorry about that." Blanket still draped around her waist, she looked down at the security feed from Merle's shop. Her head still hurt; ached mostly, but it had subsided enough for her to take something over-the-counter rather than prescription. "My eyes could actually focus this morning, so I thought I'd pick up where you left off with the security footage."

"I crapped out around two." He stretched his arms over his head. "Morning, Ms. Moxie."

"Morning, young man." Moxie touched a hand to his shoulder. "I'm also feeling adventurous this morning. How do pancakes sound?"

"Heavy," Riley muttered as she rubbed her stomach. She was still bloated form the late-night pizza and pasta binge.

"You have leftover kombucha in the fridge," her great aunt suggested.

"Yeah," Riley cringed. "I'd be better off sipping gasoline out of my car. Don't worry about me."

"Quinn?" Moxie asked. "Pancakes?"

"You can call him DSP," Riley teased. "He likes that."

"Not outside this apartment, I don't," Quinn warned. "But it has a certain ring when you say it." That damnable grin of his could almost convince her some maniac hadn't tried to kill her yesterday. "Pancakes sound delicious, Moxie, thank you."

Prince Charming, it seemed, had nothing on Detective Quinn Burton. Riley frowned. She wasn't getting used to him, was she?

"How's your head?"

"Huh? Oh, better." She moved her head around just to test her statement. "Aches still, but some aspirin should do the trick so you can stop asking."

"Acquiescing to take a medication. Maybe I can sleep tonight." Before she responded, he shifted to check the computer screen. "You find what we were looking for?"

"Oh, yeah. I did. I just wanted to wait until Moxie was out of the room. She's stressing enough over all of this. Kid with box." She stretched and set the laptop back on the coffee table. "Merle was off on his timeline. Nestor came in more than a week before Merle sold me that film." She realized her mistake the instant she said it. She sat back and glanced up at him, offered a somewhat apologetic smile. "Oops. I forgot to mention his name, didn't I?"

"That's more than an oops, Riley," Quinn said quietly. Too quietly.

"What film?" Moxie asked.

Riley squeezed her eyes shut. Of all the maladies that struck older people, Moxie's hearing had actually improved with age. "Nothing important."

"Sounds important to me," Moxie said. "Is this film what that young man was after yesterday? Film you got from Merle?"

"You make him sound like the paper boy collecting for rounds. He was a little fu—"

"Riley Jessica Temple, you watch your language!"

"How about we call him LF instead?" Quinn suggested. "All of the accuracy without the profanity."

"Speaking of film." Moxie circled around and perched on the arm of the sofa beside Quinn. "I remember a movie from the early eighties, I think. Something about a snake and film hidden in a pack of cigarettes."

"That was *Foul Play*," Riley said as she rested her head in her hand. "And as far as I know, I haven't encountered any albinos or dwarves or—"

"I don't believe that word is appropriate anymore," Quinn said.

"Really?" Riley glared.

"Yeah." He shrugged. "According to our department sensitivity training—"

"That wasn't the point of..." She sighed. "This isn't a movie, Moxie. I'm not Goldie Hawn, he's not Chevy Chase, and you're definitely no stand-in for Burgess Meredith."

"Ah, Burgess." Moxie patted her heart. "I worked with him on an episode of Batman. Did I ever tell you about that? I was one of his birds. What a charming Penguin he made. What that man could do with a monocle—"

"TMI." Her headache was coming back. In spades. "You don't have to worry about what we're talking about, Moxie, okay? We're taking care of it."

"Donkey nuggets," Moxie declared. "Some maniac tried to strangle you right here in this building yesterday, Riley. Darned straight I'm going to worry until he's held accountable for his actions and I'm convinced you're safe."

"I'll make doubly sure of it, Moxie. But Riley's right." Quinn riding to her verbal rescue notched up her irritability factor. "There's no point in you worrying about anything." He leaned over, peered at the screen. "Looks like the box that was in your car. It's a good shot of him, too. Could be he's a street kid. Clothes are pretty ragged. And he's way too skinny to be getting any steady nutrition. Could be a tweaker. Won't know until we talk to him. I'll send a screenshot to Wallace, have him get it out to some patrol officers to see if they recognize this Nestor."

"Or." The way he said the teen's name had Riley cringing. "We could go to the storage facility and ask where he might have come across the box."

Quinn pursed his lips. "Let me guess. You already have that information."

"Constant Care Storage over off Western. Merle might have mentioned—"

"Don't." Quinn held up a hand and shook his head. "Just don't. I've had enough of what Merle might have said that you haven't yet told me. This gives us a place to start, at least, and I'll start with a BOLO out on the kid. In the meantime, I'd kill for a shower."

"I'll take that as my cue to start breakfast." Moxie removed herself from the living room and busied herself in the kitchen.

"The guest bath doesn't have a shower." Riley unfolded herself from the sofa and stood up. "You're welcome to use mine. Just give me a few minutes to tidy up. Oh, and leave the Princess Leia shampoo bottle alone unless you want to smell like a kickass female space general." She gathered her blanket, folded it up and tossed it over the back of the sofa. When Quinn's hand locked around her arm, she feigned surprise. "What?"

"You and I need to have to have a conversation about sharing information, Riley."

"Okay." She reached over and pried his fingers free, trying to ignore the fact her skin was warm from wherever he touched her. When she sat back down, she made certain their thighs touched. Cop or not, the sizzle was definitely crackling between them. It would be easy, so easy, to let herself forget what was really behind their connection: that she'd uncovered evidence about a potential wrongful conviction. And that someone wanted her dead. Adrenaline, she reminded herself. Adrenaline and fear endorphins combined to heighten her awareness of him. The nearness of him.

"Yes, let's share, Quinn. Exactly what did your father say when you showed him the photographs I developed. You did show them to him, didn't you? If not, I'd love to be in on *that* conversation. If you have—"

"I thought we were done playing games." His voice was low, almost a growl and she shivered at the sound. Why did she like it when there was an angry edge between them? Because it felt so much like another form of friction?

"Au contraire." Riley rested her hand on his knee and squeezed, lifted her chin to look into his eyes. Eyes that saw entirely too much. "I'd say the games have only just begun. But to be fair, Nestor and that storage facility are the only bits of information I have at this point that needed sharing. I'm going to assume, on what little you've told me, that your father is on board with our deal about getting the truth out there. Unless he's not. Or I've misinterpreted your offer. Ball's in your court, DSP." Because she couldn't resist, she bounced up and gave him a quick kiss. A kiss that, despite its length, left the tips of her toes tingling. "You can have the bathroom for fifteen minutes. After that, if you are not done by then, I'm coming into join you." The first kiss had been to surprise him. This time—oh, this time was all for her. She snaked a hand around to the back of his neck, held her mouth against his for as long as she dared to, before slipping back and taking more than a little pleasure in the way he struggled to maintain a stern expression. "Consider yourself warned."

Quinn had never been more tempted to ignore a time restriction, but now wasn't the time for hydroponic dalliances with a sexy photographer. Besides, shower sex required trust, not to mention a solid equilibrium and seeing as they were currently in short supply of both, he was aiming, not for Riley's shower, but for her bed.

As he climbed out of his personal SUV—he'd left his department-issued car back at the station house—he pocketed his keys and watched Riley walk around the back of the vehicle to make sure the bags she'd brought with her couldn't be seen under the security cover. The Constant Care Storage facility had definitely seen better days. The worn blue and white paint spoke more of neglect than security, and the bright yellow doors left Quinn wincing against the sunlike glare. It was barely even ten in the morning and he was twinning the headache Riley still had to be experiencing.

"Do you really need all that equipment?"

She hiked her worn silver-gray pack over one shoulder and joined him. In this neighborhood, filled with more warehouses and office buildings than homes and apartments, crosswalks were either faded into extinction or had never been drawn in the first place.

"I have two appointments later today," she shrugged at his scowl. "I wasn't sure if we'd get back to Temple House before then, so better safe than sorry." She rolled her eyes. "You're the one who said you're sticking to me like a discount price tag on glass."

"I'm pretty sure I didn't say that."

"Maybe I just dreamed it." She dropped mirrored sunglasses over her eyes but not before he caught her wince. "You're just cranky because I ate some of your pancakes."

"Only because you said you didn't want pancakes, then you ate mine." The foil-wrapped package of three chocolate chip pancakes—his favorite incidentally—had been lovingly presented to him from Moxie's grateful hands. On their way out, she'd caught his arm, tugged him back and asked her to please take care of her girl. The request had both touched and concerned him, as did the worry he'd seen in the old woman's eyes. "It's been a long time since a woman made me breakfast."

"That explains a lot."

The verbal banter was going to be exhausting if one of them didn't surrender, so Quinn took the hit. As they crossed the street, his mind was filled with comebacks he made certain to file away for later.

"Let me start the conversation with the manager," Riley suggested. "When I spoke with her on the phone yesterday—"

"When you did *what*?" Quinn stepped onto the curb. "When did that happen?"

"Yesterday, in the hospital. When I was waiting on my scan results."

Those damned glasses on her face prevented him from seeing what was going on with her eyes. Probably part of her evil plan, he told himself. He muttered something that should not said in polite company.

She grinned. "Just … let me take the lead, okay? And you try looking less …" She moved her hand up and down at his physique. "… cop-like."

He pulled out his own glasses and slid them on. "Better?"

"Not even remotely."

"You do know most people don't share your aversion to my professional species." But Quinn fell in line behind her, ready to pounce with his trained professionalism securely in his back pocket.

The rusted-out gate did absolutely nothing to bolster Quinn's opinion of the storage facility. It was a drive-through location, with an ancient keypad secured on one shoddy and knocked around metal post, and the knob on the walk-through gate rattled when Riley twisted it open.

He elbowed through after her, already wanting a decontamination shower as they pushed through the grimy glass door with a crooked hours sign.

The warning buzzer that announced their arrival sounded like a constipated pig with its drawn-out whine. The nose-tickling aroma of burnt onions and overcooked eggs churned Quinn's pancakes in his stomach. "I may never eat again."

"Good," Riley beamed at him with an overly bright smile. "Then I won't have to stop at the grocery store on the way home." She rang the bell on the counter. "Hello?" She flipped her glasses on top of her head and shoved her hands into the back pockets of her jeans as an utterly disinterested attendant strode out of a back room. "Are you Denise?"

"Yeah." The attitude evoked in that solitary word couldn't have been a better fit for the middle-aged, defeated-looking woman who had a good two months' worth of gray growing out beneath the violent violet of her hair. "Who's asking?"

"It's so nice to meet you in person. We spoke yesterday. Riley Temple. I'm so sorry about how our conversation ended. That stupid sister of mine just can't keep her nose out of my business."

"I hear that," Denise sent him a side-eyed glance before easing her expression and focusing on Riley. "You were asking me about that Nestor kid that hangs around here with his crew."

Nestor had a crew, Quinn thought. Interesting.

"That's right." If Riley already had that bit of information, she didn't let on. "I know this sounds crazy, but he sold a box of stuff to my grandfather. I mean, most of it was junk. A bunch of paperbacks—the shoe box filled with crap. But you know what he did find inside? This beautiful jewelry set—only one of the earrings was missing."

"Not surprised." Denise tugged on the hem of the polyester zip-up shirt that matched the storage facility paint job. "Those old folks' units are always a mess. Nestor's a good kid, you know." She shot another look at Quinn. "He stays out of the way of the police. Purposely."

"I told you you look like a cop," Riley grumbled and shot him a look that had him easing his stance. "He didn't believe me and now look. You think we're police hunting Nestor down, when all we want to know is what unit he found that box in. For the record, this guy is in the money-lending business. If you get my drift," Riley said as she lowered her voice. "If I could find that missing earring, my grandfather would be so grateful." Riley inclined her head. "Like reward money grateful."

"Yeah?" The woman's eyes brightened. "How much we talkin'?"

Quinn had no doubt if Denise had had any, she'd be snapping her gum about now.

"Well now, that we won't know until we get the full set appraised," Riley said. "Could you show us the unit?"

"Could." With those narrowed eyes, Denise still didn't look convinced about Quinn's occupation. "That unit's been pretty popular as of late. That's how Nestor ended up with all that stuff, you know. It was part of what was left after the auction we had a couple weeks back."

"Auction. Right." Riley glanced away. "Like for when people stop paying their bills."

"That's right. We give them six months. Sometimes the payments just stop. Other times, the automatic withdrawals don't go through. Case in point, that DePalma woman's unit. Not my fault she couldn't pay anymore. We run a business, not a charity."

"How do you know it was her unit?" Riley asked.

"Cause it's the only one whose payment defaulted in the last few months. Only had like two people show up to bid on it. Winning guy took a few pieces of the furniture and walked away from the rest. I told Nestor if he got everything ready for the junk truck, he could fill a box and take what he wanted as payment."

"And the junk truck came when?"

Denise eyed her. "Funny you should ask." Quinn swore he heard a cash register ca-ching somewhere. "Truck's scheduled to come tomorrow."

"So the rest of the stuff is still here?"

Quinn marveled. Riley was so cool that penguins could have skated on her.

"Yep." Denise glanced at each of them, sizing them up. "I'd be happy to let you take a look. For the right price."

"That would be fabulous. Would fifty do?"

"Hundred would do better."

Quinn chewed on the inside of his cheek. At this rate he was going to gnaw through his face before they actually had some answers.

"Hundred it is." Riley pulled a hundred dollar bill out of her back pocket. "What unit is it?"

"Sixty-three." Denise shoved the bill under the strap of her bra. "Out this door, take a right, then a left and go pretty much to the end. Lock's busted, so no key. What's there is up for grabs. Help yourself."

"Thanks so much." Riley planted both hands on the second glass door leading into the storage facility.

"Had a feeling that box had something important in it."

"What makes you say that?" Quinn ignored Riley stepping back on his foot.

"For one, you aren't the first people to come asking questions. Young couple was here a few days back—no, make that about a week ago. Squirrely. Not street squirrely, just . . . off. Not polished like you two."

Polished meaning they hadn't looked like they could pay for information. Or admittance. Denise didn't know how lucky she was to still be breathing.

"I told them the place was cleaned out, that Nestor took what he wanted, and I hadn't seen him since. And that's the truth. Kid hasn't been back."

Quinn's stomach tightened. "You tell them anything else about Nestor?"

Denise shrugged. "Only that he hung out here a lot and if he wasn't here, he was up at that teen shelter on Mulholland."

"Ask about that did they?"

Denise shrugged. "None of my business. Come to think about it, I might have mentioned that old, abandoned movie theater a few blocks down? Place is just begging to be torn down. Shame, too. Did a brisk business especially back in the day. Makes for a good runaway squat." Denise smirked. "That info's on the house."

"How generous of you," Quinn said with a forced smile before he followed Riley outside and into the fresh air.

"You thinking what I'm thinking?" Riley asked as they hurried away. Quinn glanced back at the office and saw Denise poke her head out the door.

"That Nestor's how our terrible two found their way to Merle's place? Yeah," Quinn muttered as they picked up the pace. "You were pretty quick with that hundred."

"I'm a paparazzo who is always ready to pay for information and a lead. I've got two twenties in each of my front pockets and a fifty in my other back one. Just needed to know what her price was."

"You are a woman of interesting abilities, Ms. Temple." He zipped his jacket up against the chill of December air. "Exactly what is it you're hoping to find in the unit?"

"Something that'll tell me—"

Quinn cleared his throat.

"Tells *us* where those pictures came from. You know it's pure luck that junk truck hasn't been by yet."

"Nothing lucky about it. Those junk haulers cost a small fortune," he said. "She'd wait to make it worth the price she had to pay. No way she has them come for one unit's worth of stuff."

"Guess maybe I just added to her fund then," Riley said. "Fifty-eight, fifty-nine. Good God, packrats have their own industry."

"Some people have a hard time parting with memories. I take it you haven't laid claim to one of those storage cages in the basement of Temple House?"

"Yeah, yeah, whatever." Riley's grumble brought an amused smile to his face. "Okay, here it is. Sixty-three."

"Hang on. I've got it." Quinn bent down and slid the metal latch to the side, then pulled the metal accordion door up until it banged open. The stacks of dented, sagging boxes along with endless trash bags filled to overflowing with clothes and old shoes reminded him of a thrift store donation drop-off. "I feel a reality show in the offing."

"It's not that bad," Riley said. "You start over there." She pointed to the pile of crap balancing on nothing more than hope.

Quinn reached up and pulled the top box down, flipped it open and tried not to acknowledge the ping of sadness at the old photo albums crammed inside. Box after box of a woman's life. More boxes of bank records and receipts. Pay stubs and tax records. "You find anything over there?"

"Pictures," Riley whispered and when Quinn looked up, he saw the grief on her face. "I've seen this face before." She shook her head. "Joyce DePalma. The name isn't familiar, but I swear—"

"I've got an old pay stub here from the late eighties," Quinn pulled one free of the box and walked across the unit. "She worked for a Bryant Photography."

"Bryant. Clinton Bryant?" Riley dropped the pictures she'd been sorting through and snatched the stub from his hand. "He and my grandfather were friends. They worked at the studio together. Back in the day," she added at Quinn's blank look. "Before he became a cinematographer, my grandfather worked as a studio portrait photographer. He and Clinton were hired around the same time."

"Could Clinton have taken those pictures of Melanie Dennings?"

"God, I hope not." She flinched. "But yeah. The timing works. He only died a few years ago. Joyce was his receptionist and booking agent." She shoved the pay stub into her pocket, then pointed to the boxes. "How many album boxes are over there?"

"Two," Quinn told her. "The rest is actual junk."

"Grab them."

"Why?"

"Because I'm not letting this woman's pictures of a lifetime end up in some truck to an incinerator."

When he hoisted them into his arms, she slammed a third one on top. When he grunted, she tisked. "If this is too strenuous for you, consider it training for sleeping with me."

"Jesus, woman, don't say things like that."

"Why?"

"Because we're trying to catch a killer, not drive me to distraction. You got that one?"

"I do." Riley hoisted a fourth box into her arms and, after showing him outside, slammed the door behind them.

Two extra-large steaming cups in hand, Riley pushed out of the doors of a Starbucks a few miles from the storage facility and made her way back to Quinn's SUV. The parking lot—if one could call eight spaces a lot—was full. People took their coffee seriously around here, as evidenced by the blue sedan pulling to a stop and blocking not only a Tesla, but a Mercedes so new it didn't even have plates yet.

"Hang up," she called to him through the open passenger-seat window. "I've got the info. Here." She shoved his cup through the window before she opened the door and climbed in. "Joyce DePalma's been a resident of Hollywood Golden Age Retirement Home for the past two years. I have the address and visiting hours just … what?" The way Quinn was looking at her had her touching her face. "Do I have a mark or something?"

"Or something." Quinn returned his attention to his own phone call. "Yeah, Wallace, never mind. Riley beat us to it." After a moment, "Do you really think I'd admit that if it wasn't true? Yeah. Talk later." He hung up and tossed his phone on the console between them. "Wallace is not best pleased."

"Told you my source was better than your source." Riley smirked, embracing the triumph coursing through her system as she dug into her pack for the bag of mini vanilla scones she'd surrendered to.

"Faster, maybe, but at least my source is legal." Quinn arched a brow. "Exactly who—?"

"Don't ask questions you won't like the answers to. Just … don't," she advised and refrained from telling him she'd also asked Cass to do some surreptitious digging into the Melanie Dennings case. She jostled the paper bag in front of him. "Want one?"

"I should take two since you ate my pancakes." But he removed only one from the bag.

Mouth full of caffeine and sugary goodness, Riley set her cup in one of the holders and settled in. "If we head over to the retirement home now, that'll put me right near Beachwood Canyon for my one o'clock photo session. Stop with the look," she told him.

"You're taking unnecessary risks for both of us." He started the car. "And your clients."

"Those appointments pay the bills for me and Moxie," Riley told him. "I can't stop living my life because someone wants to end it."

"Yes, actually," Quinn argued as he pulled out of the lot and headed north and into the land of endless palm trees stretching for the sun, "you can. You might also want to consider you aren't the only one involved with these shoots of yours. Pun absolutely intended."

"You wanted me to trust you. This is me trusting you." She wasn't about to admit she almost had called and cancelled today's session more than once since leaving Temple House. "It's your job to keep me, keep *us,* safe while I work. Besides, if all I do is hang around the apartment, Moxie and I are going to drive each other batcrap crazy. And even you, with your—Wait, how long have you been a cop?"

"Some days it feels like decades." He glanced at her. "Little over ten years."

"Not even a decade's worth of experience as an LAPD police officer can prepare you for me and Moxie in close quarters for an extended period of time."

"Did your *source* give you any other information about Mrs. DePalma?"

"Ms.," Riley corrected. "She never married. No kids. No living relatives. She worked for Clinton Bryant for thirty-two years. Before moving into the retirement home, she lived in the same house since 1976. According to her bank statements, she lives on her social security and a meager retirement pension set up by her former boss."

"Hmmm. How meager?"

Riley rattled off some numbers.

"Hollywood Golden Age is one of the best retirement homes in the city."

"Yeah, I know. Sutton contracts out of there. She does private consultant work sometimes and advises on their menus."

"What I'm saying is no way that's a social security, small-pension kind of place. We're talking five to eight thousand a month. To start with."

"Shit." Riley took a large gulp of coffee. "Getting old doesn't just suck, it's expensive. How do you know about Golden Age? Uncle Silas again?"

Quinn shook his head and turned onto Melrose Avenue. "His sister, my Aunt Shirley. She was a bit player back in the day, but squirreled away every penny she could. She lived there the last couple of years of her life and had a ball. It's the retirement home to the stars. Place is a palace compared to most old folks' homes."

Riley sat back in her seat and stared out the window. Yet another reason she was determined to hold onto Temple House. Moxie wasn't ending up in a retirement home. Not only because Riley had promised her grandfather, but because as far as she was concerned, they were death's waiting rooms. She'd much rather Moxie spend what time she had left flitting about for lunch dates with her ancient agent and … "Shoot. I knew I forgot something." She quickly dialed her aunt. "She's not answering. Hey, Moxie. Nothing's wrong. I just forgot to ask: pretty pretty please, if you could bring me home some of Rao's lemon chicken for dinner? Unless you want leftover pizza—"

"Pizza's gone," Quinn said. "I finished it after my shower. And you have the 'coming together of the minds' tonight, remember?"

"A what?"

"Laurel and Mabel said something at the hospital about a meeting."

"You really do remember everything you hear." She'd totally forgotten. Still, leftover lemon chicken was a refrigerator bonus. Especially if Quinn was going to be hanging around for the foreseeable future. "Moxie, make that two orders of chicken, please. I'll be forever grateful. Okay." She hung up. "That's dinner sorted. Now let's pull up Golden Age and see what we're walking into."

# CHAPTER TEN

QUINN hadn't been to the Hollywood Golden Age Retirement Home since before he'd become a detective. The only difference he noticed, after their meandering drive up into the Hollywood Hills, was a softer white paint on the building that rivaled most Hollywood estates, much taller trees, and thick, lush landscaping. It was as if time had filled in all the gaps. With columns rivaling the Acropolis and thick, heavy paned windows giving residents a stunning view, he half-expected a royal trumpeter to announce their arrival.

"Doesn't look like any retirement home I've ever been into," Riley murmured as they stepped into the marble foyer. "It's like a movie set. I feel like I should be whispering."

Not having been on many movie sets, Quinn was more likely to compare it to an old library, but her analogy made more sense. He dragged his gaze around the elegant gold, white, and silver décor, heavily accented with punches of holiday color.

He'd been in enough nursing homes to know what they normally smelled like—stale and medicinal, all in an effort not to smell like anything. But there was no assault of the senses in this place. Instead, the filtered air was tinged with the faintest hint of cinnamon and spice, and the ever so faint strains of instrumental Christmas music playing over the sound system.

"Hello." A young woman in a tidy navy suit with bright brass buttons approached, her pointed designer pumps clicking along the floor. With her gold hair tied back low against her neck, she offered a friendly smile. "Welcome to Golden Age. I'm Yvonne, the assistant administrator. Are you here about a loved one?"

"Actually—" Quinn's hand went for his badge, but Riley shifted slightly in front of him, planting a foot on his.

"Actually, we were hoping to visit with one of your residents. She's an old friend of the family," Riley managed effortlessly. "Joyce DePalma? She and my grandfather worked together back in the day. We're in town for a few days and thought we'd say hello."

"Oh, Joyce." Yvonne's face relaxed and she smiled. "How lovely. I can't recall the last time anyone came to visit her. She'll be tickled. Won't you sign in?" She led them to the rounded desk topped with a seasonal array of poinsettias. "Nancy, the guest book, please."

"Yes, ma'am." Nancy's acne-scarred cheeks flushed as she jumped to her feet and retrieved a leather embossed register from the workstation behind her.

"Nancy, these are guests of Miss Joyce's. I'd appreciate it if you showed them to her suite once they've signed in."

"Of course." Nancy's spine straightened and she brightened. "I'd be happy to." She touched a hand to the long dark ponytail trailing down her back. "If you'd just print your name here and sign here." She pointed a trembling finger at the columns.

"Like signing into prison," Quinn murmured under his breath and earned another firm step on his foot and a not-so-gentle elbow in his stomach. "Ow."

"Excuse me?" Nancy blinked as if she'd misheard.

"He's teasing," Riley assured her as she picked up the engraved pen. "Don't mind him. I try not to."

"Yes, ma'am." Nancy said with a nervous smile.

When Riley was finished, Quinn accepted the pen, hesitating only a moment to read the name she'd scribbled, then, biting back a smile, added his Clyde to her Bonnie. "Anything else?"

"No, sir. Thank you." Nancy took the book back and set it behind her.

"If you'll excuse me," Yvonne told them. "I have some calls to return in my office. Please let me know if I can be of further assistance."

"Thank you, we'll do that," Riley said.

Quinn leant over to her, whispering. "Is it me, or do these two remind you of one of the Redrum twins all grown up?"

"Seriously?" Riley gave him a wide-eyed glare before her lips twitched. "Okay, yeah. Maybe you're right ..." She turned back to Nancy, plastering her most welcoming smile on her face. "Could you show us the way?"

"Certainly. If you'll follow me?" Nancy darted around the desk and—clutching the skirt of her plain blue cotton, button-down dress in her hands—led them through the spacious sitting area dotted with residents and brimming with Christmas cheer.

An enormous tree had been arranged in the window, covered tip-to-stem in radiant, glowing ornaments and lights. The sharp-pointed star on top seemed determined to pierce the ceiling and below it, a collection of beautifully wrapped gifts was waiting for Santa's blessing.

Quinn kept a hand on the small of Riley's back. Memories flooded back, only his featured darker hallways, louder ambiance, and definitely older carpet. Now he saw cheer and brightness, and apartment doors bearing pine wreaths decorated in Christmas red and green, or Hanukkah silver and blue.

"Have you known Miss Joyce long?" Nancy had a bit of a squeak to her voice, like an uncertain mouse being granted access to a room full of cheese. Poor kid probably spent most of her day trapped behind that desk.

"She's a family friend." Riley clung to her story which, Quinn now realized, was actually the truth. "I came across some old photos of her and my grandfather recently. I was thrilled to hear she was still with us."

"Oh, yes." Nancy turned right at the end of the hall. "She had a stroke last year, sadly, and doesn't make it out of her rooms very often, but she's one of our favorite residents. Here we are." Nancy stopped at an actual front door situated in the wall. With the smattering of shelves on either side boasting an array of collectible snowmen, and a small red awning above, Quinn definitely got front-porch vibes.

Nancy knocked twice before she pushed the door open and stepped inside. "Miss Joyce? It's Nancy. I have some visitors for you today. I'm sorry, I didn't note your names."

"It's fine," Riley said without answering the silent question.

Quinn kept a few paces back, letting Riley approach the old woman sitting in a rocking chair in front of a large bay window overlooking what the brochure advertised as one of many private meditation gardens.

"Hello, Joyce." Riley set her bag on the floor and, walking around in front of the old woman, crouched down.

"I think we'll be fine from here, Nancy, thanks." Quinn stepped back to let the attendant leave.

"Oh, certainly. Of course." Nancy practically curtsied on the way out, leaving the door slightly ajar—probably, Quinn thought, a Golden Age House policy. Quinn joined Riley by the window and as he looked down at the former photographer's receptionist, felt his hope for answers dim. The button-down housedress she wore was a mishmash of pink and lavender, with an embroidered collar. Her silver-streaked hair was neatly styled, and the scent of rosewater drifted off her skin.

The suite was of a simple layout, and filled with antique, no doubt familiar furniture, and framed photographs sat on every shelf. The walls, painted a soft yellow, were accented with various photographs of Joyce and famous faces from Judy Garland and Mickey Rooney at a piano, John Houston on the set of what would be one of his final films, to a preteen Joyce standing between a Robin Hood-clad Errol Flynn and Olivia de Havilland. Quinn marveled at the history in the room. What stories this woman must have, somewhere in that mind of hers. What a life she'd lived.

"Joyce?" Riley laid gentle hands over the woman's trembling ones. The soft blue crocheted blanket over her legs cascaded down to the floor. "My name's Riley. Riley Temple. I wonder if maybe you remember me? I'm Douglas Temple's granddaughter."

Joyce blinked, her bright blue eyes suddenly coming into focus and she smiled. "Douglas. I remember Douglas."

"You do?" Riley beamed up at Quinn. "What do you remember?"

"Oh, a gentleman. Such a gentleman." Joyce lifted her chin and looked at Quinn for the first time. "Handsome devil, too. Not quite as handsome as you." She stretched out a hand, which Quinn stepped forward to take. "My goodness, you must be giving Douglas a run for his money. Who are you, young man?"

"My name is Quinn." Quinn smiled.

"Do I know you?" By the look in her eyes, it was clear she hoped she did.

"This is the first time we've met, ma'am."

"Ma'am. Now none of that. I'm just Joyce." She seemed to fade for a moment. "Simple, plain, ordinary Joyce."

"There's nothing simple or plain about you in your pictures." Quinn inclined his head at Riley, silently urging her to explore. "You've had quite an adventure of a life, haven't you? And it's all been caught on film."

"They tell me so. Do you know about it?" With her attention firmly fixed on him, Riley stood and wandered the room. "Could you tell me the stories? I can't seem to remember many anymore."

Riley pointed to the bedroom and Quinn nodded before she disappeared.

"I hear you danced with Gene Kelly at the premiere of one of his movies, Joyce."

"Oh! Yes." Joyce's eyes filled with misty tears. "Now that you say, I do recall that. He was handsome too. And so kind. And when he walked, it was as if he had clouds in his shoes. Just ..." she sighed and got lost in the memory.

"We have some questions for you, Joyce," Quinn told her. "About your work with Clinton Bryant."

"Clinton." Joyce's voice faded.

"He was a photographer, wasn't he? And you helped him with that? You ran his business, didn't you?"

Joyce blinked, nodded, but looked more disconnected than before. "I was his secretary. And his confidant. Never anything more or untoward," she added. "He didn't like girls. That was our secret," she murmured. "One of our secrets." She began to hum.

"What other secrets did you keep for him, Joyce?" Her humming grew louder, the song faintly familiar but Quinn couldn't identify it. "Did he take secret pictures, Joyce? Do you remember—?"

"Quinn?" Riley was standing in the bedroom doorway and waved him over. "You need to see this."

The irritation over being interrupted didn't quite materialize. Not when Joyce hadn't seemed to hear him. "I'll be right back, okay, Joyce?"

She smiled, nodded, and continued to hum. The carpet muffled his steps as he joined Riley in the bedroom. The elevated bed was covered in a muted green cover with lacy pillows placed in careful positions. The pictures, much like in the other part of the suite, were many, framed, and showcased a full life lived in both Technicolor and black-and-white.

"What is it?"

"This one." Riley picked up a small silver frame. The picture of Joyce was different, shockingly so. All the rest were candid shots, but this one, she was made up, her hair was pinned into large curls, and the black dress she wore elegant and classic. "Is it me," Riley kept her voice low. "Or does Joyce look very like Melanie Dennings here?" To prove her point, Riley pulled out her phone and opened to one of the photographs she'd developed. "This was taken by the same camera," she murmured. "This discoloration here, in the corner, above the logo. That's a lens scar."

"How would that happen?" Quinn asked.

"Bunch of different ways. Wear and tear. Could be it got cracked when it was dropped. Happens all the time, especially on an older lens. They're expensive to replace, so most photographers find a way to work them into the images."

"Like with that logo. CRL. You ever hear of that before? See this logo before? Maybe in your grandfather's photos?"

Riley shook her head. "Not that I remember. Should we ask her about this?"

Quinn shrugged. "No telling what kind of answer we might get. She's not all there, Riley."

"I know." Riley's smile was sad. "But maybe there's enough left to grab hold of. Come on." She carried the frame with her and they found Joyce sitting forward in her chair.

"Oh, there you are." Joyce sank back and rested a hand against her heart. "I thought I'd imagined you. I do that sometimes. See people who aren't here. Or so they tell me." Her thin lips stretched. "I don't get many people coming by. You're Riley, Douglas's granddaughter."

"Yes." Riley crouched back down. "Joyce, can you tell me anything about this picture?" Joyce's gaze dropped to the frame in Riley's hand.

"This is you, isn't it, Joyce? Do you remember who took it?"

Joyce nodded. Then brought a finger to her lips.

"It's okay if you tell us," Riley assured her. "Clinton won't be upset, I promise. Did he take this picture?"

Joyce nodded then turned her head to look at the door.

"What about this picture?" Riley turned her phone around and displayed the image of Melanie Dennings. "Do you know this girl? Did Clinton know this girl?"

The old woman began to hum again, her head moving back and forth, peering around them, then back to the door. "Shhhhh," she said when Riley tried another question. "They'll hear you. They'll hear you and they'll come. Never alone. None of us are ever alone."

"Who'll come?" Riley's voice sharpened and Quinn stepped in.

He pulled Riley up by her arms and set her aside, and took her place in front of Joyce. "Who won't leave you alone? Joyce? I promise no one's going to hurt you."

Joyce shook her head. "You don't know. You. Don't. Know."

"We need you to tell us." Riley's frustration mirrored his own, but this wasn't the way to get the information they needed. "Where can we find them?"

"Everywhere," Joyce whispered.

"Dammit." Riley muttered. "She's too far gone."

And Riley was too impatient.

"Joyce, did Clinton take this picture of you?" He removed the frame from Riley's hand, held it up next to her phone. "Did he take both these pictures?"

Tears welled in her eyes. She nodded.

"And he gave you the film of this girl, didn't he?" Quinn kept his voice calm, soft. "You kept it safe for him. You kept his secret."

"He was so scared," Terror coated Joyce's whisper. "So scared. And so tired. He was so, so tired. He just wanted it to stop. I was his friend. So I took them away and hid them so he didn't have to worry anymore."

"What about his bookkeeping? A list of his clients? Did you do anything with those, Joyce? Do you still have them?"

All she did in response was stare at the photograph of herself in the frame.

"Well, my goodness, look who's had a popularity surge." Assistant Administrator Yvonne pushed through the door, a large glass vase filled with a bouquet of flowers held between her hands. "Nancy just accepted this gorgeous delivery for you at the front desk, Joyce."

Quinn stood and backed away as Yvonne circled around.

"I've seen my share of flowers," Yvonne declared, "but never this shade of lily. Just look at that red."

The humming in Joyce's throat stopped, replaced almost instantly with what he could only describe as a strangled scream. Her eyes went wide. All the color in her face drained. She struck out with both hands, caught the edge of the vase and nearly knocked them out of Yvonne's hands.

"Joyce!" Yvonne jumped back, clearly shocked and borderline horrified. "What on earth's gotten into you? You've gone and spilled water all over yourself."

"I'll get a towel." Riley disappeared into the bathroom off the bedroom.

Joyce turned that terror-filled gaze on Quinn. A gaze that then dropped to the frame and phone in his hands. Tears filled her eyes and spilled over.

"I'll take those." Quinn pocketed Riley's cell and took the vase and while Yvonne and Riley cleaned up the water, he set the flowers and frame on the table by the door. Buried deep in the arrangement of delicate, blood-red lilies he found the enclosure card. He opened it.

No writing. No message per se. Only a solitary tattoo-like image in red. He looked back at the flowers, then the image again. "It's a lily." His mind raced. He turned, caught Riley watching him, but there was nothing he could convey without words. That said, she caught on well enough and while she kept Yvonne distracted, Quinn pulled out his own cell and snapped a photo before replacing the card.

He'd have taken one of the envelope as well to get the florist's address, but it was blank. He checked the ribbon tied around the neck of the vase, looking for a sticker, some identification as to where the flowers had come from. Nothing there. Nothing on the bottom of the vase, either.

"I can't imagine what's gotten into her," Yvonne declared. "She's normally not like this, I assure you. There, there, Joyce." She crouched down and touched two fingers to the side of her neck. "I'm going to call one of the attending nurses. She might need some medication. Would you stay with her for just a moment?"

"Of course," Riley said.

Quinn left the flowers and frame by the door and rejoined Riley as Yvonne left the suite. Joyce was sitting forward again, on the edge of her chair, rocking back and forth. The edge of her housedress had slipped down, and with her hair swooped up into a loose knot, the back of her neck lay exposed.

"Riley." Quinn's insides tightened as he angled his phone and took another picture.

"What?" She walked around, gasped, and touched gentle fingers to the back of Joyce's neck.

Joyce's scream was anything but muffled this time. She lurched forward, slapping a hand against the back of her neck and nearly slid off the chair before Quinn caught her.

"Take my picture," Joyce whispered as the sound of hurried footsteps echoed in the carpeted hallway.

"You want me to take your picture?" Riley was pulling out her cell as she asked.

Quinn pushed her hand down. "I don't think that's what she means." Quinn's eyes darted back to the framed photo he'd set down beside the flowers. "Your picture in the frame? You want us to take that with us?"

Joyce's eyes seemed to clear, like a morning haze burned off by the rising sun. "I'm going to die now."

Chills raced down Quinn's back. It wasn't terror he heard in her voice now.

It was acceptance.

"Joyce—" Riley attempted to take her hands again, but Joyce batted her away.

"Go." Her eyes were clear now. Her voice was as well. The trembling had stopped and she looked, to Quinn's eyes at least, like a different woman. "Go. Now. Riley." The clarity with which she spoke was jarring. "Please go."

"I can't imagine what's going on with her," Yvonne's voice had Quinn and Riley stepping away from Joyce as she sank back in her rocking chair.

Quinn slid his hand around Riley's as the two orderlies and nurse hurried into the room, Yvonne right at their heels. Together they moved to the door and, with Riley blocking Quinn's actions, he picked up the frame and slipped it into his inside jacket pocket.

"I think it's best you leave," Yvonne told them.

"Of course," Quinn said. "I hope she'll be all right."

"I'm certain she will be," Yvonne said and pushed them out of the room. "Please, let us help her." She shut the door in their faces.

"Quinn?" Riley's voice was filled with an uncertainty nearly as chilling as Joyce's warning.

"Not here." Still holding her hand, Quinn led down the hall, back through the facility and out the front door. It took a moment for his eyes to adjust to the sun, and as he shielded his eyes, he scanned the parking lot. There. Back left corner. A new car had parked as far away from where he'd parked as possible. There were plenty of other spaces closer to the facility, but the sedan had chosen that spot. Like they didn't want to be spotted. "Joyce was right." He squeezed Riley's hand and tugged her closer. "We need to get out of here. But first, you need to call your client and reschedule your photo session."

Riley sighed. "I already told you, I'm not—"

"This isn't a suggestion, Riley. Do it."

"Does that order come with a side of fries?" She actually batted her lashes, but when she locked her gaze on his, the humor faded. "What? What did I miss?"

"Blue sedan." He shifted to stand in front of her, rested one hand on her cheek. "Back left corner of the lot, closest to the entry gate. You see it?"

"Yes." Her eyes narrowed. "I've seen it before. At the parking lot when I got our coffees." The rage rose in her eyes like a deadly tide. "It's the Little Fucker, isn't it?"

"That's what I'd bet on." He slid a hand down her arm, clasped her hand again. "Just act normally. Once we get in the car, you're going to call your client to cancel and I'm going to call my LT."

"Why? What can he do?"

"Hopefully prevent any collateral damage." He pulled open her door and waited for her to climb in. "Riley, I need you to trust me and say you agree to what I plan to do."

"Okay. What are *you* going to do?" There wasn't concern or fear in her eyes, but suspicion, which for some reason bolstered his confidence.

"The one thing I swore I wouldn't." He leaned in and kissed her, not only to keep her from asking more questions, but to steady himself. "I'm about to use you as bait."

# CHAPTER ELEVEN

"CONSIDER me intimidated." Riley hung up after cancelling with her two clients. "I just passed along a potential gold mine of a customer to one of my competitors." She didn't feel nearly as sour as she sounded.

"I'm sure your client will appreciate not being used for target practice." Quinn glanced in the rearview mirror but kept his foot steady on the gas. "Those flowers arriving for Joyce when they did—that wasn't a coincidence."

"I'll take it one further." Riley glanced in the side mirror and kept her own eyes on their tail. "I don't think they were only meant for her."

"Agreed. It also proves that her comments about being watched weren't paranoid or delusional."

"Why is he following us?" Riley could barely breathe around the knots in her stomach. "I've already told him I gave you the photographs. And even if I hadn't before he popped up at Temple House like a demented Whac-A-Mole, I sure as hell would have after the fact." It didn't make any sense. Why was he following them around when doing so only did one thing: risked exposing himself. "They always demand a sacrifice."

"What are you talking about?" Quinn asked. "Who demands a sacrifice?"

"It was something he said in the basement." Riley's mind raced. "They always demand a sacrifice." She turned in her seat and looked at him, but when she opened her mouth, something else her assailant had said flashed in her mind. She reached over, clicked on and cranked up the radio, sending pulse-thumbing bolts of bass and drums pounding through the car.

"What the hell—"

She slapped Quinn's hand away when he glared at her.

"Riley—"

She shook her head and grabbed her phone out of her purse, opened the notes app and typed. When he stopped for a red light, she showed him her screen.

*They overheard us at lunch. They were listening. I think they* are *listening!*

His gaze locked on hers. For one, long moment, the world came to a slow-motion halt. She could see so much in his eyes: comprehension, anger, acceptance. Horns blared from behind. The light had changed. "Okay." He gave her a nod of understanding as he drove through the intersection. "Okay, I've got an idea." He leaned forward, pulled his cell out and handed it to her. He scanned their surroundings, nodded again, then grabbed her arm and tugged her close so he could speak directly into her ear. "Text Wallace. Tell him we've picked up a tail and that I'm going to head … shit!" He looked over his left shoulder as the blue sedan suddenly switched lanes and blasted past them. "Guess that proves your theory right. Hang on."

Riley grabbed hold of the chicken bar and pushed back in her seat.

"How did he hear us over the music?"

"He didn't," Quinn yelled. "The music probably tipped him off."

"Don't you have a siren or spinning lights?" Riley yelled back as the city sped past her.

"Personal vehicles aren't supposed to …" He swore again, zoomed in and out and around to keep up with the sedan. "Little Fucker's got some wheel talent. Call Wallace." He pointed at his phone.

She flipped through his contacts, found Wallace's info and dialed, then held it up to Quinn's ear so he could keep both hands on the wheel. "Wallace? Yeah. It's me. We're in pursuit of male suspect from Unburied Treasures. Blue Ford Taurus, license number ..." He squinted as he tried to read. Riley snatched the phone back and rattled off the number, held the phone back up to Quinn's ear. "Yeah, you get that? Great. I'm going to try to drive him toward a blockade. Send units to ... hang on." Quinn sped up, cut off two cars as he plowed across to the right lane and took a hard right.

"There!" Riley yelled and pointed.

After another hard left that tested the limit of a red light, he slipped in a few cars behind.

"Wallace, I need units to cut him off and lock him in around West Sunset Boulevard. Yeah. See you there."

"You think he's headed for the freeway?" Riley's voice belied the adrenaline surging through her system as she hung up and set his phone in the cup holder in the center console.

"I think he's headed for the overpass," Quinn said. "The freeway won't get him anywhere in a hurry. He needs to disappear, and he can only do that across the highway."

His phone buzzed. Riley grabbed it and scanned the message. "Wallace has patrol units on their way. Special response team? What's that?"

"SWAT." He eased his foot off the gas a bit, but it was too late. The sedan took off again, right through a red light and triggered a blast of horns and screeching tires.

"There!" Riley pointed off to the left as the sedan took a hubcap-spinning right onto North Highland Avenue. "You were right. He's headed for the .... Can we catch up?"

"We're gonna try."

Riley tightened her grip on the bar overhead as Quinn turned left near the Hollywood Heritage Museum. At least one of his tires spun right off the asphalt.

"I thought you were supposed to keep me alive, not accelerate my demise."

"Don't worry." His grin was quick and far from amused. "I aced my defensive driving training."

"Yeah?" She didn't believe him for a second. "How long ago?" She checked his phone. "Wallace says to try to push him down Camrose. They've got multiple patrol cars up ahead."

"We're already there." Quinn slowed as they approached the freeway overpass. "What the hell is the Little Fucker doing?" Quinn slammed on the brakes when the sedan whipped into a side skid and came to a stop. Cars behind him did the same, slipping and sliding. Drivers spilled out of their cars, shouting, cursing at their suspect.

The smell of burning rubber arced into the air. On the other side of the overpass, police cruisers, lights spinning, had blocked the road. "What the . . . ?"

He flipped off the music.

Riley winced as the sudden silence hurt her head nearly as much as the pounding drumbeat.

Police cruisers zoomed up behind him, blocking traffic from getting through as Quinn unbuckled his belt, withdrew his sidearm, and shoved open his door.

"Quinn?"

"Stay here." He stepped around and, after a glance back at her, appeared to move clear of the SUV, weapon raised and aimed at the suspect's car as the young man leapt out and backed up to the side curb.

"Quinn? Don't kill him!" Riley yelled. So many questions. She had so many questions to ask. "We need him alive! Don't—" She was so distracted by the man's face, it took her longer than it should have to see the gun in his hand.

He kept it down at his side, but even from this distance, she saw his fingers tighten around the hilt.

More sirens. More shouts, mostly from Quinn ordering drivers back into their cars. The suspect watched, and remained silent.

"Put down your weapon!" Multiple voices shouted the order at him. Riley dared to shove open her door and carefully slid to the ground.

Quinn and the other officers advanced.

The suspect stepped closer to the railing.

"Nobody fire!" Quinn shouted to his fellow officers.

"Shit." She twisted to look behind her as numerous patrol cars came to a halt behind Quinn's SUV. When she looked back at the suspect, she could see it in his eyes. The absolute dead calm of a man whose plan had worked. Her entire body went ice-cube cold. "He's still playing the game."

A game Quinn didn't realize he'd just become a part of.

A game the suspect had no intention of losing.

"Quinn!" Riley darted around the car door, but the second she was out from the protection of the SUV she realized her mistake.

The suspect's eyes gleamed with something akin to triumph.

Riley stood, frozen, hands open and in front of her as if she could somehow stop the bullet his twitchy hand was clearly itching to fire. Her heart couldn't seem to make up its mind between over-beating and coming to a complete stop.

She kept her focus on Quinn, who inclined his head, anger clenching his jaw, but didn't take his eyes off the suspect.

"Drop the gun!" Quinn yelled again as Riley's assailant took one more step backward until the overpass railing hit his back. Three patrol officers moved in, flanking the suspect, who suddenly straightened as if appreciating his situation.

"All right!" The suspect finally yelled and held up both hands, released his hold on his weapon. "All right. I'm putting it down." He stooped and set the gun on the ground.

Quinn shifted his stance and moved in but not, Riley realized, in a straight line. He was heading for her. "Riley, get back to the car! Move! Now!"

"I—" It wasn't his order that caught her off guard, but her inability to move. He kept his distance from the suspect as he took a wide path toward Riley, placing himself between her and the gunman.

As the suspect stood, he dropped one hand behind his back.

"Hands where we can see them!" an officer yelled.

But the second weapon was already in his hand. As he fired, the world skidded into slow motion. Multiple shots rang out, but all she saw was the flash of the Little Fucker's gun at the same time she watched Quinn turn and dive for her. As his arms locked around her and knocked her to the ground, she felt the white-hot air of the bullet soaring past before it plowed into the tire of Quinn's SUV.

She hit the asphalt with a *wumph* and lay there, stunned. Quinn bounced right back up as the sound of gunfire erupted across the overpass. She shoved herself up, instinctively scampered back and pushed her hair out of her eyes while she watched the suspect be shot once, twice, three times in the upper torso. His body twitched each time, blood splattering with force before pooling across his light-colored shirt.

Riley watched, horrified, as he seemed to be frozen in time, his gaze pinned on Riley as a slow, peaceful smile stretched across his mouth. Their eyes met and she stared, transfixed, into the deep-set eyes of resolve as the cops raced toward him.

"No," she whispered into the wind.

He closed his eyes and stretched his arms out wide. The gun clattered to the ground and he tipped himself back.

And dropped off the overpass, out of sight.

Riley caught a sob behind her trembling hand, unable to process what she'd seen even while she felt the double gut punch of relief and revulsion. The broken violin-string screech of brakes from cars on the freeway exploded up and over the overpass. She hadn't heard the body hit. At least … she didn't think she did.

"Riley, what the fuck?!" Quinn's blast of anger barely singed her as he stalked back to her. He bent down, locked his hands around her upper arms and dragged her to her feet.

He shook her. Hard. Hard enough to make her teeth vibrate. "What the *fuck* were you thinking, distracting me like that?"

"He wasn't done," she whispered. Her knees felt like rubber bands.

"Of course he wasn't done."

"You knew?"

"That's my job." There was so much to unload from his voice. Anger. Frustration. Fear. "He was waiting for a shot at you, and you walked right into it. You didn't put just yourself at risk but every cop on this overpass." She opened her mouth to protest. "No! Stop!" Quinn gave her another hard shake and only then did she open her eyes. "Riley—" There was fury in his gaze, but there was also a sudden flash of relief. He hauled her against him, and locked his arms around her so tightly she lost what was left of her air. "Jesus, Riley. Jesus."

"I know. I'm sorry," she whispered even as her arms came around him and she clung. He was all right. Somehow, he was all right and that was all that mattered. What would she have done if …? She drew in a shuddering breath. "Sorry. I didn't think. I just …"

"No, you didn't think. You didn't think about anything but …"

"You."The admission felt ripped from her soul. As if uttering that one word had somehow torn her life into two pieces and neither half was ever going to be the same.

She felt his anger subside even as it surged into her own marrow. But still he held on.

And so did she.

Riley had always prided herself on being able to handle whatever situation she landed in. It had become a point of character contention, certainly. She was a challenge for most people and she willingly and happily accepted that. Being difficult was, in a lot of ways, a badge of honor for her.

For years she'd grabbed opportunities, jumping into spaces that might not have been created for her, but fit nonetheless. Her "leap first, think later" approach to life had, until today at least, proved without a hint of doubt she'd been living in a self-created bubble of arrogance and, in some ways, ignorance.

She was not ignorant, however, as she climbed the stairs to her apartment, as to the tension nipping at her heels in the form of one very stoic Detective Quinn Burton. The silence in the patrol car that had driven them home to Temple House had been suffocating, stealing virtually every breath left in her already tight lungs. Breath that didn't return until she entered her apartment and tossed her keys into the ceramic bowl on the table by the door.

"Moxie home?"

Over her shoulder, Quinn's deep voice made her shiver.

"Ah, no." She'd texted her aunt while she'd been waiting to give her statement. "She's making a longer day of things with her agent. Said something about dinner—"

That was as far as she got before Quinn grabbed her arm, spun her around and dropped his mouth down on hers.

It wasn't a questioning or tentative kiss, but rather one that left her head spinning as if she'd taken an unexpected drop down a steep roller coaster. The breath that had returned, vanished once more, and she found herself gripping his arms as he pushed her lips apart, dived in and took control.

She could feel so much in his kiss, in the way his mouth moved urgently, possessively over hers. There was something else, something unexpected and sobering as she grabbed onto him and held on. Need.

Pure, unadulterated, overwhelming need.

He pushed her back against the wall, pressed his body utterly and completely against hers as his hands moved up her arms, caught the sides of her face. Only then did his hold loosen and his touch gentle.

He pulled back just enough so they weren't touching, but remained so close she could feel his hot breath brushing against her now-swollen lips. Lips she pressed together so tightly they went numb. Eyes wide, breathing labored, she stared at him, but he didn't look at her. Instead, he pressed his forehead to hers as his hands flexed, as if attempting to grasp control.

"Two seconds," he breathed, squeezing his eyes even tighter. He shook his head as if trying to dislodge the thought. "If I'd been two seconds later, he wouldn't have missed. That bullet—"

"But you weren't." She released his arms, grabbed his face between her hands and forced his head back, waited until he blinked open his eyes. "You weren't too late, Quinn. I'm here. I'm alive. I'm okay. Because of you." She'd never kissed a man before because he seemed to need it. But she did so now and felt some of the tension melt out of his body. "I'm sorry I scared you. I just ..." she didn't know how to explain, so the words just spilled out. "I saw you walking toward him and all I could think to do was stop you. Somehow," she added on a laugh. "You know what? I think we could both use a drink." A big one.

She pushed him back, moved around him and headed down the hall into the kitchen.

"A drink might be better than the silent treatment you were giving me in the car."

"I wasn't giving you the silent treatment." She shrugged out of her sweater, tossed it over the back of one of the barstools, yanked open the fridge and pulled out beer and wine. "I was thinking. Deeply."

"About?"

It would be so easy, she thought as the silence stretched, to admit the truth: that he was right. She could have died. She could have left Moxie alone. That she … her hand gripped the door of the refrigerator until her knuckles went white. "Right now, all I can think about is that kiss you just planted on me."

"Try again." Looking as if he were traversing a minefield, he joined her in the kitchen. He pulled one of the beers toward him, snapped off the cap. "What are you thinking deeply about, Riley?"

"My Christmas to-do list, what else?" She forewent her usual wine glass and instead chose one of the full-bottle ones Sutton had gifted her as a joke. As she poured, she could feel his gaze on her. "Don't judge."

"Not about to." But she heard the concern in his voice. It both calmed and unsettled her. Clearly he'd gotten some of his own pent-up frustration out of his system, even while hers began to rebuild.

She drank, long and deep, set the glass carefully on the counter. Looking into its liquid depths, she said, "They sent you home."

"They did. It's procedure for when any cop fires his weapon," he said as casually as he might have discussed recent sports scores.

He had fired, Riley thought to herself. The second he was back on his feet after tackling her to safety, he'd rolled over and fired. Second nature, she realized now. Protecting her had been second nature.

"IA and Professional Standards are examining the dashboard footage from the patrol units. I'll be cleared and back on active duty soon."

She drank, wincing against the red's tannins as her system finally began to chug to a stop. Her insides felt as if an entire hive of bees had set up housekeeping, frenetically searching for a way out. She pressed a hand against her belly. "I'm finding it difficult to process everything. What you—" She drank again, wincing at the dull clink of the glass as she set it down again.

"We didn't do enough." His voice was flat, devoid of the emotion she herself couldn't process. "The suspect's dead—as are any leads he might have given us."

She didn't give a damn about leads right now. "You could have died." And that, more than anything, was what left her shaking.

"We both could have." He took a pull of his beer, leaned an arm on the counter as she circled around and toward him. "Cops don't court death, if that's what you're thinking. I can count on two hands the number of times I've actually fired my weapon."

"Good to know." The caution she'd witnessed, the training. She'd never experienced what police officers did from their side of things before. It was sobering. Illuminating. Eye-opening.

"Don't push the pendulum all the way over, Riley. We aren't superheroes any more than we are villains. We're just men and women trying to do the best job we can in the middle of this crazy world. Some days the results are better than others." But she knew what else he was thinking. That today was not one of those days. "You sure you're in the right frame of mind to talk about this now?"

"Actually," she gulped down more wine, and set her glass aside. Keeping her eyes on his, she crossed her arms, reached down, and pulled her shirt up and over her head. "Since you got the ball rolling, I don't want to talk at all." She kicked out of her shoes, unzipped her jeans and shimmied them down over her hips.

She advanced on him, feeling both powerful and anxious. Nervous and angry. Her emotions were ping-ponging all over the place, but beneath them all lay one, unarguable fact.

She wanted him.

His entire body tensed, his fists clenching as his gaze dropped to the barely there hot-pink lace bra and panties set she'd chosen this morning. The set that had been crammed in the back of her underwear drawer for longer than she cared to admit. The underwear that had brought a devilish smile to her lips the second her fingertips had grasped it.

"Detective?" She knew forced nonchalance when she saw it. She appreciated it. Most of the time. But right now? She didn't have time for games. "You're overdressed."

He set his bottle down with a clack, pulled off his LAPD windbreaker and tossed it over her sweater. "Better?" His arched brow felt like a tightly bowed erotic challenge, one she was more than willing to answer. She could hear the almost rugged edge of his breathing as he took a step closer, hands still fisted at his sides as if unable to decide what direction to advance from. His pupils had already gone wide, as if filled with the promise of the fire he'd ignited moments before by the door.

She forced herself to slow down. Quinn Burton was not a stupid man. He knew precisely what he was doing, and the effect it was having on her. She could already feel the tightening and anticipation surging through her as he slipped out of his weapon's harness. That tingling that would only be satiated by his touch. His hands. His fingers. His mouth. His cock.

"Keep looking at me that way and this is going to be over sooner than either of would like." He pulled his shirt free from his pants, giving her a glimpse of tanned, toned skin beneath. Unable to resist temptation any longer, she walked over, covered his hands with hers and together, removed the impeding fabric. The low growl in the back of her throat as she got her hands on him, felt the strong, beating heat of him was pure female instinct and attraction, pulsing as if it were a separate life force inside of her.

"If that happens, we'll just have to start again," she breathed against his chest when she pressed her lips against his bare flesh.

With the sun still shining through the leaded windows, she slid her hands up his chest, around his shoulders and down his arms.

"We have as much time as we want," she whispered, reveling in the way his muscles tightened beneath her touch. "Only one problem." Her hands traveled lower, down his waist, shifted and met at his belt buckle. Before one hand slipped down and cupped the firm hardness of him. "I want fast." She squeezed and felt her feminine power surge as his eyes darkened and his breath quickened. "I want fast and hard. I want you inside of me."

She rose up on her toes, teased her lips against his jaw before licking his lips with the tip of her tongue. "I don't want any thoughts in my head except what you're doing to me ..." She kissed him, swept her tongue into his mouth and smiled against his lips when he gave in and gripped her hips with trembling, strong hands, kissing her passionately for a long moment until she pulled back again. She could feel his fake nonchalance fracturing. "I want no thoughts other than what I'm doing to you." She bit her way down the side of his neck and this time it was he who groaned, almost growled, pulled her even closer. "Can you handle that, detective?"

"I can handle everything you've got." His gaze blazed into hers. She could all but hear his heart pounding for her. Feel his body hardening for her. "Right now there's only one thing I want."

"Oh?" She was already itching to get at him. For him to get at her. "What's that?"

"This." He reached up and tugged the band in her hair free. It spilled around her shoulders, the ends brushing against the tops of her breasts. Hands deep in her hair, he dipped down and captured her mouth, engaging her tongue in a dance she never wanted to end. There wasn't a part of her that didn't feel as if it were on fire. Inside and out, she could feel him, coaxing the passion out of her even. "Bedroom," he murmured against her mouth as if he didn't intend to let go. His hands left her hair, skimmed down her sides and, as she shivered, slipped around to cup her ass, hoisting her up and onto the edge of the counter. "Or here. Your choice." His mouth locked against her throat and she gasped, arching her back.

"Bedroom." She grabbed hold of his head, peered into his eyes as if diving into a pool of unending arousal. "Go."

He lifted her again, and this time she locked her legs around his hips, trying desperately not to rub herself against the steel hardness pressing toward her. He didn't make it far down the hall to her door before he pressed her back against the wall and, bracing her with one leg, used his other hand to slip beneath the band of her panties and dip into her heat.

She groaned, and when her head dropped back, she winced. And he froze. "Dammit. Your head. I forgot."

"Don't you dare shift tactics now." She tightened her core, bucked her hips against him and sank her teeth into his neck. "You started it. Finish it." She bit harder. "Finish me."

"Jesus," he breathed as she lifted herself up, using her hold on his neck as leverage. One finger, two, pressed into her, higher, harder as she rode his hand, imagining what it was going to feel like with his cock inside of her. "Riley."

The pressure built, white hot pleasure shooting through her as she came, her cry caught in his mouth as he kissed her again. Her legs went limp, and for a moment she felt every bit of energy drain. But his body offered more temptation. "Your turn," she murmured against his lips and smiled.

"We'll see." He picked her up again and this time they made it into her bedroom. He kicked the door closed behind them, and strode across the room like a man on a mission. "Condoms?" he asked as he reached the bed. She lowered her legs and felt the mattress bump up against the backs of her legs.

"Nightstand." She remained where he'd placed her while he retrieved the box she kept on hand. "Take as many as you need," she teased as she stepped out of her panties.

His lips curved even as his eyes darkened once more. "You want to do this?" He dropped one of the packets on the bed and returned to her, stood in front of her and offered himself by placing his hands on his hips. "Or should I?"

"Mmmm." Her own smile felt lascivious. "I'll let you do the honors." She sat on the edge of the mattress and laid back, stretching her arms over her head and arching her back. She could feel the lace edge of the bra lower, and saw his eyes follow that path. She brought her hands down, running them over her eager breasts until she unclasped the center hook and, never breaking eye contact, slowly pushed aside the fabric. "You're taking your time, detective." She replaced the bra with her palms, pushing herself up and tweaking her nipples with her fingers. "I believe I said I wanted fast. Don't make me do this on my own."

"You had it fast," he said as he unbuckled his belt and, after toeing out of his shoes, divested himself of pants and briefs in one movement. "Now we'll try a different way."

"God." It was definitely a prayer, marveling at the sight of him. The strength, the hardness, the absolute promise of filling her with every inch of himself. He was beautifully made, from his chiseled arms to his muscular legs, to the taut stomach perfectly topping that which made him utterly and completely male. "If you don't come down here—"

"I'm coming down. Don't you worry."

She gasped as he dropped to his knees, caught hers in his hands and parted her legs. She'd never before ever felt worshipped, but as she felt his mouth touch, ever so slightly, against her, she felt her head spin. She squirmed, wanting, needing to draw her knees up, to give him fuller and better access as his tongue dipped and swirled, and teased her clit. But he kept her knees in place, drawing out the beautiful torture he applied to her.

She whimpered. He licked. She cried out. He bit. And when he pushed her over the edge once more, he sat up and watched her soar.

There wasn't an inch of her that wasn't tingling, wasn't trembling beneath his touch and as she caught her breath and opened her eyes, she saw him covering himself and, as she finally floated down to earth, he lowered himself on top of her. Before her heart could catch up, he eased inside of her with a barely suppressed growl. He was so taut, so controlled, so … he surged forward, stealing her of even the thought of breathing again.

She fisted her hands in the bedspread, finally giving into the need to bring up her legs, and this time she locked them around his hips. He filled her. Stretched her. And she welcomed every pleasurable inch as he kissed her.

He thrust into her, again and again, each time too much. It was too much. And not enough. She wanted everything. She wanted to surround him. All of him. She met him move for move, once again feeling that promise of relief climbing to a peak so high, she wasn't sure she'd survive the fall this time. He thrust faster, and she hung on, memorizing every moment as if capturing it on film. She wanted—needed—to remember this feeling. Of being alive. Of being with him.

Of being loved.

They crested together, each with the other's name on their lips. Each uttering an unspoken promise of connection neither one would be able to deny. When he pulled out of her, he rolled off, drawing her into the circle of his arms in the middle of her bed.

For the first time in her life, she felt … whole.

"I'm glad you didn't die today, Quinn." She pressed a kiss into his shoulder.

"Me, too." He sank his hand back into her hair, feeling protectiveness and contentment in equal measure. "Go to sleep, Riley. Recharge." He kissed her forehead. "We're only just getting started."

# CHAPTER TWELVE

"IF you don't answer that, I'm going to smother you with a pillow."

Quinn's grumpy voice startled Riley out of a semi-sound sleep. She sat up, grabbed what little she could of the sheet and searched for her phone. Now that the sun was descending, she clicked on the bedside lamp. "What the hell—"

"Not your phone." Quinn threw an arm over his face. "Someone's knocking on the door."

"Oh." She shoved her hair out of her face as a fist hit the door.

"Riley Jessica, we need to talk!" Moxie shouted. "Put on some clothes and join me. Now."

"Uh-oh." Riley nudged Quinn. "She's mad about something."

"Sure sounds like it." He nudged her back. "Better go see what she wants. Seems safer for me to stay in here."

"My hero," she muttered. "Walks right into a psychopath's firing zone and yet won't play buffer to an octogenarian."

"Hey, I offered to do that before and you turned me down." He rolled over and hugged her pillow. "Much safer in here. And cozy too. Nice mattress. Definitely holds up."

Riley snort-laughed and untangled herself from the sheet before dragging on a clean pair of yoga pants and an oversized sweatshirt.

Barefoot, she stopped at the door and looked back at the bed. The sight of Quinn Burton, naked, satiated, and yet still incredibly tempting, triggered this odd, giddy, spinning-top feeling inside of her. "Sure you don't want to join us?"

"I'll wait for the news report." He chuckled at her glare. "I'm going to grab a shower and head back into the station."

"I thought they had you on desk duty for a while."

"They do. But I can still get some information and we've got some mysteries to solve where Joyce DePalma is concerned. Or did you forget about that burn mark on the back of her neck."

"Like I could." Darcy shuddered. "Why would someone do that to another human being? I'd think a tattoo would be enough of a statement."

"You're assuming she got that mark by choice." Quinn's eyes shifted back to cop mode. "No one reacts the way she did to anything that was a choice. And now I'm fully awake."

"Yes," Riley teased. "You are. Funny how that worked. Feel free to raid the fridge when you're done in the shower."

"I will take you up on that."

"Riley!" Moxie's voice echoed through the door.

"Eeesh. She must not have had a good meeting with her agent. Good thing IA has your gun."

She pulled open the door and, after taking a steeling breath, headed into the kitchen. She uttered a silent "Oh" at the sight of half of hers and Quinn's clothes covering the kitchen floor. She bent down and scooped them up—only when she stood up, she found Moxie standing right behind her. "Hi. How was your lunch with Ernie?"

"Revealing," Moxie said. "You. Sit. There." She pointed at the stool holding Quinn's LAPD jacket.

Feeling all of ten years old again after having been caught pilfering the Mickey Mouse cookie jar, Riley did as she was told. Normally Moxie was an open book, her moods easily decipherable, but, at the moment, Riley couldn't define any of the expressions crossing her aunt's face.

"Ernie received a registered letter the other day." She whipped it out as if from thin air and placed it on the counter beside Quinn's badge.

Riley winced. Dammit! She was off her game. She should have anticipated Powell Studios sending the letter about the Sally Tate movies to Moxie's agent.

"Aren't you going to open it to see what's inside? Don't you want to know what it says?"

Moxie inclined her head, her green eyes glowing with the bitter intensity of a comic book super villain. "Or maybe you already know."

"I was going to talk to you about Granger Powell's offer to buy Temple House," Riley said. "I got distracted. You know, the whole basement thing and … stuff." Now was not the time to tell her aunt she'd been shot at by a maniacal hitman.

"If that's an attempt to make me feel sorry for you—"

"It's not." Riley rarely interrupted her aunt, but she wanted to nip that idea in the bud immediately. "I had planned to talk to you about it during dinner last night and, well—that didn't happen. Also," she shrugged, "maybe I didn't want to bring it up because I was afraid of what you might say. It's a good offer, Moxie. It's a great offer. I didn't want to argue over whether to accept it or not. I'm sorry."

"You should be," Moxie snapped, but some of the vehemence had evaporated. "What on earth do you think of me if you believe that I'd even consider selling this place for a part in a movie?"

"It's Sally Tate," Riley said as if that explained everything. "It's what you've been wanting, isn't it? Another big spotlight. A chance at a return to the big screen. How could I not understand that after living with you for the past twenty-something years?"

"Sometimes I don't know where you keep your brain, Riley. Temple House isn't just our home. It's our family legacy. It's what we built these past few generations, and our legacy isn't for sale." She stepped close and caught Riley's chin in her hand. "For any price. Understand me?"

Riley's heart flipped over. Moxie's response was what she'd hoped it would be, even as she worried it wouldn't come to pass. "I should have had more faith in you. In us."

"Damn straight, you should have. Now, I'm going to put a stop to this Granger Powell nonsense once and for all. I've already spoken to Laurel. She's going to draft an official letter to him and warn him to back off and, if that doesn't work and the letters continue, she's going to pay him a visit in person."

Riley's eyes went wide. "Wow. Okay." That prospect almost, *almost* made her feel sorry for Powell.

"Temple House is staying with the Temples. End of story. And if the letter and Laurel's visit don't work, I'll march right down to that studio and give him what for."

"Yes, ma'am." Riley pressed her lips into a thin line, trying hard not to laugh. Siccing Laurel on Granger Powell could be one of Moxie's greatest moves ever. "Are you done being mad at me?"

"I suppose." Moxie sighed. "To be honest, it's exhausting. And I've got to save up my energy if I'm going to beat out Gloria Malfort for the lead in that play."

"Gloria Malfort? I haven't heard that name in ages." Riley looked at her aunt. "Didn't you two have some kind of rivalry back in the day?"

"Nineteen fifty-six to be exact." Moxie retrieved a normal-sized wine glass and pushed Riley's half-full one toward her. "Studio was threatening to replace me in the Sally Tate movies because I'd demanded a raise on my new contract. Considering I'd beaten Gloria out for the role in the first place, the studio heads thought they were being cute. Ernie and I showed them the error of their ways."

"I'll bet you did." Riley was always finding new reasons to admire her aunt. "Hollywood was a lot different back then."

"It was and yet it wasn't." Moxie said. "The shadows aren't so dark anymore. They're still there, though. Just better hidden."

Riley chewed on her thumbnail, countless thoughts racing through her mind. "I went to visit an old friend of Grandpa's today up at Golden Age."

"Oh?" Moxie dug into the refrigerator and started pulling out leftovers. "Who's that?"

"Joyce DePalma. She worked for Clinton Bryant. Do you remember her?"

"Of course I remember Joyce." Moxie grabbed another bottle of wine and examined it. "Haven't seen her in a while. Heard she had a stroke a while back. Poor woman. She's always been alone."

"That is sad." Inspired, and curious, Riley realized they probably had the perfect source of information living right under this roof. The tricky part was asking questions without piquing Moxie's curiosity. "Her memory's not the greatest and I think she has some dementia issues. I've never seen anyone get so spooked at a bouquet of flowers."

"Flowers?" Moxie glanced up and frowned. "What kind of flowers?"

"Red lilies."

The bottle slipped from Moxie's fingers and shattered on the bamboo plank floor. "Oh. Oh, no!" her aunt cried. "I'm sorry. I—"

"Everything okay?" Quinn, hair damp and wearing only his jeans, emerged from the bedroom. "What happened?"

"Nothing. Stupid, really." Moxie's voice trembled even as she attempted a shaky smile at Riley. "Sugar my coconuts, I've made such a mess. Oh, look." She plucked red-wine splattered gray slacks away from her leg, looked down at her ruined shoes. "These'll never come clean."

"I'll get the mop and broom," Riley said as Quinn made his way around the kitchen island and gently took Moxie's arm.

"You come out of there and let us take care of this." He drew her back, but given the look he shot Riley, he saw that the color had drained from her aunt's face as clearly as Riley had. "Are you all right?"

"I'm fine." She batted his hand away. "Such silliness. Old hands can't even hold a bottle of wine."

Riley didn't believe that for a second. The only thing that made Moxie Temple old was her age. Mentally, physically, aside from her cholesterol medication, she functioned at peak performance.

"Why don't you go and change, Moxie?" Riley told her. "I'll find another bottle for us to open."

"Yes, yes, all right." She started to walk past Quinn, then seemed to realize he was there. She stopped, looked back at Riley, then at Quinn. "Took a tumble together, did you?"

"Moxie," Riley warned, but Quinn only grinned.

"Yes, ma'am."

"Good. She needed it. Sex is good for the blood pressure," she added at Riley's frustrated huff. "Don't know why you young folks think you invented sex. I've had plenty of it myself, you know."

"Yes, I know," Riley sang as if that would magically change the topic of conversation. "I'm meeting the girls at Cassia's for dinner in a little bit, but I'll get something ready for you before I leave. What should I set up for streaming for you? Are you still watching *The Office*?"

"Finished that last week. Now I'm watching *Stranger Things*. Got me a thing for that Sheriff Hopper," Moxie announced as she patted a hand on Quinn's arm. "I'll be seeing you around, I take it?"

"That's the plan."

"Good, good." Moxie seemed distracted again. Riley headed for her, but Quinn held up his hand to keep her at bay. Together they watched her aunt shuffle off to her room as she lifted trembling fingers to the back of her neck.

"We'll figure this out." Despite standing out in the hall in front of Riley's apartment, Quinn kept his voice down. He ran his arms up and down Riley's sweatshirt-clad arms, wishing he could do something, anything to erase that distraught expression on her beautiful face. "I promise."

"Seeing that look on Joyce's face was bad enough," Riley whispered almost desperately. "Seeing it on Moxie's? Quinn, what the hell is going on? What happened to them?"

"I don't know. I'm going to do some discreet checking, see if I can find anything—"

"I can't believe I'm saying this, but … be careful." She stepped into his arms and held on tight. "Right now I feel like you're the only anchor I've got."

"Hey. Where's that spitfire Riley Temple I fell so hard for, huh?" He kept his tone light, teasing, and forced a smile that felt like an absolute fraud. "Don't go wussing out on me now. Not when we've got a mystery to solve."

"Don't call me a wuss." She jumped back, those green eyes of her sparking like bottle glass in the dark. "After the last few days, I think I've earned a bit of self-doubt and fear."

"You absolutely have." He was dealing with a good dose of both himself. "But your spine is going to be what gets us through this.

We've got one issue behind us. The Little Fucker's in the morgue, so we can relax about something."

"Great. Maybe I can get my lost client back."

"Don't push it. I want you sticking close to home for a bit longer. Just a little while," he added at her frown. "I'm heading in now to talk to Wallace. Check the preliminary coroner's report—"

"He was run over by a semi, once he … landed," Riley reminded him.

"I'm more interested in his identity than the cause of death." Honestly, he didn't care whether it was the bullets, the fall, or the truck that had killed him. The man responsible for attacking Riley in her own home was gone.

As for who sent him after Riley in the first place …

"Are you coming back here when you're done?"

"As much as I'd like to, I think it's best if we both get a good night's sleep." He bent down and pressed his mouth to hers. That instant spark of desire proved him one hundred percent right. "Sleep won't come anywhere near us as long as we're around each other."

"No." Her laugh sounded almost genuine. "I suppose not. Will you ca—"

Someone stomped up the stairs. When a familiar dark-haired feminine figure stepped into view, Quinn relaxed. "Laurel. Hey."

"Well, I guess I know why you aren't answering your phone. Not a cool move considering you were in the ER recently. Or did you forget your head got bounced around like a LeBron James special?" Laurel looked far from amused at having to make the trek up from her apartment.

"My fault," Quinn volunteered. "She's all yours."

"Not in the same way she's yours, I'm sure," Laurel observed.

"I'll call you when I'm caught up." He kissed Riley again, stroked his thumb down her cheek and once again wished he could make that fear in her eyes vanish. "Moxie'll be fine. We'll make sure of it."

She nodded and hugged her arms around her torso. "I need to get Moxie settled," he heard her tell Laurel as he took the stairs down. "Come in and keep me company and I'll fill you in."

Quinn would have liked to have been in on that update, but given he had four missed calls from Wallace, one from his LT, and one from his father on his own cell, he needed to get back to work. He was about to call his father first when he hit the lobby landing and found Blake Redford up on a ladder, attaching what looked like a micro-surveillance camera over one of the windows. Despite the former military man giving no indication of wrongdoing, Quinn could not shake the feeling something was off with him.

"What's going on?" Keeping it casual, he acted as if he had all the time in the world. "Did Riley approve this?"

"Not that I know of." Blake tightened a wire connection, then pulled out his cell to check something. "I was ambushed by four of the tenants earlier today, including Laurel Fontaine. Apparently, they decided that the building needed an upgrade on the security angle. I was told they would fill Riley in on the details."

Judging by the empty, tossed away boxes, he'd been given quite the job. And quite fast, too.

"Laurel works fast." He crouched, examined one of the boxes and let out a low whistle. "And at the high end of things." Quinn could only imagine Riley's reaction at the price tag for this multilateral Wi-Fi system. "This had to cost a pretty penny."

"From what I understand, one of the tenants is covering the cost. Not my business," Blake said. "I'm just a man who follow orders."

"Yeah, about that."

"Let me guess." Blake made another adjustment, then pocketed his phone and climbed down. "You ran a background check on me and you'd like to discuss it."

"Partially correct." He wasn't about to deny it. "It's being run. I'm heading in now to see if it's back."

"Glad to hear it."

"You are?"

"It's what I would have done in your place." Blake picked up a large garbage bag and shook it out. "Majority of the tenants in this building are women, plus there's a number of kids. Your badge makes you naturally cautious and your attention to Riley protective. Given what happened to her, you're on high alert with anyone around her, especially someone new. I don't mind your suspicion because I know what you'll find. But to ease your mind ahead of time, I'm just a guy trying to find his footing. As well as where he fits. Been a long time since I stayed put anywhere. Temple House seemed a good place to start."

"Appreciate the honesty." Quinn nodded, some of his concerns addressed. "I'm still going to read that report."

"And I'll still be around if you want to discuss. Until then?" Intense eyes narrowed and sharpened. "What happened to Riley is not going to happen again. Not to anyone who lives here. Not to this place. No one's getting into Temple House who shouldn't be here or isn't invited. You've got my word on that."

"Don't make promises you can't keep. You've got to sleep, sometimes."

"No." Blake resumed cleaning up the trash. "I don't. Good night, detective."

"Yeah, night." Feeling strangely reassured as he headed out, he took note of the new interior keypad as well as the cameras set up inside the lobby, aimed to cover the entire front landing.

His unease revolving around leaving Riley at home abated. A different sort of tension knotted in his stomach when he called his father, who was no doubt expecting an update from the overpass incident as well as why he'd been incommunicado for the last few hours. Regret was nowhere in sight. He couldn't think of anything he'd enjoyed more than spending time in Riley's bed. Unless it was her shower. With her. Testing both their equilibriums to their limit.

If only he could erase the goofy smile he suspected was permanently plastered on his face.

"Dad. Sorry. Had my phone off." He keyed into the parking lot and headed for his car, which was now sporting its spare tire in place of the one currently in evidence. "Didn't mean to miss your call."

"Picked a bad day to get selective," Alexander said. "Another close call for you and Ms. Temple, from what I hear."

Didn't get much closer, Quinn thought as he climbed behind the wheel. "Crazy couple of days, for sure. Did you need a report from me?"

"No. I have one for you."

Quinn started the car, but when his father remained silent, he kept it in park. "Silence is never golden with you, Dad. What's up?"

"I reached out to the warden at CSP about Dean Samuels."

"Great. And?" He was already mentally clearing his calendar in anticipation of either a drive or flight to wherever the convicted murderer of Melanie Dennings was residing.

"It took some pushing, but he finally came out with it. According to his predecessor's records, Dean Samuels was transferred out of the prison's custody a few weeks after he landed inside."

"Transferred where?" Quinn demanded. "By whom?"

"No idea. Records end with his transfer. I'm sorry, Quinn." His father sighed. "Dean Samuels is gone."

"So?" Laurel nipped at Riley's heels like an overeager gossip-craving Chihuahua. "Did you and Detective Sexy Pants hit a home run or what?"

Riley closed the door to her apartment. "I am not going to—"

"The hell you're not," Laurel ordered. "Do you know how long it's been since I've even picked up a bat? Sixteen months. Sixteen, three weeks, twelve hours—"

"Fine." Riley held up her hands in surrender, even as her cheeks went hot. "No details, but I will say he was frequently at bat and had no trouble sliding into home." She smirked. "Multiple times."

"Oh. Damn." Laurel fanned herself, then sniffed the air. "I smell wine. Why do I smell wine?"

"Because you're you? Moxie dropped a bottle." Try as she might, Riley couldn't shake that dread that had descended. She wished Quinn hadn't had to leave, but that thought only irritated her. Since when did her coping capabilities have anything to do with a man?

"Moxie doesn't drop things." The humor faded from Laurel's face. "What's wrong?"

*Oh, so much,* Riley thought. "I don't suppose you saw a report on the news about a jumper—"

"The swan dive off the overpass? Oh, yeah. Local news is all over it. Oh, for Christ's sake, Riley," she snapped. "Were you there?"

"Up close and personal." Keeping one eye on Moxie's closed bedroom door while she dug out the makings for a quick, high-protein salad for her aunt, Riley tried her best to keep her voice from shaking. Sex with Quinn had been a phenomenal distraction and stress reliever, but now that he was gone, the stress was back, and it had brought this odd, churning panic along for the ride. "The jumper was the guy who attacked me in the basement."

Laurel opened her mouth, closed it again, then plopped down onto one of the stools at the kitchen island. "You have got to be shitting me. And here I thought Moxie giving me a potential ball-kicking session with Granger Powell was going to be my surprise of the day."

"Not shitting you. If only I was." What she wouldn't give for a do-over of a day—well, except for that one part. "I don't want Moxie hearing any of this. Even by accident," she murmured.

"No, of course not." Laurel insisted. "We're supposed to meet at Cass's in an hour anyway. You can fill us all in at once."

"Crap." Riley cringed, then sighed.

"You forgot, didn't you?"

"Yeah. I'm sorry. I had remembered earlier, but then .... I don't like the idea of leaving her alone." But considering Moxie had decided to spend the rest of the evening in her room, lurking out here wasn't going to do either of them any good. "Today's been a bitch."

"Hey." Laurel reached out and held out her hand, palm up. When Riley grabbed hold, she squeezed, and felt surprise tears tighten her throat. "You're entitled, Riley. And you need a break. Not to mention a verbal purge-and-confession session, which is exactly what's on the menu tonight. Just be aware, Cassia's has been doing a bit of digging into some of those questions you had about Joyce DePalma. She's oddly excited over what she found."

"Wait, what?" A new surge of panic struck, this one making her knees go weak. "I only asked her to see how Joyce was paying for her room at Golden Age. I didn't ask her to ..."

"You didn't ask her to do what Cassia was pretty much put on this earth to do?" Laurel eyed her with something akin to disappointment. "Please."

"She was careful, wasn't she?"

"It's Cass. Of course she was careful—and what the bloody hell is that look on your face?" Laurel shifted into lawyer mode. "Okay, you're officially scaring me, Riley."

"That's probably because I'm scared." And admitting that, even to herself, pushed her further off balance. "At first this whole thing was ... and then it ..." How did she begin to explain what had been going on? Even to Laurel, who was already in the know for most of it. “I didn’t want any of you involved in this. It’s bad enough I am.”

“Well, suck it up and spit it out. Our default position is by each others’ sides.” She stood up and walked around, exchanging the comforting hand-holding with a hug.

“I’m not a hugger,” Riley muttered over her shoulder.

“I know.” Laurel patted her back as if she were a cranky Keeley fighting her naptime. “Tell me what you need.”

She needed to go back a week and not buy that film off of Merle. She needed to carve out anything resembling curiosity out of her personality because so far it had led to not one, but two deaths. She needed to stop her mind from spinning like a brakeless Tilt-A-Whirl and land on something solid. Something good.

Except she’d found something good. She’d found Detective Quinn Burton. And didn’t that both elate and burn.

“That’s the problem, Laurel.” she whispered. “I’m not sure.”

But if anyone could help her figure it out, it was her Temple House Girls.

“Somehow I anticipated you being in a better mood when you came back to work.”

Wallace’s observation was tinged with his trademark humor that, honestly, Quinn didn’t have time for. Normally being back at the station brought him a strange sense of peace; as if this was where he belonged. Not tonight, however.

“Life’s full of disappointments.” Seated at his desk, he glared alternately between the computer screen that wasn’t giving him the information he wanted and the phone he was attempting to avoid using. His father had let him know IA was not going to open an investigation into the overpass incident. Between dashboard cam footage, cell phone videos and witness statements, it was an open-and-shut ending to the afternoon’s chaos. The only thing that mattered to Quinn, at this point, was he was clear to return to duty. But doing so felt like climbing on board a slow-moving iceberg in the arctic. “How long does it take for a prelim ID take, anyway?”

"Normally not this long but there was a triple homicide over on Fountain. Quite the mess, apparently. Susie's team got called over. She stayed back to work our jumper."

Quinn picked up his phone. "Maybe I should call—"

"Don't," Wallace warned, then shrugged when Quinn looked at him. "I've already checked in with her twice. She said if I showed up a third time, she was going to bury the evidence so deep my grandchildren *might* get the results. I need coffee. You want?"

"Desperate times. Yeah, I'll take one. Thanks," he murmured as Wallace got up and walked past him into the break room. He sighed. "This is just great." His chair squeaked when he sat back. A triple homicide, along with the hour, explained the lack of activity at the station, something he'd normally be thrilled by. Instead, the silence left him far too much time to think. And stew.

First, the Little Fucker's flying Wallenda off an overpass, and now he'd learned Dean Samuels had vanished out of a California State Prison facility shortly after being sent there twenty-five years ago. His intention to question both of them—dead end after dead end. Literally, figuratively, and everywhere in between.

He shifted, felt something hard and unforgiving press into his side. "What the—"

Reaching into his inside pocket, he found the framed photograph Joyce DePalma insisted they take. He hefted the frame in his hands, searching for the older woman in the face of the younger one in front of him. The ghost of her was there, but that lively expression caught on film had been tainted by age and life. And, given her reaction to those flowers, more than a fair share of darkness.

"Pretty lady."

"Yes. Very," Quinn agreed and accepted the toxic swill that passed loosely for coffee in the station house.

"Who is she?" Wallace asked. "Or am I not allowed to know?"

His partner was getting better with the snark, which earned him some good will. "Her name is Joyce DePalma. She's an old friend of Riley's grandfather."

"Did he take the picture?" Wallace asked.

Quinn blinked. "What?"

"Riley's grandfather. Did he take the photo?"

"No." A tingle of doubt tickled the back of his mind. "Another photographer did. Someone they both worked with." He angled the frame into the light, examined that lens scar Riley had pointed out earlier. Against his fingers, he felt a slight bulge beneath the velvet backing. "What comes to mind when I say the word lily?"

"Death."

Quinn's head shot up. "Really?"

"Yeah. My mother calls them funeral flowers. Not exactly something you see a lot of outside a florist or a memorial service."

"Right." Quinn nodded. "Yeah, you're right."

"So this Joyce chick—"

"And you were doing so well."

"Sorry—lady. The name's not familiar. She part of this hushhush thing you've got going on with Riley."

"Possibly." He flipped the frame over, slipped the metal hinges to the side and popped off the back. "Well, shit." He stared down at an old, plastic, 3 1/2 inch floppy disk. Pulling it free, he felt as if he'd yanked something significant out of the past. He was right. She wasn't as far gone as they'd been led to believe. "Thank you, Joyce."

"Thank you for what? What do you think is on it? Besides the DOS operating system."

"No idea," Quinn lied as he pocketed the disk, then reassembled the frame.

"You're still not going to share any of this with me, are you?"

"Keep whining. That'll convince me to change my mind." A shadow fell over his desk. "Susie." He almost knocked over his coffee cup when he stood. "We could have come to you. You have something for us?"

"I needed to get some fresh air. And yes, this stinky bullpen qualifies." She pushed her glasses up higher on her nose. "Besides, sometimes I like giving verbal reports. Please, no applause, despite this being a personal best, timing wise." She held up the solitary file in her hand and shot Wallace a smile. "Although that nice bottle of Scotch was a lovely nudge. Thanks, detective."

Quinn looked at Wallace, who shrugged.

"You wanted them fast," his partner said. "I got them fast."

The kid was racking up bonus points.

"Hmm." Susie didn't look as impressed as Quinn. "Okay, here we go. Your jumper's name is Holden Tomkin. Age thirty-four—"

"Really?" Quinn sat down to make notes.

"No. I made that part up," Susie said. "Born 1988 to a Fred and Thelma Tomkin from Pasadena. One sibling, a sister. Beth. Parents deceased as of 2004. Sister remains only relative on file. As far as Holden—current residence? Unknown. Current employer, unknown. Credit report, cell phone record, driver's license, current anything …? Other than the location of his body which is at the morgue—all unknown." She pulled out a solitary piece of paper and dangled it in the air. "Never has so little been produced for so large a price."

"So we've got nothing." Dammit! Quinn blew out a harsh breath. One more dead end.

"Would I have come all the way up here if I had nothing?" Susie asked in a way that said she'd expected exactly that comment. "Here's why you all pay me the big bucks. All this 'unknown' on Mr. Tomkin is effective only since 2006. Prior to that—"

"There has to be a juvie file on this guy," Wallace jumped in.

"Exactly. Not sure it'll do you any good, though," Susie said. "Record's been sealed. Restricted even. I attempted to gain access but was blocked. In a way, I might add, I've never been blocked before. Whatever info is in that file, someone locked it down, but long before any of us joined the force. Perhaps someone with a lot more pull than me." She eyed Quinn. "If you think it's that important, you might know someone who can help get you access. Or," she pulled out another piece of paper and handed it to Quinn, "you could come at Holden in an entirely different way. The sister. Beth Tomkin."

"You know where she is?"

"No. But I know where she was. Right up until 2006. Her whereabouts mirror that of her brother's. Beginning with the day they were born."

"Son of a bitch." Quinn scanned the printout and looked up at his partner.

"All this time I was looking for a couple in relation to Merle's attackers," Wallace said. "Never crossed my mind we should be searching for siblings."

"Not just siblings," Susie said with a smirk of satisfaction. "Twins."

There were only few certainties in life for Riley, one of which was that stepping into Cassia Davis's second-floor apartment in Temple House resulted in sensory overload. Not just tonight, Riley thought as she set her bag on the table by the door. Not just on special occasions or during the festivities of the holidays. But every single time.

Elliot, Cass's golden retriever, let out a muted woof and beelined right for them, anxious for his welcome pets and "good boy" comments. Laurel and Riley crouched to give the animal a deep fur scrub welcome in exchange for wet, friendly kisses.

Once sated, Elliot huffed and walked off, and took up sentry duty at the end of the counter from where food would no doubt fall.

Hard to believe the space was generally designed with the same layout as Riley's, but where Riley and Moxie had their separate bedroom suites and cordoned off areas, Cass had downsized the personal bedroom and bath to one corner of the dwelling and left the rest, with the exception of a guest bath by the front door, open.

No walls. No barriers. Nothing to hide behind or walk around other than meticulously placed furniture. The leaded high-arching windows had been fitted with custom light-blocking shades that engaged with the flip of a switch. A switch that had already been flipped and left the majority of lighting to come from the endless strings of Christmas lights and not one, but two giant silver, fiber-optic trees bookending the galley style kitchen.

"How does it feel homey?" Riley asked herself for the millionth time. So much metal and sharp angles and coldness, and yet, because it was Cass, she found comfort and welcome in every inch.

"Because it's Cass," Laurel echoed her thoughts.

Ruthlessly segmented areas unfolded in front of her. Kitchen, check. Seating area with drop-down big-screen viewing arena, check. Virtual classroom instructor's office filled with the latest lighting and microphone equipment, double check. Computer workstation that could have easily landed the space shuttle? White boards covered with scientific hieroglyphics? Countertop filled with equipment suitable for a research lab? Check, check, check.

"It's like she's Tony Stark and Professor X's love child."

"Who's to say she isn't?" Laurel slid the metal farmhouse door closed behind them.

"Don't lock it!" Cass called all the way from the kitchen. "Nox is on their way back. I sent them out for one of those double chocolate fudge cakes from Pervis Bakery."

"Damn," Mabel groaned as she paused cutting up what looked like a produce stand worth of vegetables. "And I thought we were eating healthy."

"We would have been if you'd let me bring over a pot of that vegetarian chili I made today," Sutton all but sang, even as she popped a corn chip in her mouth.

"After the week we've had—" Mabel pouted.

"It's only Wednesday," Laurel reminded her.

"Yes, I know." Mabel popped a carrot in her mouth, then tossed one to Elliot who jumped up and gobbled it down. "Your point?"

And just like that, the bees swarming in Riley's system calmed. She was safe here. Probably safer than she was anywhere in the world. But beyond that, nothing brought her more peace and solace than her friends.

Except maybe … she couldn't have dislodged the sudden thought of Quinn Burton with a mental crowbar. How was it possible after only a few days he felt as if he'd always been a part of her life? How was it possible that Quinn, a cop no less, fit? Not just into her bed.

But into her life?

Her cell phone vibrated and she pulled it out of her back jeans pocket, checking the screen. "Dammit." She declined the call—and the tip that would have gotten a coveted photo of mega-mogul and starlet Clarice Prince hooking up with her on-again—mostly off-again—ex.

It was on the tip of her tongue to complain about how much business this situation she found herself in was costing her, but some things—things that could, peripherally at least, involve her aunt—were more important that taking pictures of people just living their lives.

"Everything okay?" Laurel asked quietly from behind her.

"Yeah." Riley shoved her phone back into her pocket along with any building resentment. Until she got to the bottom of things, until the whole creepy death photos issue was resolved, work was going to have to come second. Good thing she'd socked a good amount of cash into savings for a rainy day because it was getting ready to dump buckets on her head. "Yeah, everything's fine," she assured her friend.

"I don't understand why your assistant doesn't just move in, Cassia." Sutton, one hand filled with additional chips observed as she tucked into the corner of one of the two extra-cushiony curving sofas. "Probably save them a small fortune in rent. If they aren't here for work, they're here for some gaming something-or-other."

"They're called online tournaments," Cass said. "And they like having their own space. As do I. It's taco night, by the way."

"With margaritas? Hot damn." Laurel slapped her hands together and rubbed. "I'm in."

"Blender's over there. Have at it." Cass washed her hands and grabbed a towel, made her way over to Riley and drew her aside. Short in stature, petite in features, and enormous in intellect, Cassia Davis could go from genius criminalistics professor to group caretaker in the blink of her doe-brown eyes. Looking at her, no one could guess her terrifying past.

Or that she hadn't stepped foot out of Temple House's front door in more than three years.

"You changed your hair color again." Riley reached out and caught the dark auburn strands in her hair. "I like it. You glow."

"Tis the season." Cass said. "You doing okay? Sorry I didn't stop by after …" She frowned, as if uncertain how to parse her words.

"I'm the one who owes you an apology." Riley touched her friend's arm as guilt scrambled into her chest. "We let a maniac into the building which means I broke my promise that you'd always be safe here. That you'd always *feel* safe."

"Don't worry about it." But her tone belied the words. She was spooked. But she was fighting it. And that, Riley reminded herself, was one of the many reasons she adored Cassia Davis.

"I screwed up," Riley added. "I own up when I do. But you don't have to worry about that guy coming back." Riley raised her voice so everyone heard. "He's dead."

"What?" Sutton spun around on the sofa. "Basement Boy's gone? How?"

Cass closed her eyes and appeared to breathe easier. Riley reached down and squeezed her friend's trembling hand.

"The jumper off the overpass." Laurel poured copious amounts of lime juice and tequila into an industrial blender. "More details to come, I'm sure. But in the meantime, we've taken steps to make sure nothing like what happened to you in the basement can ever happen again in Temple House."

"What—?" Riley started to ask.

"The four of us took a vote to install a new security system," Cass said. "Or did you think our new building manager came equipped with one?"

"I bet he's equipped with a lot of things," Sutton then went wide-eyed with horror. "I said that out loud, didn't I? Oh, my God."

"Let me guess," Mabel teased. "Illicit thoughts about our new building manager?"

"What?" Sutton looked horrified. A bit too horrified. "No, of course not." But her cheeks still went chili pepper red. "It's finally happened. My filter's gone. I've turned into Riley."

"Oh! Did you spend the afternoon in bed with Detective Burton, too? Popular guy." Laurel only grinned at Riley's glare. "Oh, come on. Like they weren't going to find out?"

"Soundproof walls don't negate airflow through the vents," Cass reminded them. "Or so I was told. Ah, that's Nox." She hurried off to answer the knock on the door.

"You slept with Detective Sexy Pants?" Sutton's eyebrows arched so high they nearly leapt off her face. "And?"

"Stop calling him that. And what do you mean *and*?" Riley asked. "As far as I know, sex works the same as it always has."

"Does it?" Sutton looked confused. "I'm going to need proof."

"It really has been a long time for you, hasn't it?" Laurel's mock sympathy earned her a perfectly aimed corn chip in the face. "How mature." Elliot raced over to snap up the chip off the floor.

"On a scale of one to ten—" Mabel pressed Riley.

"Since we have completely veered off the topic at hand …" Riley was not ready for a group share regarding her suddenly vigorous—and more than satisfying—sex life. "What does this security system require and entail?"

"It passes the Cass test," Sutton informed her. "That was all I needed to know. That and the camera feeds filter in through those two monitors right over there." Sutton pointed to the two new—or at least new since Riley had last been to Cass's—large computer screens in the far corner of the room. Sure enough, the screens were siphoning through eight different camera feeds at a time. "No one's getting in this place without being looped in on film that caches into the system for … how long?"

"Stays retrievable via remote access for six weeks," Mabel said with more than a bit of "I actually understand this" attitude. "After that it backs up to a drive on a local server until it's deleted."

Riley's stomach dropped all the way to the floor. "How much—"

Laurel hit the blender and let it rip at top speed.

"Nothing," Cassia yelled over the racket as she slammed the door shut, slid the four bolts into place and grabbed one of the reusable grocery bags from Nox. "It costs you nothing. I've taken care of it. It's an extension of my personal security."

"Translation," Sutton leaned over and half-shouted, "She found a way to make it a tax write-off so you're off the hook."

"My accountant self didn't hear that!" Mabel called after the blender went silent.

"Ears like a bat, I swear," Sutton said. "The building improvements should get you a discount on your insurance. Look into it."

"I'll add that to my list. Hey, Nox." Feeling restless, Riley got back up and happily lifted the turquoise cake box out of their hands. "How was your trip back east to visit your folks?"

"Long," Nox said. "Endlessly, excruciatingly long." They tucked their pixie-short hair behind ears accented with a painful collection of small silver rings. "Took my moms all of fifteen minutes before they were trying to take me shopping for new clothes."

"Instead, they got a new tattoo," Cass grinned and headed back to the kitchen.

"Yeah?" Riley said.

"Yeah." Nox started to hike up their shirt.

"No!" Cass shouted when Nox grabbed the hem of their metal death t-shirt. "Not for public viewing."

"It's like I'm back with my parents," Nox teased as they emptied their cargo pants of their cell and wallet, set them on the edge of the kitchen counter. "Mmmm. Tacos and margaritas. If I never see a block of tofu again it'll be too soon."

Riley carried the cake into the kitchen and stashed it in the fridge. When she turned, Nox and Cass had their heads together, whispering.

"Have you two started to mind meld?" Riley accused.

"I think you mean hive-minding and no, we haven't," Cass said. "Not yet anyway."

"I was just asking her if she showed you the board yet," Nox said with such caution, the hair on the back of Riley's neck prickled.

"What board?" Laurel asked before Riley got the chance.

Sutton got up off the sofa and Mabel stopped cutting, reaching for a towel for her hands. "What's this about?"

"I didn't think you'd want to get into this before dinner." Cass tossed an irritated glare at her assistant.

"Because it's more of a dessert presentation?" Nox argued. "Cass, this is potentially—"

"Didn't want to get into what?" Mabel demanded. "This has to do with what happened in the basement, doesn't it?"

Cass turned to Riley. "Do you want to tell them? Fill 'em up, girls, cause you're gonna need it."

"All right, long story short," Riley said, even as her mind began to spin anew, "I guess I'll start with this canister of film Merle sold me a little ways back." Once she started, the events of the past few days spilled out, right up to and including Moxie retreating to her bedroom for the rest of the evening. By the time she was finished, Laurel was pouring the last of the blender's contents into Mabel's glass. "This thing has taken on a life of its own," Riley admitted. "And I probably shouldn't be telling you all any of this. God only knows what it's all leading to." Or what she was exposing them to.

"Somewhere big if it involves the police commissioner and a possible wrongful conviction," Mabel said.

"Not just somewhere big," Laurel said. "Somewhere dangerous. I warned Riley about this before, and I'll warn you all about it now. Melanie Dennings's murder sliced through this city like a plastic surgeon's scalpel. From that party she attended right through to Samuels cutting a deal, we were saturated with it. I don't relish being party to bringing all that up again."

"Yeah, well, I think it's too late for that." Cass eyed Nox. "Might as well show them what we discovered."

"Well, it was Cass's theory that gave us a jumping-off place," Nox said and motioned them all to follow. They stopped in front of the bank of computers and trio of office-sized white boards. "Keeping in mind that the Dennings's case is more than twenty-five years old. The internet wasn't anything near what it is today, so we went digging into old newspaper archives and public records that have since been digitized. Seriously old school," Nox said with a bit of grump in her voice. "Someone didn't think hacking into the police database for the Dennings file was appropriate."

"Yet," Cass said. "I said yet. Riley, Joyce DePalma's banking records are a puzzle unto themselves. She's getting money from somewhere or someone we can't identify at this time."

"But I will," Nox announced. "I've got something running on that as we speak."

"But our initial findings into Joyce's accounts brought up some interesting connections," Cass said. "Between Joyce and Melanie Dennings."

"What kind of connections?" Laurel definitely had her lawyer hat on.

"Weird ones," Cass said.

"I wrote an algorithm for an online search," Nox announced. "Nothing too fancy. Just a database search of online information using certain keywords and phrases that popped up, both in regard to Melanie and Joyce DePalma. Things like disappearances, their physical descriptions, ages, addresses, even any recent appointments or activities they may have participated in. Names, businesses, dates. We threw everything we could think of into it. Even now, after what

Riley just told us, I can think of more to add to refine the search and get us even more data."

"You wrote a program that searched all of the internet," Sutton commented. "Today?"

"Yeah." Nox shrugged. "Like I said, nothing fancy and it's still running. But what we found so far—"

"What did you find?" Riley asked, dread clawing its way through her chest.

"Not *what,* Riley." Cass spun the first white board, then the second, then the third. *"Who."*

# CHAPTER THIRTEEN

QUINN stared down at his cell phone and waited for Riley's information to land.

He'd heard what she'd said. He'd heard each and every breathless, nearly whispered word and yet …

And yet, he wasn't entirely sure he'd accepted it.

His hand fisted around his cell until his fingers went numb.

"Hey, so I'm not getting any hits on a Beth Tomkin," Wallace said as he returned from the break room, yet another cup of coffee in his hand. "I'm wondering if maybe the sister was adopted or changed her name or …" His eyes searched Quinn's face. "What's going on?"

"That was Riley. There have been some … developments." There was no other way to describe what she'd told him.

What he was faced with investigating. If he was even allowed to investigate.

Quinn looked at his partner. For the first time, Quinn actually looked at the younger man's face and, removing his reluctance to bond, assessed his ability to trust.

"I have to go." Turning his back on Wallace, Quinn shoved his phone in his pocket, grabbed his jacket, the computer disk, and the framed photo of Joyce DePalma. He touched a hand to his weapon, reverent fingers to his badge, waiting for the surge of doubt that never came. He needed help. Help his partner could give him. Help Riley couldn't provide. No, not help, he told himself.

Quinn needed backup.

"You want in? All the way in?" Quinn asked his partner. "Before you answer, you should know there's a good chance we're stepping into something that'll blow up in our faces. You come with me now, there's no telling how this ends. Our careers might be the least of it. Just so we're clear."

Wallace gave no outward appearance of being dissuaded by Quinn's diatribe as he yanked his own coat off the back of his chair. If it was possible, Wallace matured right before his eyes; the over-eager enthusiasm of a new detective eager to impress his partner vanished beneath the one who had earned Quinn's respect. "I'm clear. Where are we going?"

"Temple House. Grab everything you've printed out or read in the past few days. Shove it in a file and don't let it out of your sight. You've got five minutes."

"I only need three."

Quinn headed to his lieutenant's office. "LT?"

"Burton." Lt. Gibson rose to his feet. "You're onto something."

"Yes, sir. I'm going to need some more cover. Not sure for how long." He hesitated. "If further explanation is needed, you might benefit from a conversation with my father." He'd leave it up to the chief how much information he wanted Gibson to have.

Gibson nodded and glanced out his office window to where Wallace was ready to go. "You bringing Osterman in on this?"

"All the way," he said without hesitation. "I need to. I'll be in touch when I can."

"Don't be too eager on that front if there is danger involved. Do what you have to do, however you have to do it. But you lock this case down ASAP, you hear me, detective? With as little collateral damage as possible."

"Understood." It was definitely understood. Whether it was possible was another question, entirely.

"I'm going to give you the CliffsNotes version," Quinn said once he and Wallace were in his SUV, thankful his vehicle had been cleared of all listening devices when he'd had the spare tire put on it, following the shooting. "We can talk in more detail about it once we've gotten a look at what Riley's got, but for now, here's what's been going on."

He broke it all down into the simplest, most effective pieces, grateful that for once Wallace simply nodded, absorbed, and stayed silent. By the time they reached Temple House, he'd run out of information to impart, save for what he was waiting to spring on Wallace once they got upstairs. He pulled into a space a block away. "Grab a couple of these boxes in the back seat." He indicated the boxes of photographs he and Riley had taken from Joyce DePalma's abandoned storage unit.

"More boxes. Must be a metaphor in here somewhere," Wallace joked as he opened the back door. "Up to Riley's?" He asked as they approached the front door.

"No, second floor. Riley wants to keep all of this away from her aunt as much as possible." Considering how many brick walls he was running into on other aspects of the case, he was beginning to think a conversation with Moxie was one way to earn a breakthrough. But he'd be saving that as his nuclear option. Riley was as invested in figuring all of this out as he was, but she was also mama-bear protective of her aunt. He had little doubt if it came down to deciding between pursuing a lead and making sure Moxie was insulated, it was a no-brainer choice, as long as it also kept Moxie safe.

Quinn kept his head swiveling as they headed across the street. Nothing out of the ordinary. No odd cars that seemed out of place. A few neighborhood locals meandering around the area, but nothing suspicious. But that didn't stop the hair on his arms from standing up, as if someone was watching their every move.

He set the boxes down to key in Riley's apartment code, but he spotted Blake behind the lobby bar rearranging the bottles. Quinn knocked and when he and Wallace stepped inside, made the introductions. "Blake Redford, this is my partner, Detective Wally Osterman."

"Good to meet you," Blake said. "Riley called down, said to give him as much access around the place as necessary. You want help with those?"

"No, we've got them. Thanks. New system up and running?" Quinn asked.

"Direct feed into Cass's system on the second floor. Backup filters into one I set up in my apartment down here." He gestured to the back of the lobby across from the basement door. "Also called a former military buddy of mine. He's going to come out next week and give the place a once over, see if there's anything else we should consider."

Even as Quinn nodded and stepped into the elevator, he hoped that wouldn't be necessary. His plan was to get this case uncovered, resolved, and locked up tight before next week rolled around.

"Nice of Riley to hire a bodyguard for the building," Wallace commented when the elevator door shut. "I anticipate he'll intimidate all living things in a ten-mile radius quite easily."

"I certainly hope so."

The idea that Moxie and Riley, in theory, would be safer eased his mind. A bit.

"FYI, the only thing that popped up on my check on Redford was personal. Lost his wife and six-year-old son in a fire back in Chicago, a few years ago."

"Shit." So the vibes he'd been reading off Redford had nothing to do with criminal activity and everything to do with grief. His radar must need serious tweaking. "That's rough. Accidental?"

"Open to interpretation, but how I read it? Negligence. The house his wife bought while he was on assignment had faulty wiring. Investigation after the fact supposed that the pre-purchase inspectors either missed it or were paid to overlook it. Insurance company sued the city over the report, city settled and, well .... I'd imagine being handed a check to cover the loss of your family a pretty harsh return to the United States, not to mention reality."

It also explained the man's obsessive attention to detail when it came to protecting the tenants of Temple House.

"Hey, Wallace?"

"Yeah?"

"I don't relish the idea of spending tonight in the elevator with you. You want to hit the button for the second floor?"

"Oh. Right. Sorry." Wallace laughed. "I'm still giddy over having earned your trust."

*Lord, let this not've been a mistake.*

Riley was waiting for them outside apartment 2A. "Hey." She smiled when she saw him, a gesture that had his heart doing an odd and inconvenient jump, but the warmth didn't come close to reaching her eyes. "Wasn't sure how long you'd be."

"You called. I'm here. Brought Sundance along with me." Quinn turned to his partner when Wallace opened his mouth. "I swear, if you ask me who that is I'm going to kick you in the—"

"No need to finish that threat, Butch." Wallace practically beamed and that youthful face of his shone brightly once more. "Okay to go on in, Riley?"

"Yeah, sure. Oh, just … tread carefully. Cass doesn't like strangers in her apartment. She's making an exception for you," she told Wallace, then looked at Quinn. "You get in because you're sleeping with me. And because you passed her very thorough background check."

"I'm just going to pretend I'm deaf for the foreseeable future," Wallace said as Riley leaned back and knocked on the door in a staccato pattern.

"Carefully, Wallace," Riley warned, "I mean it. That's her sanctum sanctorum. Do not take that lightly. And don't make us regret this."

The door popped open and Laurel, wearing an expression Quinn could only describe as skeptical, stepped back to let him them. "Hurry up," she told them before she closed the door. "Dinner's still waiting."

"It's been waiting for almost two hours. Tacos," Riley told Quinn. "We didn't exactly have much of an appetite after Cass's big reveal."

Quinn set the boxes down, and before he even faced her, found his arms filled with Riley.

He folded her into him, held her close and, bending his head over hers, reveled in the very idea she felt secure enough with him to seek comfort. He closed his eyes, inhaled that orange blossom scent that sent inappropriate images surging through his head. "Rough night?"

"They found twenty-three of them." Her voice was muffled against his shirt and jacket, but she clung to him, fingers tensing and pulsing as if incapable of making a fist. "Twenty-three women who are just gone. It's as if they stepped off the edge of the world. What the hell did I stumble on to, Quinn? How did one roll of film bring us here?"

"We're going to find out." He pressed his lips into her hair. "Thank you for calling me."

"It irritates me that it's the first thing I thought to do when I saw those pictures. All those faces. I wanted you with me, because I knew you'd feel it too. They need us, Quinn. Those women need someone to find them." She stepped back, but continued to hold on to him. Even as she lifted hopeless eyes to his. "Promise me—"

"I promise."

"You don't know what—"

He caught her face in his hands and met her gaze. "I promise we will find the answers to all of this. Together." He pressed his mouth to hers, waiting until her lips softened and she let him in. Finally, he pulled back. "Did you say tacos?"

"Did you seriously stop kissing me to ask about food?"

He shrugged, delighting in the irritation in her voice. An irritated Riley was a predictable Riley. Was a perfect Riley. Perfect for him, at least. "What can I say? I'm hungry."

"Should have had you stop by my place for more tequila. We've almost cleaned Cass out. Oh, about Cass." She grabbed his arm when he bent to retrieve the boxes. "I meant what I said, warning-wise, earlier. She's ... well, there's a lot of history behind her. It's not my story to share. Just keep in mind there's a reason behind her visual madness and her lockdown behavior."

"I've been a cop in Los Angeles for more than ten years, Riley. I've seen it all." He followed her into the apartment that at first glance reminded him of Riley's. "Then again, maybe I haven't."

The golden retriever from the holiday party in the lobby approached instantly, giving Quinn a good sniff of approval before he plopped his butt down by the open door, tail banging against the hardwood floor.

"He won't move from there as long as the door's open." Riley pushed Quinn further inside and slid the metal door shut. Elliot chuffed, sniffed, and walked past them back into the apartment. Quinn followed, somewhat transfixed by what greeted him.

"Did I just step through some kind of sci-fi portal?" He couldn't begin to process the bells-and-whistle technology arranged in various spaces around the room.

"Welcome Detective Se .... I mean, welcome, Quinn." Laurel motioned for him to set the boxes down on the other side of the tables filled with computer monitors. "Just a few quick introductions. Over there on the sofa with Elliot-the-attention-seeking-hound is Sutton O'Hara."

"Right." He nodded at the woman whose blonde highlights caught against the Technicolor Christmas lights glowing around the room. "You're the dietitian and personal chef."

"Nice to meet you, DSP." She toasted him with a half-filled margarita glass and a teasing glint in her light-brown eyes. "We haven't heard nearly enough about you."

"I'd tell her to stop, but you're the first man any of us have dated in more than a year, so consider yourself the sacrificial lamb," Riley told him.

"Just don't tell Wallace about that nickname," Quinn murmured with quiet desperation. "I am begging you."

Her grin informed him he'd have to work to earn that request.

"I'm Mabel Reynolds."

"Of course." Quinn held out his hand to the familiar blonde. "We almost met the other evening when you were going out. Your daughter, Keeley, is delightful."

"Delightful? Really? Not trouble?" Mabel blinked her blue eyes and shook her head. "Welcome to ... whatever the hell this is."

"Mabel ..." Riley's voice held a level of concern he'd only ever heard her use with Moxie.

"I'm fine. Or not." Mabel clutched at the half-heart pendant around her neck. "Yeah, let's go with not. Nothing like discovering twenty-three missing and presumed dead girls and women to make you feel alive," she said, tears shining in her eyes. "You know what? I think I'm going to head home." She shoved her glass into Riley's hand. "I have a sudden urge to hug my delightful daughter into oblivion and fill her full of chocolate. Just tell everyone I—" When she shook her head again, two tears plopped onto her cheeks. "Sorry. I need to go."

"Mabel, don't—"

Quinn caught Riley's arm as Mabel grabbed her things and left. "Let her go, Riley."

"You don't understand—"

"She lost someone." He didn't need years of experience as a cop to see that. Or to feel it. "And considering what she does in her spare time, this probably hit way too close for her. She needs to process what's over there on that board and she needs to do it on her own. She'll come back," he said quietly and pulled her close again. "When she needs you, she'll come back."

"Detective Burton."

"Yes." He turned to the woman who spoke and, felt Riley's arms tighten around his waist. This must be Cassia Davis. The caution on her face was couched only with uncertainty and a good case of not-so-hidden nerves. Her hands flexed at her sides, a coping mechanism he recognized from his post-traumatic stress informational seminars. "Ms. Davis. I appreciate you opening your home to us. To me and Wallace." He didn't offer his hand, and purposely kept his distance. "I hope we won't intrude on you for very long."

"I appreciate that, detective."

Something in her tone added to the mystery of the woman. But Riley was right: Cass's story was Cass's to tell. It was Quinn's job to earn the right to hear that story firsthand, not go poking around in something that wasn't his business.

"Your partner is already working with Nox over here," Cass said. "Nox?"

Cass motioned Quinn over to computer central where Cass's assistant was busy clicking keys and reading multiple screens. But all that faded into the background when he saw the boards. "Jesus," he whispered as he released Riley and stared at the newly printed faces looking back at him. "What the hell did you uncover?"

"Someone's well-kept secrets I'm guessing," Wallace said from where he stood over the person named Nox's shoulder. "She's good. Nox, I mean," he clarified. "The LAPD could use a computer whiz like her."

"They," Riley corrected him. "Nox's pronoun is they."

"Huh?" Wallace blinked, then, looking at Nox, went wide-eyed and his cheeks flushed. "Oh, geez. I'm sorry. I shouldn't have assumed—"

"You're cool." Nox lifted one hand off the keyboard and offered a fist bump. "Know better, do better. Speaking of—I've plugged in a few more data points after talking with Riley. I've got some new names to play around with."

Compartmentalizing, Quinn turned away from the board as Nox printed out a new list off their screen. "More missing women?"

"No. Not yet anyway." Nox snatched the multiple pages of paper out of the printer and set the stack on the desk. "Suspects."

"Give me a minute?"

With midnight looming and his energy level on empty, Quinn left Riley by the door with Elliot and approached Cass in the kitchen. With Laurel and Sutton already back in their apartments, only Nox remained behind, continuously tap-tap-tapping on their keyboard and uttering frequent cries of triumph, frequently followed by more tapping, then multiple groans of frustration.

"How good are they?" He asked Cass as she finished drying the dinner dishes.

"Be clear with what you're asking, detective." Cass set a stack of forks in the drawer. "Specifics lead to the most comprehensive answers."

Quinn ducked his head and smiled. He liked this woman. While it was clear Cass had some anxiety issues, and that she didn't like having one, let alone two unfamiliar men in her apartment, she was pushing herself through the situation because she believed it necessary to do so. "You're a scientist. An exceptional one from what I've witnessed."

"Riley's right. You are a charmer."

"I haven't known her long," Quinn observed. "But I can't imagine Riley has ever said that."

Cass shrugged. "Not in so many words. She'd see blatant charm as a flaw, not an appealing characteristic. That doesn't mean you aren't above using the talent to get what you want. So what do you want, detective?"

"I came across something that might be a missing piece to what we're looking for." While he continued to debate his options where the disk from the frame was concerned, after watching Cass and Nox work, he'd landed on a decision where the floral delivery card was concerned. "If it is, I'm fairly certain there will be triggers lurking for when people go searching for it. Cyber traps, for want of a better term. If there's such a thing as that?"

"There is. Given what we've started to uncover, I'd venture to say you're right, because of the sheer amount of crime clearly being covered up." Cass nodded. "You don't want any search of whatever you have to alert anyone it's being looked for."

"They're—"

"They?" Cass's brow arched.

"Not pronoun specific. They as in multiple individuals. I believe we aren't looking for one person. Someone hired Holden Tomkin to get that film back by any means necessary. Maybe he decided suicide-by-cop was easier than admitting he'd failed. Maybe he did it because he believed he wouldn't live long enough in custody to tell what he knew." Or maybe the man had been batshit crazy and pretty much begging cops to shoot him seemed like a good idea at the time. They'd never know.

"That is a lot of maybes, detective," Cass observed. "With no scientific basis for backing any of them up."

"We know that Dean Samuels was involved in Melanie Dennings's murder, whether intentionally or not. Even if the newspaper date on the photo is confirmation he likely wasn't the one to do the actual deed. We know that someone got him transferred out of the California Prison System or maybe changed his identity to hide him in the system. Either implies help from at least one other person higher up in the procedural food chain." He grimaced. "But, testing that theory in the open could very well expose more than we want it to," Quinn said. "Would you agree that thirteen years in a profession allows me some leeway in convincing you my gut feelings are worth listening to?"

"You're talking about instinct. Honed instinct," Cass said. "Yes. Perhaps some leeway."

"Tomkin wasn't hired by one individual. Riley told me what he said in the basement. He only ever said they. Nox's pronoun aside," he said quickly when she started to speak, "I'm going to take Riley's recollection at face value and posit Tomkin was referring not to one person pulling his strings, but to a group. And groups, at times, use symbols to represent themselves. Religions for example, have their own symbols. The military, Vikings, The Masons …"

"In recent years, hate groups in particular have embraced semiotics, even perverted them to their cause," Cass agreed, folding her arms over her chest. "Intriguing. Go on."

"Instinct tells me this is something." He showed pulled out his phone and handed it to her, open to the picture he'd taken of the card. "There's power in imagery. No message. No signature. Just this flower image. The sight of those red lilies were enough to send Joyce into full-blown panic mode." He closed his phone again. "From what I saw with Moxie, the mere mention of a red lily before I arrived affected her the same way." It was all he could do not to ask Moxie about her reaction, but right now wasn't the time to alienate Riley by pressing her great aunt for potentially emotionally damaging information. "I want to know what this image is. Beyond what it looks like. I want to know what it means, who it represents—and what 'they' are. I want to know everything possible.

"What I *don't* want," he added in a lower register. "Is for *anyone* to know we're looking at it just yet. Wallace and I are too visible to research this without alerting anyone. But from what I saw tonight—"

"Nox is good enough to not get caught. Even on the dark web." Cass retrieved her own phone from the side counter and asked him to bring up the photo again. She took a picture of his picture. "Best we keep things clean with no digital footprint between us," she said. "Nox is still focused on running the data sweep for possible victims and suspects. But I'll get them on it as soon as I see they're focused enough not to make a mistake with this."

"You want my number?"

"Detective, please." Cass smiled the smile of the superior. "I'll let you know when we've got something."

"Appreciate your help with all this, Ms. Davis."

"Dr. Davis," she corrected, then, for the first time, her face relaxed and her eyes softened. "But you can call me Cass, Quinn."

Feeling as if he'd just successfully leaped a giant hurdle, he headed out, letting Riley take the lead until he met up with Wallace out in the hall.

"I've got an idea," his partner said once the door to Cass's apartment was closed. "I recognize some of the names on this list from my time in Vice. I want to touch base with my old partner, see if anything bumps with them."

Doubt circled like a hungry shark. He shook his head. "I don't know—"

"You trusted me enough to bring me with you tonight." Wallace's tone was far more determined than Quinn had heard before. "Trust me with this. I know what you suspect we're dealing with. That we need to stay under the radar. My old partner? She lost her college roommate to a repeat sex offender. She's good people, Quinn. She can keep her mouth shut."

Riley's hand on his arm felt like a gentle, encouraging touch. "Okay. Just be careful, okay? Don't talk to anyone about any of this if you don't trust them with your life. Or with mine."

Wallace nodded. "I'll grab an Uber back to the station for my car and I'll be in touch after I go through my list. Night."

"Good night, Wallace," Riley called as he headed down the stairs. She looked at Quinn, then the elevator and sighed. "I had the passing thought of taking advantage of you in the elevator, but I don't think I'm up to it this evening."

"I don't blame you." He kissed her, lingering for longer than planned. "You're a good friend, Riley Temple."

"You think?" She scoffed. "Sure doesn't feel like it. A good friend wouldn't drop their best friends into the middle of a potential serial-killer case."

Serial killers, plural, Quinn almost corrected. Melanie Dennings's case was more than two decades old. Some of those women had gone missing before Melanie had even been born. Others? As recently as two months ago. As capable as Quinn believed older people were, he found it hard to believe a serial killer could have been working the Los Angeles and Hollywood area without someone noticing before now. More evidence to add to his group theory. His generational theory.

"You've got everyone in one place, where they're protected. More protected than they were just a few days ago." He slipped his arms around her waist. "If they didn't want to be involved, they'd have left before Wallace and I arrived. Instead, they stayed. And their input is going to help us get to the bottom of all of this."

"Unless it's a bottomless pit of despair and we'll keep falling for the rest of our lives."

He couldn't help it. He laughed a sad laugh that tugged a small smile out of her. "I think someone needs a nap. Come on—I'll walk you to your door."

They forewent the elevator and took the stairs, but when they reached the landing and her door, she refused to relinquish her hold on him. "I don't want you to go."

It was what he'd wanted to hear; what he'd hoped to hear. But now that he did, he felt something akin to a tectonic shift in their relationship. "I'm going to do something I've never done before and say something I probably shouldn't say."

"I swear to God if you propose—"

He touched a finger to her open lips, amused—and intrigued—that her thoughts had taken her there. "I care about you, Riley. More than probably either of us are comfortable with at the moment. I want more than just sex. I want a shot at something real." A week ago—hell, a few days ago—he couldn't have fathomed uttering these words to anyone, let alone Riley Temple. "If I stay, I want it to be the start of something. Not because I'm a distraction for whatever thoughts you can't silence in your head."

She frowned. "How did you—?"

"How did I know that's what this afternoon was about? Because it was for me, too." He kissed her again "But now I want more. You take me in there, that's what you're agreeing to. Something more."

"You mean a relationship." She said the word as if tasting it, testing it. When she lifted her gaze, he couldn't for the life of him identify her expression. "You want to be in a relationship. With me." Her disbelief was almost enchanting. "Me, as in Riley Temple."

"Yes."

"Oh, you poor, deluded, sexy-butt detective." She shook her head. "You don't have any idea what you're getting in line for."

"Maybe. Maybe not." But he definitely wanted to get on the ride.

"Far be it from me to stop a man from making a huge mistake with his life." She sighed. "All right. What the hell. I haven't done that relationship thing in a while. Might as well give it another shot."

"Even if I am a cop?" he challenged.

She smiled. "Maybe because you are."

*She couldn't breathe.*

*Somewhere, in the last endless minutes she couldn't recall, she'd lost the ability to draw air into her lungs. Instead, water bubbled and gurgled and lapped at her face with stinging, frigid promise.*

*She opened her mouth, ordered her lungs to expand, to draw in air, but nothing happened.*

*Gasping, choking, she tried to move, but her arms, her legs, even her head wouldn't obey. She lay there. Frozen. On a slab of freezing concrete as the water climbed higher.*

*She sobbed against the horrifying conclusion that this was the end. No one was coming for her. No one was going to rescue her from that which threatened to claim her.*

*She was, at the end, all alone.*

"Riley. Riley—wake up."

Riley's eyes snapped open. She shot up in bed, dragging in a throat-scorching rasp of breath that had her clutching at her chest.

"You okay?" Quinn's voice both soothed and triggered her as he sat up and slid his arms around her, half pulling her into his lap.

"What the fuck was that?" She touched tentative fingers to her face, drew away tears and clenched her fist. "Seriously, what the hell?!"

"An overactive imagination attempting to purge some pretty horrific information and visuals."

"Psychoanalysis in bed. Awesome." She struggled to break free of him, to scramble out of bed and escape that cold, clammy sensation clinging to her damp skin. "Let go of me, Quinn."

"No." He lifted a hand, caught her chin and turned her face to his. He pressed his lips to her cheek. Her nose. Her lips. Again. Longer this time, until she whimpered and her body went limp in his hold. "There you go." He stroked his other hand down her arm, turned her and deepened the kiss. "Better now?" he murmured.

"No. Not enough." She moved over him, kicking free of the sheets and, straddling his hips, reached down and pulled her sleep shirt over her head. "Wear me out, detective." She bent over and nipped at his chin as his hands smoothed down her naked flesh, cupped her hips in his palms.

"I'm not exactly in a position to do much of anything at the moment." His grin made her laugh, which broke the final fragments of the nightmare into smoke.

She reached behind her, found him and, with fingers as nimble as they were determined, coaxed him into hardness with barely a touch. He swore, released his hold on her and fumbled for the nightstand drawer. When she leaned over to help, her hair draped around them like a curtain. Their hands met over the condom box. "Whoever opens it first gets to put it on," she whispered into his ear.

He yanked his hand back, held them both up for a moment as she shifted enough to retrieve one of the packets and turn on the light. "I want to see you," she told him. "I want to see your face when you slip inside of me."

"You don't get that condom on me soon, it'll be too late."

She slid down, her moisture leaving a trail of arousal on his skin as she positioned herself before him, locking her gaze on him as she ripped the packet open.

"You are an evil creature," he groaned as she rolled the condom onto his cock. "I may never let you sleep through the night again."

In the past, with other men, the implication of forever would have sent her running out of the room. Certainly scrambling out of the bed. But hearing it from this man, at this moment, something inside of her broke open.

She took hold of his hands, slid her fingers through his and raised them up as she moved once more, forward, open. And down.

His back arched as she lowered herself, filling herself with his hard strength. Her nipples went so hard they ached, begging for attention even as she clasped his hands and, keeping their gazes locked, she rose. And rode.

Slow at first. So slow she made her entire body ache for him. It wasn't enough, never enough, but as she moved faster, the buildup began, surging from the very core of her soul to the very center of her being. His eyes glowed and danced with arousal, a fleeting smile of marvel on his face as his body tensed beneath her. Before he came, he tugged one hand free.

"Come with me." It only took one touch. One small, quick brush of his finger over her clit that sent them into rapture, their bodies trembling against one another before she, still holding him inside of her, collapsed on top of him.

It seemed an age before their breathing eased. Before either of them could speak.

"Nightmare gone?"

"I think my bones are gone." She lifted herself off of him, reached to help with the condom, only to have him push her hand away.

"You do that, it'll be round two and, honestly, I need more sleep to work on this case with a sharp mind." He took care of himself, then rolled back to her and drew her into him, curling around her. "Go back to sleep, Riley. No more bad dreams."

"Promise?" she asked with a shiver.

"I promise."

She knew when Quinn drifted off, but as he did so, his hold didn't ease. If anything, his embrace tightened—he pulled her closer. She touched her fingers to his hands, closed her eyes, and with a sleepy smile, joined him.

# CHAPTER FOURTEEN

"DON'T you have a job to get to, detective?"

"In a way, I'm doing it. I'm on special assignment." He released her as she stretched and squirmed out of his hold, then turned over and faced him. He tucked her hair behind her ear, marveling at the morning wonder of her. "How is it you're so pretty first thing in the morning?"

She snorted. "How many margaritas did you have last night?"

"None." He touched her face and thought about how nice it would be to see it first thing every morning, even if—in its own way—that thought was also a little scary. "What do you and Moxie do for Christmas?"

"Christmas?" She shrugged. "Nothing special, really. Sometimes we host a dinner here for tenants who don't have anywhere else to go. A few years, we've gone on a cruise. Oh, the year before my grandfather died, we went to Edinburgh for the holidays. Have you been?"

"To Scotland? No. I've only ever left the country a few times, and none of the trips were particularly memorable. You like to travel then?"

"I do. Someday, I'm going to travel the world taking pictures. Not the usual pictures, but far, out-of-the-way places, showcasing people from all over. Maybe turn it into a book."

"Stalking celebrities not doing it for you anymore?"

"It has its benefits." She touched her hand to his chest, right over his heart. "But if I had a choice, I'd rather not be part of the problems in this town. I'd love to do my own thing and have it be financially viable."

"So do it. Quit the paparazzo stuff and focus on your art."

"Easy for you to say."

But there was something in her voice. Something unexpected and curious.

"What, Riley? What are you thinking?"

"It's stupid." Except her dismissive laugh sounded anything but. "Something Joyce said—something in her eyes, when she asked me to take her picture. I know what I heard isn't what she meant, but ..."

"But?"

"All of the pictures in her room were from the past. Nothing recent. Nothing that shows who she is now. I've always wanted to find a niche, for when agents or curators might come calling or show interest in my work. Youth is everywhere in this town. What if I took an honest look at what it's like to age in Hollywood. Like Joyce. Like Moxie. Why shouldn't we embrace who they've become, rather than obsess over who they were? Hmm ... I wonder." She turned her head, rested her chin on his chest. "Is it you or the sex that has me thinking like this?"

"Can it be both?" He liked the idea of being both anchor and inspiration for her.

"Sure." She pushed up and kissed him, then spun out of bed so fast he didn't have time to grab the sheet. "Share the shower?"

"I thought you'd never—"

"Riley? I've made breakfast." Moxie knocked softly on the bedroom door. "Would you and Quinn care to join me?"

"If we have shower sex before breakfast, I won't be able to look her in the eye," Quinn whispered with a cautious glare at the door.

"Please. She probably invented shower sex. But I get your meaning." She raised her voice. "We'll be out in a few minutes, Moxie! I'll be two minutes." She dashed into the bathroom and closed the door.

It was more like fifteen and when they finally joined Moxie in the kitchen; the simple cheese omelets she'd made them were stone cold. He didn't care in the least, given Moxie had taken the trouble to think of him.

"This looks delicious, Moxie." Quinn took a seat at the kitchen island. "Appreciate it."

"It was the least I could do after last evening's ridiculousness."

Quinn glanced at Riley, who was busy eating. Either she was ignoring the opening Moxie had offered or .... No. She was definitely ignoring it. "You never have to apologize for reacting to things that upset you, Moxie." He accepted a hot cup of coffee with what he hoped was an understanding smile. "Do you mind me asking what—?"

"Yes, she probably does," Riley cut him off and gave him a good kick in the shins. "And if she doesn't, I do."

"Riley, be nice," Moxie chided. "I'd rather you not chase this one away, if you don't mind."

"Yeah, Riley. Be nice." Quinn drank his coffee, trying to understand why Riley was resisting them finding out more about her aunt's reaction. It could be what breaks the case, to help them apprehend the killers earlier, preventing more deaths. *Or it could just put Moxie directly in danger,* the cop part of his brain whispered. He sighed. Now he understood her fear. It was more than just upsetting her aunt—it was about putting her at risk. He would tread carefully. "Tell me something, Moxie. Were you and Joyce DePalma good friends?"

"Dammit, Quinn—"

"Hush, Riley." But even as Moxie said it, her brow furrowed. "Not particularly. She was around when Douglas and Clinton were working together, but—"

"Did they do that a lot? Work together?"

Riley's fork clanked on the counter, but Quinn ignored her irritation. He had questions he wanted answers to.

"Off and on, over the years. More so before Riley was born. Back in my studio years, mostly." She busied herself by wiping off the already-cleaned countertop, raising her other hand to brush it against the back of her neck. The same way she had done the day before.

"That would be in the 1940s and 50s, correct?" He veered off more personal details to prevent Riley from stabbing him with her fork. "That was at the height of studio operations."

"It was definitely a different time. A more controlled time," Moxie confirmed. "Back then, studio representatives kept a pretty close eye on their contracted talent. They created the image for each individual actor or actress, regardless of the truth. The only information that got out about us was what the studio wanted out. There was no internet to reveal the truth."

"And none of those pesky paparazzi lurking in bushes, huh?" Riley attempted to tease.

"There were plenty of those," Moxie argued. "But a lot were also paid by the studios to feed the public what they wanted them to see. They were told where to be, who to expect. What to focus on. Don't get me wrong," Moxie went on, "we were protected as much as we were exploited, and the exploitation was part of the deal. It wasn't all bad, just as it wasn't all good. Everything about Hollywood was very manipulated, back then," Moxie said. "Especially for women."

"It's *still* very manipulated," Riley commented. "Especially against women."

"Spoken like someone standing on the outside looking in," Moxie said. "Forgive us, Quinn. This is a frequent conversation around the house. It's also an argument my niece is incapable of winning, due to her continued involvement in that offensive 'profession' she claims to abhor."

"Look out, she's using the air quotes," Riley muttered.

"You don't like her being a paparazzo?" *Interesting.*

"I think she's far too talented to be wasting her time finding starlets who keep losing their underwear."

"And here we go." Riley polished off her breakfast and carried her dish over to the sink. "For the record, that only happened once, and that young woman knew exactly where the cameras were aimed. She also landed a significant movie roll shortly after, so don't tell me it wasn't planned."

"I wouldn't care to think about it," Moxie huffed. "Thank you very much."

"Oh, come on, Moxie. You cannot tell me you never went commando back in the day."

"Of course I did." Moxie reached for her tea. "Panty lines were the devil's work. One of my costumers told me that." She gave Quinn a wink and a smile. "But I had the good sense not to go climbing out of a limousine when I did so. Decorum. Class. Elegance. That's what we were meant to convey. It was the illusion we were paid for and expected to project. Even women like Joyce DePalma. She might have worked behind the camera, but she maintained the same image the rest of us did. It was just understood: if you work for the studio, they call the shots. End of story."

Riley stood behind Moxie, glaring at Quinn as if silently asking, "Where is all this going?"

"You said Joyce worked behind the camera." Quinn reached behind him into his jacket pocket, pulled out the framed photo of Joyce and set it on the counter. "If that was the case, why would she need a studio portrait taken?"

"Quinn—" Riley stepped forward, but Moxie held up her hand, stopping her great-niece before she could snatch the frame away. "Quinn, she shouldn't have to talk about this if she doesn't want to."

"You're right." Quinn didn't take his eyes off of Moxie. The shock was there; the shock he'd seen the remnants of last night, but there was also grief. Anger. And fear. "Moxie, what was this picture for? What studio?"

Moxie shook her head. Her hand trembled as she lifted her teacup, spilling tea over the edge.

"What?" Quinn pushed.

"Stop it," Riley ordered.

"I can't find any record of a studio with the initials CRL," Quinn said.

"There ..." Moxie cleared her throat, seemed to steel herself as she stood up straight. "It wasn't a studio. That's all I'm going to say." She lifted a hand to the back of her neck, clenched her fist and lowered it slowly to the counter. "And that is the last time you're going to ask me about any of this. Or ask anyone." The tremble in her voice vanished behind the intensity in her eyes. "It's not for you or anyone to know of. It's in the past. It's over and done. No more. Do you hear me, Quinn?" She spun on her great-niece, who looked as surprised as Quinn felt. "Riley? Do you understand?"

"Yes, ma'am," Riley whispered.

"Yes, ma'am," Quinn lied when Moxie turned that penetrating gaze on him. It wasn't the comprehensive answer he'd hoped for, but it was one that eliminated at least one line of inquiry. He'd planted the seed with her; let her know he, that they, were on the hunt for answers. It would have to be enough for now. "I understand."

"Good." Moxie sipped the last of her tea, set her cup down. "Now, if you'll excuse me, I have a script to review. I'm having dinner at Gloria Malfort's this evening. She's hosting a number of us involved with the play. I expect I'll be out late," she added with a knowing look at Riley. "Feel free to make the most of your private time. Sex is a great way to work off a good mad."

Quinn stayed where he was as Moxie retreated back into her rooms and closed the door. The second she was out of earshot, the tension in the kitchen amped up to eye-wincing level. "Riley—"

"Don't!" The warmth and concern in her gaze vanished beneath the heat of anger. "Don't you dare sit there and pretend you didn't just try to browbeat an eighty-year-old woman into giving you answers she didn't want to give."

He couldn't very well deny it. But he was curious. "Did you see it?"

"See what?" She challenged. "Her fear? You bet your ass I did."

"No." Not the fear. "The mark."

She glared at him, crossed her arms over her chest and closed into herself like a turtle seeking protection.

"It's what you were looking for, wasn't it?" he asked. It surprised him, how easily he could read her. How well he understood her after only a few days. "When you were standing behind her. The same mark that Joyce has on her neck? Was it there?"

Riley's jaw clenched.

He carried his dishes to the sink, nudged her aside so he could wash up. "A nonanswer is enough of one for me. She's hurting, Riley. Surely you had to see that."

More silence.

"She may need help. Professional help. If it's connected even slightly—"

"You don't know that."

"The only reason Moxie would warn us off is if she understood how dangerous what we're investigating is. She knows more than we do, Riley—about women being branded by powerful people who are part of some select group, but not part of a specific studio. And while you and I have agreed to work together, I still have a job to do. I'll go wherever the evidence leads me."

"That's what this all comes down to for you, isn't it, *detective?* Your job."

It wasn't so much what she said, but how she said it that set alarm bells to blaring. "My job is part of it, yes. And I know what you're doing. What you're thinking."

"Oh, really?"

It was as clear to him as the sky above Temple House. "You're scared."

"For Moxie? You bet I am."

"I'm not talking about the pictures, or your aunt, or those twenty-three women pinned to a board downstairs." He dried his hands. "I'm talking about us."

"Good Lord." She dropped her forehead into one hand. "Ego, party of one, your table is ready. This conversation doesn't have anything to do with *us*."

"It has everything to do with us. Keep punching, Riley. Punch up, punch down, whatever makes you feel better." He placed his hands on her shoulders and turned her to face him. "I'm not going anywhere."

"Is this part of your job, detective?" Her eyes narrowed. "Handling a source and potential witness by taking her to bed and filling her head so full of you that she can't think straight? Keeping me in line, are you? Doing all you can to close your case, earn your cop wings, and protect your father from the fallout over his role in convicting an innocent man?"

Anger swirled inside of him, like a hot tornado whipping across the plains. He'd goaded her into taking a swipe at him, and she'd lived up to the frustrating promise of Riley Temple in a full-scale emotional panic. It might have been entertaining if her accusation hadn't left a gaping wound across his heart. "Sleeping with you has nothing to do with wanting to control you, Riley."

"Doesn't it?"

"If that was the case, I can assure you, I'd be doing a much better job." He released her, stepped away and slipped Joyce's picture back into his jacket. "I meant what I told you the other day over lunch. Not everyone has an agenda. I'm fully capable of working this case, protecting my father, making sure your aunt is safe, and caring for you, all at the same time."

"Anytime you want to get started on that third task, you let me know." She moved in front of him, blocking him from leaving. "Don't use my family to protect yours, Quinn. Do not. Do it."

It hurt, far more than it should have, that she thought him capable of such a thing. But it begged the question he'd been avoiding the past few days. How far was he willing to go to make sure his father escaped this mess—the impending scandal—unscathed? He had no words—at least none that wouldn't make the situation worse between them.

"I thought you said you weren't going anywhere," she called after him as he headed to the front door.

"As you have reminded me, I have a job to do." He turned, motioned to the thirsty Christmas tree sagging in the corner. "I was trying to find a diplomatic way of telling you this, but that seems unnecessarily polite right now. Stay close to home." He made certain she heard the warning in his voice. "Get that tree set up, embrace whatever holiday cheer you can, commiserate with Cass and Nox, or get drunk with Laurel, but don't step foot out of this building until you hear from me. Holden Tomkin has a sister." He took some comfort in the shock on her face, but it wasn't enough to convince him she heeded his caution. "We're pretty sure she's the other half of the pair who attacked Merle and killed Dudley, and she's still out there. Do us all a favor? Don't make it easy for her to kill you, Riley. I don't think Moxie would appreciate having to plan your funeral. I know I sure as hell wouldn't."

He knew, down to his marrow knew, that a quietly closed door made far more impact than a slammed one. It didn't lessen the disappointment and anger swirling inside of him though. Dammit, he didn't like the way she twisted his head around. Twisted his heart around that snarky, albeit talented, little finger of hers. Who in the universe had he pissed off to have him falling for the most stubborn, irritating, enraging …

Standing out in the hall, he felt the last few days move into a controlled spin around his head. The only way to get beyond all this was to bulldoze his way through it. Once they got out of this case and onto the other side of things, they could take a step back and examine what, if anything, remained between them.

Descending the stairs, he pulled out his phone and called Wallace. "What did your friend from Vice say?" he said in way of greeting.

"Guess I don't have to ask how your evening went," his partner muttered, his voice thick with sleep.

"Hang on a second." Quinn stopped on the second floor, wandered to the side window and looked at the surrounding buildings. "Okay, I'm back." Quinn heard the distinct sound of something being slurped. "Ronnie marked off some of the names on that list as having definite potential as suspects. Others she said we could disregard. I'm creating a culled-down list now. Where are you headed?"

"I'm going to see if I can find out how a prisoner goes missing from a state prison and no one notices for two decades." He had his suspicions, but confirming them was going to take some clever footwork. "Can you give me Nox's number?"

"What makes you think—"

"Wallace," Quinn warned.

"Eesh. Fine. Texting it to you now. Got it?"

Quinn checked his phone. "Yeah."

"Great. I'm going back to sleep. Catch me up later, yeah?"

"Will do." Quinn hung up and immediately texted Nox, asking if they could meet. As he headed back to the stairs, Cass's door popped open and Nox stuck their head out. "How did you—"

"Elliot," Nox explained as the dog nosed his way through the space in the door. "He likes you and he's been parked in front of the door for a few minutes. What's up?"

"Want to take him for walk?" Quinn suggested. "There's a coffee place down the street."

Nox's small eyes narrowed. "What's the catch?"

"No catch." He pulled the computer disk out of his pocket. "I've got another job for you, if you're interested." It went against instinct, running so much evidence through outside sources, but until he had a better handle on what they were dealing with, he preferred to keep the circle of information as tight as possible.

Excitement burned away suspicion. Nox nodded, have him a quick signal to stand by and, a few minutes later, leash in hand, they led Elliot out of the apartment. "Your call, your treat. Let's book."

"Deck the halls with crap and bullshit, Fa-la-la-la-laaa, la-la-la-laaaa." Riley's updated version of the Christmas carol didn't quite live up to holiday expectations, but the handfuls of tinsel she tossed on the now-decorated tree brightened her surly mood. She had the patience of a toddler when it came to decorating and, since it had taken her more than an hour to untangle the lights alone, she was more than ready for her nearly daylong shift as a crabby little elf to be over.

How one man could, within such a short time, insinuate himself into her life in a way that left her following a cop's orders was beyond her. "A better question might be how can one man, even hours later, make me feel like an overboiled teapot."

"That looks absolutely lovely, Riley." Moxie's voice was warm.

"Yeah?" Grateful to hear her endless hours hadn't been for naught, Riley stepped back, plucked an errant piece of tinsel out of her mouth and looked at her aunt. "Wow. Spiffy. Haven't seen that outfit in a while." The emerald-green pantsuit matched Moxie's surprisingly lively eyes. She'd added a bit of holiday-flair glitter in her hair with a floral pin reminiscent of one of those British fascinators that had earned their own social media following. "You feeling better?"

"Better than what?"

Was she being purposely opaque or unknowingly forgetful? "That conversation with Quinn at breakfast. I hope he didn't upset you too much."

"Oh, that." Moxie waved her concern away. "That's just family being family, isn't it? He was concerned and I told him not to be."

"And Quinn strikes you as the kind of man to let something like that go?" Her skepticism clearly didn't land with her aunt.

"He's a man who respects his elders," Moxie said without looking at her now. "As I hope you do. Let it be, Riley. I don't wish to discuss this further."

Dammit! She didn't want to admit Quinn was right about anything, let alone everything, but watching her aunt clearly struggle to put something traumatic into a compartment she couldn't access had her thinking that he was right about something.

"Would you like me to drive you to Gloria's?"

"Ernie is sending a car for me." She checked the clasped silver bag she'd chosen for the evening. "All these years, and he still treats me like a queen. It'll be nice spending part of the holidays with old friends."

"Maybe you could host the dinner here?" Despite her determination not to let Quinn Burton get so deeply into her head, Riley couldn't help but worry about her aunt leaving Temple House. "I don't know that—"

"Gloria would never forgive me for usurping her dinner party," Moxie said with a disbelieving frown on her face. "And I won't be that far away. If you need me, just call."

Riley bit back her response, the urge to tell Moxie that needing her wasn't Riley's biggest concern. Moxie's safety was. "I guess maybe I'd feel better if you weren't going alone."

"As much as I would love to have you accompany me," Moxie's tone held a bit of a warning. "I'm not entirely certain Gloria's forgotten that Christmas you knocked down her custom decorated tree at her holiday extravaganza."

"Oh, for cripes sake," Riley muttered. "I was nine. And it was her pampered poodle that knocked into the stupid thing." And sent beautiful crystal ornaments smashing onto the floor.

"Some memories linger stronger than others. I'll be fine. And if it makes you feel better, Gloria still has those personal bodyguards of hers." Moxie shook her head. "She's such a show-off. But I'll admit they are very nice to look at."

"I guess I'll just say enjoy yourself, then." Riley kissed her soft cheek and gave in to the impulse for a hug. Her heartbeat didn't steady until Moxie patted her arm, then her cheek.

"You're a good girl, Riley. I love you to pieces. Now do me a favor."

"Anything."

"Fix whatever you broke with Quinn."

"There isn't anything to fix," Riley said. "And why do you assume—"

"You've had a shield around your heart since we lost your parents," Moxie said. "Oh, you've dropped it for some people. Laurel, Cass, Mabel, and Sutton. Me. Your grandfather. But you've been on lockdown where everyone else is concerned for years. That's a lonely way to live. Love, trust—it's a fragile thing. Especially at the start. But the more you fight for both, the stronger it becomes." Moxie cupped her chin, the gesture both loving and chiding. "He's a good man. You'd be a fool not to see it, and you, Riley Temple, are no fool. Now," she stepped away and made her way to the door. "you wallow if you want, but not for long. Tomorrow I expect to see that man back here with a Santa hat on his head. I mean it," she added before she walked out the door.

"Santa hat." Riley snorted. "Yeah, right." But she had to admit something to herself.

The idea definitely made her smile.

"Well, ho ho ho, bro."

"Hey, Cheryl." Quinn walked into his parents' house and greeted his sister not with a kiss on the cheek, or a quick hug, but a familiar pat on her very large belly. "How're they baking?"

"Nearly overdone." Cheryl Burton waved him inside with a half-eaten candy cane in her hand. His sister's Amazonian presence had frequently intimidated yet always impressed, both him and anyone who ever met the prosecuting attorney. "Mom and Marcie are in the kitchen. We're baking super-spicy-eat-yourself-into-labor chocolate chip cookies if you're interested."

"If it works by proxy, I'm in." He looked around the house, smelled the holidays wafting out of the kitchen. "Where's Dad?"

"Office. He's seriously and abnormally grumpy." She closed the door, eyed him as she did anyone she suspected of wrongdoing. "You responsible for that?"

"I plead the fifth. Go eat your cookies." He touched her arm and ignored the frown on her face as he walked around the staircase and knocked twice on the closed door at the end of the hall.

"Come!"

Quinn cringed. He was all too familiar with that tone. When he opened the door and walked in, however, he found his father struggling with a tape dispenser and a roll of snowman wrapping paper.

"Close the door," Alexander ordered. "Then shut your eyes. I told your mother I'd wrap your gift. Act surprised when you get this, okay?"

"Didn't know I needed a mando … what the heck is that?" He walked over to the desk and read the box.

"Something apparently every kitchen requires, plus William Sonoma was having a sale. My guess? It'll slice the fingers right off your hand." He attempted once more to position the box correctly, then stood up and headed for the bar. "Maybe it takes alcohol. You want one?"

"I'd prefer two," Quinn said.

"That kind of day?"

"That kind of week. Spoke to the warden up at the state prison today. Don't worry," he added at his father's expression. "I was careful how I asked about Dean Samuels, and she had absolutely no answers or explanation. Not that she's eager to explain. She's definitely not anxious for word to get out she or any of her predecessors misplaced a high-profile prisoner." It made absolutely no sense how something like this could happen.

Although it did. If one considered the higher-ups that would need to be involved to make it happen.

"That was the impression I got when I spoke to her." Alexander handed Quinn a glass of Scotch, which Quinn downed in one shot. "Want to talk about what else is bothering you?"

"Oh, believe me." Quinn walked to the double French doors behind his father's desk and stared out into the yard that doubled as his mother's prized hobby. The sun had made an uncharacteristically early night of it and the stars were emerging in twinkling perfection. "You do not want me to open that can of worms."

"Something's brought you here," he said as he folded his body into the sofa beneath a large painting of the Griffin Observatory. "You come to tell me it's time to fall on my sword?"

"No." Even as he said it, Quinn thought of Riley's accusation that he'd instigated a relationship with her to protect his father. Ridiculous, he thought and dismissed the idea yet again. Even if his father was ready to fall on his sword over the Dennings's case, Quinn wasn't going to accelerate the action by giving credence to the notion.

"Not yet." Hopefully not ever. There had to be a way to protect his father's reputation and see this case through. "We don't know enough to take this public." The pieces weren't necessarily coming together, but they were multiplying. More pieces meant a bigger picture at the end.

He'd heard from Nox twice since he'd loaded them up with a triple shot espresso; once to confirm that the files on that disk Joyce gave him were indeed client and accounting records from Bryant Photography. Then a second time to say they'd run into a bit of an issue tracking down the image from the floral card. Two steps forward. One step back.

That fact that most of Quinn's hope was pinned to Wallace's list of suspects spoke volumes. "We need to have answers in place for whatever questions that will come flying at us." And they were going to come flying. From every conceivable direction. Preparation was going to be key to all of them coming out of this with some kind of future in place. "There is something else you need to be aware of. Something that could complicate things down the road."

"Sounds serious."

"Doesn't get more serious." Quinn laughed. "I slept with Riley Temple."

The ice in his father's glass tinkled like muted sleigh bells. "I see." He paused, each moment ticking in Quinn's ears like a time bomb. "Is this a one-night kind of thing or—"

"It's definitely an or." He still couldn't decide if that was good news or bad. "Did you mean it the other day when you said you liked her?"

He glanced over his shoulder in time to see his father's brow arch. "I did, actually. But even if I didn't, your personal life is—"

"Please. The second mom and Cheryl hear about this, it's going to be open season on my love life. Riley's it." All his life he'd known when the right woman presented herself, he'd know it. And dammit if Riley Temple hadn't made herself known. "Thought maybe in case you were just being polite, I'd give you some lead time to get used to the idea. I'd like to invite her for Christmas Eve. Her and her aunt." When Alexander didn't respond, Quinn turned around. "Is that a problem?"

"No." His father rested his elbow on the arm of the sofa and covered his mouth with his hand. It wasn't until he saw his father's eyes twinkling that he realized Alexander was laughing. "I'm sorry." His dad stopped trying to hide his reaction. "I've just never seen you quite this confused and miserable before. It's—"

"Entertaining? Yes, I can see that." But his lips twitched all the same. "I do not know how to do this, Dad."

"Do what?"

"Love someone." And there it was. The admission he'd been fighting all day. The acceptance that plunged him straight into an unknown terror more frightening than the idea of a multi-generational serial killer on the loose in Los Angeles.

The fact Riley had all but manufactured an argument with him should have ticked him all the way off back to bachelordom. Instead, he found himself coming up with ways to surprise her with the admission that she'd hooked him. All the way down to his … toes. "I already blew one marriage in what was probably record time. I don't want—"

"What you had with your college girlfriend didn't last long enough to qualify as a marriage. Heck, you two got married after graduation and by Christmas—"

"By Christmas she realized she couldn't be married to a man who got shot at for a living." On the bright side, dividing up his and Erica's assets had taken as long as a trip to the DMV for Quinn to sign over his rights to their car.

"The fact you're concerned about repeating past mistakes is already proof you're not who you were then."

"You think?" Quinn wasn't convinced.

"Hell son, this isn't something you think to death. You just do it. Look," Alexander said, "I'll tell you what I told Cheryl when she and Marcie hit a bump in the road a while back. There is nothing as equally terrifying and exhilarating as finding the person you're meant to be with. You either face it, accept it, and embrace it, or you walk away from it. Either way you'll never be the same. That said"—Alexander motioned for him to sit—"I look forward to meeting your

Riley in a setting other than through the two-way glass of a police station's interrogation room. I'm also anxious to see your mother's face when you tell her about this new relationship of yours."

"Feel free to do it yourself," Quinn muttered as he sat beside his father. "I don't think I can have this conversation twice." Especially since he also brought less amusing news. He grasped his empty glass between his palms. "Riley and I have been doing some … investigating. Without going into the details as to how and where, I think you should know. Whoever truly was responsible for killing Melanie Dennings, they didn't stop with her. She wasn't the only one, Dad. There were more. Before and since."

Silence landed in the room like a bomb. He swore he could hear his father's pulse skip a beat.

"How many more?" Alexander rose and, after Quinn declined a refill, returned to the bar.

"So far, we believe we're up to thirty-one."

Alexander drank then set the glass aside. "I take it there's more information than just a potential body count." Voice detached, the commissioner side of him had taken over the room as he strode to the window and looked out at the garden his wife, Quinn's mother, meticulously tended.

"We're compiling a report. Organizing information." Adding to the horror that had been the Melanie Dennings murder. "I should have something cohesive and solid in the next few days. It's bad, Dad. Really bad. And it's only going to get worse."

"Digging up the past often makes things worse." He was quiet for a long moment. "All right. Tell me. What do you anticipate needing?"

Quinn's cell rang. "Hold that thought," he told his dad when he read the screen. "Yeah, Wallace, what's up?"

"Gibson just called. They've found Nestor."

"The kid who sold the pictures to Merle? Where?" He checked his watch. "I can be there in—"

"There's no rush," his partner said in an all-too-familiar tone. "He's in the morgue."

"Thanks for following me over, Mabel." Riley hit the lock on her car, and they headed out of the parking lot of Cedars-Sinai into the main hospital. It hadn't taken long for her to feel as cooped up as a starlet just out of rehab. Funny how even in the home you loved, the walls could start closing in. Hearing from Merle's floor nurse that he had definitely turned a corner and was as cantankerous as Riley had warned, she couldn't stay away another moment.

"I've been meaning to visit Merle again. It's just … things got crazy and, well, hell." Riley huffed out a breath. "If Quinn found out I came out here alone, he'd skin me. And not in a good way."

"Is there a good way to be skinned?" Mabel's attempted joke was a sign last night's melancholy had lifted. "And don't think twice about it. There's a night-shift nurse I've been wanting to talk with about dedicating some private space for assault victims. You gave me the perfect excuse to finally mark it off my list."

"I doubt this'll take long. Merle's nurse said he's still mildly sedated, but that he's been asking for me." She checked her watch. After finishing with the Christmas decorations in hers and Moxie's apartment, she'd run a set of the photographs up to Cass's, after which she'd landed at Mabel's for an old-fashioned pity-party bitch session. "Visiting hours are only for another hour, so—"

"Stop worrying about me," Mabel insisted. "Go and enjoy some time with your friend."

"You're the best." Riley took the stairs, after which she was reminded she'd let her exercise regime lapse for far too long. Although last night should have more than made up … "Oh, for the love of Mike, stop obsessing." She flashed a quick smile to the shocked orderly who passed her in the hall. "Just working out my personal drama with the only person who can stand to listen to me. Evening, officer." She nodded at the young, uniformed woman seated just outside Merle's room.

"Ms. Temple." The officer nodded and returned to her paperback puzzle book.

Finding Merle attempting to change the TV channels with his bed remote lifted her spirits almost to pre-photograph levels. A painful pressure she hadn't realized had been pressing against her heart eased. "Well, you're looking considerably better than the last time I saw you."

"Riley!" The relief on Merle's face brought tears to her eyes. "Where on earth have you been, girl? I've been worried you up and disappeared on me."

"Never." She dropped her pack on the floor and went to him, leaning down to kiss his whisker-covered cheek. "I brought you some Christmas cheer." She hoisted the small rosemary bush dotted with tiny ornaments and set it on the table by the window. "What do you think?"

"It's perfect." He let out a sigh. "I'm so glad to see you." He held out his hand and she walked back to the bed, grabbing hold as she sat on the edge of the squeaky mattress.

"I'm glad to see you, too. How are you feeling?"

"Like a sheep that's been sheered too close for too long." He sagged back against the pillows. "My shop—"

"Don't you worry about the store. I've already been in touch with a company that's coming in next week and will get everything cleaned up for you. By the time you're ready to leave here, home will be waiting."

"They're sending me to rehab for a few weeks," Merle grumbled. "Might not be going home until after the first of the year."

"We'll make it work, I promise. I'm so sorry I've been scarce. I've been trying to help find the people who did this to you. Good news. We're getting close."

Whatever color the old man had in his face drained. His monitors beeped and alarms blared. He locked a hand around her wrist and squeezed. "Riley, no."

"Hey, Merle, what … what's going on?" It wasn't the pain from his squeezing her hand that worried her, but the abject terror on his face. "Merle, breathe. Don't … come on, Merle. There's nothing to get upset—"

"They killed Dudley," Merle whispered urgently. "You stay away from them, do you hear me? You stay away from her!"

"From which her?" Riley glanced at the monitor as the alarms continued to ring. "Okay, okay, I'm fine, Merle. I'm not going anywhere. I'll stay away."

"You promise? You promise me you'll stay away, Riley." The desperation in his voice trailed off as he struggled to catch his breath.

She pried his fingers loose. "Promise me you'll forget about those pictures and leave this alone!"

"What's happening?" Riley demanded of the nurses who rushed in.

"Move, please." Riley was elbowed out of the way as they dropped the head of the bed flat and maneuvered around the numerous lines and wires. The medical jargon flew faster than Riley's mind could process.

She picked up her bag, stepped back, blanketed with the knowledge one careless statement on her part may very well have cost her friend his life.

Heart hammering so hard she felt dizzy, Riley backed out of the room, hugging her bag against her chest as another wave of medical personnel swarmed into the room.

She stood in the hallway, frozen, staring helplessly into the room teeming with lab coats and odd-colored scrubs. Faces blurred until a young man came out and touched her arm.

"He's stabilized for now."

"For now." She shuddered out a breath. "What does that mean? What happened?"

"It means he's being put under sedation again until we can get his heart rhythm back under control. They are considering a pacemaker and returning him to ICU." He gently steered her to the elevator.

"You're kicking me out."

"It's late," he said kindly. "And yes. Call the nurse's station in the morning. They'll give you an update then. Do you have the—"

"Do I have the number? Yes. Memorized." She winced at her snarky tone. "I'm sorry. Thank you for taking care of him. If he comes around, would you or someone tell him I'm going home and that I'll stop looking? He'll understand," she added at nurse's obvious confusion.

"I'll make sure someone does."

She rode the elevator down as if in a fog. Upon reaching the lobby, she looked around for signs to the ER, to where Mabel was meeting with her nurse friend. When her cell rang, she didn't think twice about answering the unknown number. "Hello?"

"Riley? This is Gloria Malfort."

"Ms. Malfort." Riley's spine stiffened. "Yes, of course. Moxie speaks of you frequently." Not necessarily in the best of terms, Riley thought. "Is everything all right?"

"I'm afraid not. I'm afraid Moxie took a bit of a spill in my hallway. Nothing serious, mind you, just a bump on the head and more than a bit of wounded pride. She was wondering if you could come get her? The car Ernie sent for her won't be back for a few hours yet and she doesn't want to be a bother."

"Of course. You're sure she's all right? She didn't pass out or anything, did she?" She dug out a pen and notepad.

"Nothing so dramatic, I assure you. I'd just feel better if you were here."

"I appreciate that." Riley dumped her bag on the registration desk, offered an apologetic smile to the frowning volunteer behind the counter. "Give me the address and I'll be right there."

Note in hand and phone call ended, Riley quickly made her way to the ER department and found Mabel at the main station. "Mabel." She practically dived for her. "I need to go get Moxie. She fell. Don't worry, she's fine," Riley added as she set the paper down on the desk and quickly entered the address into her phone. "I need to go get her. I didn't want to leave you—"

"I'll come with you." Mabel reached for her bag. "This can wait."

"No, it can't." Riley wasn't about to drag her friend away from something important. "I'll be fine. I'll call Quinn if I need help," she added as she pulled the directions up on her app. "Okay, Castilian Drive. I know where that is. I'll see you when I get her home."

"Call me if you need anything," Mabel called after her.

Riley barely heard her. She was already running.

# CHAPTER FIFTEEN

"NESTOR Campbell, age fifteen. Two shots. One to the head, one to the heart."

"Just like Dudley." Quinn stared down at the body of Nestor Campbell. The ashen face. The too-long dark hair. The scrawny, frail body that had probably withstood its share of abuse, whether self-inflicted or otherwise.

Quinn had lost count of the times he'd stepped into the medical examiner's domain. Lost count of the times he'd stood across a metal table from Dr. Kimberly Masters. How many bodies had it been, he wondered as he gazed upon this latest one with regret and dispassionate grief. "Dammit. We should have done more to find him."

"Not much more we could have done beyond the BOLO," Wallace told him. "When kids like him don't want to be found, they aren't. Until they are."

"Really not up to you being wise and logical right now," Quinn told his partner. "He got to him. Holden must have gotten to him before we could." When neither Wallace nor Kimberly responded, Quinn glanced up. "What?"

"His body was still warm when the patrol officers found him this afternoon," Wallace told him. "He'd been dead one, maybe two hours tops."

"Holden was dead by then, so he couldn't have killed him." He looked down at the metal table tray displaying Nestor's meager belongings. A beat-up Velcro wallet. A tarnished Celtic-inspired medallion. A crumpled pack of cigarettes. "What about the weapon? Same one that killed Dudley?"

"Quinn," Kimberly warned. "You know bullet comparisons take time. I can't just guess—"

"Yes, you can." His voice was as cold as the steel table holding the boy. "Surmise. Estimate. Guess—whatever you want to call it. Gut feeling, Kimberly. Same gun?"

"If I had to *suppose,* I would expect the bullets to come back as a match to the ones that killed Dudley Wankier. But we won't know for sure until—"

"I know." He had no doubt who was responsible. "Next of kin?"

"Still looking."

"Let me know when they've been located. I'll do the notification myself."

"All right." Kimberly drew the white sheet up over Nestor's face. "Quinn—"

"I'm fine." Except he wasn't. There was absolutely no reason he could think of that Nestor would have been a threat. Not at this point. The only reason they'd have to kill him was to tie up loose ends. His stomach pinged with the panic of nauseating certainty.

There was only one other loose end he could think of. "I have to get to Riley."

"Wait for me." His partner hurried after him.

"Wallace, I don't think—"

"I'm enjoying being a third wheel," Wallace insisted. "Can I drive?"

"No." Quinn had his phone out and dialed Riley's number as they walked through the offices back to the parking lot. "Dammit. Voice mail." He waited for the beep. "Riley, it's me. Call me back immediately. I'm headed your way, but …" He didn't want to tell her in a voice mail that a fifteen-year-old kid was dead. "Just call me when you can." He hung up and glared down at the phone as they reached his car. "I bet she's still ticked at me."

"What for?" Wallace buckled in.

"Telling the truth." He checked his watch. It was after nine. Bad time of night to just show up, but with Nestor dead and Merle under guard at the hospital, there were too many people who had seen the film at this point to make an educated guess as to where they'd be hit next. "Do me a favor. Keep calling her while I drive."

"You could just use the ..." Wallace pointed to the online speaker system.

Quinn's patience stretched spider web thin. "Call on *your* phone so she doesn't know it's me."

"Ah. Right. Got it."

With the traffic gods firmly in control, by the time Quinn pulled up in front of Temple House he hadn't had time to drop into complete panic. Not that he would have. No. Now was the time for control and composure. For clear-headed thinking. But none of that was going to happen until he heard the sound of her voice. They were out of the car in record time, racing up the stairs and punching in the new security code to gain entrance. "Anything?"

"Voice mail." Wallace shook her head. "Maybe she has it turned off."

"She never turns it off. Damn thing's an appendage for her." He was headed for the stairs when he spotted Blake coming out of the basement door. "Blake, you seen Riley?"

"You mean since she left with Mabel? No. Why? What's going on?"

Dammit! She did leave. He should have low-jacked her car. "She's with Mabel. Okay, that's good." That was good. She wasn't on her own. "Where did they go?"

"No idea." Blake's chiseled features hardened. "Why?"

"When did they leave?"

"Couple of hours ago. You going to tell me what's ..." He looked over Quinn's shoulder. "Mabel." He frowned and pushed past Quinn. "Where's Riley?"

Mabel pulled her phone away from her ear. "I was just calling her. Her car isn't in the lot. I figured she and Moxie would be back before me."

"I thought Moxie had dinner plans at a friend's," Last he'd heard the unmarked unit his LT had approved to watch over Moxie had been sent into the Hollywood Hills.

"She did." Mabel's frown intensified. "She called Riley while we were at the hospital visiting Merle. Riley said she'd fallen and that she was going to pick her up. She didn't call you?"

"No," Quinn said. "She didn't. Think carefully. Did Riley speak to Moxie directly?"

"I …" Confusion marred her delicate features. "I don't know—I wasn't there for the call part. Quinn, what's going on?"

They all turned to the sound of the lobby door opening, to where a laughing Moxie and an elderly gentlemen strode in, arm-in-arm, looking blissfully carefree.

"Moxie." Mabel's breathy prayer barely reached his ears before Quinn turned and ran up the stairs, paying little attention to the activity behind him. He skidded to a halt in front of Cass's apartment and banged a fist against the door.

One of the doors across the hall was yanked open. "Hey!" Laurel shouted at him. "Respect, detective."

"Riley's in trouble." The fact he could get the words out amazed him. "Mabel and Moxie are downstairs," he added to a suddenly alert Laurel.

The bolts on Cass's door snapped open on the inside before it was pulled open barely an inch. "Explain." The dead calm in Cass's voice didn't come close to reaching the restrained fear in her dark eyes.

"Riley's missing." He took a deep breath, forced himself to calm down. He wasn't getting past the threshold unless he was in control. "I need your help to find her."

"Your destination is on the right."

"Finally." Riley slowed the car and hunched over the steering wheel. "Give me a freaking downpour over this fog any night of the year." She rolled to a stop, outside the access gate of the palatial estate in the Hollywood Hills. Ahead, she could see the outline of the house thanks to the lights burning inside. She tried to recall having been here before, all those years ago, but honestly, these estates started to look alike after a while especially at night. The gate dragged itself open before she could press the intercom. "Guess I just go on in."

She drove around the circular path, pulled to a stop near the front door. She turned in her seat, first one way, then the other, looking for other cars. Other guests. But she only saw a small compact parked almost out of sight on the other side of the house. "Guess Gloria's party ended sooner than expected." She set the car into park, left the lights on and the engine running, and shoved out of the door.

Her cell rang yet again as she circled around to the porch steps. She clicked the green button. "Wallace, hey—sorry I didn't pick up. The reception around here—Wallace?"

Garbled voices, followed by white noise static erupted in her ears. The call went dead.

"Okay, either I need some serious feng shui or I need a sage bundle the size of Texas." She rang the doorbell, then called the detective back. No connection. "Dammit." She took a step back, one step down on the porch, angled around until she caught a bar. "There you are. Okay, this time we try—"

The porch light blinked on.

Riley glanced up. Every cell in her body froze.

"Riley?" Quinn's voice exploded through her cell and left her shaking. "Riley, where are you?"

"Quinn." Riley took a step back, eyes glued to the stained-glass window and the telltale flower of the dead above the front door that had just opened.

It took Riley a moment to place the young woman standing in the light of the foyer. The eyes, Quinn had said about her basement assailant, the eyes never lied. "Nancy." She looked different than she had at the reception desk at the Golden Age Retirement Home. Her features were similar, but rather than round, full of innocence and naiveté, Riley now saw gaunt angles and shadows sharp enough to draw blood. She was taller than Riley remembered and, in fact, if Riley had passed her on the street, she wouldn't have recognized her at all.

"Beth, actually." She smiled a practiced, patient smile that almost distracted Riley from the gun aimed directly at her chest. "Go ahead." She motioned to Riley's cell phone. "Say goodbye."

"Quinn?" Despite her best effort, her voice shook.

"Riley." His voice carried the sound of relief she only dreamed of feeling. "Where are you? Are you safe? Can you talk?"

"Not really, no." She'd never tried to think so hard in her life. "I met up with an old friend of Mr. King's. I'm going to hang out with her for a while. Sorry I'll miss your birthday dinner." She swallowed around the lie. "I was really looking forward to singing Happy Birthday to you. Oh, and Quinn?" Her heart seized.

"Riley, tell me—"

"I love you."

Quinn stared at the disconnected phone in his hand.

"What did she say?" Laurel demanded.

Standing opposite a frenetically typing Nox, Quinn asked, "Did you get it? Can we trace the call?"

"Almost," Nox murmured. "Signal's weak. Probably why Wallace's calls kept dropping. Last strong ping was further south ..."

"Quinn, what did she say?" Mabel grabbed his arm.

*Sorry I can't sing happy birthday to you.*

"She's in trouble." He spoke as if from outside his body. "She hates that song." But she'd also told him something else. Something else that didn't make any sense ... "A friend of Mr. King's. I've heard that somewhere." He began to pace, knocking a fist against his forehead. She wouldn't have wasted her potential final words on something frivolous. They would have meant something.

"Friend of Mr. .... Son of a bitch. Cass, pull up the Golden Age website. Their list of employees." How could something be both stupid and brilliant at the same time? He stalked around to the second bank of computers where Cass was seated, read over her shoulder. "Scroll down, down." Faces and names streamed by, nothing taking hold until ... there. "Nancy." She had to be one of the Redrum twins. "Stupid misconception. We assumed Holden was the dominant twin."

"Where's Moxie?" Mabel asked Blake as he stepped into the apartment.

"Her agent's with her upstairs." Even from a distance, Quinn recognized the combination of rage and fear in the other man's eyes. "Did you find Riley?"

"Almost." Nox's eyes were moving so fast it was as if she was REM-ming. "Got it. Thirty-seven-ninety-six … hang on. I've seen that address before."

"So have I." Wallace shoved around and started sifting through the copy of the list Nox had printed out the previous evening. "It came up again while I was doing research today on the Denning's case. Give me a second." He dragged a finger down the spreadsheet, then poked one of the cells. "Anthony Tenado, former agent. Died three years ago. Drowned after suffering a heart attack in his pool. House has been vacant ever since, sale currently pending."

"Tenado." Quinn's ears roared. "Melanie Dennings's agent was named Tenado."

"That's where the party was held that Melanie attended that night," Wallace confirmed.

'Let's go," Quinn ordered his partner.

"What can we do?" Laurel demanded.

"Take care of Moxie," Quinn said.

Blake grabbed his arm before he could run out the door. "I'm coming with you."

"You have a weapon?"

Blake reached into the back waistband of his jeans and pulled out a Glock. "Don't worry, detective. It's registered."

As if he cared at this point. "You're with us. Wallace? Let's go."

"You really didn't have to give me the tour." Every step Riley took inside the mausoleum of a house was a stark reminder of just how careless she'd been. She tried to keep track of the rooms, the hallways, the staircases leading down, over and beneath the living area.

The house was empty of furniture. Dust and cobwebs clung to the corners and window ledges. The lights burned a harsh glow into the vast emptiness as she was maneuvered through the maze. She could smell must and dirt. There was an odd metallic taste in her mouth and for an instant, she thought it was blood. Just her imagination playing tricks, Riley told herself. Please, God, let it only be her imagination.

Her pulse had taken to fits and starts. When, when, when was she going to learn to think first and jump second? Her fists clenched at her sides. Nancy had taken her cell phone the second she'd hung up. Taken it, stomped on it. Killed it. "How did you know about my aunt's dinner with Gloria Malfort?"

"Everything is connected." Beth walked a few steps behind, stopped briefly and, after flipping a switch in a metal box on the wall, plunged the house into darkness. Riley tensed, ready to run, but Beth pressed the barrel of the gun against the base of her spine.

Without her purse, without her phone, she was left only with herself and her wits to get her out of this. Or to at least stall long enough for Quinn to get to her. If he got to her. "Everything is connected with The Circle. Surely you must see that by now."

Riley squeezed her eyes shut, forced herself to remain calm as she moved deeper into the unfurnished, candle-lit house. "No, actually. I don't. You work for the person who killed Melanie Dennings don't you?"

"She was one of the Chosen." Her voice carried a haunting hint of reverence. "Sacrifices must be made."

"I take it you aren't one of them? You aren't a Chosen? Seeing as you're still alive." Riley cringed. Might not be a great idea to tick off the psycho with a gun to your head.

"It was Holden's and my responsibility, our birthright, to protect The Circle. And we did. For more than ten years."

"Bang-up job you did, too." The Circle. Riley could only hope she lived long enough to expose every last one of them. "I take it me finding those pictures of Melanie's murder screwed with your legacy?"

"Not murder," Beth insisted. "Sacrifice. Our responsibility has ended. I have only one task left to complete." She stepped closer, pressed the barrel of the gun against Riley's back as she made her take one last turn at the end of the hall. "One last sacrifice to make. We will earn forgiveness. I will earn it for both of us."

Riley stood in the doorway to yet another darkened staircase. Just how deep down did this house of horrors go? "Got a flashlight?"

Beth nudged the muzzle against her spine. "Walk or tumble. Your choice." There was an odd cantor to Beth's voice. A cadence that spoke more of obedience and routine than impulsive utterance.

"Walk, it is." Riley was not going to cower. She was not going to crumble. And she was not going to die easily. She could smell the earth now. Thick, damp, dark earth that had been covered and coated in stone. As she descended the stairs, the dim light from below grew brighter and cast shadows against the darkness. "He failed, you know. Your brother. He's dead."

"Yes. There are others waiting to take our place. There are many." Beth stepped closer and breathed into Riley's ear. "We are everywhere."

"Everywhere? Really?" Riley trailed her hands along the walls that cooled as they descended. "Everywhere as in everywhere or just in Los Angeles? Because if this thing of yours is global—"

"Those who speak do not see."

"Will not see what?" The large wooden door at the foot of the stairs loomed like a portal into the past. The smell of death wafted from under the door. She covered her mouth, tried not to gag.

"Open it."

"Yeah, I don't think—"

Beth pressed the barrel of the gun harder into Riley's back. "Open. It."

"This is one messed up *Let's Make a Deal.*" She clicked the handle and shoved open the door. Wood scraped against cement, the noise echoing into the cavern ahead. A cavern twisting and turning into the distance. The stench hit instantly. She retched, covered her mouth and nose and did her best not to vomit.

"Left."

Riley stumbled forward. Yet another door at the end of the hall.

She squinted into the darkness, her eyes burning at the strain. She looked for anything to grab hold of, to use against her captor. As long as Nancy—no, Beth—had that gun in her hand, as long as she held her finger on the trigger, Riley was trapped.

"Let me guess," Riley said as they reached the door. "Open it?"

She didn't wait for an answer. What waited for her on the other side robbed her of words. Robbed her of thought.

A bedroom, of sorts. Elegant, with hues of golds and white draping across the bed, accenting the beautiful frames hanging on the stone wall. Endless, countless frames filled with only a fraction of the faces Riley had seen last night in Cassia's apartment.

Not twenty-three. And not thirty-one.

But more. So many more.

"You are Chosen," Beth murmured and pointed to a black velvet dress hanging over the vanity.

"Chosen for what?" Riley hugged her arms around her torso, determined not to look at the countless pairs of eyes silently screaming at her. But she couldn't help it. She crept closer to the wall and saw the thin trickles of red staining the stone. It was then she realized she shouldn't have asked.

"The Circle demands a sacrifice to set things right." Beth motioned the gun toward the dress. "Put it on." Her smile was slow. "And then we'll begin."

"Fucking California fog," Quinn muttered as he took too sharp a right turn and had to steady the car.

"Is now a good time to say I get carsick in the backseat?" Wallace called.

"Not really, no." Blake stared out the windshield. "Curve coming up to the left. Take it slow."

"Yeah, see it." It was all Quinn could do not to floor the gas pedal, but getting the three of them killed wasn't going to help Riley. If anything, he'd be killing her as well. "Wallace? Where's our backup?"

"Ten minutes behind us." His partner cringed. "Lt. Gibson put out the call all units. We'll get to her, Quinn."

He sure as hell hoped so." If they didn't, he was going to have to live the rest of his life without her and that was not something he planned to do.

"Slow down. We're close," Blake ordered and rolled down his window. "Next house on the right. Stop here." He indicated the stone wall. "We should go in on foot."

"Right." Quinn pulled over, killed the engine. "Wallace?"

"Thank God we've stopped moving." His partner shoved open the door and practically dropped to his knees. Quinn climbed out and retrieved three flashlights out of the back of his car before he stood over him. "When this is over," Wallace panted, "I'm driving. And just so we're clear: driver picks the music, shotgun shuts his cakehole. Got it?"

"Got it. Bitch," Quinn said with an appreciative grin.

Wallace snorted and held out his hand. "Jerk."

Finally, the kid got something right. Quinn grabbed hold and hauled him up. "We get Riley out of there, you can have anything you want."

"Great." Wallace smacked him on the chest as he passed. "I'll start a list. Let's go get your girl."

"If Riley hears you called her a girl, she will kick your nuts into your throat."

"Can't wait," Wallace tossed over his shoulder. "You two coming?"

"Yeah." Blake cocked his gun and assumed the position. "Let's go."

# CHAPTER SIXTEEN

"IF this is supposed to be some kind of virginal sacrifice, I've got bad news for you." Riley kicked her jeans away. They landed in a pile on top of her tank and jacket. Buying time, she unzipped the velvet dress and stepped into it, drew it up and over her shoulders with a shudder. "Zip me up? No?"

Beth stayed where she was, gun unwavering.

"All right." Riley twisted her arms until she pulled the zipper up to the back of her neck. She couldn't feel her fingers. She couldn't feel much of anything. The numbness and cold had taken over as she became the current object of attention for the countless pairs of eyes staring down at her from the framed photos. Photos of women Riley assumed had been in precisely this same place over the years. They hadn't made it out, had they? Riley wondered as she fought to keep her mind clear. But she would. She had to. "Tell me, is this a makeup and hair kind of event, or …"

Beth grabbed a bottle of water from the table near the door, brought it over to her. "Drink."

"Not thirsty, thanks." Behind her in the mirror, Beth's eyes sharpened like obsidian. Black. Dark. Sharp.

Empty.

"Drink," she repeated and this time she held the gun against Riley's head.

Riley wasn't stupid. There was no reason for Beth to force her to drink the water unless it was drugged. "This really isn't a good idea."

Beth cocked the hammer.

"All right." She took a sip. Then another, wincing at the bitter taste.

"Come with me." Beth grabbed her arm and hauled her out of the room. Barefoot, Riley stumbled and when she caught her balance, found herself back in the curving stone hallway.

The dark-robed figure shifted into sight so fast she screamed and jumped back. Beth shoved her forward. Riley fell to her knees, her stomach revolting around the water as she scrambled back to her feet.

Another shadow. And another. They swarmed around her like bats; countless, overwhelming, soundless creatures she could only pray were figments of her imagination. Her ears roared with the sound of running water.

"Move. To the light," Beth ordered as she stepped between the shadows and herded Riley down the corridor into a cavern as wide as it was deep. Candles burned in every niche, on stands and tables, illuminating the cavern in unholy light.

"There." Beth pointed to the raised platform in the center of a filling cement pool of water.

Unable to speak, Riley shook her head. She recognized this house of horrors from the photos she'd developed, now—from Melanie Dennings's last moments. She opened her mouth, tried to force out the words, but she couldn't push them free. The energy drained from her body and she collapsed on the ground. For an instant, she felt the strangest sensation of relief. Of release. And then she was flying, soaring into the air as the nausea churned in her stomach.

She felt the cement platform against her back. Looking up, she saw the tiniest, darkest window overhead, even as she heard the low, guttural chants echoing above the rush of the water.

Droplets coated her skin. Refreshing cool water that for a moment promised relief. The all-too familiar dry mouth warning hit with the force of a brick against her skull. She tried to cry out, to scream, but the only thing she could do was bring one foot up and shove herself onto her side as she vomited into the rising water.

Choking, coughing, dragging in razor sharp breaths, Riley pushed herself up with one hand, her arm trembling with effort. The water was rising, churning around her as she sank back and felt it close over her body.

Beth loomed over her, eyes triumphant as she lifted both hands into the air, raised her eyes to the moon-glazed window Riley now saw was in the same flower pattern as the window over the front door.

A red lily.

"Behold! My sacrifice!"

*Both hands.* Riley thought dully. *Both hands up. No gun.*

It took a moment for the thought to penetrate the fog evaporating from around her head. She didn't wait. She didn't think. She reared up and grabbed Beth's head and yanked her forward with every bit of strength she possessed.

She heard Beth's head smack hard against the concrete pedestal even as Riley rolled off the other side and dropped into the rising water.

She dropped for a moment, the instant pleasure of release tempting her to surrender before she surfaced, gulping in giant lungfuls of air. Beth, face dripping with water and blood, clawed her away across the pedestal.

She dived at Riley, taking them both under. Arms and legs tangled as Riley tried to stay on top and shove Beth beneath her.

The robed figures just watched.

Beth broke away, grabbing for the pedestal and hauled herself up, kicking at Riley as she tried to get another, better, stronger hold. Adrenaline surging, Riley launched herself at Beth, locked one arm around the smaller woman's neck and pulled her straight back into the water with her. Before she went under, she heard a voice.

Heard *his* voice.

Quinn.

Beth continued to struggle in her hold, but Riley squeezed her arm harder, even as her own strength began to ebb.

*Happy birthday to me …*

Quinn, Blake, and Wallace stopped at Riley's car.

Quinn quickly opened the driver's side door, ducked in and killed the headlights and the engine. The silence that dropped over them left them with nowhere to hide. Every step they took would be heard.

But every move Riley and Beth Tomkin made, Quinn would hear.

The house was pitch-black and silent; as if they were too late. Quinn refused to believe or accept that. He wasn't too late until …

"Be ready for anything," Quinn murmured as the three moved in unison to the front door, guns poised, close to their bodies, and steady. "Blake, go right once we're inside. Wally, go straight through. I'll take the left. Anyone comes across a fuse or breaker box, flip the switch and try to get us some light."

Wally clicked his tongue. "Place has been abandoned and locked down for three years—"

"No, it hasn't." Blake cut him off. "Fresh oil stains all over the gravel in this drive. Plenty of cars have been here. Recently."

"Go." Quinn took the lead and stepped in through the glass entry doors first, his blood freezing when he saw a familiar flower gracing the glass panel above the doors. Blake and Wallace vanished down either end of the hall while Quinn shook off his unease, and stepped cautiously into the sunken living room.

From somewhere in the house, he heard a shriek.

Quinn moved lightning fast, pressed himself against the wall as he ducked around corner after corner. Went down one staircase, then another. He clicked off his flashlight, stood in the darkness.

Gun raised, he slowed his breathing, pricked his hearing, and waited.

He heard footsteps behind him. Slow, muffled. He clicked on his light, shot it to the side as Blake rounded the corner. "Rest of the house is clear," Blake whispered. "Wallace went out to wait for backup and fill them in once they're here."

"I'm not waiting." Quinn angled his light down the hall. "They're down there."

"I've got your six." Blake added his light to Quinn's. Two more levels down and Blake's hand landed on his shoulder. He pointed toward the metal box on the wall.

"Do it." Quinn kept moving while Blake hit the lights.

He clicked the flashlight off, but kept it out as he pulled open another door. They went down another staircase that opened up into a stone passageway that smelled of death.

"What the hell is this place?" Blake's whisper of a question sent chills down Quinn's spine.

"Which way?" The passage curved out in both directions. Damp earth coated the air as he turned one way, then the other.

"Behold, my sacrifice!" The shout echoed down one passageway like an audible beacon.

"Right!" Blake shouted as they ran full bore toward the voice.

The sound of rushing water greeted them as they skidded to a halt inside the cavern.

"Riley!" Quinn's voice bounced off the walls, erupting around them as they raced down the stairs. "Riley!" He skidded to a halt at the pool's edge, scanned the water.

"There!" Blake pointed to the nearly completely submerged platform. A hand reached up, fingers twitching.

"Jesus." Quinn jumped in, went all the way under before he sprung back up and shoved himself across to the hand. He grabbed hold, pulled hard.

Riley erupted up and out of the water and straight into his arms.

Choking, gagging, sputtering, she struggled for a moment.

"Riley, it's me. I've got you." He hung on tight as he dragged them both through the water to Blake. The velvet monstrosity they had put on her was weighing her down. "Take her!" He passed her off to Blake, who reached down and grabbed hold of both of Riley's wrists and plucked her almost effortlessly out of the water.

Quinn returned to the platform, reaching for the prone female figure bobbing to the surface, face up. Eyes wide open, she stared vacantly up at the moon-filled window overhead.

Footsteps echoed down the stairs. Shouts and yelling in various tones of urgency as Quinn returned to Blake and Riley. She barely waited for him to drag himself out of the water before she threw herself at him.

"Quinn." She grabbed hold and clung to him as he dragged her into his lap. "I heard you. I heard you call for me. You came." She trembled so hard he was afraid her bones might break. "I wasn't sure—"

"Hey." He pried her back and caught her face in both hands as Wallace and a dozen uniformed officers spilled into the chamber. "I will always come for you, Riley Temple. Do you hear me?" He kissed her quick and hard, afraid that once he started, he wouldn't be able to stop. "I will always come for you. I have to—because you love me." His grin earned that sharp glare of irritation he adored so much. "Ah, there you are." He tucked her in close.

"Ambulance is on the way," Wallace announced as he dropped down beside them. "Hey, Riley. You good?"

"Good? She thought she could drug me," Riley slurred a bit. "She made me put on this dress." She plucked the heavy, soaked fabric away from her chest. "Get it off of me, Quinn. Get it—"

He caught her flailing hands. "We'll get it off. I promise. I just don't think you want to get naked in front of all these cops, do you?"

That calmed her down.

"Where are they?" She asked dazedly, succumbing more to the drug now that her fight/flight response was fading.

"Who? Beth? She's dead." Quinn couldn't imagine a better end to this nightmare.

"Not Beth. The others. There were others here." She tried to sit up, but her rapid blinking told him more of that drug had been consumed than she'd thought.

"No one else was here," he told her, looking confusedly at Blake. "Did you see anyone?"

"No. I didn't."

"They were here," Riley insisted.

"All right, I hear you. But they aren't now. You're safe. Riley? Do you hear me?"

"I heard you. Safe," she murmured before she passed out.

"Quinn?"

"Yeah?" Quinn stepped away from the back of the ambulance where Riley had been loaded. She was still out cold, but her vitals were good. She wasn't going to be happy when she woke up in the hospital, but wasn't that just too damned bad. "You find something, Blake?"

"Yeah." The former Naval Intelligence investigator waved Quinn over to where they'd cordoned off Beth Tompkin's car.

The property looked like a Hollywood murder mystery set with patrol cars, emergency vehicles, and helicopters circling overhead. Lights spun and blazed bright enough to blind everyone in sight.

Quinn followed Blake around Beth's car, then stopped a few more feet in. "You're going to want your techs back here." Blake shone his light against the ground. "I'm seeing four, maybe five distinct tire treads here. Fresh ones. Footprints, too. Not clear enough to get casts of, but they're there." He angled the light up into a grove of trees. "I took a walk. This skirts the edge of the property, and leads right back up and around to the main road."

"Riley's shadows?"

"Shadows don't leave footprints."

"Shit." He rubbed hard fingers across his forehead. "So much for this being over."

"Quinn?" Wallace jogged over. "LT's on scene. Your dad, too."

"Awesome. Thanks, partner. Can you head back to Temple House? Fill them in on what happened. Maybe censor what you tell Moxie?"

"Consider it done." He headed off into the throng of cops and crime scene techs.

"Blake?" Quinn said.

"Yeah?"

"Thanks for the assist."

"Yeah."

Quinn's feet felt as if he were wearing cement boots. "Loo. Commissioner." He greeted both men as professionally as his exhaustion would allow. His father rested a comforting hand on his shoulder.

"How's Ms. Temple?" Lieutenant Gibson asked.

"Alive. She nearly drowned down there. Some kind of crazy-ass sacrifice ritual .... I don't know." He shook his head. "Riley should be able to fill in the blanks once she's awake. I was going to go—"

"To the hospital," his father finished with a nod. "Of course. Do you have any more information on that topic we discussed earlier this evening?"

"Not yet, sir, no." Quinn wasn't sure what he should tell his father right now. "There's evidence Beth Tompkins wasn't acting alone here tonight. Whoever else was here, got away. And …"

"And what?" Lieutenant Gibson asked.

"It's going to take days, if not weeks, to process this scene, sir. There's a room …" He ducked his head, chose his words carefully. "There's a room of pictures, sir. Of the women we believe went missing over a period of time." Far more than their growing list included.

"How long are we talking? Weeks? Years?" Lieutenant Gibson looked between father and son.

"No, sir." Quinn looked at his father. "Decades."

There wasn't any way to stop what was going to happen. Word was going to leak out. About this place. About the cavern. About the Melanie Dennings pictures. The explosion and fallout were imminent.

There was only one thing he could do about it and that was stand by his father's side. No matter what.

"Hey." From her confinement in what had to be the most uncomfortable bed in the history of hospitals, Riley nudged Quinn's foot with hers and nearly sent his legs crashing to the floor. "How are you at prison breaks?"

"As a rule, I'm against them." Quinn readjusted his position and kept his eyes closed. "And I'm under orders not to bring you home until you are back in tip-top shape. Moxie's orders."

Riley snapped her blankets back in shape. "This sucks. I've been in here for two days! Two days! I'm fine!"

"You were drugged with a toxic dose of Scopolamine and nearly drowned."

"And?"

He sighed and opened his eyes. "And I'm done taking chances with you."

She snorted and plucked a container of orange Jell-O off her table. "You are not. Unless you're changing your mind about moving in?"

"Moving in with my girlfriend after less than a week." He sighed and dragged his feet to the floor. "Seems like a sane decision given recent events."

"And it has nothing to do with the fact the lease on your apartment is up." Her smirk turned to a frown when she couldn't find a spoon. "You're living dangerously, you know. Moving in with me and Moxie."

"Your aunt adores me."

"Of course she does." Riley beamed at him. "You saved her favorite niece from a psychopathic killer. Everyone at Temple House loves you. What?" She blinked. "Too soon?"

"And they say cops have macabre senses of humor. Okay. I surrender." He reached into his back pocket and pulled out a cell phone. "Brand new. souped-up according to Cassia, who took care of it. Who, may I ask, is Carlos?"

She grabbed for it like a toddler after ice cream.

"Why?" She opened her missed calls. "Eesh. That's a lot of activity."

"Carlos?"

"Night manager at the Fairfront Hotel. He gives me tips on celebrities staying at the hotel." She scanned through the messages, then started on her emails. "Don't worry. I haven't changed my mind about quitting. My days of celebrity stalking are over."

"Find something else to hide behind?"

His concern wasn't new. She'd heard it in his voice every time he spoke to her now. Yes, she'd almost died. And yes, she was already having flashbacks and panic attacks that left her huddling in bed and wanting to scream. But she'd also been visited by every single one of her friends and tenants save for Cassia, and even wheeled herself down to Merle's room for an extended, reassuring chat.

The pawnshop owner had been given the same edited story Moxie had been, along with the renewed promise of Christmas Eve dinner at Temple House. The prospect of Christmas Day with Detective and Chief Burton, on the other hand, could very well be the second most terrifying thing to happen to her this week. She was ready for new. A new job paying tribute to Moxie and her contemporaries. A new grateful attitude to still be alive. And most importantly, a new love.

"If it'll make you feel better," Riley said quietly at Quinn's raised brow. "I have a therapy appointment later this week. Laurel's suggestion," she added at his approving nod. "So it's not like I had much of a choice."

"I find I like that woman more every day." Quinn got to his feet, stretched, then motioned her to move. "Scoot over."

"What? Here? Now?" Her pulse kick-started and her cheeks warmed. "Quinn, I don't think—"

"I haven't slept in a real bed in two nights, Riley. I'm tired and …" He glanced up at the television, frowned, then reached for the remote. "What the hell?" He clicked the volume up as a special report interrupted the *Real Housewives* rerun she'd been forcing him to watch.

"Local KFRB news has confirmed that an anonymous source has come forward with explosive new evidence in the infamous Melanie Dennings murder. These images, obtained by one of our lead reporters, call into question the timing of Ms. Dennings's death. We can also report that Chief Alexander Burton, who himself led the original investigation, has requested that the District Attorney appoint a special investigator to determine whether any prosecutorial, judicial, or investigative misconduct took place."

Quinn turned off the television. "Never mind." He sat back in the chair. "I think I'm awake now."

"How did they get the pictures?" Riley whispered. "Quinn, I swear, I didn't—"

"I know you didn't, Riley." He sank his head into his hands for a long moment, sighed. Then looked at her. "There's nothing anonymous about those pictures getting out. My father did it."

"Why?" She sat up straighter. "Why on earth …?"

"Because he's a good man." His smile was faint. "He would have done it sooner, but he was waiting for me to decide what I'm going to do about my future. With the department," he added at her frown. "Promotions board is coming up. I needed to decide if I was going to take the command route or stay where I am in homicide."

"Oh." She blinked, uncertain how to feel. "Did you decide?"

"I did. I probably should have talked to you about it first."

"No." Riley reached out her hand and waited until he grabbed hold. "No, this is a decision you have to make, Quinn."

"Maybe I want you to have a say."

"It's too early for me to have a say in what you want from your career. I want you to be happy. I happen to think you're an excellent detective, but if that's not what—"

"It is." He squeezed her hand. "I'm not going to move up. I don't want to. And besides, this case is only going to get bigger and more complicated. I'm not letting it go. We have dozens of faces who need identifying. Women who need to come home. I'm not abandoning them now."

"Neither am I." She assured him. "As someone with special insight into this case now—"

"Oh, boy. Here we go." He actually chuckled when she tugged him forward and into bed with her. "I have a feeling my life just got even more complicated than I anticipated."

"Maybe." She shrugged and snuggled against him as he wrapped his arms around her. "But it's not going to be boring. I love you, Detective Quinn Burton." She lifted her chin and kissed him.

"Love you, too. Now go to sleep."

"Yes, sir, detective." She closed her eyes. "Yes, sir."

# EPILOGUE

*Three days before Christmas*

MABEL Reynolds climbed out of her ten-year-old minivan and stared at what Riley called Hollywood's true house of horrors. Keeley was elbow-deep in baking Christmas cookies for the Temple House holiday party tonight. She and Addie and Lucas had taken over Sutton's kitchen, allowing Mabel to take advantage of the free hours to meet Riley and Quinn.

They'd been acting squirrely for the past few days. Well, after Riley had been discharged from the hospital. She'd assumed it had to do with their new all-in relationship that had Quinn moving into Riley and Moxie's apartment last weekend, but then Laurel and Sutton had trouble meeting her eyes whenever they spoke and frankly, she was getting sick of it.

"Are you two finally going to tell me what's going on?" she asked as they stepped down off the front porch. "What on earth am I doing here?" She looked up at the stained-glass window over the front door. At the red lily that was as deep as the blood thankfully still running through Riley's veins. When her friend ducked her head and rocked back on her heels, Mabel sighed. "Quinn, what's going on?"

"There's no easy way to tell you," Quinn said. "It was easier to show you and we needed to wait until the techs were mostly done. You'll need to put these on." He handed her a pair of fabric booties to fit over her shoes.

"What on earth could you possibly have to …" Mabel's breath froze in her chest. "Sylvie." She clasped the charm she always wore between her fingers, held it so tightly she was afraid it might shatter. "Is this where—?" She couldn't bring herself to finish the sentence. But inside her mind, her heart, she screamed out for her twin.

"I didn't know." Riley's eyes filled with tears. "Not until I came back a few days ago. Mabel, I'm so sorry I didn't—"

"Riley, stop." Mabel grabbed hold of her friend's hand, not because Riley seemed to need it, but because she did. "Show me. Quinn?"

"Yeah." The sadness in his voice touched her. "Follow me."

Mabel couldn't, no matter how hard she tried, imagine the terror Riley must have felt being taken through his house at gunpoint, in the dead of night. Down darkened corridors and staircases, winding her way down, down, down into the unknown.

Except it wasn't unknown. Mabel knew what had happened. News stories and gossip aside, she'd heard the whole and full truth from Riley herself just a few nights ago during one of their wine and whining parties at Cassia's. Riley hadn't been one for purging scary thoughts and emotions before, tending to usually bottle them up, but nearly dying at the hands of a crazy woman had her turning over a new leaf. Hell, she'd turned over an entire tree.

Mabel's feet slowed as she stepped into the stone and dirt passageway. Shop lights had been set up, removing the shadows and darkness. "It's just down here," Quinn urged and held out his hand. She grabbed hold and, walking between Riley and Quinn, they made their way into the makeshift bedroom.

She felt it the instant she stepped inside. Almost as if she could hear her sister's voice screaming into the stone walls. She sobbed, her arms trembling as she tried to pull herself free, but her friends held on and moved in around her as tears blurred her eyes. "She was here. Oh, God." Her entire body shook. "I can feel her." Her knees buckled, but she righted herself almost instantly, refusing to cower at the truth. "It's okay." She squeezed their hands and nodded. "I'm okay. Let me …"

She stepped clear of them, walked toward the big brass bed covered in a blood-red comforter. A pair of chain shackles had been pounded into the stone wall and the cuffs hung over the edge of the railing.

The vanity sat in the far corner, covered with bottles of makeup, curlers, curling irons. It was scattered with bobby pins and hair ties. A small velveteen chair and matching ottoman filled the back corner, but it was the display of framed photographs hanging on the stone walls that had her stumbling back.

Her eyes scanned the faces—too many faces. Their eyes filled her with sorrow, the pictures only hinting at the horrors this room had witnessed. She could, if she let herself, hear the screams even now.

"How many?" Her whisper of a voice echoed against the stone.

"There are sixty-seven photographs," Quinn said.

"Sixty-seven." Mabel wondered how long it would take her to find her sister in the crowd, but even as she did, a cool breeze wafted its way through the door. She lifted her chin and immediately met the eyes of the sister she hadn't seen in more than eight years.

She caught the sob in her palm, stumbling back as she saw the mirror image of the half-pendant she wore. "Sylvie." She wanted to touch her. To hold her. But she couldn't. She couldn't do anything except look at a picture. "Where is she?" The question was a whisper of thought at first, then it grew louder. "Where is she?"

She swung on Quinn. He was a detective. A policeman. Someone who was sworn to protect the innocent. The victims of this cruel, harsh world.

"Where. Is. She?"

He shook his head. "We don't know, Mabel. I'm sorry. As of now—"

"As of now the only lead you have is a picture on the wall." She pointed up at Sylvie. "What does that tell you? Anything?"

"Mabel."

"Don't!" Mabel lashed out and hated herself for it. "Don't tell me what to think or how to feel about this. Some monster, some group of monsters, took her away from me, from our parents, from Keeley—from her future—and all they left us was that!"

"I know." Riley's voice was filled with sympathy.

"How does this happen?" Mabel stalked over to Quinn, stood in front of him. She hated the stoicism. The acceptance. The understanding. "How does this happen? Sixty-seven women; daughters, sisters, friends, and they're just … gone! How?"

He shook his head. "I don't have any answers for you, Mabel," he said. "Not yet."

"Maybe not ever," she snapped. An unfamiliar warmth, maybe rage, maybe it was an all-encompassing sensation of vengeance, washed over her. "Sixty-seven women do not just vanish without a trace." Although, apparently they did. She did—her other half.

"I want her found. Do you hear me?" Mabel couldn't stop the tears as they flowed. "I want them all found. Are you going to do it?"

"I'm going to do my best," Quinn assured her. "I promise you, we're going to do our best."

"I want to help."

"Mabel—"

"I'm going to help," she told Riley without a tremor in her voice. "She's *my* sister. *Mine.* My blood. My t-twin." Grief stole her breath, then, looking back at Sylvie's picture, she found it again. Her determination. Enough for both of them. "Whatever it takes, I'm going to find her."

# VANISHED

## Circle of the Lily: Book Two

She'll risk everything to expose the truth

Since her sister's disappearance seven years ago, single mother Mabel Reynolds has turned grief into action and become a strong voice for victims of violence and abuse. When new revelations in the case surface, Mabel's hope for answers is reignited. But the DA overseeing the investigation seems more interested in a quick, rather than an accurate, resolution. With little faith in the system, Mabel is willing to go up against anyone—even a smug, irritating, tempting DA—to get justice.

Open-and-shut.

That's what Assistant DA Paul Flynn has been told about the house of horrors case. With a high-profile conviction at stake, Paul can't afford to make a wrong move, but Mabel Reynolds has his attention. All of it. Attraction aside, the woman knows far more than what's in the official files which makes her even more intriguing and valuable.

But using Mabel as an asset means exposing her and her daughter to danger. Danger that is closing in on them from every side. The closer the darkness gets, the more Paul realizes he's risking not only his career, but also the one thing he never anticipated losing: his heart.

# ACKNOWLEDGEMENTS

IT would be impossible to thank every single person who has helped me along my publiciation journey, especially after almost fifty published romances. *Exposed* and the Circle of the Red Lily novels, start a new phase for me, one I hope will continue for a long time to come. I'm so excited to begin this series and take readers on an escape I hope you'll all love.

This book in particular would not have been possible without the continuous and encouraging support of a number of people.

To my mother, Marjorie McLetchie Stewart and late grandmother, Ruby Hunker, who raised me on Shirley Temple, Errol Flynn, Marilyn Monroe, and Bogart & Bacall. My love of all things Hollywood stems from those years of watching Saturday movies curled up on the sofa.

Authors Melinda Curtis and Cari Lynn Webb, who are always a text away, especially when the doubts creep in. Loucinda McGary for her early, honest eye and support. Hannah Gunsallus, thank you for your guidance through the dark pages. Mary Helfrick, best friend forever, who has always believed and is always willing to head to the theater. The Northern California Romance Writers, the greatest group of writers and authors around.

To Authors on a Dime for the fantabulous cover and attention to detail. Working with you is so much fun!

Shoutout to Mickey Mickkelson of Creative Edge Publicity. Your enthusiasm is contagious and your dedication, inspiring.

Lastly, and most importantly, to my warrior editor Lezli Robyn and publisher, Shahid Mahmud. Being part of the Arc Manor family, and Caezik Romance in particular, is an honor. Thank you for asking "What do you want to write?" Because of you, the Circle of the Red Lily was born. I endeavor to make you proud.

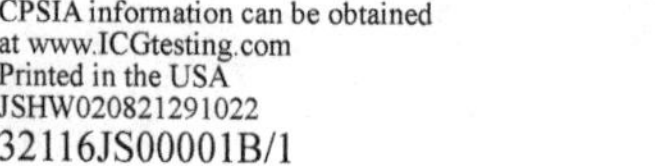

CPSIA information can be obtained
at www.ICGtesting.com
Printed in the USA
JSHW020821291022
32116JS00001B/1

9 781647 100674